Susanna Gregory was a police officer in Leeds before taking up an academic career. She has served as an environmental consultant, doing fieldwork with whales, seals and walruses during seventeen field seasons in the polar regions, and has taught comparative anatomy and biological anthropology.

She is the creator of the Thomas Chaloner series of mysteries set in Restoration London as well as the Matthew Bartholomew books, and now lives in Wales with her husband, who is also a writer.

Also by Susanna Gregory

The Matthew Bartholomew Series

A Plague on Both Your Houses
An Unholy Alliance
A Bone of Contention
A Deadly Brew
A Wicked Deed
A Masterly Murder
An Order for Death
A Summer of Discontent
A Killer in Winter
The Hand of Justice
The Mark of a Murderer
The Tarnished Chalice
To Kill or Cure
The Devil's Disciples
A Vein of Deceit
The Killer of Pilgrims
Mystery in the Minster
Murder by the Book
The Lost Abbot
Death of a Scholar

The Thomas Chaloner Series

A Conspiracy of Violence
Blood on the Strand
The Butcher of Smithfield
The Westminster Poisoner
A Murder on London Bridge
The Body in the Thames
The Piccadilly Plot
Death in St James's Park
Murder on High Holborn
The Cheapside Corpse

A POISONOUS PLOT

The Twenty-first Chronicle of
Matthew Bartholomew

Susanna Gregory

SPHERE

First published in Great Britain in 2015 by Sphere

1 3 5 7 9 10 8 6 4 2

A CIP catalogue record for this book is
available from the British Library.

ISBN 978-0-7515-4977-5

Typeset in Baskerville by Palimpsest Book Production Limited,
Falkirk, Stirlingshire

Printed and bound in Great Britain by Clays Ltd, St Ives plc

Papers used by Sphere are from well-managed forests
and other responsible sources.

MIX
Paper from
responsible sources
FSC
www.fsc.org   FSC® C104740

Sphere
An imprint of
Little, Brown Book Group
Carmelite House
50 Victoria Embankment
London EC4Y 0DZ

An Hachette UK Company
www.hachette.co.uk

www.littlebrown.co.uk

For Brad and Mary Anne Blaine

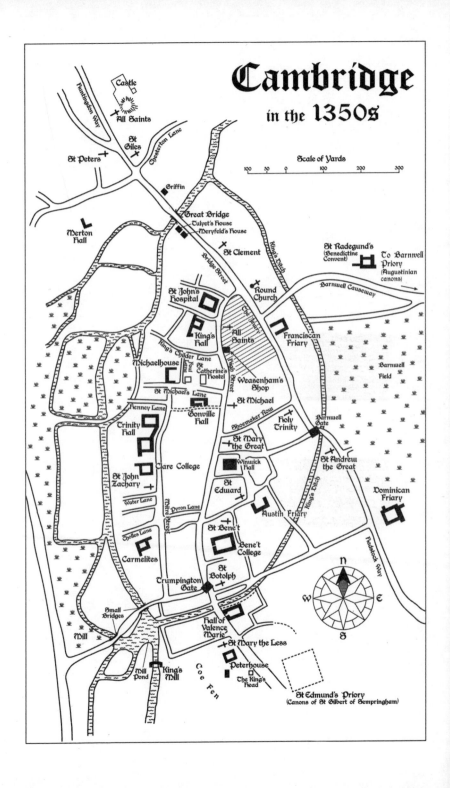

PROLOGUE

Barnwell Priory, near Cambridge, September 1358

Nigellus de Thornton eyed the dying Augustinian dispassionately. What had started as a mild fever a month ago had gradually progressed to violent stomach cramps, agonising headaches and a debilitating weakness. Nigellus had been a physician for many years and he knew the signs: John Wrattlesworth would not live to see another dawn.

'He has eaten nothing for days,' whispered Prior Ralph de Norton, hovering anxiously on the other side of the bed. He was fond of Wrattlesworth and was distressed by his plight – Wrattlesworth had been a kindly and unassuming presence at Barnwell for nearly three quarters of a century, and Norton had not forgotten the older man's support and guidance when he himself had first come to rule. 'And he has drunk nothing but your medicine and our elderflower wine.'

Nigellus winced on Wrattlesworth's behalf. The Augustinian canons were very proud of the acidic brews they fermented themselves, although few who tasted them thought they had cause to be. 'How much elderflower wine?'

'One or two cups a day. The vintage this year is unusually fine, and we hoped a few sips of such sweet nectar would help him rally.'

'Christ God,' muttered Nigellus. He cleared his throat. 'What about the remedies I prescribed? Has he had those?'

'Of course – every electuary, tonic, infusion and decoction.

1

Yet still he continues to sink.' Norton's voice cracked as he added pleadingly, 'Do you have *nothing* that works?'

Nigellus was affronted. 'The fault does not lie with my medicines. If they have not done what was expected, it is because they have been improperly applied.' He raised an imperious hand when the Prior began to object. 'We shall try Gilbert Water next. However, it is costly – it contains crabs' eyes, ambergris, ground pearls and other expensive ingredients.'

'I care nothing for the price, not if it makes him well again. But perhaps we should summon another physician. Cambridge is less than two miles away, and Bartholomew at Michaelhouse or Rougham of Gonville Hall would—'

'Neither will do anything that I have not already tried,' said Nigellus shortly. He was tired of hearing about the University's *medici* and their legendary skills. He had more experience than Bartholomew and Rougham put together, and considered himself by far the superior practitioner. 'Besides, one is away and the other is far too busy to trail all the way out here.'

Unhappily, Norton watched him write more instructions for the apothecary. Nigellus exuded the arrogant confidence that was often found in members of the medical profession, but Norton was far from convinced that the man's hubris was justified, and heartily wished one of the College men had been available instead. When Nigellus had finished, Norton escorted him to the gate.

'I understand you will become a member of the University yourself this term,' he said, good manners compelling him to make polite conversation, despite the apathy he felt towards the man. 'You have been offered a post in Zachary Hostel, and will leave our village to take it up.'

'Yes,' said Nigellus, gratified that the Prior had heard about his good fortune. After all, what greater acknowledgement of his abilities than to be courted by one of the *studium generale*'s richest and most respected foundations? 'New patients from the town will flock to me, of course, but I shall not abandon my old ones.'

'Oh, I am so glad.' Norton tried to inject a note of grateful enthusiasm into his voice, but did not succeed, and received a sharp glare in return.

Nigellus climbed on his horse. Although Barnwell was tiny, comprising just the priory, a few cottages and a leper hospital, he would never demean himself by making his rounds on foot. He rode to his next patient, a woman with symptoms not unlike Wrattlesworth's. Olma Birton was the reeve's wife, a lady who had never enjoyed robust health, and who had taken a downward turn over the past three or four weeks.

'How is she?' he asked as he entered the stone-built house that nestled prettily in a copse of ancient oaks. 'Any better?'

'Worse,' replied Birton tersely. 'And Egbert died last night.'

'Egbert?' queried Nigellus blankly.

Birton scowled at him. 'My uncle. You came three days ago to calculate his horoscope.'

'Oh, yes.' Nigellus recalled an ancient person with wispy white hair and no teeth. 'He was unable to supply me with the dates I needed for an accurate forecast, and I did warn you that any treatment I prescribed might not be effective.'

'Well, it failed completely,' said Birton. 'So I hope you do better with Olma. The last time you were here, you told me that she and Egbert were suffering from different ailments, but you are wrong. They fell ill within days of each other and—'

'The timing of their maladies is irrelevant,' said Nigellus sharply, annoyed that the reeve should dare presume to tell him his business. Did *he* dispense advice about harvesting crops or mending fences? No, he did not, and Birton should mind his tongue.

'They both had headaches, pains in the innards and weak limbs,' the reeve persisted. 'And what about Canon Wrattlesworth? He is suffering from the same symptoms that—'

'His illness is none of your affair. Now, do you want me to see your wife or not?'

Nigellus could see that Birton itched to send him packing, but the curmudgeonly reeve loved his wife, and would never do anything that might be to her disadvantage. Nigellus was glad: Birton was wealthy, and no physician liked to lose a good source of income. He followed the reeve to a pleasant bedchamber on the upper floor, where Olma lay grey-faced and barely conscious.

'Did you rub her cheeks with snail juice, as I ordered?' he asked, laying two fingers on her neck to assess the strength of her life-beat. He could barely feel it at all.

'No,' replied Birton in a strangled whisper, gazing at the woman who had shared his life for the past three decades. 'She would not have liked it. She is a fastidious lady.'

'Then it is your fault she has slipped into this fatal decline,' said Nigellus brutally. 'You promised to follow my orders, but this is the third time you have flouted them. How can you expect her to recover when you withhold the treatment that will save her life?'

Birton hung his head while Nigellus busied himself about the patient, but there was nothing he could do, and it was not long before Olma breathed her last. Nigellus left Birton to his grieving and rode to Cambridge, aiming to inspect his new quarters in Zachary Hostel – they were being redecorated and he was keen to ensure that the right colours were being used. He would collect his fee from Birton the following day: he was not so insensitive as to ask for it while the man was still in a state of shock.

4

'I have had a trying morning,' he sighed when he arrived at Zachary, hoping to find a sympathetic ear in John Kellawe, the hostel's theologian. 'Olma Birton died an hour ago, while Canon Wrattlesworth will follow her to the grave tonight.'

Kellawe raised his eyebrows. He hailed from the north, and was noted for his sharp tongue and brusque manners, along with a religious fanaticism that even pious men found alarming. He was an unattractive specimen, with a pugnacious jaw and wild eyes.

'You lost two patients last week as well,' he remarked. 'The Prior's cook and gardener. That makes four dead – a lot gone in so short a space of time. Especially in a small place like Barnwell.'

'Five, not four,' sighed Nigellus. 'Birton's uncle is dead, too.'

'Of the same disease?' asked Kellawe in alarm. 'There are rumours that the plague is poised to return . . .'

'These patients do not have the plague: they died of completely separate causes,' declared Nigellus confidently. He glanced up as an exhausted messenger staggered through the door, breathing hard. 'Yes? What is it?'

'Prior Norton needs you again,' gasped the lad. 'Another canon is ill, suffering identical symptoms to Wrattlesworth. You must come at once.'

'"Completely separate causes", Nigellus?' asked Kellawe sharply. 'Are you sure?'

'Of course I am sure,' snapped Nigellus, nettled. 'Norton is not a physician – he is not qualified to say whether the symptoms are identical or not.'

'Then let us hope you are right,' said Kellawe grimly.

CHAPTER 1

Cambridge, All Hallows' Eve 1358

Matthew Bartholomew, physician and Doctor of Medicine at the University in Cambridge, had never liked the three-day festival of Hallow-tide. To him, it was a reminder that the warm reds and ambers of autumn were about to fade to the cold grey fogs of November, and that the days would soon grow depressingly short.

No one else at the College of Michaelhouse shared this opinion, however, and an atmosphere of happy expectation blossomed as the Master dismissed his scholars from the breakfast table. There would be a feast that night, and as such extravagance was rare, students, Fellows and servants alike could hardly contain their excitement. All Hallows' Eve would be followed by All Saints' Day and then All Souls, the latter of which was particularly important to Michaelhouse, as it was the anniversary of their founder's death. Usually, they spent the day on their knees, saying masses for his soul, but things were going to be different that year.

'I am not sure whether to be pleased or worried,' said Brother Michael to the other Fellows as they repaired to the conclave – the comfortable chamber adjoining the hall that was off-limits to students. Michael was a portly Benedictine who taught theology, and was Bartholomew's closest friend. 'On one hand, I am delighted that we won the honour of hosting the reception after the All Souls' debate this year, but on the other, it will cost a lot of money – money we do not have.'

'It is an investment,' said Ralph de Langelee, the Master.

He had been chief henchman for an archbishop before deciding that life as a scholar would be more interesting, and still looked more like a warrior than an academic. He knew little of the philosophy he was supposed to teach, but he was fair and level-headed, and his Fellows had no complaints about his rule. 'When the town's wealthy elite see the princely show we put on, they will fall over themselves to give us money.'

'Will they?' asked Bartholomew doubtfully. He had never understood economics. 'What if our ostentatious display makes them think we have too much already?'

'It is a matter of confidence,' explained Langelee. 'No one wants to fund a venture that is on the brink of collapse – which describes us at the moment, unfortunately – but they will certainly want to be associated with one they think is flourishing.'

'Because of their sin-steeped souls,' elaborated Father William, a grubby Franciscan whose oily hair sprouted untidily around a tonsure that was never the same shape two days in a row. 'Which need prayers if they are to escape Purgatory. The rich are eager to support foundations that will still be saying Masses for them in a thousand years, and our ruse will convince them that *we* are such a place. Our gamble will pay off, you can be sure of that.'

'I hope you are right,' said Bartholomew, less sanguine about the risks they were taking. If they failed, Michaelhouse would never repay the debts that were accumulating, and the College would be dissolved.

Langelee waved away his concerns. 'I have invited a whole host of prosperous merchants to our feast tonight, in the hope that they will brag to their cronies about the lavish way in which they were entertained. And more of them will experience our generosity at the student debate—'

'At the *disceptatio*, Master,' corrected William. 'It sounds more illustrious, and we should do all we can to stress the grandeur of the occasion.' He grinned impishly. 'Even if it is only one where a lot of youths pontificate on matters they do not understand.'

'—when we shall provide refreshments fit for a king,' finished Langelee. 'Of course, we have other irons in the fire, too. Namely Prior Joliet and his fellow Austins.'

The Austin friars, unlike their monastic counterparts the Augustinian canons, lived in the town among the people to whom they ministered. The Order had arrived in Cambridge almost seventy years ago, and occupied a tract of land between the King's Ditch and the Market Square.

'They will give us money?' asked Bartholomew, surprised. Priories did not usually extend their largesse to Colleges – they had their own communities to fund.

'Not money,' explained Langelee. 'Labour. First, they have agreed to teach all the new theologians we enrolled last year—'

'The ones we took to get the fees,' put in William, lest the physician should have forgotten.

'—and second, they are painting that lovely mural for us in the hall,' finished Langelee.

Bartholomew regarded him in alarm. 'They have not donated this labour – they expect to be paid! Prior Joliet was telling me only yesterday how he plans to spend what they earn. They give more alms than all the other convents combined, and if we default, it will be the poor who suffer.'

'We will not default,' said Langelee impatiently. 'We will pay the Austins the moment the benefactions start flowing in.'

'Which they will,' avowed William. 'Thanks to the mural.'

Bartholomew shook his head in bewilderment. 'How will the mural help?'

'In two ways,' replied Langelee. 'By showing prospective patrons that our finances are healthy enough to afford such a luxury; and by demonstrating that we are men of great piety – it depicts St Thomas Aquinas, you see. The rich will certainly want prayers from our priests when they see that fresco.'

'But what if this scheme fails?' asked Bartholomew worriedly.

'It will not fail,' said Langelee firmly. 'It cannot.'

'I am looking forward to the *disceptatio* this year,' said Michael, before Bartholomew could argue. 'It is a great honour for Michaelhouse to be one of the two foundations chosen to take part.' He shot the physician a grin. 'As you and Wauter are on the committee that selects the topic, you can tell our lads what it is in advance. Then they can prepare, so will defeat Zachary with ease.'

Bartholomew sighed. 'How many more times must I say it? The subject will be announced on the day. No one will prepare, which is the point – to test the participants' mental agility when dealing with an entirely new thesis.'

'But Principal Irby has already told *his* scholars,' said William crossly, 'which means that Zachary will emerge victorious, while our boys end up looking like fools.'

'No, he has not,' argued Bartholomew. 'He cannot – we have not chosen the question yet.'

'Really?' asked Michael, frowning. 'But the *disceptatio* is scheduled for the day after tomorrow. Are you not leaving it a little late?'

'A little,' admitted Bartholomew. 'Unfortunately, we cannot agree on a topic. But we are meeting again this morning, and I hope it will be decided then.'

'Do not fret,' said Langelee to William, who was redfaced and indignant. 'If Bartholomew will not tell us, we shall have it out of Wauter. *He* will not be hobbled by foolish principles.'

He turned to where Michaelhouse's newest Fellow, John Wauter, was reading in the window. Wauter was an Austin and a geometrician, and it had been his idea to hire priests from his own Order to help teach Michaelhouse's overly abundant theologians. He had cropped black hair and a ready smile. He became aware that he was the subject of discussion and looked up.

'I was just telling William that you will not let us down,' said Langelee. '*You* will tell our students what they will be discussing at the *disceptatio*, so they can practise.'

Wauter blinked his surprise. 'You mean cheat? Really, Master!'

Langelee regarded him frostily. 'You were a member of Zachary Hostel before accepting a Fellowship here. I hope you know where your loyalties lie.'

It was a nasty remark and Wauter would have been within his rights to object to the slur on his integrity, but he merely closed his book and stood up.

'With Michaelhouse – a College that will win honourably or not at all.' He turned to Bartholomew. 'The committee is due to convene soon. Shall we walk there together?'

'Walk where, exactly?' asked William casually.

'To a place where *you* cannot eavesdrop,' replied Bartholomew curtly.

Hallow-tide was popular in the town as well as in Michaelhouse. It meant time away from work, so folk could visit friends and neighbours, where soul-cakes – sweet spiced biscuits with a cross cut into the top – would be given in exchange for prayers for the dead, and there would be both laughter and sadness as lost loved ones were remembered. That evening, bonfires would be lit on street corners, and there would be a torchlit procession led by the parish priests.

'Half the town is drunk already,' muttered Wauter

disapprovingly, as Bartholomew pulled him out of the path of an erratically steered handcart bearing a barrel of ale.

'My remedies for sore heads will be in demand tomorrow,' agreed the physician.

'Good! The College needs every penny it can get. How much will you charge?'

Bartholomew smiled ruefully. 'Nothing, because most of those who summon me will be unable to pay. Any spare funds they did have will have been spent on Hallow-tide treats, and who can blame them? This is the last fun they will have until Christmas.'

Wauter opened the door to St Mary the Great, where the meeting was to be held. The other committee members were already there, standing in a huddle in the centre of the nave, a place chosen specifically to thwart spies – the *disceptatio* always brought out the worst in its participants. Bartholomew and Wauter exchanged a wry glance when they spotted a Zachary Hostel lad lurking behind a pillar.

'Can he read lips?' asked Bartholomew.

'Yes, quite possibly.' Wauter raised his voice. 'Do not think you are hidden there, Yerland, because I can see you. Now go home before I tell the Senior Proctor that Zachary is resorting to unscrupulous tactics.'

'And that goes for you, too, Melton,' called Bartholomew, aware that one of his medical students had been trailing him ever since he had left the College.

Scowling, both youths slouched away, fortunately towards different doors. Although the *disceptatio* had originally been established to pit two randomly selected foundations in an innocent and enjoyable battle of wits, it was being taken more seriously that year, because one contestant was a College and the other was a hostel. Colleges were larger, richer and more secure – by virtue of their endowments, a perpetual source of money that hostels did not have – while hostels tended to be smaller and much less stable. Rivalry between the two had always been intense.

However, in a curious inversion of the usual state of affairs, Michaelhouse was on the brink of fiscal ruin – although only its Fellows knew the true extent of its problems – while Zachary was noted for its affluence. Zachary liked to gloat about its wealth, which Michaelhouse resented, so spats nearly always followed when their students met.

The debate committee, or *consilium*, comprised five members: two from Michaelhouse, two from Zachary and a chairman. Zachary was represented by Principal Irby and Nigellus de Thornton, while the chairman was Prior Joliet of the Austins.

Irby was a dreamy grammarian who was far too gentle to rule a hostel, particularly one with a reputation for feistiness like Zachary. He was famous for always wearing a cloak – in his hostel's colours of grey and cream – no matter what the weather, and never went out without a wineskin clipped to his waist, which he claimed was necessary for good health. The remedy was not working as far as Bartholomew was concerned, because Irby never looked well, and he was sure the man was suffering from some chronic and debilitating illness.

By contrast, Nigellus was squat, fierce-faced and aggressive. He was sensitive about the fact that his late entry into the University had brought him the title of Junior Physician, particularly as he was older than the other *medici* by a good twenty years. The Colleges, quick to sniff out a sore point, rarely missed the opportunity to jibe him about it.

'We are all here at last,' said Prior Joliet, who had a round little head perched atop a round little body. He had a reputation for piety, sincerity and generosity, and he and his flock had gone hungry the previous winter so that beggars might eat. He was also a talented artist, and it was he who was painting Michaelhouse's mural. 'Shall we begin?'

'Yes – and may I reiterate that we *must* make our decision today,' said Nigellus, all brisk business. 'I am tired of discussing it, to be frank. It is time we made up our minds.'

'I say we gauge the mood of the audience on the day,' countered Wauter. 'We can determine then whether to pick a topic that will make them laugh, one that will provoke intelligent reflection, or one so tedious that it will quell any desire to engage in fisticuffs.'

'That is a good point,' said Irby, nodding approvingly. 'We all want the occasion to pass off peacefully, and emotions do seem to be running unusually high this year.'

'Nonsense,' snapped Nigellus. 'We should decide now, and I recommend *nemo dat quod non habet* – "what you do not own you cannot give". It is high time we had a legal debate.'

'You have been fighting for *nemo dat* ever since this committee was formed,' said Wauter suspiciously. 'Would there be a reason for that – such as that Zachary has been practising it?'

'How dare you question my honour!' cried Nigellus furiously. 'It is not—'

'Gentlemen, please,' interrupted Joliet sharply. He waited until Nigellus spluttered into angry silence and then continued. 'Even if we do make our final decision on the day, we should still have a shortlist of questions ready. We have not agreed on a single one so far.'

'Then put *nemo dat* on it,' ordered Nigellus stiffly. 'It will be the one chosen, because it is the most suitable, and any fool should see it.'

With a pained smile, Joliet began to write, and while he did so, Bartholomew took the opportunity to study

14

Nigellus. He had been delighted when he had first heard that another *medicus* was to enrol in the University – there had been a desperate shortage of them after the plague – but it had not taken him long to learn that Nigellus epitomised the very worst of the medical profession. The Junior Physician was brash, condescending, closed to new ideas and saw his patients purely in terms of their fees. His cosy practice at Barnwell had made him very rich, which was why he had been invited to join Zachary Hostel, a place where the size of a member's purse was much more important than his academic credentials.

'What else?' asked Joliet, pen poised expectantly.

'How about a medical question?' suggested Irby. 'I have always found the subject fascinating. Bartholomew, did you moot something to do with diet the last time we met?'

Bartholomew nodded, and was about to elaborate when Nigellus cut rudely across him. 'I have never been convinced by all that rubbish. A man should eat what he feels like, on the grounds that the body knows best. The notion of good and bad foods is a nonsense.'

Bartholomew could not help himself. 'So you think that a man who eats nothing but red meat or marchpanes will be healthy? Surely it is obvious that a balanced diet is extremely important.'

'An excellent thesis,' said Joliet, writing it down before Nigellus could object. 'The students will have a lot of fun with that. Any more suggestions?'

There were, but none of them were suitable, and when he felt the discussion was starting to go around in circles, Joliet called the meeting to a close.

'I recommend we go away and think very carefully,' he said, folding the parchment and slipping it in his scrip. 'Our shortlist needs to be longer than two.'

'Yet more wasted time,' grumbled Nigellus. 'I would not have agreed to serve on this stupid committee if I had known how much indecision there would be. May I go now, Father Prior? I have patients waiting – *paying* patients.'

He gave a superior smile before turning to strut towards the door, his remarks designed to remind Bartholomew that *he* did not demean himself by tending paupers like his Michaelhouse colleague, and that all *his* clients were from the very highest echelons of society. Bartholomew watched him go, eyes narrowing when the ousted Zachary student and several cronies hurried to cluster around the Junior Physician the moment he stepped outside.

'They just want to know when his next lecture will be,' explained Irby quickly, seeing what Bartholomew was thinking. 'I assure you, they are not asking the outcome of this meeting.'

'Of course not,' said Wauter, uncharacteristically acerbic. 'After all, being mobbed by pupils clamouring to know our teaching plans is an occupational hazard, is it not? However, regardless of Nigellus's popularity in the classroom, I should not like to be physicked by him. It is said that a lot of his Barnwell patients died before he took up his appointment here.'

'Lies,' said Irby firmly. 'Put about by bitter people who cannot afford his horoscopes. He is very good at them, and no one who follows his advice ever becomes unwell. He is of the admirable opinion that it is better to prevent sickness than to cure it once it has arrived.'

'Perhaps I shall commission one, then,' said Joliet. 'I dislike being ill. It is time-consuming, unpleasant and a nuisance. How expensive are his predictions?'

'Very,' replied Irby. 'Although I shall have to invest in another soon, because my last one has expired and I have been feeling shabby of late. Will anyone join me for a drink at home? My brewer makes a lovely apple wine, and I broached a new cask last night.'

* * *

16

It was too early for wine, as far as Bartholomew was concerned, so he left Wauter and Joliet to accept the invitation while he set off for Michaelhouse, intending to put the rest of his free day to good use by preparing lectures for the following week.

He had not taken many steps before he heard his name called, and turned to see Michael waddling towards him. The monk had an office in St Mary the Great – besides being a member of Michaelhouse, he was also Senior Proctor, a post he had manipulated to the point where he ran the entire University. The Chancellor, who should have been in charge, was a mere figurehead, there to take the blame if things went wrong. Bartholomew had once asked the monk why he did not apply his skills to improving Michaelhouse's precarious finances, and had received a rueful reply: Michael knew how to control people; he did not know how to generate vast sums of money.

'I am on the run from Thelnetham,' Michael explained, falling into step at Bartholomew's side. 'He wants me to persuade Langelee to take him back.'

He referred to William Thelnetham, a Gilbertine canon who had resigned his Michaelhouse Fellowship to take advantage of a better opportunity. Unfortunately, the new offer had fallen through, leaving Thelnetham in limbo. He was desperate to be reinstated.

'It was his decision to go,' Bartholomew pointed out. 'And he went eagerly, after calling us thieves, fools and lunatics. His spiteful tongue caused a lot of unhappiness, and the College is better off without him. Besides, Wauter has his post now and we cannot afford to fund another.'

'I agree and so does Langelee, but that does not stop Thelnetham from pestering me at every turn. And it is not as if I have nothing else to worry about either. Hallowtide, for example.'

'Are you expecting trouble?' Bartholomew stifled a

yawn. He had been summoned by a patient in the small hours, and he was tired. Unfortunately, he would not be catching up on sleep that night because of the feast: even if he managed to escape early, there would be far too much noise for peaceful repose.

Michael shot him a sour glance. 'How can you even ask such a question? The town is furious with the University over the business with King's Hall, and there will certainly be skirmishes later, when too much wine and ale have been swallowed by both sides.'

'What business with King's Hall?'

Scholars and townsmen were always at loggerheads, and Bartholomew found it difficult to keep track of all their disagreements, especially during term time, when he was struggling to balance classes containing an impractical number of students with the demands of an enormous medical practice.

Michael regarded him balefully. 'Have you listened to nothing I have told you this week? It is the latest crisis to assail our poor *studium generale.*'

Bartholomew racked his brain for answers. 'Do you mean the case of trespass that King's Hall has brought against some drunken brewer?'

'That "drunken brewer" did a lot of damage. He let the pigs out, chased the geese, and terrified John Cew out of his wits by leaping out at him from behind a buttress. Indeed, Cew has still not recovered, and his colleagues want you to visit later, to see what can be done.'

Bartholomew nodded, but thought the antics of one silly townsman should not have been given so much attention. In his opinion, John Wayt, who was in charge of King's Hall while its regular Warden hobnobbed with royalty in Winchester, should have ignored the matter in the interests of good relations.

'Cambridge has never wanted us here,' Michael went

on bitterly. 'Sometimes I wonder whether our ancestors should have chosen another town. Peterborough, for example. I liked what I saw when we were there last summer.'

'It is a pretty place,' agreed Bartholomew. 'But I imagine its people would have objected just as vigorously to a lot of noisy and opinionated academics descending on them.'

'I suppose so.' Michael frowned worriedly. 'I have had to order all my beadles to work tonight, because there is a rumour that Frenge – the marauding brewer – plans a repeat performance, and there are plenty of hotheads in the town who are eager to join him.'

Bartholomew regarded him in alarm. Of all the Colleges, King's Hall was best able to protect itself, not only because it boasted sturdy walls and a powerful gatehouse, but also because many of its scholars were the sons of noblemen, well-versed in the art of combat. Frenge and his supporters were likely to get themselves killed if they staged an invasion.

'A massacre will do nothing to calm troubled waters,' he said worriedly. 'Let us hope your beadles can talk some sense into them.'

They reached Michaelhouse to hear a lot of noisy activity emanating from the kitchens. Agatha – technically the laundress but in reality head of the domestic staff – was in the midst of the maelstrom, screeching orders as she oversaw preparations for the festivities to come. Bartholomew smiled at the cacophony, and surveyed the College that was his home.

Its core was a fine hall with an oriel window, where the scholars took their lessons and meals. Adjacent to it was the conclave, while beneath were the kitchens and a range of pantries, butteries and storerooms. At right angles to them were the two accommodation wings, the older, smaller north wing more dilapidated than the newer southern one. A wall completed the square, against which had been built stables and a porters' lodge. There were more outbuildings behind the hall, as well as a long garden that ran down to the river.

The Hallow-tide celebrations were to begin with a special Mass in church, and most scholars had already donned their finery, ready to go. Those in holy orders were bedecked in their best habits, while the seculars wore their College uniform of black, but with ceremonial fur trimmings to mark the special occasion. Langelee saw Bartholomew and Michael, and came to talk to them, William trailing at his heels.

'Have you heard the rumours?' the Master asked. 'That Frenge the brewer will lead another assault on King's Hall tonight?'

Michael nodded. 'My beadles will stop him.'

'They had better,' said Langelee. 'I do not like the mood that bubbles here at the moment, and another raid by Frenge will certainly ignite a spat.'

They all jumped when there was a sudden roar of delight from the High Street. Then smoke wafted into the sky above the rooftops, a few wisps at first, followed by bigger billows.

'Will Lenne must have lit the bonfire that he and his apprentices built at the back of our church,' said Langelee angrily. 'I asked him to move it to a safe distance, but he refused, on the grounds that that particular plot is common land. I hope it does not do us any damage. We cannot afford repairs – at least, not until we have secured some wealthy benefactors.'

'We should have dismantled it, as I suggested,' growled William. 'Because the town will not pay if anything goes wrong. And if you want an example, look at how Frenge is refusing to make good on the destruction he wreaked on King's Hall.'

'If we had destroyed Lenne's handiwork, he would just

have rebuilt it, and then there definitely *would* have been harm to our church,' said Langelee. 'He has been very crafty: the fire is as close to St Michael's as it can be, without one twig over the boundary and—'

He broke off when there was an urgent hammering on the gate. Walter the surly porter emerged grumbling from his lodge with his pet peacock under his arm, a bird that possessed a temper every bit as irascible as his own. He listened to the message that was delivered, then hurried towards the little knot of Fellows.

'Trouble,' he reported grimly. 'Frenge has been murdered in the Austin Priory, and the town is saying that King's Hall did it.'

Besides being a physician and teacher of medicine, Bartholomew was also the University's Corpse Examiner, which meant it was his responsibility to declare an official cause of death for any scholar who died, or for anyone who breathed his last on its property. He was paid three-pence for every body he inspected, money he used to buy medicines for his poorest patients. As it had been a busy few weeks and his funds were low, he was grateful for the opportunity to replenish them, and fell into step at Michael's side with something approaching enthusiasm.

Unfortunately, the post did nothing for his reputation among the wealthy, who disliked the notion of being treated by a man whose last client might have been a cadaver. The poor were not too happy about it either, but as no other physician was willing to treat them free of charge, they tended to keep their reservations to themselves.

Rumours about Frenge's demise were already circulating, and the atmosphere was darker and more menacing than it had been earlier. Scholars no longer walked singly or in pairs, but formed larger groups for protection, while the town's malcontents gathered in sullen gangs that loitered in doorways or under trees.

Then Michael saw that a group of academics had cornered two bakers' apprentices in St Michael's churchyard, their antics partially concealed by the wafts of dense smoke that billowed from the bonfire at the back.

'Stop,' he commanded. The students turned in surprise. They were from Zachary, and their leader was Yerland, the lad who had tried to eavesdrop on the *consilium*. The bakers' boys took the opportunity to flee.

'We were only warning them to be mindful of the flames, Brother,' said Yerland, all wounded innocence. 'That fire might be on common land, but its sparks are flying towards University property. Look at them!'

He was right, and Bartholomew noted with alarm that bright cinders were not only dancing over the top of St Michael's roof, but were flying towards Gonville Hall and Michaelhouse, too. Several townsmen, careful to stay on their own side of the invisible line that marked the boundary, made challenging gestures that turned into jeers when the Senior Proctor and his Corpse Examiner declined to respond. Zachary's lads bristled, though.

'Ignore them,' ordered Michael sternly. 'Brawlers will be fined – as will anyone not wearing his prescribed uniform.'

The students had flouted the University's ban on ostentatious displays of wealth, and had augmented their grey and cream livery with fashionably pointed shoes, feathered hats, a plethora of jewellery and multicoloured leggings.

'It is Hallow-tide,' explained Yerland petulently. 'The townsmen are wearing their best clothes, so why should we not do the same?'

'Because they are not scholars,' retorted Michael. 'Now go home, before your rule-breaking costs you a penny apiece.'

The lads slouched away, although not without muttering that it was a Michaelhouse ploy to unsettle their opponents before the *disceptatio*. Michael treated the remarks with the contempt they deserved by pretending he had not heard.

'Perhaps I was wrong to coax Wauter from their fold to ours,' he sighed. 'Irby is too gentle to be effective, and struggles to keep order without Wauter's support.'

'You *poached* Wauter?' Bartholomew was shocked: there was an unwritten law in the University that foundations did not steal each other's members.

The monk shrugged. 'We needed to fill the vacancy left by Thelnetham, and I adjudged him to be the best candidate. It was a good decision: he is a fine teacher, an excellent geometrician and his company is a pleasure. Besides, he was glad to escape – Zachary had offered Nigellus a place by then, and Wauter does not like him.'

Bartholomew hoped such underhand tactics would not cause trouble at the *disceptatio*. He changed the subject as they walked away, tuning out the taunts from the folk around the bonfire.

'If someone from King's Hall did murder Frenge, why did it happen in the Austin Friary?'

'King's Hall did not kill him,' said Michael impatiently. 'At least, I hope not, because it will create a rift that will not be easily mended. So bear that in mind when you make your report, please, Matt: accident or suicide, but definitely *not* murder. Is that clear?'

Bartholomew winced. He was not a good liar, and hoped such a deception would not be necessary. He walked faster, wanting the matter resolved as quickly as possible. Moreover, he disliked the uneasy mood in the streets. He was more popular than most members of the University, partly for his care of paupers, but also because he had kin in the town – a sister, who had recently assumed control of her late husband's cloth business. But there was no point in courting trouble, and the wisest course of action was to go home as soon as possible and stay there.

They arrived at the Austin convent, which was shielded from the outside world by high walls and two gates: the main entrance on St Bene't's Street, and a smaller one at the back, although this opened on to the canal known as the King's Ditch and could only be reached by boat. They knocked at the front gate, and were admitted by a burly friar named Hamo de Hythe, one of the two Austins who often accompanied Prior Joliet to Michaelhouse.

Like Joliet, Hamo was also a talented artist, although it seemed impossible that such huge fists could produce such beautifully delicate images. He rarely spoke in more than monosyllables, and was a great mountain of a man who could have done with a much larger habit.

Inside, the Austins' domain was much like any other Cambridge convent. Its chapel formed the heart of the community, and huddled around it were dormitory, refectory, kitchen, stable, storehouses and sheds. Most were timber-built with thatched roofs, although the chapel was of stone, an intimate, pretty place pierced by lancet windows and famed for its fabulous murals. The sound of chanting emanated from within.

Hamo led the way inside, and the clanking of the door made two of the kneeling brethren break off their prayers to greet the visitors. One was Prior Joliet, and the other was his almoner Robert, a tall, rangy man with a shock of long white hair and the eccentric bearing of the dedicated academic. Robert was the other friar Joliet took to Michaelhouse, although to teach rather than paint. He was responsible for distributing alms, which he did with a quiet, kindly compassion that did much to make the Austins the most popular Order in the town.

'We were praying for Frenge's soul,' Joliet explained. His round face was pale, and his hands shook as he

24

plucked agitatedly at a loose thread on his sleeve. 'It seemed the right thing to do, although we have no experience of violence committed on holy ground.'

'The Dominicans, Franciscans and Carmelites are used to it,' elaborated Robert. 'But we have always managed to remain aloof from the spats between University and town.'

'"Aloof" is the wrong word,' said Joliet unhappily. '*Apart* might be better.'

'What happened?' asked Michael, unwilling to waste time on semantics.

Joliet rubbed his eyes with unsteady fingers. 'The town feels oddly dangerous today, so just before sext, Hamo went to check that our back gate was shut and found . . .' He trailed off.

'Frenge,' finished Hamo helpfully.

Robert hastened to supply a bit more detail. 'The gate was open and Frenge was lying there, dead. The town is saying that he was murdered by King's Hall, because of his vow that he would never pay for the damage he did there.'

Joliet looked as though he might be sick. 'When we heard Hamo shout, we raced to see what was the matter. We did our best to revive Frenge, but he was well past any help we could give.'

'When terrible things like this happen, it makes me wonder whether our predecessors might have been wiser to found our University out in the Fens,' said Robert. He fingered the cross he wore around his neck; it had been carved of wood so dark that it appeared black.

'It would certainly have made for a more peaceful life,' agreed Michael.

Joliet led the way out of the chapel to the greasy grey snake of the King's Ditch, an ancient waterway that had been built to defend the town from attacks from the east. It was as wide as the river but its flow was sluggish, which meant that anything tossed in it tended to stay. As a result, it comprised a reeking, sulphurous sludge of sewage, entrails from the slaughterhouses and miscellaneous rubbish.

As they approached, they saw they were not the first to arrive. Sheriff Tulyet was already there. Tulyet was slightly built with a boyish face, and more than one criminal had lived to regret making the assumption that youthful looks equalled weakness. He and Michael had worked hard to develop an efficient working relationship, one unblighted by the usual jurisdictional spats.

Puzzled, Bartholomew wondered why Joliet had not stayed with him – it was rude to leave a high-ranking official on his own – but the answer soon became clear: Tulyet had brought his son. Dickon was only ten years old, but was already taller than his father, and was a mean-spirited bully. Because he bore no resemblance to either of his parents, in looks or temperament, there was a rumour that he had been sired by the Devil. By rights, he should have been sent to another wealthy household to begin knightly training, but his reputation had gone before him and Tulyet had been unable to find one that would take him.

'This is bad news,' said Tulyet without preamble. 'Even if Frenge's death is natural, the town will assume the worst. Dickon! Do not prod the body with your sword. It is disrespectful.'

'I hope people do not think that *we* had anything to do with the poor man's demise,' said Joliet unhappily, as Bartholomew, one wary eye on Dickon's blade, knelt next to Frenge and began his examination.

'They will certainly suspect a scholar,' replied Tulyet. 'If not an Austin, then someone from King's Hall.'

'They will deny it,' said Michael.

'They will,' agreed Robert. 'I have already heard several holler that Frenge broke in to make good on his threat to damage more University property, and was struck down for his temerity.'

'The town will not appreciate *that* being said about one of its favourite brewers,' said Tulyet. He scowled when Bartholomew jerked backwards suddenly. 'Dickon! Step away from the corpse and let Matt work in peace. And sheathe your sword this instant!'

Bartholomew waited until Dickon had complied before resuming his inspection, much happier once there was no longer a sharp weapon waving about so close to his head.

'So why was Frenge here?' asked Michael of the Austins. 'Was he visiting or was he intent on mischief?'

'Mischief,' replied Hamo tersely.

'Hamo is right,' said Robert. 'As you know, there are only two ways into our grounds: the main gate and this one. Frenge did not come to the front, which means he must have crossed the ditch in a boat – slyly and secretly.'

'I cannot imagine why,' said Joliet tearfully. 'We brew our own ale, so we are not among his customers. None of us know him other than by sight – and only then because his spat with King's Hall earned him a certain notoriety.'

'What about your servants?' asked Tulyet.

'We do not have any,' replied Robert, slightly smug. 'We prefer to channel our resources into alms, rather than catering to our own comforts.'

'Well, Matt?' asked Michael, as Bartholomew stood. 'What can you tell us?'

'Frenge has not been dead long,' replied the physician. 'The damp mud on his boots indicates that he was walking around in them not long since, and there is a residual warmth in his body, despite the coolness of the day.'

'More importantly, how did he die?' asked Tulyet.

'Poison,' replied Bartholomew. 'There are burns on

his mouth and hands, and considerable damage to his throat. I have never seen a clearer case of murder.'

'Damn it, Matt!' muttered Michael. 'I thought I told you to declare it accident or suicide.'

The reeking King's Ditch was no place for a serious discussion, so once Frenge had been loaded on to a stretcher and taken to the nearest town church, Joliet invited everyone to his house, which transpired to be a modest cottage with spartan furnishings. It was spotlessly clean, though, and the only extravagance was a small collection of theological tomes.

'I agree with Michael,' said Tulyet, once they were settled with cups of watery ale. The convent did not run to cakes, so pieces of bread dusted with herbs were provided instead. Dickon took one bite, pulled a face and lobbed the rest out of the window, much to his father's chagrin. 'We cannot let this be murder: Frenge must have taken this toxin by mistake.'

'I do not think so,' said Bartholomew. 'Finger-shaped bruises on his jaws suggest that he was forced to drink it. And even if I am wrong, and he did swallow it willingly, why would he kill himself here? It is not on the beaten track, so I sincerely doubt he just happened to be passing when he was overwhelmed by a sudden desire to commit suicide.'

'He would *not* have killed himself here,' stated Joliet firmly. 'We have done nothing to earn his ire. If he had wanted to make that sort of point, he would have gone to King's Hall.'

'But security has been increased at King's Hall,' countered Michael. 'He may have tried to break in, but failed, so came here instead.'

'But why?' pressed Joliet. 'Why not another College? Or better yet, a hostel – few of them have walls or fortified gates.'

'Perhaps he *did* break into King's Hall,' suggested Tulyet soberly, 'but was caught. Then, keen to avoid trouble, the scholars brought his murdered corpse here.'

'They are not stupid,' said Michael bitingly. 'They would have dumped him in the town, not in another part of the University.'

'Assemble our brethren, Hamo,' ordered Prior Joliet tiredly. 'Perhaps one of them knows something that will allow us to solve this mystery. I am afraid I have nothing to report – as I said, I knew Frenge by sight and reputation, but I never met him.'

'Nor had I,' said Robert, watching Hamo shuffle from the room. 'He never came here for alms. Well, why would he? Brewers are not poor.'

Michael turned to Bartholomew. 'Tell us about the poison. If we can identify it, perhaps it will lead us to the culprit.'

'It will not,' predicted the physician. 'It was the kind of caustic substance that can be found in many homes and businesses – used for cleaning, scouring, killing fleas and dissolving residues. Some everyday solutions are extremely toxic.'

'So it might have been something Frenge owned himself?' pounced Tulyet. 'All brewers like to sample their wares, so perhaps he gulped down a jug of this stuff before he knew what he was doing, and staggered here in search of help.'

'Staggered across the town, into a boat and over the King's Ditch?' asked Bartholomew. 'That seems unlikely for a dying man.'

'But we *cannot* allow a verdict of murder!' said Tulyet irritably. 'The town will blame scholars, regardless of who is the culprit, because of the bad blood between Frenge and King's Hall. And then we shall have another of our interminable spats.'

'So what do you suggest, Dick?' asked Michael. 'That we lie?'

'I have heard worse ideas. And in the interests of keeping the peace . . .'

Michael considered for a moment but then regretfully shook his head. 'We would never succeed in keeping it quiet, not when a whole convent knows what really happened.'

'My friars can be trusted,' objected Joliet, offended.

'Even so, the truth will out,' said Michael. 'It always does. The best we can do is stress that the Sheriff and Senior Proctor will leave no stone unturned in their pursuit of the truth.'

'Very well,' said Tulyet reluctantly. 'Although the villain will not be a townsman. This crime has University written all over it.'

Michael regarded him coolly. 'I beg to differ, but we shall see. Ah! Here is Hamo with the other Austins. Let us hope they know something useful, because the best way to avert trouble will be to arrest the culprit as quickly as possible.'

Unfortunately, none of the twenty or so friars could help. No one had been near the back gate that day, because they had either been beautifying the chapel for Hallow-tide, or helping to cook the huge vat of soup they planned to distribute to beggars as a special treat.

'I am sorry,' said Joliet gloomily, after the last one had gone. 'Obviously, if we knew such a terrible thing was in the offing, we would have been more observant.'

'We had better lock the back gate from now on, Father Prior,' said Robert worriedly. 'We do not want this happening again.'

'No,' agreed Joliet fervently, and then sighed. 'Perhaps you are right to wish that our University had been founded in the Fens, Robert. I dislike living in a place that does not want me.'

'It is unfortunate,' agreed Michael. 'But the town will accept us eventually.'

'Will it?' asked Joliet bleakly. 'We have been here for a century and a half, and it shows no sign of welcoming us yet. I am beginning to think it never will.'

'Look!' cried Dickon with sudden glee, pointing a plump and grubby finger at the sky. 'Sparks and flames! All coming from St Michael's Church. It is on fire!'

CHAPTER 2

St Michael's Church was a pretty place, and Michaelhouse revelled in the fact that it alone of the eight Cambridge Colleges actually owned the place where it performed its daily devotions. But it was more than a status symbol to Bartholomew: it was a haven from the hectic round that comprised his life, and the final resting place of many much-loved colleagues. Heart in his mouth, he raced towards it, hating the notion that it might be lost.

'Thank God,' gasped Michael, when they arrived to find the bonfire blazing merrily but the church unscathed. 'I was sure disaster had struck.'

Bartholomew nodded as he leaned against a buttress to catch his breath, thinking sourly that there had been no need for the townsfolk to have built their pyre quite so high. Perhaps they *did* hope it would damage University property, which was galling, as Michaelhouse had tried hard to win their affection. Not only did he physick many of them without charge, but Michael ran a choir that was essentially an excuse to provide the needy with free food, while the other Fellows gave money they could ill afford to charitable causes or said free Masses for anyone who asked.

'People have short and selective memories,' said Michael soberly, reading his friend's thoughts. 'But our church still stands – for now, at least – so we had better visit the brewery to break the news of Frenge's death before they hear it from someone else.'

They began to walk along the High Street. It was busy with people who were either 'souling' – earning cakes in return for prayers for the dead – or making last-minute adjustments to their bonfires. Those who were to take part in the torchlit procession were beginning to assemble, but the atmosphere was more menacing than celebratory, and both scholars were glad to turn down a road that was devoid of revellers.

Water Lane, where Frenge's brewery was located, was one of several alleys that ran between Milne Street and the river. It was fairly well maintained because it was in constant use by the wagons that carried goods to and from the wharf, and boasted a number of fine houses. Some belonged to the merchants whose warehouses stood nearby, but most had been bought by scholars after the plague had emptied the area, and were now hostels. The largest and grandest was Zachary, which had recently been fitted with new window shutters – a gift from one of its many wealthy members.

Unlike most of the river thoroughfares, Water Lane did not end in a muddy slope and a rickety pier. It finished in a spacious cobbled yard dominated by two very different but equally handsome buildings, and a spanking new jetty. Of the buildings, one was the brewery, while the other was owned by Bartholomew's sister, Edith Stanmore.

A few weeks before, Edith had startled her brother and everyone else who knew her by announcing a decision to expand her late husband's highly profitable cloth business. She had achieved this by entering the dyeing trade, and had acquired premises, equipment and a workforce before anyone had really understood what she was doing – which was unfortunate, as the venture had aroused a lot of ill feeling. There were two main reasons for this: first, dyeing was a noxious process, and generated a lot of bad smells and unwholesome effluent; and second, she had chosen to hire staff from a controversial source.

'Prostitutes,' said Michael, as two women emerged. 'I understand Edith wanting to do something good for the town's downtrodden, but did she *have* to open her doors to harlots?'

'They are not harlots,' objected Bartholomew. He loved his sister, who had raised him after the premature death of their parents, and disliked anyone disparaging her. Moreover, helping the women had allowed Edith to think of something other than how much she missed her beloved Oswald, and he was glad to see the sparkle back in her eyes after so many weeks of sorrow. 'They might have walked the streets once, but now they are gainfully and decently employed.'

'Perhaps,' said Michael, although doubt was clear in his face. 'However, the place reeks *and* it fouls the river. All dyeworks do, which is why there are laws stipulating that they must be sited well away from any settlement. It is unfortunate she managed to find a way around them.'

'You make her sound sly,' said Bartholomew resentfully. 'She is not.'

'Not as a rule. However, she did commission Cambridge's most slippery lawyer to look for a legal loophole – and Stephen's contention that dyeworks are clean because they use a lot of water is disingenuous. I am surprised you support her in this, because such disgusting waste must surely be harmful to health.'

Bartholomew did not reply, because the truth was that he *was* concerned about the dyeworks' effluent. He and Edith quarrelled constantly about it, so it was a sore subject for him – he hated being at loggerheads with her, and wished she had never started the scheme in the first place. Oswald Stanmore had not dyed his own wares in the middle of the town, so why did she have to do it? He supposed he would have to try again to persuade her to shut the place down, or move it somewhere out of sight and mind, although it was not a prospect he relished – Edith had thrown herself wholeheartedly into saving 'her ladies'.

Seeing the physician was unwilling to discuss it further, Michael marched towards the brewery and rapped on the door. 'Frenge owns . . . *owned* this business with a man named Shirwynk,' he said. 'Shirwynk is a very unpleasant individual, and I have had several altercations with him over the last few weeks.'

'What about?'

'Selling inferior brews, picking fights with scholars, grazing his horses on College land. I hope he does not turn violent when he learns that Frenge is dead.' Michael glanced up at the sky. 'And I hope our interview with him does not take long, because I should hate to miss the feast.'

Bartholomew regarded him askance. 'You think about your stomach as you are about to deliver news of an untimely death? Not to mention the fact that the town is on the verge of a riot, you have a murder to solve, and there is a bonfire next to our church that may set it alight at any moment?'

Michael shot him a disagreeable look and hammered on the door again. 'I notice you say that *I*, not we, have a murder to solve. I shall need your help if I am to find the culprit.'

'I cannot, Brother. Nigellus and Rougham are coming to put my students through a mock disputation in the morning, so I will be busy.'

'You plan to let Nigellus loose on your pupils?' asked Michael in disbelief. 'Why? The man is an ass, and I would sooner die than call on him for medical assistance.'

'Those are strong words, Brother. What has he done to vex you?'

'He is smug, arrogant, overbearing and as clever as clay. He is probably an Oxford man.'

Bartholomew laughed. 'As am I, Brother, in case you had forgotten.'

'Yes, but you had the intelligence to abandon the Other

35

Place and come here as soon as you were qualified, whereas Nigellus has been stagnating at Barnwell for the past forty years. So am I right? *Did* Nigellus learn his medicine at Oxford?'

Bartholomew nodded. 'Followed by practical training in Norwich. Or so he says.'

'You do not believe him?'

'He is probably telling the truth. Unfortunately, he seems to have learned nothing since, and some of his skills could do with updating.'

Michael grimaced. 'Zachary should never have recruited him. His abrasive personality does nothing to make our University more popular among the townsfolk.'

'He is not an easy man, which is why I must be there tomorrow, to make sure everything goes smoothly.' Bartholomew sighed ruefully. 'And to ensure that he and Rougham do not teach my lads a lot of nonsense. I should have refused when they made the offer, but I did not want to offend the only two other *medici* in the University.'

'Your boys are more than capable of distinguishing the intelligent from the twaddle, and I need you. Besides, you always object to lending a hand but we both know you will do it in the end. We go through the same charade every time there is a suspicious death.'

'I do not—' began Bartholomew indignantly.

'Just agree to help me, Matt,' said Michael testily. 'It will save us both a lot of trouble.'

Bartholomew knew the monk was right, although it galled him to admit it. He leaned against the wall and kicked moodily at the cobbles, resenting the loss of precious teaching time. Then there was a loud clatter from the dyeworks, followed by a rank smell that grew stronger with every breath. He detected the distinct tang of old urine, mixed unpleasantly with brimstone and something so powerful that he wondered if it was melting his lungs.

He and Michael were not the only ones who thought the dyeworks should move away from the town, and dozens of people had gathered to protest when Edith had first opened her doors. Most had given up when they realised the place was there to stay, but a few diehards persisted. That day, they comprised a handful of scholars from the nearby hostels, who claimed the fumes were distracting them from their studies, and an equal number from the town, who objected to the fact that laws had been twisted to allow Edith to start the business in the first place.

Bartholomew watched them wave their fists as the reek rolled out, although it was not long before the angry voices turned against each other – the two sides might have a common cause, but they still could not bring themselves to join forces. All he hoped was that the dyeworks would not provide the spark that would ignite the latest trouble that was bubbling.

It was some time before the brewery door was hauled open – by a great bear of a man who wore a sleeveless leather tunic that revealed hairy shoulders; his features were blunt and pugilistic.

'You again,' he said coolly to Michael. 'What now?'

'We bring sad news, Shirwynk,' said Michael kindly. 'May we come in?'

'If you must,' replied Shirwynk ungraciously. 'Although no decent townsman likes having scholar-scum on his property, so say your piece quick and get out.'

He turned and stalked inside, leaving Bartholomew and Michael to follow as they would. The place smelled strongly but not unpleasantly of barley and yeast, and was full of the huge vats used to ferment ale. A lad of eighteen or nineteen lounged against one. He was unshaven, dour-faced, and he looked like the kind of youth who would find fault with everything. He scowled at the scholars and spat, narrowly missing Bartholomew's foot.

'My son Peyn,' said Shirwynk, nodding towards him with obvious pride. 'He is going to Westminster soon, to work in the Treasury.'

'Is he?' asked Bartholomew, startled. Such posts were highly sought after, and the slovenly Peyn did not look like the kind of person who would appeal to the fastidious and exacting officials who ran the country's finances.

'Yes,' said Shirwynk tightly, sensing an insult in the response. 'Now what do you want?'

'It is Frenge,' began Michael, but then could not resist taking the opportunity to fish for information before breaking the news. 'Do you know where he might be?'

'We are not his keepers,' replied Peyn insolently. 'All we can tell you is that he went out just after terce – five hours ago now – to deliver ale to King's Hall.'

Bartholomew did some quick calculations: that left a three-hour window between when Frenge had left the brewery and when the Austins had found the body.

'Why would he go there?' asked Michael suspiciously. 'He hates the place.'

'Perhaps the barrel was a peace offering,' said Peyn, with the kind of smirk that suggested he thought it highly unlikely.

Bartholomew experienced a growing sense of unease. Had Frenge done something sly to the ale, something that would lay an entire College low? And if so, had King's Hall seen through the plot and forced him to swallow the stuff himself? It would certainly explain the bruises on his jaw. But then how had Frenge's body gone from the College to the Austin Priory?

'I am afraid Frenge is dead,' said Michael gently. 'He was taken ill near the Austin Priory, and although the friars did their best to help him, it was to no avail. I hope you can take comfort from the fact that they are praying for his soul as I speak.'

'We already heard,' said Shirwynk. He seemed more irked than distressed. 'Although it is hard to believe – he was perfectly well earlier.'

'He was poisoned,' Michael went on. 'My Corpse Examiner here—'

'Your *what?*' interrupted Shirwynk, regarding Bartholomew askance.

'Matt inspects all those who die on University property,' explained Michael. 'He—'

'In that case, I do not want him near Letia,' said Shirwynk firmly. 'Not if he has had his hands on cadavers.'

Bartholomew regarded him blankly. 'Letia?'

'My wife. Nigellus did her horoscope, see, and he says she will die before tomorrow. I was considering getting a second opinion, but I do not want one from a Corpse Examiner.'

The last two words were spoken with considerable distaste.

'I am a physician first,' said Bartholomew, hoping Nigellus had done something more useful for the poor woman than predict the time of her passing.

'Perhaps,' said Shirwynk with a shudder. 'But you will stay away from her – now *and* when she is dead. Is that clear? Now get out.'

He began shoving both scholars towards the door before Bartholomew could say whether it was clear or not.

'Wait,' ordered Michael, resisting. He was a large man, and all but impossible to budge if he did not want to go. 'Your friend was *poisoned*, Shirwynk. Surely you must want to help us catch the culprit? You can do it by answering questions.'

'I already know who is the culprit,' snarled the brewer. 'King's Hall.'

And with that, he gave Michael a push that sent him staggering into the street, a feat that revealed him to be a very powerful man. Bartholomew was thrust out after him and the door slammed closed. Michael straightened his rumpled habit.

'He was very determined that an expert on death should go nowhere near his ailing wife,' the monk remarked. 'It was suspicious.'

Bartholomew agreed, but could hardly insist on seeing the woman against her husband's wishes, and his immediate concern was King's Hall. He broke into a run, aware of Michael struggling to keep up, but the monk had enjoyed too many sumptuous meals at University expense, and his girth had expanded accordingly. He was a long way behind by the time Bartholomew reached Cambridge's largest and most influential College, and rapped on the gatehouse door.

'Thank God you are here at last, Doctor!' cried the porter who answered. 'Come in quickly. Master Cew is dying.'

King's Hall was proud of its royal connections. It had been founded by Edward II forty years before, and was the College of choice for the kin of barons and high-ranking churchmen. Grateful alumni showered it with gifts, and it occupied by far the most sumptuous buildings in the town, set amid beautifully manicured grounds. Each Fellow had the unthinkable luxury of one or even two rooms to himself, and its table was among the finest in the country.

Bartholomew saw none of the tastefully understated elegance as he hurried through the College on the heels of the porter, but he did notice the students. All wore some form of armour and carried weapons, even though University rules forbade it. A few were in major holy orders, but even these had donned leather jerkins and toted thick wooden staffs.

'We are expecting trouble,' explained the porter. 'There is a tale that Frenge is dead, and we will be blamed, even though we had nothing to do with it. Rough men from the town have been drinking all morning, so it is only a matter of time before they attack.'

'Have you received a delivery of ale today?' Bartholomew asked urgently. 'From Frenge?'

'We would not have accepted anything from him! He might have spat in it – or worse.'

'Then what about from another brewer?'

The porter shook his head. 'The only thing to arrive was a horoscope from Nigellus for Master Cew. Then Acting Warden Wayt said we should not open our doors again – other than to you – because too many townsmen are stupid with drink.'

'Very wise,' said Bartholomew, sagging with relief. 'Now tell me what ails Cew.'

'Impending death,' came the unhelpful reply. 'Would you like a soul-cake?'

'What?' asked Bartholomew, bemused by the non-sequitur.

'A soul-cake,' repeated the porter, stopping to take one from a platter that stood on a table in the hallway; the air around them was rich with the scent of butter and spices. 'Then you can say a prayer for my mother, who died last year.'

He turned at the sound of footsteps – Michael had caught up at last. Without a word, the monk snatched the biscuit from the porter's hand and rammed it into his own mouth.

'I need nourishment,' he muttered, spraying crumbs down the front of his black habit as he spoke, 'if I am to gambol around the town like a spring lamb.'

'Then take several,' said the porter, beginning to hurry forward again. 'It is a shame to waste them, and I doubt we will be giving them to friendly callers *this* Hallow-tide.

41

Wise scholars will stay home and townsmen will not be welcome. Not if they plan to accuse us of murder.'

'That is a pity, because these are very nice,' said Michael, who considered himself an expert on pastries. 'A little sweet, perhaps, but there is a good balance of cinnamon and nutmeg.'

'I am sorry Warden Shropham is away,' whispered Bartholomew as they followed the porter through a labyrinth of corridors and halls. 'He is much more reasonable than Wayt, and would never have sued Frenge in the first place.'

'Wayt is a menace,' agreed Michael, almost indecipherable through his next cake. 'Shropham should have appointed someone else as his deputy, although from what I understand, Wayt simply announced that he was doing it and Shropham was too taken aback to object.'

Eventually, they reached the library, a huge room with a magnificent hammer-beam roof and purpose-built bookcases. Bartholomew frowned his puzzlement when he saw that Cew was not breathing his last, but standing on a shoulder-high windowsill with a dish on his head, a poker in one hand and an apple in the other. John Cew was a small man in his fifties, and the physician wondered how he had managed to scramble up there.

Two men were pleading with him to come down. One was Acting Warden Wayt, who was distinctive by having an unusually hairy face. The other was Geoffrey Dodenho, whose academic prowess was nowhere near as impressive as he thought it was.

'Your porter told me that Cew was dying,' said Bartholomew, rather accusingly.

'He is,' averred Wayt. 'Every day that passes sees more of his mind destroyed – and it is all Frenge's fault. Cew was the greatest logician our College has ever known, but now look at him.'

'He thinks he is the King of France,' elaborated

Dodenho. 'The bowl is a crown, and the poker and apple his sceptre and orb.'

'Have you come to pay homage to your monarch?' demanded Cew in a booming voice that he would never have used had he been well. 'Then kneel before us.'

'Lord!' muttered Michael, watching Bartholomew push a table under the window so that he could stand on it and help Cew down. 'He has been like this ever since Frenge startled him?'

Wayt nodded. 'I have heard that a violent fright can turn a man's wits, and that is what happened when Frenge hid behind a buttress and leapt out. I saw it happen, and I witnessed the terror on Cew's face. It was a wicked thing to do.'

Bartholomew climbed on the table and offered Cew his hand. With great solemnity, Cew gave him the apple to hold while he made his descent. When he was down, he reclaimed the fruit and went to sit by the hearth, where he recited a list of all the French barons who had lost their lives at Poitiers, complete with a description of the armour they had worn. Unlucky chance had put Bartholomew at that particular battle, so he was able to say with certainty that Cew's analysis was uncannily accurate.

'He is very pale,' he observed. 'Has he been eating properly?'

'He will only accept oysters and soul-cakes,' replied Dodenho. 'He says those are all that is fit for the royal palate.' He lowered his voice. 'But they block his innards, and he has not been to the latrine in days.'

'We summoned Nigellus the day Frenge did this terrible thing to Cew,' Wayt went on, 'because he is the most expensive of the University physicians and therefore must be the best. He spent hours calculating a horoscope, then told us that Cew would only recover if we took him to stand under an oak tree in the light of the next full moon.'

'But it was raining on those particular nights,' added Dodenho. 'And Cew refused to leave his rooms anyway. He thought the Prince of Wales might be out there, and he is wary of him after what happened at Poitiers. Do *you* have any advice, Bartholomew?'

Bartholomew was tempted to say that he had, and that it was never to hire Nigellus again. But diplomacy prevailed and he kept his opinion of the Zachary *medicus* to himself.

'Ailments of the mind are a mystery to me, I am afraid, and you are already doing what I would recommend – making sure his needs are met, and preventing him from harming himself.'

'These rumours about Frenge,' said Wayt, turning to Michael. 'Are they true? *Is* he dead in the Austin Priory?'

Michael nodded. 'He was poisoned – murdered.'

'I do not believe that, and neither should you,' scoffed Wayt. 'I imagine he broke in intent on mischief, but was struck down for his audacity – God had obviously had enough of him. There was a tale that he planned to raid us again tonight, so I cannot say I am sorry he is no longer a threat.'

'Do not blame Frenge's death on the Almighty,' warned Michael sternly. 'If you do, we shall have even more trouble with the town.'

'I do not care. If they do not want a war, they should not have applauded Frenge's crime.' Wayt rounded on Bartholomew. 'And speaking of crime, can you do nothing to stop your sister from killing us all? Her dyeworks are poisoning the river.'

'It is true, Matthew,' said Dodenho. 'All the fish are dead, and I am sure she was responsible for that bout of sickness at Trinity Hall last week. After all, it happened after they drank ale made with water from the river and—'

'That ale was from Frenge's brewery,' interrupted Wayt. 'Doubtless he and Edith conspired together to bring Trinity Hall low.'

'Actually, the culprit was a syllabub,' said Bartholomew coolly. 'Which had nothing to do with my sister or Frenge. I tasted it myself and the cream was bad – not to mention the fact that it was so sweet as to be unpleasantly cloying.'

'Probably because it was stuffed full of sucura,' said Dodenho.

'Sucura?' queried Bartholomew.

'The sweet powder from Tyre that Sheriff Tulyet has recently deemed illegal,' replied Wayt. 'It is smuggled through the Fens to avoid import tax, so you will not see any in King's Hall.'

'Tell me again what happened when Frenge came and did all that damage,' ordered Michael, whose refined palate told him that sucura had been in the soul-cakes he had just eaten. However, he was unwilling to waste time on the argument that would follow if he said so.

'It was a week ago now,' obliged Dodenho. 'We were all at table, and did not know he was here until we heard the pigs rampaging in the yard. We hurried out to see Frenge driving them towards our hall. He turned his attention to the geese then, and chased them into the orchard.'

'We followed, but he managed to evade us,' said Wayt. 'Then I saw him hiding behind the buttress. Cew was nearby, but before I could shout a warning, Frenge had ambushed him.'

'Frenge escaped in the ensuing confusion,' finished Dodenho, 'and poor Cew has not been in his right mind ever since.'

'It was an outrage,' said Wayt angrily. 'We are right to sue Frenge for damages.'

'You cannot sue him now he is dead,' said Michael. 'He—'

'Oh, yes, we can,' countered Wayt. 'We shall transfer our claim to his estate – the brewery he part-owned. That will show the town that they cannot get the better of us, not even if they die.'

'In the interests of good relations—' began Michael in alarm.

'No,' hissed Wayt. 'We will *not* withdraw. Frenge did us a lot of harm, and we intend to ensure that he pays for it. His death is irrelevant as far as I am concerned.'

'There are rumours that King's Hall murdered him,' said Michael, also growing angry. 'If you persist with this lawsuit, everyone will believe them.'

'Do you think we care what townsfolk believe? Their opinions matter nothing to us.'

'Well, they matter to me,' said Michael, controlling his temper with difficulty. 'And my investigation must be one of which they will approve or we shall have a riot. That means interviewing every member of King's Hall about the crime, which we shall do at once. Assemble them, if you please.'

'What, *all* of them?' asked Dodenho, startled. 'This very moment?'

'If you would be so kind.'

Interrogating every member of King's Hall was a daunting task, as there were more than forty Fellows, all of whom had at least two students, not to mention an army of servants. Fortunately, the College had held a feast to mark the beginning of Hallow-tide, so most had an alibi for the three-hour window in which Frenge had died.

Michael was thoughtful when he and Bartholomew eventually left. 'Only three of the Fellows cannot account for their whereabouts: Wayt went to attend urgent College business in his quarters; Dodenho disappeared to practise a lecture; and Cew was left unattended in his quarters, so no one knows whether he stayed there or went a-wandering.'

'Can you really see any of them invading the Austin Priory to commit murder?' asked Bartholomew doubtfully.

'Oh, yes,' replied Michael. 'Very easily, if you want the truth. Wayt is viciously spiteful, Dodenho thinks he is

46

cleverer than the rest of us, while Cew is insane. Or is he? He might be pretending in the hope that we will exclude him from our enquiries. Well? Is it possible?'

'I suppose so. Can we go home now? It is getting dark, and it is reckless to be out while so many drunken townsmen are spoiling for a fight.'

'I ordered a curfew for all scholars between dusk and dawn, and it would not do for the Senior Proctor to set a bad example.' Michael grinned at Bartholomew. 'Which means I have the perfect excuse to stay in and enjoy tonight's celebrations.'

The High Street was teeming, pitch torches bobbing in the gathering gloom as folk gravitated towards St Mary the Great, outside which the procession would start. Many folk were also still traipsing around the homes of friends and relations, and as refreshments invariably included a drink as well as a soul-cake, few were sober. Bartholomew was right: it was no time for two scholars to be abroad without good reason.

'There are those Zachary men again,' said Michael irritably. 'What are they doing out in defiance of my instructions?'

Bartholomew's stomach lurched when he saw that the scholars in question had gathered in a circle around two women, one of whom was his sister. Without considering the consequences, he surged towards them, shoving them away from her with considerable vigour.

'It is all right, Matt,' said Edith quickly, as blades appeared in a dozen outraged hands. 'We are only discussing a consignment of red cloth.'

'Were you?' asked Michael, hurrying over to regard the hostel men archly. 'Why, when your uniform is grey and cream? And speaking of academic tabards, you seem to have forgotten yours. Where are they?'

'We decided to dispense with them.' The speaker was an older man, a master rather than a student. He wore

47

a black and yellow gipon – a knee-length tunic with sleeves. Its colour, coupled with his small size and bristling demeanour, were redolent of a wasp.

'You cannot dispense with them,' said Michael irritably. 'They are—'

'We do not answer to you, Brother,' interrupted the man sharply.

'Oh, yes, you do,' countered Michael. 'I am the Senior Proctor.'

'And I am John Morys, bursar of Zachary and kin to the Chancellor,' the wasp flashed back. 'We make the rules for our own scholars, and care nothing for your silly strictures.'

'Too right,' agreed the second older man among the throng, who was remarkable for a pair of startlingly purple lips. 'I am Peter Segeforde, Zachary's philosopher. What Morys says is true.'

'Is that so?' asked Michael mildly. 'And does Principal Irby agree?'

'Of course he does,' replied Segeforde shortly. 'He is no fool.'

'Then he is included in the fine I am about to levy,' said Michael sweetly. 'A penny from every man in your hostel, for insolence and flouting University rules.'

'You cannot,' said Morys coldly. 'Not without the Chancellor's agreement – and Tynkell and I have recently become kin by virtue of his mother's latest marriage. He would never dare cross a member of her new family, because she would skin him alive.'

'She is Lady Joan de Hereford,' said Segeforde, puce lips curling into a smirk. 'Not only is she formidable, but she is also a friend of the Queen, and thus in a position to make life difficult for any man who dares cross her. So go home, Brother, and keep your nose out of our affairs.'

'I think you will find that Tynkell fears me a lot more

than his dam, no matter how ferocious and well-connected she happens to be,' retorted Michael. 'Now will you return to your hostel willingly or will you bear the shame of being marched there by my beadles?'

While they argued, Bartholomew turned to Edith. He peered at her in the darkness to reassure himself that she was well – he had not forgotten the depth of her sorrow during the first few weeks of her bereavement.

'You scholars!' she whispered, and he smiled when he heard the laughter in her voice. 'If you are not arguing with us, you are squabbling with each other. I have never known a more quarrelsome horde.'

'It is because they have too much time on their hands,' explained the woman who was with her. 'They would not be so querulous if they did an honest day's work.'

'This is Anne de Rumburgh, Matt,' said Edith. 'I told you about her the other night.'

'Did you?' asked Bartholomew, then remembered his manners and bowed politely.

Anne favoured him with a smile that was, by any standards, full of sensual promise. She was taller than Edith, and her kirtle was cut to show off the voluptuous curves of her figure; its neckline was lower than was currently fashionable and certainly lower than was decent. Her lips were red and full, and her eyes bright with the suggestion of fun.

But Bartholomew only inclined his head in a brief nod before turning back to Edith. He had suffered some recent mishaps with his love life, which had wounded him deeply, and he was unwilling to risk another encounter with the opposite sex just yet.

'Yes,' said Edith, a little crossly. 'She runs the sales side of the dyeworks for us, and I praised her financial acumen to you for at least an hour. You gave every appearance of listening. Was your mind on something else, then?'

'Of course not,' mumbled Bartholomew, although he

49

felt the colour rise into his cheeks at the lie. He had been thinking about his lost loves, Matilde and Julitta, as he always did when he was not occupied with patients or teaching.

'Good,' said Edith coolly. 'Because I have better things to do than chat to myself. The dyeworks are a major undertaking, and there are many issues that require my attention.'

'You mean like finding ways to avoid tipping waste in the river?' asked Bartholomew.

Edith shot him a sour look. 'Such as who to hire. So many Frail Sisters have applied to work with us that we are having to make some very difficult choices.'

Bartholomew experienced a sharp stab of loss. 'Frail Sisters' had been Matilde's term for the town's prostitutes, and she had championed their cause, organising them into an unofficial guild whereby they united to create better and safer working conditions. Now Edith was a widow, there was no one to tell her that they were unsuitable company for a respectable lady, and she had elected to take up where Matilde had left off. Bartholomew glanced at Anne, wondering whether she was one of them.

'No,' said Edith, reading his thoughts. 'She is the wife of William de Rumburgh the goldsmith. You know him – he is one of your few wealthy patients.'

'The one with the inflamed gums,' supplied Anne, seeing Bartholomew rack his brains.

'Oh, yes.' The physician was often better at recalling ailments than the people who displayed them. 'He has trouble eating.'

'That is the least of his problems,' said Anne with a grimace. 'More annoying is that his condition adversely affects his performance in the marriage bed. You suggested ways in which we might remedy the matter, but none have worked. I am now a lonely and desperate woman, especially in the evenings when he is out at the guildhall.'

Another sultry smile came Bartholomew's way.

'Are you going to watch the procession, Matt?' asked Edith, deftly changing the subject, clearly fearing he might be tempted by Anne's none-too-subtle invitation.

'No scholars can go,' he replied. 'The University has imposed a curfew.'

'Ignore it,' suggested Anne with yet another smouldering look. 'And come to my house instead – to keep me company until my husband returns. He will be *very* late and—'

'You heard him – he is obliged to stay in tonight,' interrupted Edith sharply. 'And you had better go home to change, Anne, or you will be late.'

Anne fluttered her eyelashes and sashayed away, hips swaying provocatively.

'Are you sure it is a good idea to employ her?' asked Bartholomew. 'She does not seem to be your sort of . . . person.'

'No,' sighed Edith. 'But so many folk want to close the dyeworks down that it is a relief to find someone who not only understands what I am trying to do, but who wants to be part of it. And do not say that you do, because you cannot see past the fact that we sometimes create a few smelly by-products.'

'It worries me – I do not want you blamed if people become ill. And you have always been a considerate neighbour, so this sudden callous indifference to their health is a mystery to me.'

'I am not indifferent to it – I just know that my dyeworks will not harm them. Ours is a *good* scheme, Matt. It has given desperate women a new chance in life.'

'I know that, but—'

'My ladies now have a regular and assured income that allows them to feed their children,' Edith continued

51

passionately. 'They are at home at night, where they belong, instead of risking life and limb on the streets. No one would question the venture if it were being run by nuns – or by scholars for that matter – but because Frail Sisters are involved, it is deemed dirty and toxic.'

'Can you be sure it is not?' asked Bartholomew pointedly.

'Yes,' replied Edith firmly. 'But I cannot debate it with you now. I need to go and make sure that all is safely locked up for the night. Good night, Matt. If you visit me tomorrow, I will mend that tear in your tabard.'

Bartholomew fingered the rip, sure it had not been there that morning. As Edith hurried away, his mind turned to the curious case of Rumburgh's gums, a complaint that he had never seen before, and that might even prove to be—

'—Matt's verdict,' Michael was telling the Zachary men, and mention of his name drew the physician from his medical reverie. 'He should know: he has inspected hundreds of them.'

'Hundreds of what?' asked Bartholomew, hoping Michael had not claimed anything too outrageous on his behalf.

'Corpses,' replied Michael. 'I was just telling these gentlemen that we *will* catch whoever poisoned Frenge, no matter who the culprit transpires to be.'

'And I was telling him that he will not,' countered Morys. 'Because *God* killed Frenge for daring to invade King's Hall.'

'That sort of remark is why the town does not like us,' snapped Michael. 'It is inflammatory and certain to cause offence.'

'Good,' said Segeforde spiritedly. 'Then let them challenge us over it. It is high time we taught them a lesson.'

* * *

52

It was now completely dark, but Bartholomew and Michael had not taken many more steps towards home before they met Nigellus, hurrying after his Zachary colleagues.

'Do not think of fining *me* for breaking the curfew,' he said archly. 'I have been on an errand of mercy to Letia Shirwynk, who was dying. Her husband refused to buy her a horoscope until it was too late to make a difference, so he should not be surprised that she is gone.'

'What was the cause of death?' asked Bartholomew with the polite interest of a fellow professional. He suspected that Shirwynk would not mourn the hapless Letia long – the brewer had not seemed particularly distressed when he had mentioned her predicament earlier.

'Dizziness,' replied Nigellus. 'A very nasty way to go.'

'Dizziness?' echoed Bartholomew. 'How can she have died of that?'

'Easily,' said Nigellus coolly. 'As she would confirm, were she in a position to satisfy your ghoulish curiosity. She reeled and fainted, and it was a blessed relief when she breathed her last.'

'What were her other symptoms?' pressed Bartholomew, sure Nigellus's diagnosis was in error. 'And how long did she have them?'

'At least a month – she was suffering long before her husband finally overcame his miserliness and agreed to pay for her stars to be read. And her other symptoms are irrelevant, because it was the dizziness that killed her.'

'Perhaps Matt can inspect her before she is buried,' said Michael, as unhappy with Nigellus's claims as Bartholomew. 'I was just telling your colleagues that he is very good at determining accurate causes of death.'

Nigellus smiled tightly. 'Which is why he holds the sinister title of Corpse Examiner, I imagine. However, I would rather he kept away from Letia. I do not want people thinking that he questions my proficiency, which is how it will appear.'

'Was Frenge your patient?' asked Bartholomew, feeling it *should* be questioned.

Nigellus regarded him coldly. 'Yes, but it has been more than a week since I saw him. I read his stars and recommended that he spent more time asleep in bed and less drinking in taverns. He would doubtless be alive today if he had heeded my advice. And now you must excuse me. I am not in the mood for idle chatter.'

He stalked away. Bartholomew glanced at Michael, and without a word they began to walk back to the brewery, both suspicious that the belligerent Shirwynk should lose his friend and wife on the same day.

'Of course, it is odd that Nigellus was *medicus* to both as well,' said Michael. 'Not to mention his order for you to stay away from Letia's corpse. He would not be the first physician to dispatch his patients, either by design or incompetence.'

'But both were wealthy,' Bartholomew pointed out. 'Nigellus would not deprive himself of a useful source of income on purpose. And as to his competence, I have not seen him at work often enough to judge. However, his diagnoses are a little unusual . . .'

'More than a little,' murmured Michael.

Once they were off the High Street, the town was quieter, as most folk had gone to watch the procession. Yet neither scholar felt any safer, knowing that while law-abiding citizens might be enjoying the spectacle, there were plenty of others who prowled the darkness in search of mischief.

'I hope you realise that I do not have the authority to look at Letia,' said Bartholomew. 'The brewery is not University property and she was not a scholar. Shirwynk has already asked us to stay away, and if he refuses to change his mind, there is nothing you can do to make him.'

'We shall see.' Michael had considerable faith in his powers of persuasion. 'But speaking of authority, I am inclined to bring mine to bear on Zachary. I have never met so many unpleasant individuals under one roof: Nigellus, Segeforde, Morys, Yerland . . . There is a feisty Franciscan named Kellawe, too – the fellow with the big jaw.'

'Yes, I have met him. He preached a sermon saying there is a sulcus in the heart that houses the soul. I told him that no anatomist had ever found such a feature, and he called me a heretic.'

'You took a risk, admitting to knowledge of the evil art of dissection.'

'I would not have spoken if the other half of his sermon had not been a diatribe against Edith for helping the Frail Sisters. He objects to them touting for business on the streets, but when someone provides them with an alternative way to earn a living, he complains about that, too.'

'I am glad I poached Wauter,' declared Michael. 'He is too decent to live in Zachary.'

'So is Principal Irby. He is on the *consilium,* and is a perfectly reasonable man. I am surprised he puts up with such colleagues.'

'I would like to close the place down,' said Michael. 'Unfortunately, Morys was telling the truth when he claimed to have Tynkell in his sway – he does. Thank God Tynkell will retire at the end of next term. He used to be an ideal Chancellor, but he has shown a distressing independence of late, and I cannot work with someone who has ideas of his own.'

'He is a scholar, Brother. He is supposed to have ideas of his own.'

'Not ones that conflict with mine.'

Both stopped when there was a sudden roar of cheering voices. Bartholomew assumed it was the procession getting under way, but the direction was wrong, and Michael gave an urgent yelp before stabbing a plump finger to where bright flames danced up the side of St Michael's tower.

'That bonfire!' he cried. 'Now it *has* set our church alight!'

It was a fraught dash back to the High Street. Three different bands of marauding townsmen tried to waylay them, and it was not easy to extricate themselves without giving cause for offence. They arrived to find a large crowd watching gleefully as fire consumed a derelict lean-to shed that sagged against the base of the church tower.

'We have been meaning to demolish that anyway,' wheezed Michael, grabbing Bartholomew's shoulder for support as he fought to catch his breath. 'So its destruction is no loss. However, the blaze might spread, so you start putting it out while I fetch help.'

Bartholomew seized a long-handled hoe and began to knock the little building to the ground. Fires were taken seriously in a town with lots of wooden houses and thatched roofs, so he was surprised when the onlookers did nothing but jeer and hoot. He glanced at them as he worked. The men were sullen and the women snide, united in their hatred of the University and its perceived affluence. One went so far as to lob a stone at him.

'I love a good conflagration,' taunted the furrier named Lenne, whose wife Isabel was at his side. 'With luck, it will take their damned church as well.'

He coughed, the deep, painful hack of a man who had spent too many years inhaling hairs from the pelts he sold. Sadly, much of his antagonism towards the *studium generale* resulted from the fact that its physicians were powerless to cure him.

'I have never liked St Michael's,' declared Isabel. 'It stinks of scholars.'

'Help me!' shouted Bartholomew, bellowing to make himself heard over the mocking laughter that followed. 'If the church ignites, your houses might be next.'

'Not with this wind,' countered Shirwynk. Bartholomew was surprised to see the brewer out and about so soon after losing his wife, and could only suppose that he had been unable to resist the temptation of joining the mischief. 'The sparks are flying towards Gonville Hall and Michaelhouse, both places we should love to see incinerated.'

Bartholomew abandoned his efforts to persuade and concentrated on the shed. Just when he thought his efforts were in vain – that the church would burn anyway – Michael, Langelee and some of their students arrived. Once they did, the lean-to was quickly flattened and the flames stamped out.

'I told you this would happen, Lenne,' said Langelee angrily. 'You promised to be careful.'

Lenne coughed again, then shrugged. 'So I misjudged – just like Wayt of King's Hall misjudged when he decided to sue Frenge for trespass. And now Frenge is dead.'

'Murdered,' hissed Isabel. 'By a scholar.'

There was a growl of agreement from the crowd, but Michael drew himself up to his full and impressive height and it gradually died away.

'We do not know the identity of the culprit yet, so I suggest you keep your accusations to yourselves. And before you indulge in any more shameful antics, you might want to remember that we cannot repair damaged buildings *and* buy bread and ale for the poor – your fellow citizens – after choir practices.'

'Nor free care from the University's Senior Physician,' added Langelee tartly. 'So bear that in mind the next time you leave us to burn.'

There were more mocking jeers, but they lacked conviction, and it was not long before the crowd began to disperse, especially when the wind changed course and blew smoke towards them. It made Lenne cough so violently that he had no breath to argue and limped away on Isabel's arm. Soon, only the Michaelhouse men remained.

'Can we leave you to finish here, Master?' asked the monk wearily. 'Matt needs to examine Letia Shirwynk, whom we believe might have died in suspicious circumstances.'

'We cannot visit the brewery, Brother,' said Bartholomew. 'Shirwynk was among the onlookers just now, so he will not be at home to give us his permission.'

Michael smiled sweetly. 'Then we shall just have to get it from Peyn instead – which I anticipate will be a lot easier than dealing with his sire.'

Once again, they hurried through the dark streets, Michael more fleet-footed than usual as he aimed to be home in time for the feast. They trotted down Water Lane, grimacing at the rank smell that seeped from the dyeworks even though they were closed, and were about to approach the brewery when Peyn emerged with some friends. He was so intent on bragging about his imminent move to Westminster that he did not notice the door pop open again after he had closed it.

'His father will not be impressed by that cavalier attitude towards security,' remarked Michael, watching him swagger away. 'But it suits our purposes. Come on.'

Bartholomew baulked. 'If I am caught examining someone's dead wife without permission, the town will rise against the University for certain.'

'Then we must ensure that you are *not* caught. I will guard the door, while you go in. Be ready to make a run for it if you hear me hoot like an owl.'

'*Can* you hoot like an owl?'

Michael flapped an impatient hand. 'Hurry up. You are wasting time.'

Heart hammering, Bartholomew stepped inside. A lamp had been left burning by one of the vats, so he grabbed it and made his way to the living quarters at the back of the house, expecting at any moment to bump into Shirwynk, back early from the festivities. But he met no one, and it was almost an anticlimax when he found Letia's body on a pallet in the parlour.

He examined her quickly, ears pricked for anything that sounded remotely like a bird. However, it was a cacophony of cheers from the High Street that eventually drove him outside again.

'That was the procession ending,' whispered Michael. 'Shirwynk will be home soon, so let us be off before anyone spots us. Well? How did she die? And please do not say dizziness.'

'I could not tell. There are no marks of violence, and certainly nothing to suggest she swallowed the kind of poison that killed Frenge. To all intents and purposes, she appears to have died of natural causes. Yet there are compounds that kill without leaving any trace . . .'

'So was she murdered or not?' hissed Michael impatiently.

'I have already told you,' said Bartholomew, equally testy. 'I could not tell.'

'But you must! You were gone an age – you must have seen something to help us find out why Shirwynk's fellow brewer and wife died on the same day.'

'It is suspicious,' agreed Bartholomew. 'But I am afraid poor Letia provided no answers.'

CHAPTER 3

'Lord, I feel sick,' muttered Michael, as the Fellows took their places at the high table the following morning. Meals in College were meant to be taken in silence, so that everyone could listen to the Bible Scholar chanting the scriptures, but it was a rule they rarely followed, and the hapless reader invariably struggled to make himself heard over the buzz of conversation. 'I think I ate something that was past its best last night.'

The Benedictine was not the only one to be fragile. The feast had been glorious, reminiscent of the splendid affairs they had enjoyed a decade earlier, when the College had been flush with funds. There had been mountains of meat and fish, wine in abundance, bread made with white flour rather than the usual barley-and-sawdust combination, and enough cakes to feed an army. Bartholomew had stayed sober, lest he was called out on a medical emergency, but no one else had demonstrated such restraint, and now there were sore heads aplenty.

Langelee was pale, and kept both hands pressed to his temples as he mumbled a grace that comprised a string of half-remembered Latin quotations, including part of a recipe for horse-liniment. No one but Bartholomew seemed to notice. Wauter had dark circles under his eyes and winced when Langelee raised his voice for a final amen, while William's habit was not only splattered with a quantity of grease and custard that was remarkable even for that foul garment, but it was rumpled, suggesting he had slept in it.

The remaining Fellows were Suttone and Clippesby, both swaying in a way that suggested they might still be drunk. Clippesby was a Dominican who talked to animals and claimed they spoke back, so was generally deemed to be insane. He had no beasts about his person that day, however, and when the College cat rubbed around his ankles, it was ignored. Suttone was a portly Carmelite famous for his conviction that the plague was poised to return at any moment.

The students were also unusually subdued, and as breakfast comprised a bizarre and unsuitable combination of leftovers, it seemed that the servants had also availed themselves of the opportunity to enjoy the festivities the previous night.

'Is it my imagination, or do our pupils get younger every year?' asked Langelee, as food worked its magic on roiling stomachs and the students began to chat amongst themselves, throwing off their malaise with the enviable resilience of youth.

'They must lie about their age,' said Michael sourly. 'That puny boy in Matt's class – Bell, is it? He cannot be more than nine.'

'Eighteen,' said Bartholomew. 'They seem younger because you are growing old.'

'That is a wicked thing to say!' cried Michael. 'I am in my prime. However, there are a few grey hairs on *your* head that were not present a decade ago.'

'Those came because he let women make him unhappy,' stated William, referring to Matilde, who had left Cambridge because Bartholomew had been too slow to ask her to marry him; and Julitta, who had transpired to be a rather different lady from the one they all thought they knew. 'Painful affairs of the heart always age a man, which is why he should give up his various amours and become a Franciscan. Like me.'

'Or better yet, find a few more,' said Langelee. Relations with women were forbidden by the University, but many scholars – he and Bartholomew among them – opted to ignore this particular stricture. 'What about that widow you were seeing earlier this year? Is she still available?'

Bartholomew was aware that the students were listening, no doubt delighted to learn that the Fellows strayed from the straight and narrow – and his colleagues' remarks, taken out of context, made him sound like an incurable philanderer. Moreover, he did not want to be reminded of the confusion and hurt he had suffered that summer. He changed the subject with an abruptness that made everyone automatically conclude that he had intriguing secrets to hide.

'The mural is looking nice,' he declared. 'The Austins are talented artists.'

'They are,' agreed Wauter, prodding suspiciously at the plate of marchpanes and cabbage that had been set in front of him. 'It is why I suggested we hire them. You should see their chapel – it is a delight.'

They were silent for a while, studying the painting. It ran the full length of one wall, and was nearing completion. There had been some debate as to what it should depict, but in the end they had settled for Aristotle, Galen, Aquinas and Plato teaching rows of enrapt scholars. The faces of many College members were among them: Bartholomew sitting near Plato but straining to hear Galen; Clippesby with the College cat; Wauter raising a finger as he prepared to tackle Aristotle; and William scowling at Aquinas's Dominican habit – he hated his rival Order with a passion that verged on the fanatical.

'I do hope our plan works,' said Suttone worriedly, lowering his voice so that the students would not hear. 'We have spent such a lot of money on it, and if we fail to win benefactors . . .'

'I know it is a risk,' whispered Langelee. 'But we have no choice. We will not survive another year if we do not replenish our endowment, and drastic situations call for drastic solutions.'

'Then we *must* remain aloof from this burgeoning spat between town and University,' said Wauter. 'No secular will give us money if we support King's Hall against Frenge.'

'Hopefully, we will not have to be diplomatic for long,' said Langelee. 'We shall put on such a grand display at the *disceptatio* tomorrow that donors will race to be associated with us.'

'They will race even faster if we win,' said William, treating Bartholomew and Wauter to a pointed look. 'Which may not happen unless our representatives on the *consilium* agree to be reasonable and tell us which question they have chosen.'

'We cannot,' said Wauter shortly. 'We have not yet made our final decision.'

'Then you had better hurry up,' said the Franciscan disagreeably. 'Or do you expect us to stand around in St Mary the Great tomorrow, waiting while you debate the matter?'

'Perhaps we should listen to them instead of the students,' sniggered Suttone. 'It will almost certainly be more entertaining.'

'Regardless of what happens in the debate,' said Michael, tactfully changing the subject, 'when they see the lavish style in which we honour the memory of our founder, every wealthy family in the town will want us to do the same for them.'

'But if not, there is always Wauter's *Martilogium*,' said Suttone. 'He confided last night that all the monies from its publication will come to Michaelhouse.'

'You mean that list of martyrs that you have been compiling for the last twenty years?' asked Langelee eagerly. 'That is generous, man!'

Wauter shot Suttone a weary glance. 'Yes, I *confided* my intentions to you. That means you were meant to keep them secret until I was ready to make a general announcement.'

'Oh,' mumbled Suttone guiltily. Then his expression became pained. 'Lord! I remember why you told me now! To cheer me up after what Stephen the lawyer said – that he plans to leave his collection of tomes on architecture to Gonville Hall instead of us.'

'Does he?' cried Langelee, dismayed. 'I thought I had persuaded him that they would be more appreciated here.'

'You did,' said Suttone. 'But he changed his mind. Personally, I suspect it was Zachary's doing – to disconcert us before the *disceptatio*.'

'It will have been Kellawe,' said William viciously. 'I cannot abide him – he is a fanatic.'

'But he is a Franciscan,' Suttone pointed out, while the others supposed that the Zachary man must be zealous indeed to have drawn such condemnation from William, who was no moderate himself. 'A member of your own Order.'

'He should never have been allowed to join,' declared William hotly. 'He should have gone to the Dominicans instead. They are the ones who love heretics.'

There followed a lengthy diatribe, during which William listed all Kellawe's failings. His colleagues were wryly amused to note that every one of them was echoed in himself – arrogance, inflexibility, dogmatism and stupidity.

'What will the Saturday Sermon be about today, Suttone?' asked Langelee, eventually tiring of the tirade and so changing the subject. 'It is your turn to preach.'

Suttone's regarded him in horror. 'Is it? Lord, I forgot, and I have nothing prepared! Perhaps we all can listen to the mock disputation that Matthew has organised instead. I know it will be about medicine, but that cannot be helped.'

'Very well,' said Langelee. 'What is the subject, Bartholomew? And do not worry about what Nigellus and Rougham will think when informed that their audience will be ten times the size of the one they are expecting – they will be delighted, as both love being the centre of attention.'

Bartholomew hoped he was right. 'Whether scrofulous sores in the throat can—'

'Oh, no,' gulped Langelee with a shudder. 'I do not want to listen to that sort of thing today, thank you very much. We shall change it to something less grisly.'

'What about one of Aristotle's medical questions?' suggested Suttone. 'Such as my personal favourite: why do women have softer bodies than men?'

'I hardly think our theologians will want to hear the answer to that, Father,' said Wauter primly. 'Moreover, our seculars will become inflamed with lust, and we shall have trouble.'

'Nonsense,' said Langelee briskly. 'Medical debates necessarily involve mention of human parts, and I am sure we can trust Rougham and Nigellus to be genteel. Besides, our clerics can always stuff their fingers in their ears if anything too shocking is aired.'

He rubbed his hands together gleefully, although Bartholomew thought that if he was expecting anything enjoyably lewd from those particular *medici*, then he was going to be sorely disappointed.

When the meal was over, the servants began to remove dirty dishes and fold away tables, turning the hall from refectory to auditorium. Bartholomew went to wait by the gate, aiming to warn Rougham and Nigellus about the revised itinerary, so they could escape if they wanted. The rest of Michaelhouse might not care about offending their sensibilities, but Bartholomew was obliged to work with them, and did not want them irked.

'I have not attended a good debate in ages,' came a cheerful voice. It was Rob Deynman, who had been a medical student himself before Langelee had 'promoted' him to the post of Librarian. He had been accepted to study because his father was rich, but the unfortunate truth was that he had no academic talent whatsoever and everyone had heaved a sigh of relief when he had agreed to care for books rather than people. 'Now we shall have two in as many days.'

'Do you plan to take part tomorrow?' asked Bartholomew, a little uneasily. Michaelhouse would be unlikely to impress potential donors if he did.

'No, because Brother Michael says it would be beneath a Librarian's dignity,' replied Deynman. 'So I shall just listen, and nod sagely in all the right places.'

'Oh,' said Bartholomew, supposing he would have to be placed where no one could see him.

'I am sorry that Stephen is giving his architecture books to Gonville,' Deynman went on, his amiable face creasing into a scowl. 'He promised them to us, and I built special shelves to house them. I imagine Rougham did something sly to make him change his mind.'

'I do not think—' began Bartholomew, but Deynman was already stamping away, having thoroughly outraged himself with the notion.

'Ah, Matt,' said Wauter, emerging from his room. 'I keep meaning to ask you about your sister's dyeworks. Are you *sure* they are safe? My former colleagues at Zachary are extremely worried by the stench. As am I.'

Bartholomew was in a quandary. He did not want to betray Edith by voicing his concerns about the venture, but nor could he bring himself to issue false assurances.

'I will try to monitor what they do,' he hedged, although he was aware that Edith would not take kindly to such interference.

'Good,' said Wauter, smiling. 'But here comes Rougham, so I shall make myself scarce. I cannot see him being very pleased to learn that his opinion on scrofulous sores is no longer required, but that Michaelhouse is instead eager to hear what he thinks about the softness of women's bodies.'

Rougham was effectively Master of Gonville Hall, because the real one had gone to see the Pope in Avignon some years before and had not bothered to come back. He was a plump, smug man who hated anything that smacked of innovation, even if it worked. Bartholomew went to greet him, but Nigellus arrived before he could speak, glorious in a green gown and scarlet cloak that were certainly not part of Zachary's sober uniform of grey and cream.

'I am a few moments late because I was with a dying patient,' Nigellus declared importantly. 'I felt obliged to linger a while, lest he asked for another horoscope, but I think he is past caring about his stars now.'

'A wealthy patient?' queried Rougham, ready to be sympathetic to an inconvenient loss.

'Naturally, or I would not have answered his summons.'

Bartholomew tried to mask his distaste by informing them of the change of plan. He was surprised when Rougham clapped his hands together in delight and Nigellus actually smiled.

'Do not be sorry, Bartholomew,' said Rougham, eyes gleaming. 'It will be a lot more enjoyable than scrofulous sores, which I have never found particularly interesting anyway. I shall go first, naturally. After all, Nigellus is the *Junior* Physician, and so must take second place.'

Nigellus scowled. 'Call me that once more and I shall savage you in this debate. And do not think I cannot do it – I know a great deal about women's bodies, despite the fact that I have never had the opportunity to couple with one.'

Bartholomew blinked, astonished by the bald confidence, but Rougham, who had a long-standing arrangement with one of the town's most popular prostitutes, smirked superiorly. 'Then let the most experienced man win.'

'So this is your home,' said Nigellus, shoving past Bartholomew to stand in the yard and gaze around disdainfully. 'It is much smaller than I expected, and you must be terribly crowded. Thank God I chose Zachary instead.'

Resisting the urge to point out that Nigellus had never been offered a place at Michaelhouse, Bartholomew led the way towards the hall. For the first time, he saw the College through the eyes of an outsider. Algae ran in streaks down the walls, while the steps were worn and narrow. The hall was pleasant, but too small for the number of students currently enrolled, and it suffered from having no glass in its windows. The rushes on the floor needed changing after what had been dropped or spilled in them the previous night, and someone had lobbed a dish of brawn at the founder's coat-of-arms above the dais, where it had lodged.

He introduced the speakers, noting that the eyes of students and Fellows alike were bright with the prospect of vulgar entertainment, while the servants loitered behind the serving screen, pretending to work but clearly hoping to hear something rude.

'No,' interrupted Nigellus curtly, when Bartholomew announced his intention to preside. 'Your non-medical members will not want three physicians holding forth, so we shall have someone else instead. Father William, perhaps. He accused my colleague Kellawe of being a narrow-minded fool, so let us see *his* intellect in action.'

William surged to his feet. 'Very well. And then you can tell that stupid oaf how a *real* scholar performs in the debating chamber.'

Presented with a fait accompli, Bartholomew had no choice but to yield, although he did so with considerable reluctance, loath for members of rival foundations to witness the friar in action. The students were sniggering helplessly, while Langelee, Michael, Suttone and Wauter looked pained, and Clippesby, unable to witness what was about to transpire, simply stood and left.

It was the president's duty to introduce the subject, and William launched into a detailed account of the differences between the sexes that had everyone gaping their amazement at the depth and breadth of his knowledge. It wiped the smirk from Nigellus's face, and his own opening statement was repetitive and uninspired. Rougham was not much better, and it was only when the Franciscan stood to summarise their preliminary arguments that matters became lively again.

'I never said that large women find it easier to grow moustaches,' objected Nigellus in dismay. 'You have misquoted me, and make me sound like an idiot.'

'You have done that all by yourself,' retorted William. 'And you *did* say it – everyone heard you.' He addressed his audience. 'Am I right?'

There was a resounding chorus that he was, and Nigellus fell silent, folding his arms with a petulant pout. His sulk lasted until William paraphrased what Rougham was alleged to have said about big hips, at which point he released an involuntary snort of laughter.

'I can stand it no longer,' muttered Michael, taking Bartholomew's arm and pulling him away. 'And we should not be listening to this nonsense when there is a killer at large anyway.'

Bartholomew was sorry to go. No one would learn anything of medical use from the occasion, but it had certainly been entertaining, and he had been maliciously gratified to see the pompous Nigellus put in his place.

The two scholars had not taken many steps across the yard before they were hailed. Langelee had followed them out. The Master jerked his head towards the hall, from which angrily raised voices could be heard. They were loud enough that the servants were no longer obliged to lurk behind the serving screen to listen, and were going about their work outside, grinning as the combatants began to make some very outlandish claims.

'We shall have to do this again,' he said. 'It is very amusing.'

'My novices do not think so,' said Michael prudishly. 'They are mortified.'

Langelee laughed. 'Nonsense! They are relishing every moment. But tell me about Frenge and the rumour that King's Hall murdered him. Is it true?'

'He was poisoned, certainly,' replied Michael. 'But we do not know by whom – yet. We are about to visit Shirwynk again. He might have more to say now that he has had a chance to digest the news of his friend's death.'

'And his wife's,' add Bartholomew. 'I found no evidence of foul play, but it is odd that she and Frenge should die within hours of each other.'

'King's Hall would not have dispatched Letia,' averred Langelee. 'So if it transpires that she *has* been poisoned, you can eliminate them as suspects – which would be good, as it might calm the bubbling unease between University and town.'

'We need to know for sure, so will you open her up, Matt?' asked Michael. 'As you did with those murder victims last summer? Your findings then allowed us to bring a killer to justice, and I should not like to think of Letia dispatched with no one any the wiser.'

Bartholomew winced. He had advocated for years that dissection was the best way to learn about the mysteries of the human body, but when the opportunity had finally arisen to put theory into practice, he had found himself unsettled by the whole business and had no wish to do it again.

'With them, I was fairly sure I would find distinctive

70

lesions,' he hedged. 'That is not the case with Letia. Besides, Shirwynk would never allow it.'

'No,' agreed Langelee. 'And I would rather you did not ask. He is a burgess, and we cannot have him carrying tales of your ghoulish habits to men who may give us money. There must be another way to unearth the truth.'

'We shall have to rely on our interrogative skills, then,' sighed Michael. 'And afterwards, I shall inform Chancellor Tynkell that if he cannot bring Zachary Hostel to heel because he is afraid of what Morys might say to his mother, then he should resign now, not next term.'

'Quite right, Brother,' nodded Langelee. 'That place's unscholarly antics will put benefactors off the whole University. Go with him, Bartholomew. He will need help if he is to catch a killer *and* restore peace between us and the town. Do not worry about your classes – I will take them.'

'No, thank you,' gulped Bartholomew, knowing that the Master would not read the set texts, but would hold forth about camp-ball, his favourite sport. And what lively young man would not rather discuss fixtures and ratings than learning lists of herbs and their virtues?

Langelee waved a dismissive hand. 'Do not fret. Being a scholar is not all about reading books, hearing lectures and learning how to argue, you know.'

'No?' asked Bartholomew warily. 'What else is it, then?'

Langelee smiled enigmatically and ignored the question. 'You have my permission to miss meals and church until Frenge's killer is caught – except for this evening and tomorrow, when you will be needed to help with the preparations for the *disceptatio.*'

He strode away, leaving Bartholomew staring after him unhappily, hating the loss of valuable teaching time. There was so much he wanted his students to know, and he was struggling to cram it all in already. Michael tugged on his sleeve, murmuring that the quicker they started, the sooner they would finish.

They walked through the gate and on to Milne Street, along which was evidence that the previous night's festivities had been wild. Pie crusts, apple cores and other half-eaten foods were strewn everywhere, along with discarded clothing and smashed pottery. Principal Irby from Zachary was picking his way through it. As usual, he was wearing his uniform grey and cream cloak, the colours of which matched his pale face and the bags under his eyes. He was drinking from a flask, and the smile he gave was wan.

'What a night! I swear people were still carousing until an hour ago – and that includes Michaelhouse. I could hear *your* celebrations from my bedchamber.'

'We did do ourselves proud,' said Michael, smiling at the memory. 'But you must have enjoyed yourself, too: you look decidedly delicate this morning.'

'Because I am ill,' said Irby coolly. He brandished his flask so vigorously that some splashed on Bartholomew, who tasted its cloying sweetness as he wiped it off his face. 'But a sip of this will put me right. It is Shirwynk's apple wine.'

'Is there sucura in it?' asked Bartholomew, wondering why it was so sickly.

'Certainly not! The Sheriff has deemed that illegal, and I would never break the law.'

'It is a pity your students and masters do not think as you do,' retorted Michael sourly. 'Not one of them sees fit to wear his uniform these days.'

Irby suddenly looked very old and tired. 'I know, Brother, but Morys says his kinship with the Chancellor exempts him from the rules. And where he goes, the others follow.'

'He most certainly is not exempt,' declared Michael firmly. 'And you had better find a way to claw back control

72

or *he* will be Principal and you will be ousted.' Irby nodded miserably, so the monk changed the subject. 'When will the *consilium* decide the topic for tomorrow's debate?'

Irby turned to Bartholomew. 'Nigellus is wrong to insist on *nemo dat* – it will be tedious, and there are far more interesting issues to debate. A medical question, for example.'

'We had better not,' said Bartholomew, recalling what was currently happening in Michaelhouse. 'Besides, the last time I discussed medicine with a layman, I was accused of heresy.'

'By Kellawe, I suppose,' sighed Irby. 'Who believes that the soul resides in a pouch in the heart. He is wrong, of course. It is much more likely to be a pouch in the head. But a debate with a medical theme *will* be best, and I shall continue to ponder until the right subject comes to mind.'

'Good,' said Michael. 'Although you might want to run it past your Senior Proctor first. These occasions can be contentious, and we do not want trouble.'

'You want to know so that Michaelhouse's students will have time to prepare,' said Irby, wagging an admonishing finger. 'But I am afraid you will have to hear it at the same time as everyone else, because no one on the committee will break his silence.'

'*He* will not,' murmured Michael resentfully, watching him go. 'Nor will you, Prior Joliet or Wauter. But Nigellus will cheat for certain. He is that kind of man.'

As they continued along Milne Street, they met the Austins from the convent. Almoner Robert was struggling to carry the large and very heavy book that he needed for a lecture on Augustine's *Sermones*, long white hair undulating in the breeze, while hulking Hamo toted pigments, brushes and boards as though they were made of feathers. Prior Joliet was empty-handed and sombre.

'I cannot stop, Brother,' he said, as Michael made to intercept him. 'I am summoned to Will Lenne's deathbed, so I dare not linger.'

'The furrier?' asked Bartholomew, surprised. Lenne had hacked horribly the previous evening, but he had not appeared to be on his deathbed.

Joliet nodded. 'He is Nigellus's patient – his ailment has something to do with metal, apparently, although I am not sure what. Nigellus's message said that death was imminent, so you must excuse me – I promised to be with Lenne at the end, and I have a feeling that the lad Nigellus hired was not the quickest. I may already be too late.'

He hurried away, while Bartholomew recalled Nigellus claiming that his failure to arrive on time at Michaelhouse was due to a dying patient. Bartholomew was unimpressed: Lenne should not have been abandoned by his *medicus* at such a time. It was unprofessional.

'Did your novices read that extract I set them yesterday, Brother?' asked Robert, grimacing when his pectoral cross caught on a corner of the book, pulling it tight around his neck. He nodded his thanks when Michael pulled it free for him. 'Or shall I give my lecture tomorrow instead? I imagine you were all busy preparing for the feast.'

'We were,' nodded Michael. 'However, you cannot teach at Michaelhouse today – or paint, for that matter – because the University's *medici* are in our hall, showing everyone how to conduct a disputation.'

Robert regarded him uncertainly. 'You mean Rougham and Nigellus? You let them loose on your students? Heavens! You are brave.'

Michael laughed. 'It will keep them occupied while we try to find out what happened to Frenge. And speaking of Frenge, we should inspect the place where he died in daylight. May we visit you later?'

'Of course,' replied Robert. 'Come at noon and share

our dinner. It is nothing like the sumptuous fare at Michaelhouse, of course, but it is wholesome and plentiful.'

'Very well,' said Michael, never one to refuse free victuals. Then he scowled. 'Here come those Zachary men, and not one is wearing his academic tabard. It seems my threats of further fines have gone unheeded.'

Robert regarded them unhappily. 'The town resents the way they flaunt their wealth with these ostentatious clothes. If our University were out in the Fens, Zachary would not feel the need to bother, as there would be no women to impress.'

'Lust,' growled Hamo, the master of the one-word sentence.

'Hamo is right,' said Robert. 'Lust would not be a problem in the marshes, and Zachary would be more inclined to concentrate on their studies.'

The Zachary scholars were an imposing sight in their finery, and anyone might have been forgiven for thinking that they were burgesses. They were led by Morys, who wore a different set of clothes that day, but ones that were still reminiscent of an angry insect. Purple-lipped Segeforde was on one side of him, while the fanatical Kellawe was on the other. Their students strutted behind, defiant and gleeful – an attitude that suggested they were out without their Principal's permission. Michael had been right to warn Irby that Morys aimed to usurp his power.

'It is a holiday,' declared Morys insolently, as Michael draw breath for a reprimand. 'And Chancellor Tynkell says we can suspend our membership of the University for Hallow-tide, so do not think of fining us again. We are no longer under your jurisdiction.'

'You cannot opt in and out as the whim takes you,' snapped Michael. 'And if Tynkell told you otherwise, then he is sadly mistaken.'

'Well, he issued a writ that entitles us to do as we please anyway,' said Kellawe smugly. He spoke with a thick northern accent that was difficult to penetrate, and had a habit of jutting out his lower jaw belligerently when he spoke. 'You may contest it if you like, but by the time lawyers have debated the matter, Hallow-tide will be over, so you may as well not bother.'

'I threatened to write to Tynkell's mother if he refused my request,' smirked Morys, 'so he is unlikely to retract what he has granted. Besides, wearing secular clothes is nothing compared to the harm *his* sister is doing.' He stabbed a finger at Bartholomew.

'She has hired whores,' elaborated Kellawe, his eyes blazing rather wildly. 'Those dyeworks are nothing but a brothel.'

He turned and stalked away before Bartholomew could defend her. The others followed, clearly of the belief that they had won the confrontation. Bartholomew started after them – no one abused his beloved Edith – but Michael stopped him.

'Ignore them: they are not worth a quarrel. Unlike Tynkell. What was he thinking to issue such a document? He cannot be permitted to make these decisions without consulting me. Does he *want* the town to attack us?'

He released Bartholomew and stamped towards St Mary the Great, Shirwynk temporarily forgotten. Bartholomew stared at the retreating figure of Kellawe for a moment, tempted to go after him anyway, but Michael was right – the Franciscan was not worth the trouble. He followed Michael instead, catching up just as the monk marched into Tynkell's office.

Tynkell was a meek, timid man who had never wanted high office, and who had been as astonished as anyone when a technicality had seen him elected Chancellor. He was thin, wan, and had an unfortunate aversion to hygiene, which meant his chamber was rarely a pleasant place to be. He was sitting at a table that was piled high with documents representing the more tedious aspects of running a *studium generale*, work that had been delegated to him by Michael.

'You have some explaining to do,' the monk began without preamble. 'Regarding Zachary Hostel's—Oh, you have company.'

The 'company' was Stephen the lawyer, a fox-faced man with sly eyes. It was Stephen who had told Edith how to circumvent the laws regarding noisome industries, and who had disappointed Michaelhouse by electing to give his much-coveted collection of books to Gonville.

'We were discussing architecture,' said Stephen pleasantly, unperturbed by the monk's whirlwind entry. 'I should have liked to have been an architect, but my tutors thought my mind was better suited to law. However, I retain a deep interest in the subject.'

'So do Michaelhouse's students,' retorted Michael pointedly. 'And they had hoped to read some books about it.'

'Then I am sorry, but Gonville is more likely to be here in ten years' time than your College,' explained Stephen. 'It is nothing personal, and I must consider my own needs first.'

Michael blinked. 'What are you talking about? We are by far the most secure College in the University. We own lands in Suffolk, Staffordshire and Norfolk, and we were granted a huge benefaction earlier this year from no less a person than the Archbishop of York.'

He was grossly exaggerating the value of the College's holdings, but Stephen remained unconvinced even so. 'I have made my decision and I will not change my mind. The matter is closed.'

'Why are you here?' asked Michael, the curt tone of his voice suggesting that if Stephen had come to beg a favour, it would be refused.

'To give you some friendly and well-intentioned advice – that King's Hall should drop their case against Frenge's estate.'

Tynkell frowned. 'But it was you who told them that death is no excuse in the eyes of the law, and that Frenge's brewery will still be liable to pay their claims for damages.'

'Yes,' agreed Stephen silkily. 'But that was before Shirwynk hired me. Now I am recommending that King's Hall settles the case out of court, before they lose a lot of money.'

'Money is not the issue here,' said Michael, making no attempt to hide his distaste for the lawyer's duplicity. 'Our relationship with the town is – so *I* shall speak to Wayt and ask him to withdraw in the interests of peace. None of us want a war. Well, *some* of us do not: I am not sure that is true of the man who allowed Edith to build her filthy dyeworks.'

Stephen shrugged. 'It was all perfectly legal, I assure you. But to return to the matter in question, Shirwynk wants compensation for the distress he has endured. I am sure we can reach a mutually acceptable arrange-ment.'

Michael gaped at him. 'You want King's Hall to *pay* Shirwynk? Have you lost your reason? He is lucky not to lose half his brewery – assuming I can convince King's Hall to do as I suggest, of course. They may decline.'

'Then on their head be it,' said Stephen, standing and making a small bow before aiming for the door. 'And yours.'

'Lord!' breathed Tynkell, when he had gone. 'He changes sides like the wind. I never know whether he is for us or against us.'

'Whichever will make him richer,' said Michael sourly. Then he glared at the Chancellor. 'But I did not come here to talk about him. I came to discuss Zachary.'

Tynkell grabbed a handful of parchments from the

table, and clutched them to his thin chest, as if he imagined they might protect him. 'My mother has recently married into Morys's family, and she told me to accommodate him in any way I could, so I *had* to accede to his requests.'

'How can you be frightened of your mother?' asked Michael contemptuously. 'She must be well into her seventh decade. Or even her eighth.'

Tynkell nodded miserably. 'But age has rendered her fiercer than ever, and only a fool would cross her, believe me. Worse, she is a close friend of the Queen, so any infractions on my part will be reported to royal ears.'

'Then send Morys to *me* when he comes with his bullying demands,' said Michael irritably. 'I do not care what your dam whispers at Court, and his behaviour is unacceptable.'

'I will try,' mumbled Tynkell. 'But he is like you, Brother – he just bursts in and starts giving orders. I cannot say I am pleased to call him kin, and dealing with him plays havoc with my nerves. I do not suppose you have any of that soothing remedy to hand, do you, Bartholomew?'

It was mid-morning by the time Bartholomew and Michael emerged from St Mary the Great, but their journey to the brewery was interrupted yet again, this time by Acting Warden Wayt from King's Hall who shoved his hairy face into the physician's and spoke in a snarl.

'Your sister's whores have filled the river with blue dye, which has stained the wood on our pier. God only knows what toxins were in it. She poisoned Trinity Hall, after all, and it is probably her fault that Cew is so sick as well.'

'You said it was Frenge's antics that turned Cew's wits,' pounced Michael before Bartholomew could respond. 'If it is the dyeworks, then you cannot sue the brewery.'

'It was Frenge who sent Cew mad,' Wayt snapped back.

'But the dyeworks have given him stomach pains, nausea and vomiting.'

'He is worse?' asked Bartholomew, concerned. 'Would you like me to visit him again?'

Some of the belligerent anger went out of Wayt, and he nodded, although Michael rolled his eyes. Muttering under his breath, the monk followed them to King's Hall, where the College continued in a state of watchful vigilance – its gates were barred, armed students patrolled the tops of its walls, and barrels of water had been placed ready to extinguish fires.

'This would not be necessary if you dropped the case against Frenge's estate,' said Michael, as Wayt led him and Bartholomew along the maze of corridors to Cew's quarters.

'Never,' declared Wayt. 'I want reparation for the terrible crimes committed against us. That snake Stephen might have defected to Shirwynk for the promise of a larger fee, but we have good lawyers of our own, so he is no loss.'

'His recommendation to sue was seriously flawed,' said Michael. 'He was motivated by personal gain, and you cannot trust his advice.'

'He always did have an eye to his own purse,' Wayt conceded. 'But—'

'What he failed to tell you was that going ahead will cost you dear, even if you win. You will earn the town's undying hostility, and will have to pay a fortune in increased defences. None of us want trouble, so abandon this foolery and—'

'I shall not,' declared Wayt. He glared at the monk. 'And we are not moving to the Fens either. If the University leaves Cambridge, it will be without King's Hall.'

'There are no plans to relocate,' said Michael, puzzled. 'Who told you that there were?'

'Weasenham the stationer.' Wayt held up a hand when Michael started to object. 'I know he is a gossip and his "facts" are often wrong, but my Fellows have heard the same tale from several other sources, too, so it must be true.'

'Well, it is not,' said Michael shortly. 'How could we survive in the Fens without the services a town provides – bakeries, breweries, candle-makers, mills, potteries, clothiers, tanneries, saddlers? I know monasteries do it, but we are different: we would founder within a year.'

Wayt sniffed. 'Then make sure you tell the Chancellor so, should he moot the idea.'

Michael's eyes narrowed as a servant hurried past carrying a bowl. It was not a very big one, but he carried it with considerable care. It was full of grainy white crystals.

'Sucura,' he said accusingly. 'The substance banned by the Sheriff, which you assured me that King's Hall would never buy, despite the fact that I tasted it in your soul-cakes.'

Wayt's expression turned shifty. 'We did not *buy* it – it was donated by a benefactor, so it would have been rude to question its origins. Besides, it is for Cew. Soul-cakes are one of the two things he will eat, so we have no choice but to use sucura. Or do you suggest we let him starve?'

Cew's peculiar diet had done nothing to help him regain his wits. He sat in his bed with the pewter bowl on his head, and swiped with the poker at anyone who came close. After suffering a nasty crack on the elbow, Bartholomew decided to question him from a distance.

'You cannot ask the King of France about his bowel movements,' declared Cew indignantly. 'It is treason. Now go away – unless you can cure our terrible pains.'

'I might, if you let me examine you,' said Bartholomew crossly.

'Very well,' said Cew, capitulating abruptly. 'But do not touch our crown. Now hurry, because we shall be sick soon.'

Unfortunately, even a lengthy examination did not tell Bartholomew what was wrong with Cew. He prescribed a mild anti-emetic of chalk and herbs, and recommended that the oysters and cakes were replaced with a simple barley broth.

'We will try,' said Wayt. 'But he is shockingly mobile for an invalid, and will simply get what he wants from the kitchens himself if we do not oblige. I suppose we could lock him in . . .'

'No,' said Bartholomew quickly. 'It would cause him distress and might hinder his recovery. Just watch him as often as you can.'

'Do not worry,' said Wayt, uncharacteristic tenderness suffusing his hirsute face. 'He is one of our own, and we look after those. He shall have whatever he needs.'

Michael and Bartholomew reached the brewery eventually, where they found business in full swing, despite the deaths of Frenge and Letia. Apprentices moved among the great vats, stirring or adding ingredients, while Shirwynk sat at a table dictating letters to his son. A quick glance told them that the brewer was illiterate – if he had been able to read, he would have ordered Peyn to redo them, as the lad's grammar left much to be desired, while his writing was all but illegible.

'*Why* must we talk about Frenge again?' demanded Shirwynk, when Michael told him what they wanted. 'It is obvious what happened: King's Hall poisoned him, and deposited his body in the Austin Priory to confuse you. Of course, they need not have bothered with such a complicated ruse – you will never find a scholar guilty, no matter how compelling the evidence.'

'I have found scholars guilty in the past,' said Michael icily. 'I could cite a dozen examples.'

'Then arrest Wayt and his cronies,' snapped the brewer. 'Frenge was perfectly healthy when he left here to take ale to King's Hall yesterday.'

'Was he?' pounced Michael. 'How can you be sure?'

'Because he was singing. People do not sing if they are ill. Is that not so, physician?'

'I imagine it depends on the person,' replied Bartholomew cautiously.

Shirwynk shot him an unpleasant look and turned back to Michael. 'He was warbling happily as he loaded the dray with ale and wine. Right, Peyn?'

'Wine,' mused Michael. 'I have been meaning to ask you about that. You are a brewer, not a vintner, so you have no right to produce wine. How do the town's vintners feel about you treading on their professional toes?'

'There is only one vintner in Cambridge, and he is a sot who would rather drink his wares than sell them,' replied Shirwynk. 'Peyn suggested that we expand into wine earlier this year, and the venture has been very successful.'

'Which is why King's Hall refuses to drop its case against Frenge,' elaborated Peyn. 'Our fine apple wine has made us rich, and they itch to relieve us of our profits.'

'Do you keep toxic substances here?' asked Bartholomew. 'Perhaps for scouring—'

He stepped back quickly when Shirwynk rounded on him with a face as black as thunder, while Peyn fingered the knife he wore in his belt.

'You think to accuse *us* of Frenge's death,' the brewer snarled. 'Well, you can think again – we would never harm a friend. But look around, if you must. You will find no poisons here.'

Bartholomew took him at his word and began to explore. However, although he peered inside every vat, pot and cupboard, he saw nothing that could have caused the burns in Frenge's mouth. Of course, that was not to say that Shirwynk and Peyn were innocent – wise killers would already have taken steps to dispose of incriminating evidence.

'Your ale-making operation is impressively hygienic,' he said when he had finished. 'But where do you ferment the wine?'

Still scowling, Shirwynk led the way to the back of the brewery, where three large lead tanks had been placed in a line.

'We bought these from the Austin Friary,' explained Peyn, leaning against one and beginning to pare his nails with the dagger. 'They needed money to buy bread for the poor, so we got them cheap. We fill them with the juice from crushed apples, add yeast, and nature does the rest. This batch is ready for decanting. You may taste it if you like.'

He filled a cup from a barrel. Bartholomew took a very small sip, but it was far too sweet for him, and he was glad to pass the rest to Michael. The monk sniffed it, carefully inspected its colour, then took a large gulp, which he swished noisily around his teeth.

'It would slip down nicely with cheese,' he declared eventually, while the others watched the performance with fascination. 'And it has an agreeable punch.'

'It does,' agreed Shirwynk, pleased by the praise, although he tried to hide it. 'It is popular with wealthy townsmen and scholars alike.'

'Although we charge the University twice as much as we do the burgesses,' added Peyn, then scowled defiantly when his father shot him a withering look – the Senior Proctor had the right to set prices for food and drink, so telling him his colleagues were being cheated was hardly wise.

'It is so well liked that scholars break in here to steal it,' said Shirwynk, going on an offensive in the hope that Michael would forget his son's incautious remark. 'Some disappears almost every night.'

'How do you know an academic is responsible?' asked Bartholomew, a little indignantly.

'Because no townsman would raid me,' replied Shirwynk, rather unconvincingly. 'Peyn has taken to standing guard during the hours of darkness, but even he is obliged to slip away on occasion, and the villains always seem to know when the place is empty.'

'Frenge,' said Michael briskly, unwilling to waste time in idle chatter. 'Did he have any friends who might be able to tell us about his final hours?'

'Well, there is Robert de Hakeney,' replied Shirwynk. 'The drunken vintner. But he will say the same as us – that Frenge was murdered by King's Hall.'

'What did Frenge eat and drink yesterday morning?' asked Bartholomew.

'Breakfast ale and sweet pottage,' replied Shirwynk. 'But you cannot blame those for making an end of him, because Peyn and I shared them with him and we are still alive.'

'I did not have the pottage,' put in Peyn. 'I prefer salty foods. But I had the ale.'

'Did your wife eat and drink with you as well?'

'She did not.' Shirwynk's voice was cold. 'She was too ill.'

'What was wrong with her?'

'Nigellus said it was a fatal dizziness, although he is a scholar, so I am not sure whether to believe him. I tried to get Meryfeld – the only physician who is not part of your damned University – but he decided to be mulish over an unpaid bill, and refused to come.'

'Other than dizziness, what were Letia's symptoms?'

'Where to start?' sighed Peyn. 'Mother was ill for as long as I can remember. Indeed, we were surprised that she lasted as long as she did, given the number of ailments she claimed she had.'

'Most recently, she suffered from pains in the stomach,

85

headaches and weak limbs,' said Shirwynk. 'She insisted on hiring a physician, and wanted Nigellus because he is the most expensive and therefore the best. But she died anyway.'

'I am sorry for your loss,' said Michael automatically.

'I am not,' muttered Peyn. 'Her constant moaning was a trial.'

There was no more to be said after such a remark, so Bartholomew and Michael left the brewery, waiting until they were well away before voicing their thoughts.

'You found no poison on the premises, but that means nothing,' said Michael. 'And I can see Shirwynk *and* that nasty little Peyn committing murder to suit themselves. It is obvious that neither cared for Letia, and they do not seem unduly distressed by Frenge's demise either. It would be a good outcome for us – townsmen dispatching each other.'

'You may be right, but how will we prove it? They were both very confident that a search of their brewery would tell us nothing – either because they *are* innocent, or because they know they had covered their tracks.'

'We *must* find answers,' said Michael worriedly. 'Because if we do not identify the culprit, rumour and suspicion will bring us a riot. Of course, that may be exactly what Shirwynk intends.'

'Why would he want something that would disrupt trade, including his own, and inflict misery and suffering on his town?'

'Because he is a vicious malcontent with an irrational hatred of our University and an agenda I do not yet understand. We cannot afford to be lax about this, Matt. We both must do all in our power to solve Frenge's murder before the whole of Cambridge erupts into flames.'

CHAPTER 4

Michael wanted to question Hakeney about Frenge at once, but Bartholomew was concerned about the accusation Wayt had made about the blue discharge, and as the dyeworks were next to the brewery, he insisted on stopping there first. The monk was not pleased by the delay, but could tell by the set expression on Bartholomew's face that there was no point in arguing.

The protesters in the cobbled square had swelled in number since the previous day. The University faction was led by Kellawe and included a number of his Zachary students, along with men from the other hostels on Water Lane. The fanatical Franciscan was stirring up their passions with an eye-witness account of the 'atrocity' committed by Edith's ladies.

'Those whores marched out with their buckets,' he railed, 'and I could see the defiance in their eyes as they hurled their vile effluent into the water. It is *their* fault that Cew from King's Hall grows worse by the day, and *they* poisoned every man in Trinity Hall last week.'

The town faction was led by a potter named John Vine, an opinionated man who had been an infamous brawler in his youth. Age and experience had taught him to express his views with his tongue rather than his fists, but he was still usually to be found wherever there was trouble. He lived with an elderly cousin who was one of Bartholomew's patients; she was an excellent and generous cook, and thus a great favourite with his ever-hungry students.

Vine had assembled his followers on the opposite side of the square, on the grounds that he had fewer of them than Kellawe, and would not fare well in any brawl that might ensue. However, they were still close enough to hear what was said, especially given that the voluble Franciscan tended to deliver his thoughts in a bellow.

'Perhaps we should be *supporting* the dyeworks then,' a baker jeered. 'If enough scholars sicken, the University might leave our town. And good riddance!'

'Yes, but unfortunately, they are not the dyeworks' only victims,' said Vine grimly. 'There is illness and death among *real* people, too – such as my poor cousin. Did I tell you that she has not been well since this filthy venture came into being?'

'Once or twice,' quipped the baker, a remark that elicited sniggers from his cronies, although Bartholomew was sorry to hear that old Mistress Vine was ailing. He wondered if it would be presumptuous to pay her an unsolicited visit, and supposed he had not been called because Vine was reluctant to beg favours from the brother of the person he held responsible for her plight.

'It is not just her, either,' said Vine, fixing the baker with a fierce eye that wiped the smile from the man's face. 'Six folk in Barnwell have died, not to mention Letia Shirwynk and Will Lenne. The dyeworks killed them all.'

'You cannot blame the Barnwell deaths on Mistress Stanmore,' objected Isnard the one-legged bargeman. He had been Bartholomew's patient for years and was an enthusiastic if untalented member of the Michaelhouse Choir. Like Vine, he had a nose for trouble, and was always to hand when it was unfolding, sometimes as an impartial spectator but more usually as a participant. 'The village is a good walk from here, all across the marshes.'

'The toxins did not cross the marshes – they were washed down the river,' averred Vine, 'which means they are even more potent than we feared.'

'But the folk at Barnwell were already ill when the dyeworks opened,' persisted Isnard. 'The reeve's wife had been ailing since the summer, and so had one of the canons.'

'Yes, they were ill,' acknowledged Vine, 'but it was the dyeworks that finished them off. Mistress Stanmore should know better, especially as her brother is a *medicus*.'

Bartholomew took an involuntary step backwards when everyone – townsfolk and scholars – swung around to glower at him.

'Well?' demanded the baker. 'What do you have to say for yourself, physician? Vine's cousin is your patient, so surely you feel some responsibility for her health?'

'Well, yes, of course,' said Bartholomew, flailing around for a way to answer without being disloyal to Edith. 'But—'

'More importantly, what about the scholars of Trinity Hall?' called Kellawe, jaw thrust out challengingly. 'Their well-being is far more important than that of mere towns-folk, and Edith Stanmore did them serious harm.'

'No, she did not,' said Bartholomew firmly. 'Their illnesses were attributable to bad cr—'

'My poor cousin became ill after eating fish from the river,' declared Vine hotly. 'Fish poisoned by *this* filthy place.'

'The river has always been dangerous,' said Bartholomew. 'I have warned you for years not to drink or eat anything from it. It is essentially a sewer and—'

'You scholars are all alike, twisting the facts with your sly tongues.' Vine turned angrily to his friends. 'Not only did Bartholomew avoid the question, but he aims to blame us – saying my cousin's illness is *our* fault for tossing the occasional bucket of slops into the water.'

'It is a good deal more than the "occasional bucket",' argued Bartholomew, but his words went unheard, because Vine drowned them out.

'Scholars are killers,' the potter roared. 'We all know King's Hall murdered Frenge—'

'The University would not dirty its hands by touching that low villain,' bellowed Kellawe, whose voice was louder still. 'He invaded the sacred confines of a priory, aiming to repeat the mischief he did in King's Hall, so God struck him down for his malice.'

'Well done, Matt,' hissed Michael irritably as the two groups surged towards each other and began to screech insults. 'I told you we should have gone straight to see Hakeney, but your appearance has inflamed these rogues, and now we have a spat.'

'They cannot blame Edith for Trinity Hall,' Bartholomew snapped back. 'That was caused by the bad cream in their sickly syllabub.'

'So you are happy with the dyeworks?' asked Michael, watching Kellawe wave his fist in Vine's face; furiously, the potter knocked it away. 'They pose no risk to health?'

'I did not say that,' mumbled Bartholomew, hating the invidious position he was in. He turned with relief when he heard a clatter of feet on cobblestones. 'Here are your beadles, come to restore the peace. Shall we go to see Edith now?'

The odour from the dyeworks was unpleasant in the street, but it was nothing compared to the stench inside the building. Bartholomew recoiled, sure the fumes could not be safe to breathe. Edith had decided to make her own dyes, rather than buy them from Ely, and it was this process, not the staining of cloth, that was responsible for much of the reek.

The woad used to make blue colouring was the worst offender. The leaves had to be mashed into balls and dried, after which they were allowed to ferment before being mixed with urine and left to steep. The madder and weld used for red and yellow respectively were less noxious, but still required generous amounts of dung, oil and alum. Each stage of production generated much smelly waste, and the river, which ran a few steps from the back door, was the obvious place to deposit it, despite the by-law that forbade the practice.

Bartholomew blinked his smarting eyes and looked around. The dyeworks comprised a long shed dominated by three enormous vats, each with a space underneath for a fire. All were so tall that the only way to see over their rims was by climbing up a ladder.

Drying racks covered three of the four walls, while the last was shelved and held the tools of the trade – buckets of the precious finished dyes, mangles, poles and dollies. Frail Sisters were everywhere, sleeves rolled up and faces shiny with the sweat of honest labour; there was no hint of the alluring creatures who haunted the streets after dark. Some stirred the contents of the vats, others stoked the fires, while the remainder scurried here and there with bustling purpose.

One was Yolande de Blaston, married to the town's best carpenter. Their enormous brood of children meant that money was always tight, so she was obliged to supplement their income by selling physical favours to various town worthies – favours she performed so well that she was in almost constant demand. However, as several of their offspring bore uncanny resemblances to prominent burgesses and scholars, Bartholomew often wondered whether her chosen method of contributing to the family purse had compounded rather than eased the problem.

'What, *again*?' he asked, when he saw the tell-tale bulge around her middle. 'How many is it now? Twelve? Thirteen?'

'The twins last year made fourteen,' she replied. 'Have you come to visit your sister?'

Bartholomew nodded. 'About this morning's spillage.'

An expression of guilty defiance flashed across Yolande's face. 'I was carrying a couple of buckets of blue sludge when I stumbled and dropped them. The same thing happened to Anne.'

'So four pails of waste "accidentally" fell in the river? No wonder people are complaining!'

'Edith will not want to see you if you are going to take that tone,' said Yolande warningly. 'So keep a civil tongue in your head or she will box your ears.'

Edith was in the annexe at the end of the building, the place reserved for the most malodorous processes. She smiled when she saw Bartholomew and Michael, although there was a guarded expression in her eyes – she knew why they were there. Bartholomew took a breath to speak, but the reek of fermenting woad was so powerful that all he could do was cough, while Michael pressed a pomander so tightly to his nose that it was a wonder he could breathe at all.

'How can you bear it?' Bartholomew gasped. 'The stench is enough to melt eyeballs.'

'What stench?' asked Edith.

'I am glad you have not set up near Michaelhouse,' croaked Michael. 'Or we would be forced to take out an injunction against you.'

'You could try,' said Edith coolly. 'But we have retained the services of Stephen the lawyer, who assures us that any such action will fail. And we are doing *good* things here, Brother. Look around you: these women have decent pay and regular meals. They are respectable now.'

'It is true,' agreed Yolande. '*And* we provide a valuable service – everyone wants our cloth, because it is cheaper than materials that have been dyed elsewhere.'

'Yes,' acknowledged Bartholomew. 'But you are not supposed to dump nasty residues in the river. The burgesses told you to ship them to the Fens instead.'

'We do, most of the time,' said Edith. 'But it is not always practical. Like this morning – all four of our best big buckets were full of spent dye, but then we had a problem with some caustic cleaner – which really does need to go to the Fens – so we had to make a strategic decision.'

'Besides, no one uses the river at night,' added Yolande carelessly. 'Unfortunately, we were a bit late in today, because of last night's Hallow-Eve celebrations, and the spent dye was rather more potent than we had anticipated . . .'

Bartholomew was exasperated. 'No one uses the river at night? Then where do you think the fish go when darkness falls? And there is the small matter of tides – anything deposited while the river is flowing will revisit the town when it ebbs.'

'We are within our rights to use the waterways,' said Edith, hands on hips and looking fierce. 'We pay our taxes. And besides, we hired Stephen to check our rights and responsibilities before we started. Everything we do is perfectly legal – other than the occasional minor breach, such as happened today.'

'Minor or not, the protesters have a point.' Bartholomew gestured around him. 'There are some very toxic substances here. Perhaps some of the illnesses or deaths in the town *are* a result of whatever you are putting in the water.'

'I did not think you would side against us, Matthew,' said Edith, anger turning to hurt. 'There is no evidence that we are to blame. People sicken and die all the time, as you know better than most. You should be ashamed of yourself for accusing us.'

Her words were like arrows in Bartholomew's heart, and he closed his eyes for a moment before continuing more gently. 'Dropping stinking waste in the Cam *will* have an impact on public health – you know it will. Moreover, the people outside watch you like hawks: they might do you or your ladies harm the next time you have an "accidental" spillage.'

'But we would *never* put anything toxic in the river,' argued Edith. 'Strong smells and bright colours do not equal dangerous, as you of all people should understand.

93

You should also know that I would never put the health of townsfolk at risk.'

'What about the health of scholars?' asked Michael.

Edith gave a wry smile. 'It is tempting to silence those men from Zachary with a dose of something nasty, but wishing is not the same as doing. And anyway, they do not use the river – they are too wealthy to eat its fish, and they have their own well for drinking.'

'I am not sure I agree that your waste is harmless,' said Bartholomew. He pointed out through the door, where the dyeworks' pier and the one belonging to King's Hall were a beautiful royal blue. 'Would you really want that stuff inside you? Or inside me?'

Edith sighed irritably. 'We will never agree on this, so let us talk about something else before we fall out. Yolande tells me that Frenge was killed by King's Hall yesterday. Is it true?'

'No,' replied Michael shortly. 'We are on our way to visit Frenge's friend Hakeney. Hopefully, he will tell us something that will allow us to put an end to these silly tales.'

'Then you will be disappointed,' said Yolande with a vengeful smirk. 'He was drunk most of yesterday. He will be a useless witness.'

'Did *you* know Frenge, Edith?' Bartholomew asked. He was still cross with her for refusing to heed his advice, so it was not easy to keep his voice even. 'You were neighbours, after all.'

'Yes, but he went out delivering ale, while Shirwynk and Peyn stayed in to brew, so I did not meet him very often. I suppose Peyn will drive the dray now.'

'He is going to Westminster,' said Michael. 'To become a Treasury clerk.'

Yolande burst out laughing. 'Him? I doubt His Majesty will let a snivelling cur like *that* near his precious money. The boy is dreaming.'

94

Recalling Peyn's appalling handwriting, Bartholomew suspected she was right. 'If you do not know Frenge, then what about Shirwynk? What kind of man is he?'

'A loathsome fellow,' replied Edith with a moue of distaste. 'Although Peyn is worse. He is a dreadful young man – sullen, arrogant and lazy.'

'He told us that he was not sorry his mother was dead,' said Michael. 'Do you think he did something to hasten her end? Or did Shirwynk?'

Edith considered the question carefully. 'It is possible. She was an awful shrew, always whining about her poor health and demanding to be waited on. Both of them grew to resent her.'

'I do not suppose you know anything about Frenge's relationship with Shirwynk and Peyn, do you?' asked Michael, rather desperately. 'Did you ever hear them fighting, for example?'

Edith was thoughtful. 'No, but I was always under the impression that Frenge was wary of them. Perhaps that is why he liked to go out with the cart – to avoid their company. I never saw any violence between them, though.'

'Nor did I, but that does not mean it did not happen,' put in Yolande. 'Shirwynk is a brute, and Peyn is no better. Perhaps *they* murdered Frenge, to stop King's Hall from suing him.'

'Then their ploy misfired,' said Edith. 'King's Hall just shifted their suit to the brewery.'

At that moment, the door opened and Anne de Rumburgh minced in. She was wearing another low-cut bodice, and when she bent to retrieve a woad ball from the floor, Bartholomew was certain she was going to fall out. She was with her husband, older than her by two decades.

'Matt is here to berate us for spilling waste in the river,' said Edith, shooting her brother a cool glance. 'While Michael wants our opinion of the brewers next door.'

'I like the brewers,' said Anne with a sultry smile. 'They are all very fine specimens. Their wares are delicious, too.'

'Then you are very easily pleased,' said Rumburgh with a grimace that revealed his painfully inflamed gums. 'Their apple wine is too sweet, while their ale is only palatable with a cake to take away the bitter taste. I am almost glad Frenge is dead, because now we shall not have to accept all those free samples he would insist on bringing.'

'He gave you ale and wine for nothing?' asked Edith, startled. 'Why would he do that?'

'I really cannot imagine,' said Anne with a sly smile.

'So Anne bestowed her favours on Frenge,' mused Michael, as he and Bartholomew left the dyeworks – by the back door, so as to avoid the protesters at the front – and began to walk towards Hakeney's home. 'Do you think Rumburgh poisoned him, and he is only pretending not to realise that the free gifts were just Frenge's excuse to visit?'

'It is possible. Poor Rumburgh is impotent, and his wife is a . . . restless woman.'

'More harlot than most Frail Sisters,' agreed Michael. 'She could not take her eyes off me. Did you notice?'

'Not really.' Bartholomew thought she had spent more time looking at *him*.

'Then watch her more closely next time. She ogled me shamelessly, and it was clear that she was desperate to get her hands on my person.'

It was not far to Hakeney's home, which stood on Water Lane, sandwiched between Zachary's elegant grandeur and an inn. It was by far the shabbiest building on the street: weeds sprouted from its thatch, and the paint on its window shutters was old and peeling.

'He used to be a respected vintner,' said Michael, while

they waited for their knock to be answered. 'But now all he does is haunt taverns. He hates the University, because our physicians were unable to save his wife and children from the plague. You might want to stand behind me when we go in.'

The door was opened eventually by a small man with the bloodshot eyes and the broken-veined cheeks of the habitual drinker. Hakeney was unhealthily thin, and his clothes were dirty.

'If your sister sent you here in the hope of currying favour among townsfolk, then she is going to be disappointed,' he snarled when he saw Bartholomew. 'You are not coming anywhere near me. It is her fault I am ill anyway – her filthy dyeworks.'

'You are sick?' asked Bartholomew politely.

'My innards have been blocked these last ten days. It is breathing all the fumes that did it.'

'I can prescribe something to ease that,' offered Bartholomew, aiming to inveigle an examination to see if Hakeney was right. If so, Edith would have to move the dyeworks to a place where they could do no harm.

The vintner immediately began to bray about why he would never permit a scholar, especially a physician, inside his home, but his constipation was painful and Bartholomew represented possible relief. The tirade petered out, and the Michaelhouse men were invited to enter on condition that they did not touch anything.

'That will not be a problem, I assure you,' said Michael, looking around with a fastidious shudder. 'My hands will remain firmly tucked inside my sleeves.'

While Bartholomew palpated the vintner's abdomen and asked the questions that might help him determine the cause of Hakeney's discomfort, Michael made a nuisance of himself by interrupting with queries about Frenge.

'Poor Frenge,' the vintner said sadly. 'He lost his wife

to a physician's incompetence during the Great Pestilence, too, which is what drew us together as friends. He liked to drown his sorrows in ale, after which he often became boisterous.'

'So he was drunk the night he invaded King's Hall?' probed Michael.

Hakeney shot him a sour look. 'He would hardly have done such a thing if he had been sober. He was not a complete fool, and breaking in there was dangerous.'

'So why did he do it?'

'Because false friends put the idea into his head, knowing he was too tipsy to see that it was a stupid thing to do. He told me afterwards that he wished he had not listened to them.'

'Then why did he refuse to apologise to King's Hall? A little contrition would have gone a long way to soothing troubled waters.'

'Because Wayt annoyed him by blowing the matter out of all proportion. And besides, the town thought him a hero, and would have reviled him if he had recanted.'

'He frightened Cew badly,' said Bartholomew, looking up from his examination. 'That is hardly the act of a hero. Neither is terrorising pigs and geese.'

Hakeney shrugged. 'Well, it is done now, and King's Hall has made him pay dearly for it.'

'There is no evidence that they are responsible for his death,' cautioned Michael.

'Then perhaps you should look at the matter a bit harder,' Hakeney flashed back.

'Do you know anything about the ale that Frenge was going to take there yesterday?' asked Michael, manfully keeping his temper. 'Peyn told us that he went to deliver a barrel.'

'If he had, it would have resulted in a sore stomach or two,' smirked Hakeney. 'However, he would not have wasted his time: he knew they would have tipped it straight down the drain.'

'Is there anyone else who might have meant him harm? Shirwynk, perhaps? Or Peyn?'

'Of course not. They were not friends, but they had worked well together for a decade.'

'Did Frenge own a boat?' asked Bartholomew, writing instructions to the apothecary for a syrup that should ease Hakeney's problem. Unfortunately, he was not sure what had caused the attack – it might have been the dyeworks, but it might equally well have been too much wine, a poor diet, a lazy lifestyle or a host of other factors.

Hakeney blinked his surprise at the question. 'No, why?'

'How well did he know the Austins?' Michael turned to another subject without giving Bartholomew the chance to explain.

'He did not know them at all – at least, not the ones in the convent. He was good friends with your colleague Wauter, though – Wauter's old hostel is not far from the brewery, you see.'

'You say he was drunk when he launched his foolish assault on King's Hall,' said Michael. 'But what about when he went to the Austin Priory?'

Hakeney raised his hands in a shrug. 'There was a lot of ale on his cart, and he was a scrupulous man – he would not have wanted to sell his customers sour wares, so of course he would have sampled them first.'

Michael regarded him thoughtfully. 'There is something you are not telling us – I can read it in your face. It is almost as if you do not want Frenge's death investigated.'

Hakeney regarded him with dislike. 'Of course I do. But if you must know, I fear that Frenge might have gone to the friary because of me. My wife had a cross, you see. She inherited it from her father, who brought it back from a pilgrimage. But Almoner Robert stole it.'

'I sincerely doubt he did any such thing!' declared Michael, startled. 'The Austins are good men. They are generous with alms, and even starved last winter, so that beggars could eat.'

'I know,' said Hakeney. 'But that does not alter the fact that Robert is wearing my wife's crucifix. It may not look like much – a simple thing of plain black wood – but it was something she cherished, and I want it back.'

'His cross *is* crafted from black wood,' said Bartholomew, recalling it hanging around the almoner's neck. 'But there is nothing remarkable about it, so how can you be sure it is hers?'

'That is what he said, but he started flaunting it not long after I lost mine, which is too great a coincidence for me. It looks smaller than I remember, and the colour is slightly different, but I am sure it is the same piece.'

'Speak to Prior Joliet about it,' suggested Bartholomew, looking around the seedy chaos that was Hakeney's home and suspecting that the original was still there somewhere; it would be found if the vintner ever bothered to tidy up.

Hakeney scowled. 'I did, but Robert produced a bill of sale, so Prior Joliet told me I was mistaken. I often talked about the injustice of the matter to Frenge.'

Michael narrowed his eyes. 'So you think Frenge might have gone to steal it back for you?'

'He might,' said Hakeney, although he spoke slyly, and Bartholomew wondered if he just aimed to exacerbate the trouble between town and University. 'But he was drunk and they caught him, so they decided to kill him – to stop him from trespassing on their property again.'

Michael eyed him balefully. 'I have never heard such arrant nonsense in all my life. The Austins are the last men to take umbrage at someone straying into their grounds. They are decent souls, Hakeney – not violent or vengeful.'

'If that were true,' said Hakeney sullenly, 'then Robert would give me back my cross.'

Bartholomew felt like wiping his feet when he emerged from Hakeney's lair, and he certainly wanted to wash his hands. He did so in a horse trough, then went with Michael to search Frenge's house, a pleasant cottage near St Botolph's Church. Apart from a dress with a low-cut front that clearly belonged to Anne, they discovered nothing of interest, and there was certainly nothing to suggest that he had poisoned himself, either by accident or design.

When they emerged, it was nearing noon, the time when they had been invited to visit the Austin Priory and examine in daylight the place where Frenge had died.

'We cannot stay there long,' warned Michael as he and Bartholomew hurried up the High Street. 'No matter how fine a repast they provide. Impressing patrons at the *disceptatio* tomorrow is Michaelhouse's only hope for the future, so we must be back to help with the preparations.'

Wryly, Bartholomew thought it would not be *he* who would linger to gorge at the Austins' table.

They arrived to find Robert waiting for them at the gate. As the almoner waved them inside, Michael pointed to his pectoral cross.

'Hakeney says you stole that from him.'

Robert winced. 'I know, but I bought this in London years ago, and I have the bill of sale to prove it. Moreover, the priest who sold it to me wrote a letter confirming my claim.'

Bartholomew reached out to take the crucifix in his hand. 'Is it valuable?'

'It is to me. It is crafted from Holy Land cedar and was blessed by the Pope himself.'

'But it is just plain wood,' said Michael, squinting at

101

it. 'No jewels. It would fetch little at the market, and I do not understand why Hakeney is making such a fuss.'

'Grief,' sighed Robert. 'He feels guilty for mislaying his wife's most prized possession in that pit of disorder he calls home, and thinks that acquiring my cross will make him feel better.'

'Did Frenge ever raise the subject with you?' asked Michael.

Robert looked startled. 'Frenge? Why would he . . . Oh, I see. He and Hakeney were friends, and they probably discussed it. But no, I never spoke to Frenge about the cross – or anything else, for that matter. Would you like to see my documents? I do not want you thinking that I am a thief.'

'Yes, please,' said Michael, ignoring the flash of hurt in the almoner's eyes.

While they waited for Robert to return, Bartholomew looked around, thinking the Austins' domain was by far the prettiest of Cambridge's convents with its grassy yard and attractive chapel. The almoner soon came back, and thrust two pieces of parchment into Michael's hand. The monk scanned them quickly, then passed them back, nodding to say they were in order.

'Poor Hakeney,' said Robert, placing them carefully in his scrip. 'Prior Joliet thinks I should just give him the cross, given that he is so desperate to have it, but I feel such an act of sacrifice will not help. His obsession with it is a symptom of his unhappiness, not the cause.'

'Is our food ready?' asked Michael, cutting to the chase. 'Or shall we inspect the scene of the crime first?'

'It is ready, but you must wait a moment, because we are burying Father Arnold. We should have finished by now, but the ceremony had to be delayed – on account of Prior Joliet being called to sit with Will Lenne while he died.'

He led the way to the back of the church, where there

was a little cemetery. All the friars had gathered there, and Joliet was intoning the final words of the burial service.

'What was wrong with Arnold?' whispered Bartholomew.

'Insomnia,' replied Robert. 'Nigellus told us he would recover if he avoided foods that had fruited when Venus was in the ascendency, but Arnold must have laid hold of some without our knowledge, because he suddenly grew feverish and was dead within hours.'

Michael waited until Robert had gone to help shovel earth into the grave before murmuring, 'That makes three of Nigellus's patients to die recently: Arnold, Letia and Lenne. And there were six deaths at Barnwell . . .'

The same thought had occurred to Bartholomew. 'Yet it might just be a run of unrelated misfortunes. Last winter, I lost four patients in one day . . .'

'Yes, but from causes that were patently obvious even to laymen – there was none of this "dizziness" or "insomnia" nonsense. So we had better make a few discreet enquiries, if for no other reason than Nigellus is a member of the University, and we should be ready with answers if a townsman raises eyebrows at his some-what alarming mortality rate.'

When the friars had finished burying their colleague, three hurried to the chapel to recite more prayers, while the rest trooped to the modest building that served as their refectory. Then four disappeared to the kitchen to finish cooking and three served the others, so fewer than ten sat down to eat. The meal was frugal, with watery soup, a few prunes and some grated onion. Moreover, the presence of guests meant there was not really enough to go around. Michael regarded it in dismay, feeling he had been misled when told the fare would be 'wholesome and plentiful'.

'We are sorry about Arnold,' he said, refusing a sliver

103

of onion with ill grace. 'Robert said he suffered from insomnia.'

Prior Joliet nodded. 'For about a month, along with pains in the innards. He would have been ninety next year, and he had planned to celebrate in style – well, what passes for style with us. It is not what *you* would consider extravagant, I am sure. I heard last night's feast was very impressive, and the reception after tomorrow's *disceptatio* is predicted to be equally magnificent.'

'We intend it to be an occasion our founder would have appreciated,' said Michael, 'as it is the anniversary of his death. Your mural is certain to draw much admiration.'

Joliet flushed with pleasure. 'Perhaps it will encourage others to hire our services, and we shall earn enough money to mend the roof in our dormitory. Another prune, Brother?'

When the meal was over, Joliet led the way to the back gate, where Bartholomew and Michael scoured the area for clues. Robert and the burly Hamo helped, but there was nothing to find. Moreover, the spot was shielded by overhanging trees, and so was invisible from the road – appealing for witnesses would be pointless.

'Is that yours?' asked Bartholomew, pointing to a boat that was tied to the pier with a scrap of ancient rope.

Robert nodded. 'We use it when one of our older residents fancies an outing. It is easier to transport them by boat than in a cart – less jostling for ancient bones.'

Bartholomew bent to examine it, noting a fresh scratch near the back, and then stared at the opposite bank. It comprised a strip of land that was too boggy for building, so was used for grazing sheep. He stepped into the boat and paddled across. There were footprints in the silt at the water's edge, and although some were smudged, he was fairly sure they came from one person. And Frenge's boots had been muddy. When a brief search of the reeds revealed a grapnel, he thought he knew what had happened. He rowed back again.

'Frenge stood over there,' he said, pointing to where he had just been. 'He tossed this hook across the water, snagged your boat and drew it towards him. That gouge on the stern is where it bit. The mooring rope is rotten with age, so it would have been easy to snap.'

'But why?' asked Joliet, his round face perturbed. 'To despoil our priory, as he did King's Hall? I know he hated the University – especially after Wayt decided to sue him.'

'I think he came for something else,' said Michael, staring pointedly at Robert's cross.

Robert blinked his astonishment, but then shook his head. 'That cannot be true, Brother. Frenge came in the daytime, when I was wearing it. If his intention *was* to steal, he would have invaded at night, when it hangs by my bed.'

'He was probably drunk,' said Bartholomew. 'Such men are not noted for their logic.'

'But the cross does not belong to Hakeney,' objected Joliet, distressed. 'Do you think I would let one of my friars keep stolen property? Hakeney is mistaken.'

'Poison,' grunted Hamo, speaking for the first time. 'Madness.'

'That is a good point,' said Joliet, although Bartholomew and Michael had exchanged a glance of mutual incomprehension. 'Perhaps it was the *toxin* that encouraged Frenge to retrieve what he thought was his friend's property – it addled his wits.'

'Impossible,' said Bartholomew. 'The poison was caustic, and Frenge would have felt its effects immediately. He could not have rowed across the King's Ditch once it was inside him.'

Robert gazed at him, blood draining from his face. 'But that means he swallowed it here – after he had snagged the boat and crossed the ditch.'

'It means he was *made* to swallow it here,' corrected Michael. 'Do not forget the bruises on his jaw. He did not drink it willingly.'

'But who would have done such a dreadful thing?' cried Joliet. 'Not only to kill, but to do it on hallowed ground?'

'Who indeed?' murmured Michael.

A soldier was waiting outside the Austin Priory when Bartholomew and Michael emerged, to say that the physician was needed at the castle. He would not explain why, but the amused gleam in his eye suggested it was probably something to do with Dickon.

'I shall come with you,' said Michael. He raised a plump hand when Bartholomew started to smile startled thanks. 'Not to protect you from that little hellion – no friendship extends that far – but to brief Dick on our investigation. Then we must return to Michaelhouse and help our colleagues with the preparations for tomorrow.'

The castle lay to the north of the town. It was a grand affair, its curtain walls studded with towers and gatehouses, and it boasted a sizeable bailey. Its function was now more administrative than military, and the Sheriff preferred to spend his budget on clerks and tax assessors than repairs, so parts of it were rather shabby. That day, however, it teemed with soldiers, some preparing to go out on patrol and others returning. All were armed to the teeth.

'The spats between town and University are escalating,' said Tulyet grimly, hurrying to greet his visitors. 'And I have the sense that we are heading for some major trouble. But that is not why I summoned you here. Come this way, please, Matt, and hurry. Dickon has had an accident.'

'What kind of accident?' asked Bartholomew warily. 'One that has injured someone else?'

Tulyet was already halfway to his office in the Great Tower, but he turned to shoot the physician a reproachful look. 'I do not know why you hold such a miserable opinion of my son. His scrapes and adventures arise from the fact that he has an enquiring mind.'

Bartholomew knew better than to embark on that sort of argument with a doting parent. They climbed the spiral staircase in silence, but when they reached the top, where two knights were standing guard, Tulyet turned to regard him and Michael bleakly.

'You will be stunned by what you see, so be warned.'

He opened the door and ushered the scholars in, closing it quickly to prevent his warriors from following. Bartholomew thought he heard suppressed laughter before it clicked shut.

Dickon was standing by the hearth, and there were two things that were notable about him. The first was that the child had poured himself a very large cup of wine; he held it in one hand, while the other rested on the hilt of his sword, so that he appeared like a miniature version of the beefy, hard-drinking warriors Bartholomew had encountered during his sojourn with the English army in France. The second was that his face was a bright and startling shade of scarlet.

'God's blood!' gulped Michael, crossing himself. He rarely swore, so the oath was a testament to the depth of his shock.

Bartholomew simply stared, wondering if the brat had also sprouted horns or a forked tail.

'It is your sister's fault, Matt,' said Tulyet, angry and defensive at the same time. 'We had a report that she was dumping waste in the river again, and when we went to investigate . . . well, suffice to say that Dickon accidentally submerged his face in one of her vats.'

'It is dye?' breathed Michael. He crossed himself again. 'Thank God! I thought it was . . .'

'Yes, it is dye,' said Tulyet coldly. He turned to Bartholomew. 'You must find a way to scour it off, because I cannot have him looking like that.'

'I like it,' said Dickon, whose small, bright eyes looked more malevolent than ever in his crimson skin. 'People will be more ready to obey me if I frighten them – which I will, if they think I am a denizen of Hell.'

'You do not need a red face for them to think that,' muttered Michael.

'It is coming off,' said Tulyet shortly. 'Today. And if it hurts, that is too bad, because your poor mother will be beside herself if she sees you in such a state.'

Bartholomew advanced cautiously. Dickon had a habit of punching, biting, kicking, clawing and scratching those who went too close, and the physician would have refused to tend him had he not been friends with his father. He stopped dead in his tracks when Dickon's fingers tightened on the hilt of his sword.

'Draw that, and I will never train you to be a knight – you will go to a monastery instead,' said Tulyet sharply. It was the voice that had instilled fear into the hearts of many seasoned criminals, and even Dickon knew better than to challenge it. The hand dropped away.

Bartholomew inspected the damage, and drew the conclusion that Dickon's 'accidental submersion' had been nothing of the kind: the dye had been carefully applied, neatly following his hairline and ending tidily under his chin.

'Nothing will remove this,' he told the horrified Sheriff. 'Well, nothing that will not harm him. I am afraid it will have to fade naturally.'

Dickon grinned, and the sight of large slightly jagged teeth in the red face was distinctly disconcerting. 'Good,' he said gleefully.

Tulyet scowled at him. 'No, *not* good! How can I teach you how to run a large and turbulent shire when you look like one of Satan's imps? People will laugh at you, and you cannot command respect if you are a source of mockery.'

'No one will laugh,' said Dickon with a determined menace that was disturbing from a child of ten. 'And if they try, I will spear them with my sword.'

Tulyet regarded him uncertainly for a moment, then turned to Bartholomew. 'How long will it take to disappear?'

'A few days. Longer, if he does not wash.'

'He will wash,' vowed Tulyet. He glared at his son, an expression that softened when the lad favoured him with a smile of great sweetness. He rubbed a weary hand over his eyes. 'Fetch us some wine, Dickon. Show our guests the pretty skills you have learned as my squire.'

Dickon obliged, slopping claret in Michael's lap when his father was not looking, and contriving to bang Bartholomew's shins with his sheathed sword. Once again, the physician marvelled that Tulyet, who was nobody's fool, should be so blind when it came to his son.

'Is this Shirwynk's apple wine?' he asked, taking a small sip and then placing the cup on the table in the hope that Michael would finish the stuff.

Tulyet nodded. 'Dickon and my wife like it, although I prefer a drier vintage. It is potent, though, and I am sure it is the reason why so many men are drunk these days.'

'It is expensive,' said Michael. 'Few will be able to afford it, especially townsfolk.'

'Actually, I was referring to scholars. Wealthy Colleges and hostels have laid in great stores of it for Hallow-tide, and I believe it has turned some of them unusually belligerent.'

'It is not just scholars who are aggressive,' objected Michael. 'The town is just as bad. Look at Frenge – invading King's Hall and the Austin Priory. And when we went to tell Shirwynk that Frenge was dead, he was unreasonably hostile.'

Tulyet was thoughtful. 'In my experience, people are hostile if they have something to hide – and Shirwynk lost his wife and business partner in the same day. Perhaps we need look no further for the killer. He would have a willing accomplice in Peyn – the lad is a monster.'

Without thinking, Bartholomew's eyes strayed to Dickon. Worn out by excitement, the boy had curled up in a window seat and gone to sleep. Even in repose, he looked dangerous, not only for the weapons he carried – two knives and a cudgel in addition to the sword – but because he still scowled and it was not a pleasant expression.

'It would be a convenient solution,' Michael was saying. 'But we have other suspects, too. Frenge made a cuckold of Anne de Rumburgh's husband and, although I hate to say it, there are three men from King's Hall with no satisfactory alibi – Wayt, Dodenho and the lunatic Cew.'

Tulyet listened carefully while Michael outlined all he had learned, although it was pitifully little. When he had finished, Bartholomew stood to leave, feeling it was time to do their share of the preparations for the *disceptatio*, but Tulyet began to hold forth about sucura.

'The import taxes are so high – ninety per cent – that no Cambridge grocer is willing to trade in it,' he grumbled. 'Yet the town is awash with the stuff, which means that every grain has been brought here illegally. If the King knew the full extent of the problem, he would have my head.'

'Perhaps His Majesty should lower his levies, then,' suggested Bartholomew. 'Ninety per cent is downright greedy.'

'I shall let him know you think so,' said Tulyet acidly, then winced. 'Even my wife bought some. Luckily, I was able to dispose of it before the servants saw. How does she expect me to confiscate it from others when it is in our own larder?'

'It would be hypocritical,' agreed Michael. 'But time is passing and we—'

'Of course, the best way to deal with the problem would be to arrest the smugglers – who must be rolling in money, given the amount of sucura they have sold – but I have no idea who they are. Or how they sneak their wares into my town.'

'Barges, probably,' shrugged Bartholomew. 'Just like any other contraband. I am told that sucura comes from Tyre, so it must be shipped across the Mediterranean Sea around Spain and France—'

'Impossible! I search every boat that docks here, and I *know* none has slipped past me.'

'Then concentrate on who is selling it,' suggested Bartholomew. 'You can start with your wife: where did she buy hers?'

'From a friend,' said Tulyet sourly. 'Who had it from a cousin, who got it from a man in a tavern. And there the trail ended. Have you attempted to investigate, Brother?'

'I do not have the time – and it is not my business anyway. It is yours.'

Tulyet shot him an unpleasant look. 'I suppose you – like most of Cambridge – think that smuggling serves the King right for imposing such high taxes. But we will all suffer if he finds out what is going on, so if you know anything, I strongly urge you to tell me.'

'I have nothing to tell,' shrugged Michael, although Bartholomew suspected Tulyet was right to imply that the monk was not being entirely honest with him. Perhaps Michael *did* look the other way because he disapproved of a levy that put sucura out of the reach of all but the very wealthy.

'Then come to me when you do,' advised Tulyet shortly.

'Because I know for a fact that scholars like sucura just as much as townsfolk.'

'Not my College,' declared Michael. 'We prefer honey.'

'Good luck for tomorrow,' said Tulyet. His sardonic expression suggested that he did not believe Michael, but was not about to call him a liar. 'I shall attend the debate with the town's burgesses, who tell me I can expect to be impressed.'

'You will be impressed,' promised Michael. 'We are the University's best and most stable foundation, and I would appreciate you saying so to your wealthy friends.'

'So they will give you donations?' asked Tulyet, amused by the bald instruction.

'So we can say prayers for their immortal souls,' said Michael grandly.

Bartholomew and Michael arrived home to find Michaelhouse in the grip of frenzied activity, and the hall was in such disarray that they regarded it in horror, sure it would not be ready in time. The Austins were at their mural, while all around them was a frantic hubbub of scrubbing, dusting, buffing and brushing. Agatha the laundress was standing on a table in the middle of the room, screeching orders at Fellows, students and servants alike.

Women were not generally permitted in University foundations, but exception could be made if they were old and ugly, and thus unlikely to inflame carnal desires among the residents. Agatha was not particularly old or notably ugly, but it would be a very reckless scholar who would foist himself on her. She had been part of the College for so long that no one recalled how she had come to be there, and she was comfortable in the knowledge that she was a permanent fixture.

'Polish the benches, Doctor,' she instructed, shoving rags and a jar of beeswax into Bartholomew's hand. 'And

112

do not stop until you can see your face in them. Brother? I need you to taste the marchpanes in the kitchen, because I think I used too much sucura.'

'Sucura?' echoed Michael in alarm. 'But the Sheriff is coming, and I have just told him that we do not have any.'

'He dislikes sweet food,' said Wauter, who was folding tablecloths. 'So I doubt he will find out. However, sucura is a sign of wealth, and if we fail to flaunt it, people will think we are poor – which defeats the whole exercise.'

'Then make sure no one offers Dick a marchpane or he may think we are so rich that we can afford to pay a fine for defrauding the King of his taxes,' said Michael, not much comforted.

'Who bought the stuff?' asked Bartholomew keenly.

'I am not at liberty to say,' replied Agatha haughtily, although the physician was sure Michael had made some sly signal to her behind his back. 'Lest someone decides to tattle and we are made an example of – which would be unfair, as we only have a few grains, while places like King's Hall buy it by the bucket-load.'

'Hakeney the vintner,' said Michael to Wauter, bringing an abrupt end to the discussion. 'He told us today that you knew Frenge.'

'Did he?' asked Wauter, startled. 'Then he is mistaken. I might have exchanged nods with Frenge on occasion – as I do with many people – but I did not *know* him.'

'So Hakeney was lying?'

Wauter smiled. 'I imagine we Austins all look alike in our habits, so perhaps he thought I was someone else.'

'He identified you as an ex-member of Zachary Hostel,' Michael persisted, 'which suggests he *can* tell you apart from the others.'

Wauter raised his hands in a shrug. 'It still does not alter the fact that I did not know Frenge. Of course, Hakeney likes a drink, and his wits are somewhat pickled.'

113

'True,' conceded Michael. 'Which is a pity, as we have no idea why Frenge should have died in the Austin Friary, and information from you would have been most welcome.'

'I wish I could help, Brother, but I know nothing about it. Yet the whole business concerns me greatly, and makes me feel that the University should leave the town and resettle in the Fens. I have heard that you and the Chancellor are considering such a move, which is excellent news.'

'It is untrue,' said Michael. 'A tale started by misinformed gossips. Pay it no heed.'

'Really?' asked Wauter, disappointed. 'That is a pity. I dislike the ill-feeling we engender among townsmen, and I have no wish to antagonise anyone unnecessarily – if they want us gone, we should accede to their wishes and leave them in peace. How is Cew, by the way? Any better? It is a terrible thing when a gifted man loses his mind.'

'It is,' agreed Michael soberly. 'Do you know him well?'

'Not *very* well, but I spent many an evening with him, debating points of logic.'

'You did not enjoy the intellects of your Zachary comrades? Kellawe, Irby, Nigellus, Morys and Segeforde. All charming men, I am sure.' Michael's dour expression made it clear he was not.

'Irby is a fine man,' replied Wauter. 'But Kellawe is quarrelsome, Morys an ass, and Segeforde dull company. And as for Nigellus, I moved here before he was officially installed at Zachary, so he was never a colleague.'

'Wauter!' called Langelee, hurrying up with bustling urgency. 'Deynman tells me that you have not put your *Martilogium* in the library, and it is a work that *must* be displayed to our visitors tomorrow. Fetch it at once!'

'I cannot, Master,' said Wauter, a little testily. 'It is not finished.'

'No one will know.' Langelee turned to Bartholomew.

'And you must exhibit that treatise on fevers you have been writing for the past five years. Its size alone will impress, although we must make sure no one opens it – Deynman tells me it contains some very nasty illustrations.'

'He is right, Matt,' said Michael, as the Master dashed away hauling Wauter with him. 'We must present ourselves as active scholars, and Deynman has all my academic scribblings. Yet I shall be glad when tomorrow is over. We have made scant progress with Frenge, and the *disceptatio* is a distraction we could do without.'

Bartholomew nodded. 'Although at least we have some suspects: Shirwynk, Peyn, Rumburgh and the three men from King's Hall.'

'And Wauter. I did not believe him when he denied knowing Frenge.'

'You would take Hakeney's word over his?' asked Bartholomew, surprised. 'A drunk, who dislikes all scholars – and Austins in particular, because he thinks one stole his cross?'

Michael was thoughtful. 'Then perhaps Hakeney is our culprit. He and Frenge were friends, but they would not be the first to fall out after copious quantities of ale, and Hakeney would certainly like the University blamed for the murder. And there is Nigellus, of course. Frenge was his patient, as were Lenne, Letia, Arnold and six dead people from Barnwell.'

'So how shall we proceed?' asked Bartholomew.

'By interviewing Nigellus tomorrow, to see what we can shake loose with a few clever questions. I shall want you with me, of course.'

'Of course,' said Bartholomew wearily.

CHAPTER 5

The College bell ensured that everyone at Michaelhouse was awake long before dawn the following morning. All Souls fell on Sunday that year, which made it especially holy, and Langelee did not want their founder forgotten in the excitement surrounding the *disceptatio.*

'We need him watching over us today,' he informed his scholars, as they lined up to process to the church. 'We cannot have him vexed, lest he hardens the hearts of potential benefactors, so I want you all to pray for his soul as fervently as you can. Is that understood?'

There was a murmur of assent, even from the servants who were waiting for Agatha to arrive so they could start preparing the expensive treats that would be served to the guests when the debate was over. Bartholomew's book-bearer was among them, touching an amulet pinned to his hat. Cynric was the most superstitious man in Cambridge, and would certainly believe that the success of the day depended on the calibre of the rituals performed that morning.

Those Fellows in religious Orders – everyone except Bartholomew and Langelee – had risen even earlier, to prepare the church for the special ceremony. Suttone had decked it out in white flowers, and the sweet scent of them filled the whole building. Michael and Clippesby had dressed the altar in its best cloth, and William had laid out the ceremonial vestments, although he had managed to spill something down the embroidered chasuble he was wearing. It was not clear what Wauter had done, although he was slightly breathless and certainly gave the impression of a spell of hard work.

Unwilling for the occasion to be ruined by a contribution from the Michaelhouse Choir, Langelee had 'forgotten' to tell them that the rite was to begin early. Its members comprised people who joined solely for the free bread and ale, and few could sing. They made up for their lack of talent with volume, and prided themselves on the great distances over which they could make themselves heard. The Master was not alone in thinking that the founder's soul might not like his Mass punctuated by off-key bellowing, and there were relieved glances among Fellows and students alike when the choristers shuffled in too late to participate.

Unfortunately, the choir was not easily discouraged, and began to warble anyway, so the scholars left the church to a resounding *Gloria* from the basses, and an Easter anthem from the tenors and altos. A good-natured competition followed, as each group tried to drown out the other, and as the music was in different keys, the din was far from pleasant. Langelee increased the pace, but the racket was still deafening in St Michael's Lane.

Bartholomew breathed in deeply as he walked, savouring the fresh scent of early morning. Then there was a waft of something vile, accompanied by a plume of oily smoke.

'The dyeworks,' said Michael disapprovingly. 'My beadles reported that a pile of waste had been assembled ready to incinerate. No doubt Edith and her lasses hope their neighbours will not notice if they burn it when most people are still in bed.'

Wauter pursed his lips in disapproval. 'You really should encourage her to move away from the town, Matt. You must see that such a reek is deleterious to health.'

'I will speak to her today,' said Bartholomew unhappily. 'Again.'

'Good,' said Wauter. 'Because our University has no

117

future in a town that chokes us with poisonous gases. If she does not leave, then we shall have to go instead.'

'We are not going anywhere,' said Michael firmly. 'We may not like our secular neighbours, but we need the goods and services they provide – food, fuel, shoes, candles, pots, cloth, beds—'

'Many great abbeys and priories are self-sufficient,' argued Wauter. 'We can be, too.'

'It takes years – decades, even – to develop that sort of community,' said Michael testily. 'What would we do in the interim? Live in tents?'

'You are clever, with a keen eye to the University's interests. I am sure you could find a solution. And then your name would be remembered for all eternity. Masses like the one we have just said for our founder will be sung for you long after your soul is released from Purgatory.'

'That will happen anyway,' said Michael loftily. 'Because I have already done much to put us on an equal footing with Oxford. However, I certainly do not intend to be remembered as the man who took our University from a perfectly good town to a bog.'

Wauter nodded to where a handful of students from Zachary were reeling along with three Frail Sisters. The lads made themselves scarce when they saw the Senior Proctor, so the women turned their lewd attentions to the Michaelhouse men instead, some of whom looked sorely tempted by the activities that were listed as on offer.

'You would not have to worry about *that* happening in the Fens,' said the Austin. 'Lads in holy orders know how to resist such invitations, but the same cannot be said for our seculars. Your students would be over there in a trice, Matt, and so, I am sorry to say, would Langelee.'

He stepped forward to distract the Master with a discussion about the *disceptatio*. It was a prudent decision, as

Langelee's lustfully gleaming eyes had been noted by several undergraduates, and it was hardly a good example.

'Wauter is an excellent teacher, a gifted geometrician and good company in the conclave,' whispered Michael to Bartholomew. 'But he is also a liar. I am unconvinced by his claim that he did not know Frenge. Moreover, he disappeared this morning while we were preparing the church, and arrived back hot, dishevelled and unwilling to say where he had been.'

'Did you ask him?'

'He said he had been removing debris from the church-yard, so that we would be "perceived as having an unstained soul despite our many blemishes". Now what is that supposed to mean?'

Bartholomew had no idea, but agreed that it was an odd remark to have made.

The procession arrived back at College to find that the servants had only just started their own breakfast, as Agatha had anticipated that the scholars would be longer at their devotions. They started to rise, but she waved them back down with an authoritative hand, muttering that they would need their strength if they were going to give of their best that day.

'But I am hungry,' objected Langelee plaintively.

'So are we,' retorted Agatha, and the Master, veteran of battles and performer of unsavoury acts of violence for powerful churchmen, backed away at the belligerence in her voice. 'We have been working hard this morning, and we need our sustenance. We will attend you as soon as we have eaten.'

Unwilling to waste time, Langelee led the way to the hall, where he and the students set out the tables and benches themselves.

'If any one of you drops so much as a crumb on the floor this morning, he will answer to me,' he growled. 'And wipe the tables with your sleeves when you have finished, because we cannot have greasy fingermarks all over them. Wauter? Go and fetch your *Martilogium*. Deynman tells me that you still have not brought it to the library.'

'I have explained why, Master: it is incomplete,' replied Wauter shortly. 'We do not want people thinking that we foist unfinished manuscripts on our students.'

'And I have told you that no one will read it,' argued Langelee. 'My own contribution is next year's camp-ball fixtures, which I would never risk being looked at, because they are confidential. But they add to the bulk, and it is the impression that is important here.'

'I will make sure no one touches anything,' promised Deynman. 'Books are far too valuable to be pawed by laymen anyway, no matter how much money they want to give us. Your list of martyrs will be safe with me.'

The hall smelled strongly of polish and the caustic substances that had been used to scour stains from the floor, so Bartholomew opened the shutters to let in some fresh air. It was a pretty morning, with the sun burning away the fog that had dampened the streets earlier. A blackbird sang in the orchard and hens clucked in the yard below. Then the porter's peacock issued a shrill scream.

'I want that thing gagged,' said Langelee. 'Who will tell Walter?'

As the porter was fond of his pet, and was inclined to be vindictive to anyone who took against it, there were no volunteers.

'Actually, Master,' said Wauter, 'the creature may serve to our advantage. Peacocks are expensive, and there are not many Colleges that can afford to give one to a servant.'

'Go and inform Walter that his bird is to have its tail on display when our guests arrive,' instructed Langelee, capitulating abruptly. 'And it is to screech and attract the attention of anyone who does not notice it.' He turned to Clippesby. 'You will repeat my orders to the peacock.'

The two Fellows nodded acquiescence and sped away. There was no more to be done until breakfast arrived, so Bartholomew leaned on the windowsill and gazed absently across the yard. He was not alone with his thoughts for long: his students came to give a report on the mock disputation with Rougham and Nigellus the previous day.

'It was great fun,' enthused young Bell. 'Father William threw open the floor for questions after you left, and I have not laughed so much in all my life.'

'It was not meant to be amusing,' said Bartholomew, wondering whether he had been wise to disappear. 'It was supposed to be an exercise in logical analysis and contradiction.'

'Oh, it was,' said Melton, the eldest, with a wicked grin. 'Rougham and Nigellus were excellent examples of how *not* to argue a case. Even Bell won points, and he has never taken part in a disputation before. You would have been proud of him, sir.'

Bartholomew groaned, not liking to imagine the intellectual carnage that had taken place. 'You did not offend them?' he asked anxiously.

'Not deliberately,' hedged Melton.

Bartholomew supposed he would have to apologise on their behalf. Rougham and Nigellus were colleagues, after all, and he did not want to be ostracised by men he might need in the future. He turned when Agatha announced that breakfast was ready, and there was the usual scramble as everyone dashed for their places. As it was a special day, Langelee was obliged to read a set grace from a book, which started well, but took a downward plunge when he turned the page and saw how much more was still to come.

'. . . *pacem et concordiam* . . . burble, burble,' he intoned, rifling through to hunt for the end, '*defunctis requiem* . . . more burble, *et nobis peccatoribus vitam aeternam*. Amen.

Oh, and we had better observe the rule of silence today, given that chatting might bring us bad luck.'

He sat, took his knife in one hand and his spoon in the other, and raised his eyebrows at the waiting servants. They hurried forward with their cauldrons, while the startled Bible Scholar, who had not anticipated that he would be needed quite so quickly, scrambled to take his place at the lectern. For several moments, all that could be heard was muted cursing and the agitated rustle of pages as he endeavoured to find the right reading for the day. He managed eventually, and soon the hall was filled with a monotonous drone that encouraged no one to listen.

'Just a moment,' cried Michael, his voice shockingly loud. 'This is pottage! Where is all the lovely food left over from the feast? It is not good enough to serve to our guests this afternoon, obviously, but it will certainly suffice for us now.'

'Gone,' replied Agatha shortly. 'Eaten.'

'By her and the servants,' muttered William, although not loud enough for Agatha to hear.

'I was looking forward to a decent breakfast after all my labours in the church,' whined Michael. 'And pottage is hardly the thing.'

'Well, I am sorry,' said Agatha, although she did not sound it. 'But Doctor Bartholomew says it is dangerous to keep leftover food too long, so we took it upon ourselves to dispose of it.'

All eyes turned accusingly on the physician, who marvelled that she had contrived to put the blame on him so adroitly. He started to explain that some foods were more susceptible to decay than others, but no one except his students were interested, and he did not try long to exonerate himself – and he was not so rash as to claim that Agatha had quoted him out of context.

'What is happening with King's Hall?' asked Langelee,

blithely forgetting his injunction against chatter that morning. Or perhaps he had simply decided that half a meal taken in silence was enough. 'I hear they plan to sue the brewery now that Frenge is unavailable. Is it true?'

'Shirwynk will not like that,' averred Wauter. 'He hates the University with a passion.'

'But it is Shirwynk's fault that Frenge invaded King's Hall in the first place,' said Clippesby, who sat with a hedgehog in his lap. 'Him and his son Peyn. The water voles heard them egging Frenge on, even though Frenge thought it was a bad idea.'

'Is that so?' asked Michael keenly. He had learned that although Clippesby had peculiar ways of dispensing information, his habit of sitting still and unnoticed for hours at a time meant he often witnessed incidents that were relevant to the Senior Proctor's enquiries. Moreover, Hakeney had also claimed that Frenge had been encouraged to invade King's Hall by 'false friends', although he had not named the culprits.

The Dominican nodded. 'As Wauter says, Shirwynk hates our *studium generale*, and the raid was his way of striking a blow with no risk to himself.'

'But it saw his business partner dead,' William pointed out. 'So there *was* a risk, and it has left him running the brewery alone.'

'Quite,' said Clippesby. 'He is now sole owner of a very lucrative concern, and he will be able to hire someone to do Frenge's work at a fraction of the cost. At least, that is what this hedgehog told me. He lives in Stephen's garden, you see, and Shirwynk went to consult him. To consult Stephen the lawyer, I mean, not the hedgehog.'

'Just a moment,' said Michael, holding up his hand. '*When* did the hedgehog hear this? Before or after Frenge died?'

Clippesby bent towards the animal, as if soliciting its

opinion, and Bartholomew saw Wauter look away uncomfortably, embarrassed by the Dominican's eccentricity.

'After,' Clippesby replied. 'While you were at the Austin Friary examining the body. However, he also says that the news of Frenge's demise was out by that time, so it is not necessarily suspicious.'

'I shall make up my own mind about that, thank you,' said Michael, giving the animal a superior glance.

'Be careful if you plan to challenge Shirwynk, Brother,' advised Wauter. 'He is not a nice man, and *I* should not like to accuse him of murder. Stephen is not very pleasant either. I saw him emerging from Anne de Rumburgh's house very early one morning, when her husband was away.'

'Well, well,' murmured Michael. 'Perhaps Stephen did not like the competition, so dispatched Frenge to rid himself of a rival. Our list of suspects is growing longer, Matt.'

Once breakfast was over, Bartholomew went to visit patients, leaving his colleagues to finish beautifying the hall. When he returned – sombre, because a burgess he had been treating for lung-rot had died in his arms – the students were standing in neat rows, clad in their best clothes, while Langelee inspected them. Several were ordered to shave again, while others were rebuked for dirty fingernails or muddy shoes. Suttone prowled with a pair of scissors, and anyone with overly long hair could expect an instant and not very expert trim.

'I shall be glad when it is all over,' said William, who wore a habit that, while not smart, at least did not look as though it could walk around the town on its own.

'So will I,' sighed Michael, watching Bartholomew emerge from his room in new ceremonial robes, a recent gift from his sister. They were in Michaelhouse's livery of black, but with the red trim that denoted a doctor of the University, and his boots shone with the dull gleam of expensive leather. He had managed a closer shave than most, being in possession of sharp surgical knives, and one of his customers had offered to cut his hair in lieu of a fee. In short, he looked uncharacteristically elegant and a credit to his College.

'Edith will have to buy you some more finery soon,' said William, looking him up and down approvingly. 'Langelee plans to change our uniform from black to green.'

'Does he?' asked Bartholomew, startled. 'Why?'

'Because Edith told him it would make us stand out from the rabble,' explained Wauter. 'And because it will look as though we have money for such vanities.'

'Regardless, I hope we win this *disceptatio*,' said William worriedly, then glared at Bartholomew and Wauter. 'But if we lose, it will be because *you* refused to tell our students what the topic will be.'

'We refused because we have been sworn to secrecy,' objected Wauter. 'Or would you have Michaelhouse adopt a less than honourable approach?'

'Of course, if it means us winning,' retorted William. 'But will you tell them now? Then at least they will be able to glance through the necessary books during Chancellor Tynkell's introductory speech. It is not much of an advantage, but it is better than nothing.'

'The committee has yet to make its decision,' said Wauter coolly. 'However, Principal Irby will not be joining us today, because he is ill. Nigellus told me earlier.'

'What is wrong with him?' asked Bartholomew, wondering if the Zachary Principal was one of Nigellus's patients – and if so, whether he was in any danger.

'Loss of appetite, apparently. I hope he recovers soon. Not only is he a friend, but he has promised to help me finish my *Martilogium*.'

'Langelee says that we must clean the hall when the guests have gone,' grumbled Suttone, slouching up and cutting into the discussion. 'He wants to avoid paying the servants overtime. So no wandering off when the event is over, if you please.'

He looked hard at Bartholomew and Michael, the ones most likely to have business elsewhere, then went to take his place in the procession. The others followed in order of seniority – William directly behind Langelee, Bartholomew and Michael side by side, Suttone and Clippesby together, and Junior Fellow Wauter bringing up the rear.

'We must interview all our suspects again as soon as we have a free moment,' said Michael, while they waited for Langelee to set off. 'I have little new to ask, but if they are guilty our questions may make them nervous – and nervous men make mistakes.'

Bartholomew listed them. 'Rumburgh, Shirwynk, Peyn, Hakeney, Stephen, the three men from King's Hall and Nigellus.'

'And possibly Wauter,' added Michael in a low voice. 'But you should have put Nigellus first. Not only for his nine dead clients, but I learned last night that he was at Trinity Hall when everyone there was poisoned. He was not ill himself, and his advice to the sufferers was to stand on their heads to let the bad humours drain out. When that failed, they called you.'

'Lord!' breathed Bartholomew. 'His "remedies" beggar belief sometimes.'

'You should be pleased by the news – if he is the culprit, your sister's dyeworks will be exonerated. And there is another thing . . .'

'Yes?'

'The only people who have died of late have been wealthy: Letia, Lenne, the Barnwell folk, Arnold and now your burgess. There is not a pauper among them. Do you not find that odd?'

Bartholomew supposed that he did.

*　*　*

126

There was to be an academic parade through the town before the *disceptatio*, although many scholars thought it should have been cancelled, given the town's current antipathy towards them. Luckily, it was only along a short section of the High Street, and the hope was that it would be over before any serious protest could be organised.

Unfortunately, the town was only part of the problem, and trouble broke out between rival factions within the University before anyone had taken so much as a step. Peterhouse thought they should lead the way, because they were the oldest foundation, but King's Hall had been built by royalty, which they claimed made them more important. Their antagonism sparked quarrels between other Colleges and hostels, and it was not long before a dozen spats were in progress.

'It is Tynkell's fault,' grumbled Michael, watching his beadles hurry to intervene. 'He should have published the order of precedence in advance, so there would have been no surprises. I reminded him to do it, but he claims he forgot.'

'Perhaps it is just as well,' remarked Bartholomew. 'It would have given resentment longer to fester, and feelings would have been running even hotter.'

Michael sniffed, unwilling to admit that he might be right. 'There is Peyn,' he said, looking to where the brewer's son was standing with his father. 'Is he about to lob mud at King's Hall?'

He was, and the missile sailed forth. Fortunately, Wayt chose that particular moment to adjust his shoe, so the clod sailed harmlessly over his head. Michael stalked towards Peyn, Bartholomew at his heels, but Shirwynk hastened to place himself between scholars and son.

'You would be wise to take him home before he spends the rest of the week in the proctors' gaol,' growled Michael.

'For what?' sneered Shirwynk. 'Accidentally flicking

127

up a little dirt? You will have a riot on your hands if you try to arrest him for that.'

'I am surprised to see you merrymaking when your wife is barely cold,' said Michael, going on an offensive of his own. 'Why are you not praying for her soul?'

'My parish priest is doing that,' replied Shirwynk. 'A man with no connections to your University, because I would not want a scholar near her.'

He stared hard at Bartholomew, who wondered with a pang of alarm whether the brewer somehow knew that Letia had been examined without his consent. Or was it a guilty conscience that prompted another warning to stay away?

'She and Frenge died on the same day,' said Michael, apparently thinking likewise, and so launching into an interrogation. 'That is an uncanny coincidence, do you not think?'

'Not uncanny – cruel,' said Shirwynk. 'King's Hall knew exactly how to inflict the maximum amount of distress on me. Thank you for the invitation to dine with you after this silly debate, by the way. However, I would sooner jump in the latrine than accept.'

'*You* were asked?' blurted Bartholomew.

'By Wauter,' replied Shirwynk coolly. 'Many of my fellow burgesses will demean themselves by setting foot on University property, but I shall not be among them.'

'My father sent me to ask if all is well,' came a voice from behind them. It was Dickon, resplendent in new clothes, and carrying a sword that was larger than the one he usually toted. However, what really caught their attention was his scarlet face and the fact that he had contrived to shape his hair into two small points just above his temples.

Peyn promptly turned and fled. Shirwynk followed with more dignity, treating the scholars to a final sneer before he went, leaving Bartholomew astonished that a boy with a dyed face and hair-horns could achieve what the

128

formidable figure of the Senior Proctor could not. Dickon set off in pursuit and Michael opened his mouth to call him back, but then had second thoughts.

'Did you see Peyn blanch when he saw that little imp?' he chuckled. 'He doubtless thought it was the Devil come to snatch his soul.'

'We should have asked Shirwynk why he encouraged Frenge to attack King's Hall,' said Bartholomew, wishing Dickon had kept his distance for a little longer. 'And why he consulted Stephen so soon after Frenge's death.'

Michael nodded to where the lawyer stood not far away. 'Shall we ask him instead?'

Stephen was so adept at twisting the law to suit the highest bidder that he was used to angry people ambushing him in the street, and was not in the slightest bit discomfited when the Senior Proctor bore down on him, all powerful bulk and flowing black habit. He smiled with smug complacency, an expression that Michael quickly determined to wipe off his face.

'I understand that you are one of Anne de Rumburgh's lovers,' he announced, loudly enough to be heard by several merchants who were chatting nearby.

Stephen's smirk promptly became a gape. 'Who . . . how . . .' he stammered.

'I have my sources. Well? Is it true that you seduced the wife of a fellow burgess?'

Stephen grabbed Michael's arm and pulled him to where they could talk without an audience. 'It only happened once,' he whispered. 'An isolated incident.'

'Frenge was also one of her conquests,' said Michael, not believing a word of it. 'Did *he* know you were enjoying her favours as well?'

'He was not!' exclaimed Stephen. 'She would never have accepted a man like him. The brewery he shared with Shirwynk might have made him wealthy, but he was hardly genteel.'

'So you know her well enough to guess her habits,' pounced Michael. He raised his hand when Stephen started to argue. 'Never mind. I would rather hear what transpired when Shirwynk visited you on the day that Frenge died.'

'You already know what transpired,' snapped the lawyer. 'Because I told you the last time we met: he asked me to abandon King's Hall and represent him instead.'

'Why would he do such a thing? Frenge was the one being sued.'

'Yes, but any compensation that King's Hall won would have come out of the brewery – the business that he and Frenge shared. Of course, he requires good legal advice.'

'You do not consider it unethical to advise one party, then slither away to act for the other?'

Stephen glared at him. 'I dislike your attitude, Brother. I shall certainly not be giving anything to your College now. Nor Gonville – they are not having my architecture books either.'

He stalked away before either scholar could ask what Gonville had done to earn his ire. Michael watched him go thoughtfully.

'He said nothing to remove himself from my list of suspects, and neither did Shirwynk and Peyn. As far as I am concerned, any of them might have murdered Frenge.'

With every University scholar and most wealthy townsmen in attendance, St Mary the Great was packed to the gills. Everyone overheated in the thick robes that comprised their Sunday best, and tempers frayed, especially when rival hostels or Colleges found themselves crushed together. The beadles struggled to keep the peace.

Bartholomew and Wauter hurried to the chancel, to meet the other members of the *consilium*. Prior Joliet looked competent and statesmanlike in his best habit, while Nigellus wore robes that would not have looked out of place on a courtier. Irby was absent.

'He is too ill to come,' explained Nigellus. 'He is suffering from a loss of appetite.'

'So am I,' remarked Prior Joliet wryly. 'Nerves. There is enormous pressure on us to choose the right subject, and I am cognisant of the disappointment we will cause if we err. However, if I can endure it, so can he, so send a messenger to Zachary and tell him to come and do his duty.'

'I am afraid his malady is more serious than yours, so I confined him to bed,' said Nigellus pompously. 'Morys will take his place instead.'

He beckoned his colleague forward. Fierce little Morys was as wasplike as ever in his trademark yellow and black; Bartholomew wondered if he and Nigellus even remembered that Zachary scholars were meant to wear grey and cream.

'No, he will not!' said Joliet crossly. 'There are procedures that must be followed before a representative can be changed. It is—'

'There is no time,' interrupted Nigellus curtly. 'Or do you suggest that we keep hundreds of people waiting while we go through a host of petty formalities? I am sure Michaelhouse will not object to the substitution, given the immediacy of the situation.'

'Do you?' asked Joliet of Bartholomew and Wauter. He grimaced. 'I confess I am worried about the uneasy atmosphere in the church today, so the sooner we start, the less opportunity there will be for trouble. It would certainly make for a quieter life if you agree to Morys's nomination.'

'True,' agreed Wauter. 'I do not mind him in lieu of Irby.'

Bartholomew did, and wished Wauter had consulted with him before replying. Uncharitably, he wondered whether the geometrician's loyalties still lay with the hostel that had housed him for a decade, rather than the College that had kept him for a few weeks. And was Irby really ill, or had Nigellus simply decided to exchange a moderate man for one with opinions akin to his own?

'The motion is carried then,' said Joliet, casting an apologetic glance at Bartholomew, whose opinion did not matter now the majority had spoken.

'Good,' said Nigellus smugly. 'Then the subject of the debate will be *nemo dat*, as I have been suggesting for weeks. Are you in agreement, Morys?'

'Yes, I am,' replied Morys firmly. 'It is by far the best idea.'

'So there are two votes in its favour,' said Joliet. 'Wauter? What do you think?'

'It *would* make for an interesting—' began Wauter.

'Three,' pounced Morys. 'Which means that the views of Bartholomew and Joliet are now immaterial. I shall inform the Chancellor at once.'

'Now just a moment!' Joliet put out a hand to stop him. 'Wauter did not say he was voting for *nemo dat* – he merely said it was interesting. Besides, I am chairman, Morys, not you, so it is for *me* to speak to the Chancellor when we make our choice.'

Morys glared at him. 'You want Michaelhouse to win because they hire you to teach and paint murals. You are unfairly biased, and should not have accepted a place on this committee.'

Joliet and Bartholomew gaped at him, astounded by such intemperate accusations.

'Steady on, Morys,' murmured Wauter. 'And Joliet is right – I did *not* vote for *nemo dat*. I want to hear a few more suggestions before making my final decision.'

'Why?' demanded Nigellus. 'Morys and I have made up our minds and we will not be swayed. Now, Joliet, will you tell Tynkell or shall I?'

'I recommend that we select a theological or a musical—' began Joliet, pointedly turning his back on the Zachary men.

'No,' snarled Nigellus. 'It is *nemo dat* or nothing.'

'Hear, hear,' said Morys.

'Then Joliet, Wauter and I will choose the question,' said Bartholomew, objecting to their bullying tactics. 'If we can agree on a subject, you two are irrelevant.'

Nigellus addressed Joliet in a voice that held considerable menace. 'Vote as I suggest or I will tell the Sheriff that you bought illegal sucura for Arnold in his final days. All the money you have hoarded to feed the poor this winter will be gone in a fine.'

Bartholomew felt his jaw drop, while the blood drained from Joliet's face.

'You would never do such a terrible thing!' breathed the Prior, shocked.

'No?' sneered Nigellus. 'Just try me.'

'You want *nemo dat* because your students have been practising it,' said Bartholomew accusingly, unable to help himself. 'Do not look indignant – we all know the truth. But there is no glory in a victory won by cheating. Moreover, the Chancellor will not stand by and let you make a mockery of—'

'He will never oppose my wishes,' interrupted Morys. 'And if you accuse us of foul play again, I shall sue you for slander. Now, Joliet, what will it be? *Nemo dat* or poverty?'

Joliet's answer was in his silence and bowed head.

'Morys, tell Tynkell that the subject is *nemo dat*,' ordered Nigellus, allowing himself a tight, smug smile of triumph. 'I shall inform our students. No, do not argue, Bartholomew – we have the necessary three votes. The matter is over.'

He and Morys hurried away. The Zachary students began to cheer when he addressed them, a reaction he

133

quelled with an urgent flap of his hand. It told Bartholomew all he needed to know about the hostel's sense of honour. Wauter watched for a moment, then ambled away to report the 'decision' to Michaelhouse, although given that every moment of preparation counted, Bartholomew thought he should have moved more quickly.

'I am sorry, Matt,' said Joliet wretchedly. 'But I am afraid we *did* buy sucura to make poor Arnold smile during his last few days. And as legitimate sources are prohibitively expensive, we were obliged to turn to an illegal one.'

'How did Nigellus know?' Then Bartholomew sighed and answered the question himself. 'Because he was Arnold's *medicus*, and took a professional interest in his diet.'

Joliet nodded bitterly. 'He recommended sucura. Now I know why – not to brighten a dying man's last days, but to blackmail me. He knew I would opt for the cheapest source – and that the Sheriff would love to make an example of us.' He looked miserable. 'I know Tulyet is your friend, Matt, but it is the beggars who will suffer if you tell him what we have done.'

'I will keep your confidence, although I am not sure you can trust Nigellus. Perhaps you should confess before he blabs. Dick is a compassionate and practical man, and will understand why you did it. Probably.'

Sniffing unhappily, Joliet followed him to where Michael stood with Tynkell, ready to set the *disceptatio* in progress. The Chancellor was almost invisible inside his sumptuous robes of office, and he looked ill.

'It is strain,' he said in response to Bartholomew's polite concern. 'Morys threatens to invite my mother here unless I do everything he says, while there are rumours that say I am going to lead the University to a new life in the Fens. Half our scholars are delighted and press me for a date; the other half accuse me of being the Devil incarnate.'

'It is just gossip,' said Michael soothingly. 'Everyone will forget about it in a few days.'

'No, they will not,' said Tynkell glumly. 'Because the town is overjoyed by the "news", and when they realise it is untrue, their disappointment will know no bounds. They will riot.'

'But not today,' said Michael. 'Now go and start the debate. The *nemo dat* principle is not my idea of fine entertainment, but I suppose the *consilium* knows what it is doing.'

Michaelhouse's students rose to the challenge magnificently, and their inability to recite long passages from legal texts meant their observations were sharper and more concise, which put the audience on their side. This encouraged them to even greater mental acuity, and it was quickly clear who was the better of the two participants. Zachary's dismayed response was to resort to personal insults that lost them marks. With grim satisfaction, Bartholomew saw that Nigellus and Morys had done their pupils a serious disservice by cheating – Zachary would have fared better if they had been left to rely on their wits.

'Deciding the victor has been extremely difficult,' announced Tynkell when it was over.

'Rubbish!' cried Wayt from King's Hall. 'There was no real contest. And I do not say I support a College over a hostel, because everyone here knows that Michaelhouse sparkled, while Zachary was pompous and dull.'

'You are entitled to your opinion,' said Tynkell, shooting a nervous glance at Morys, whose eyes were like gimlets. 'But Zachary is adjudged the winner, because—'

Cries of 'shame' boomed through the church, which Tynkell was unequal to quelling. Michael let them mount

135

until it was obvious that most support was for Michaelhouse – even from the hostels – and only then did he take pity on the beleaguered Chancellor. He ordered silence in a stentorian bellow.

'You did not let me finish,' bleated Tynkell. 'Zachary is adjudged the winner in *quotes*, but Michaelhouse made more convincing arguments. So it is a draw.'

'You cannot have a draw,' yelled Wayt, while Morys's expression was as black as thunder. 'Do not be a fool, man!'

There was a resounding chorus of agreement, which Michael again allowed to run before calling for order, hoping that Tynkell would come to his senses in the interim.

'Very well,' conceded the Chancellor feebly. 'Michaelhouse wins.'

There was a loud cheer, and Bartholomew was disappointed but not surprised to see that Zachary were poor losers. They shouldered their way out of the church, sullen and angry, and the look Morys shot Tynkell was enough to make the Chancellor wilt.

'I shall be glad when he retires,' said Langelee, watching in disapproval. 'Tynkell is a dreadful weakling, wholly unsuited to the post.'

'He is,' agreed Wauter with a tight smile. 'But justice has been done, so let us forget about the debate and concentrate instead on convincing all these wealthy burgesses that our College is a worthy recipient for their spare money.'

The beadles cleared the church quickly after Tynkell had announced the result, aiming to reduce the chances of fights breaking out. Langelee rounded up his scholars and guests, and led them back to Michaelhouse at a jaunty clip. They were greeted by the peacock, which was indeed standing in full display by the gate. Clippesby was with it, and Bartholomew was not the only one who wondered if the Dominican *had* somehow persuaded it to do as the Master had ordered.

The hall looked better than it had done in years – bright, clean and welcoming. The mural was spectacular in the full light of day, with the four great thinkers holding forth under a spreading oak while the Fens stretched away in the distance. Prior Joliet stood next to it, accepting the praise of admirers, while Robert and Hamo served wine, managing it better than the students who had been allotted the task – they were more interested in reliving the triumph of the debate. Then Hakeney appeared, and shoved himself to the front of the queue.

'Who invited him?' hissed Langelee, glaring accusingly at his Fellows. 'He is not rich – not now he drinks wine rather than makes it.'

'No one did,' surmised Wauter. 'He just sniffed out free victuals.'

'I see you wear my wife's cross, Robert,' the vintner said aggressively. He was already drunk, although Bartholomew's remedy seemed to have worked on his constipation, as he looked better than he had when they had last seen him. 'When will you return it to its rightful owner?'

'I bought it in London,' said Robert with weary patience. 'You have seen the bill of sale.'

'That is a forgery,' stated Hakeney, staggering when he tried to lean against a table and missed. 'And so is the letter from that so-called priest who you claim sold it to you. That cross belongs to me, and I demand it back.'

'It does not,' said Tulyet quietly. 'I looked into this matter at your request. Do you not recall my verdict? Robert can prove ownership; you cannot. So stop this nonsense and let us enjoy this splendid repast.'

'Unless you would rather talk to me instead,' said

Dickon. His evil leer turned into a grin of malicious satisfaction when Hakeney took one look at the crimson face and backed away.

'Christ God, Tulyet,' breathed Langelee, staring at the boy. 'What have you done to him? Or is that his natural colour, and you have been deceiving us all these years?'

'His mother insisted that he come,' replied Tulyet stiffly, which Bartholomew interpreted as meaning that she wanted the brat out of her house. She, unlike her husband, was beginning to accept that there was something not very nice about their son. 'Personally, I thought he should remain indoors until it wears off.'

'Well, just make sure he does not fly up to the rafters, trailing his forked tail behind him,' ordered Langelee. 'I do not want potential benefactors frightened out of their wits.'

He turned abruptly to usher members of the wealthy Frevill clan towards the cakes, leaving the Sheriff scowling his indignation.

For the next hour, Bartholomew made polite conversation with the guests, who were so numerous that he wondered if Langelee had invited everyone with two coins to rub together. Edith was there with Anne and Rumburgh. They were talking to Wayt from King's Hall, and he went to join them quickly when he saw anger suffuse his sister's face.

'I was telling her that Cew is getting worse,' explained Wayt, when Bartholomew asked what was the matter. 'He might have recovered from the fright Frenge gave him, but the dyeworks poison the air he breathes and send him ever deeper into lunacy.'

'If that were true, you would be showing symptoms of madness, too,' retorted Edith.

'Perhaps he is, and he came here for a remedy,' purred Anne, running one finger down Wayt's sleeve, so that Bartholomew was seized with the sudden conviction that she already counted the Acting Warden among her conquests. 'I know one that is better than any physick.'

'In that case,' Wayt said smoothly, 'perhaps you will enlighten me, madam. Shall we step outside to discuss it? It is overly warm in here.'

Rumburgh started to protest, but Anne and Wayt sailed away without so much as a backward glance, leaving the burgess bleating his objections to thin air.

'It would not surprise me to learn that *he* killed Frenge,' Rumburgh muttered resentfully. 'After all, I did overhear them arguing shortly before Frenge died – Frenge was telling Wayt that if he continued with his lawsuit, he would reveal a nasty secret about King's Hall.'

'What secret?' asked Bartholomew keenly.

'I did not hear, but Wayt was livid.' Rumburgh clenched his fists in impotent fury as his wife and the Acting Warden reached the stairs and disappeared from sight.

'And Frenge?' asked Bartholomew. 'How did he seem?'

'He yelled like a fishwife.' Rumburgh lowered his voice. 'I should not speak ill of the dead, but I could not abide him either. He had designs on my Anne, and she was hard-pressed to repel him on occasion. He was very persistent.'

'What happened when he and Wayt parted ways?' asked Bartholomew.

'I do not know. I could not bear to be in the same vicinity as either, so I walked to the dyeworks, where I listened to Edith and Anne talk about woad balls for the rest of the day.'

Edith confirmed Rumburgh's tale, which meant that he – and Anne – had alibis for Frenge's murder. Bartholomew was thoughtful. Had the burgess witnessed the quarrel that had led one man to poison another, and he and Michael need look no further than the Acting Warden of King's Hall for their culprit?

* * *

A little later, Bartholomew saw Rougham, and supposed he had better apologise for what had happened the previous day. He was surprised to see him talking to Nigellus, though, because no one else from Zachary had accepted Langelee's invitation. As Bartholomew seriously doubted that Nigellus was a more gracious loser than the rest of his colleagues, he was instantly suspicious.

'I hope your lads learned something useful yesterday, Bartholomew,' said Rougham pleasantly. 'Nigellus and I certainly put them through their paces. Indeed, there were several instances when they were stunned into silence by the beauty of our logic.'

Bartholomew breathed a silent prayer of relief that Rougham was so full of hubris that he had failed to realise what was really happening. 'They told me they had enjoyed themselves,' he replied ambiguously.

'You can thank me by explaining why Stephen has withdrawn his offer to give Gonville his books,' said Rougham. 'I saw you talking to him earlier. Did he mention it?'

'I know why.' Nigellus spoke before Bartholomew could answer. 'Because Michaelhouse made such a fuss about you having them that Stephen decided to disinherit both Colleges.'

Rougham eyed him coldly. 'Do not try to stir up hostility between Bartholomew and me, Nigellus. It is unbecoming. And speaking of unsavoury antics, I am unimpressed with Zachary's fervour for decanting to the Fens as well. It is a stupid notion, and you would be wise to drop it.'

'On the contrary,' growled Nigellus, 'it is the most sensible idea I have heard since I enrolled in the University. But do your objections mean you will not be coming with us?'

'They do,' averred Rougham. 'I am not going anywhere, and neither will Michaelhouse, King's Hall, Bene't College or any other quality establishment. Your new *studium generale* will comprise nothing but a lot of ruffians from the lowest kind of hostel.'

'Is that so?' sneered Nigellus. 'Well, we shall see. However, I am delighted to learn that we shall soon part company permanently. To be frank, I do not respect either of you as *medici*.'

'There speaks the *Junior* Physician,' scoffed Rougham. 'However, it is not we who have lost so many patients of late – Letia, Arnold, Lenne, six clients from Barnwell . . .'

'None of them would have died if they had followed my advice,' snapped Nigellus. 'I calculated their horoscopes with great precision, and outlined exactly what they needed to do to save their lives. Is it my fault that they elected to ignore me?'

'You mean they declined to take the medicines you prescribed?' probed Bartholomew, thinking of the arsenal of potentially toxic ingredients that was available to physicians, many of which would not be detectable even if the victim was dissected.

'I do not prescribe medicine,' replied Nigellus haughtily. 'If a patient needs some, then he is past saving and it would be a waste of his money.'

'Lies!' cried Rougham, while Bartholomew regarded the Zachary man askance. 'You *do* dispense cures, because I saw you at the apothecary's shop only today.'

'Yes – buying liquorice root for sweetmeats,' Nigellus flashed back. 'Not that it is any of your concern. Irby has a fondness for them, and I thought they might cheer him up. He is a colleague, you see, so I am prepared to go the extra mile for him.'

'How is he?' asked Bartholomew, wishing some of Nigellus's clients were listening, as he was sure they would defect to another practitioner if they knew their current one did not consider them worthy of his best efforts.

'Ill,' replied Nigellus shortly. 'He has lost his appetite.'

141

Bartholomew waited for a fuller report, and when none came said, 'What ails him exactly?'

Nigellus regarded him askance. 'I have just told you: loss of appetite. It is a nasty disease.'

'It is not a disease,' said Bartholomew impatiently. 'It is a symptom.'

'Nonsense,' declared Nigellus. 'But I expect him to die of his malady, and then we shall have Morys as Principal. I cannot say I am sorry. Zachary needs a strong man at the helm, and while Irby is a kindly soul, he is hardly what you would call an inspiring leader.'

'Would you like Rougham or me to visit him?' asked Bartholomew, alarmed. Irby had not been in good health when they had last met, but he had certainly not been dying. Did it mean that Nigellus *was* the killer, and was in the process of claiming yet another victim – one whose death he had just said would suit him very well?

'I do not. He is *my* patient, and I shall thank you not to meddle.'

Bartholomew went on the offensive. 'You claimed that Letia died of dizziness, but—'

'Dizziness?' blurted Rougham. 'I have never heard *that* ever given as a cause of death.'

'Then you are a poor physician,' sneered Nigellus. 'Next you will say that there is no such disease as metal in the mouth, which killed Lenne. Or insomnia, which took Arnold. Or pallor, which carried away so many at Barnwell, although I bested it when it struck Trinity Hall.'

'But they are *not* diseases,' cried Bartholomew. 'And what is "metal in the mouth" anyway?'

'I am shocked that you should need to ask,' declared Nigellus. 'Call yourself a *medicus?* Clearly, you have a very long way to go before you match me in experience and skill. Now, if you will excuse me, there are wealthy burgesses who may need to buy a disease-preventing horoscope.'

'Lord!' breathed Rougham, watching him strut away, while Bartholomew supposed the last remark explained why Nigellus had accepted Langelee's invitation. 'If I am ever ill, promise you will not let him anywhere near me. I shall do the same for you.'

Bartholomew made the vow with all sincerity. Then Rougham went to refill his goblet, and Bartholomew turned to see that Michael had overheard the entire conversation.

'Even I know you cannot die of pallor, insomnia and dizziness,' said the monk. 'While "metal in the mouth" is a nonsense.'

'He should not be allowed anywhere near the sick,' stated Bartholomew. 'Unless we can believe his claim that he does not bother with medicine.'

'Well, I do not,' said Michael. 'Perhaps we need look no further for our poisoner. But would Nigellus be strong enough to force a fit man like Frenge to swallow something deadly?'

'Yes, if the first mouthful was taken willingly. Then, when Frenge collapsed from the shock, Nigellus could have grabbed his head and poured the rest into his mouth. But why would Nigellus do such a thing? He has no reason to inflict such a terrible death on a client.'

'Actually, he has – I have just learned that Irby bought ale from Frenge, but it was bad. Several Zachary masters stormed to the brewery to demand a refund, but Frenge refused. The confrontation grew quite heated, by all accounts.'

'And you think this is sufficient to drive a healer to murder?'

'I think it is sufficient to drive *Nigellus* to murder. Apparently, he was most indignant about the wrong that was done to his new hostel. Perhaps it is his way of demonstrating loyalty to the foundation that brought him from a dull country practice to the hub of academia.'

'He was not the only one who quarrelled with Frenge.' Briefly, Bartholomew told the monk what Rumburgh had confided, but when they went in search of the Acting Warden of King's Hall, it was to discover that he had left early. Someone else had left early, too.

'My wife has gone home,' said Rumburgh. 'She found your hall a little too warm.'

'So did Wayt,' said Michael. 'And I imagine they are both busily dispensing with unnecessary clothing as we speak.'

It was late by the time the last of Michaelhouse's guests went home, leaving their hosts with a mass of dirty goblets and a crumb-strewn floor. Wearily, Fellows and students began setting all to rights, while the servants were packed off to bed before they could claim overtime.

'That went well,' said Suttone, whose idea of clearing up was to eat the leftovers. 'No one will think we are on the brink of bankruptcy now, and benefactors will flock to us.'

'Have any flocked so far?' asked Wauter eagerly.

'Not yet,' replied Langelee. 'So we must continue the illusion for a little longer. Our next ploy will be to change the colour of our tabards from black to green.'

'We cannot buy new cloth for sixty students and Fellows, Master,' said Michael impatiently. 'The expense would finish us for certain.'

'And therein lies the beauty of my plan,' said Langelee smugly. 'We will not have *new* tabards made – we shall dye the old ones. Edith has offered to oblige for a very reasonable price.'

'But they are black,' Bartholomew pointed out. 'The colour will not take.'

'I am sure she knows what she is doing,' said Langelee. 'She would not have accepted the commission if she did not think she could do it.'

'Then I hope your trust is not misplaced,' said Wauter worriedly. 'Or we shall have no tabards at all, and our students will have to wear secular clothes.'

'Like Zachary,' said Father William disapprovingly. 'Not one was in his uniform today, and if we had lost the *disceptatio*, I was going to demand that they be disqualified on the grounds of illegal attire. But as we won, I decided to overlook it. Still, I am surprised that Tynkell did not order them home to change.'

'It is time we were rid of Tynkell and had a proper Chancellor,' said Suttone harshly. 'One who is not afraid that Morys might carry tales to his mother.'

'Incidentally, Irby summoned you earlier,' said Langelee to Bartholomew. 'He claimed he was dying and wanted you to visit. I was on my way to fetch you, but Nigellus intercepted me and volunteered to go instead. I did not think you would mind, as they are members of the same hostel.'

Alarmed, Bartholomew grabbed his cloak. 'I had better go now.'

'Unfortunately, there is no longer a need,' said Langelee. 'There was another message within the hour to say that Irby had passed away. It was very sudden, apparently.'

'Well,' breathed Michael, while Bartholomew gazed at the Master in dismay. 'Yet another of Nigellus's patients dead in curious circumstances.'

'We should go there now,' determined Bartholomew, donning his cloak. 'Nigellus was very open in wanting to be rid of Irby so that Morys could be Principal. Well, this is one death that will *not* go unremarked.'

'Would he have expressed such an opinion if he were the killer?' asked Langelee doubtfully. 'It would be reckless, would it not, to announce a motive for murder before the event?'

'He thinks we are stupid,' said Bartholomew. 'He does

not fear an investigation, because he believes he can outwit us.'

'Then he will learn the perils of underestimating the Senior Proctor and his trusty Corpse Examiner,' vowed Michael. 'But it is very late, and Irby will still be dead in the morning. I recommend we wait until tomorrow before beginning our assault – when daylight will assist in telling you what really happened to the unfortunate Principal of Zachary Hostel.'

CHAPTER 6

The All Souls' Day celebrations marked the end of Hallowtide, and the scholars of Michaelhouse woke the following morning aware that it was time to return to their usual routines. There were groans from Bartholomew's students when the bell rang to call them to church, and everyone was tardy about assembling in the yard. There were sore heads aplenty, and no Fellow thought it would be a good day for teaching.

It was William's turn to take the church service, and as he prided himself on the speed at which he could gabble through the sacred words, it was not long before everyone was walking back to College for breakfast. Any food left over from the reception had been eaten by the servants by the time they returned, so they sat down to watery oatmeal flavoured with cockles, cabbage and nutmeg. The dismal fare told them for certain that the holiday was over.

'I thought about Irby all night,' said Bartholomew unhappily, setting down his spoon when he found a slug in his bowl. 'When Nigellus told me that he had confined him to bed, I assumed it was part of the ploy to foist *nemo dat* on us – to dispense with a member of the *consilium* who would have voted against it. I wish to God I had gone to see him at once.'

'I wish you had, too,' said Michael. 'Then he might still be alive.'

'He tried to summon me,' Bartholomew went on wretchedly, 'which suggests he was dissatisfied with Nigellus's care. And with good cause.'

Michael nodded. 'He is the tenth of Nigellus's patients

147

to die – the eleventh if we count Frenge. It cannot be coincidence, and he did say that Irby was not the leader he wanted for Zachary. I imagine we will find motives for the other deaths, too, if we dig deep enough.'

'We might.' Bartholomew was still racked with guilt for not going to Irby's assistance.

'But why *kill* them?' Michael went on. 'He must realise that people will notice if he loses more clients than other *medici*. Then the surviving ones will desert him, which he will not appreciate, given how much he loves the fees they pay.'

'He practised at Barnwell for years before coming here,' said Bartholomew. 'He could not have dispatched those customers at this sort of rate, or the whole village would be in their graves. We must be wrong, Brother. He is a physician – a healer.'

'Of sorts – even I can tell that he is barely competent. Hah! Now there is a thought . . .'

'What is?'

'Perhaps he dispatched them to conceal evidence of his ineptitude – his failure to cure them. After all, if he used poison, who would know? You detected signs of a corrosive substance on Frenge, but there was nothing on Letia, so perhaps he learned from his mistake. Meanwhile, Arnold and the Barnwell folk are buried, so unless we exhume them . . .'

'No,' said Bartholomew firmly.

'Then maybe the dyeworks are responsible,' said Michael. He held up his hand when Bartholomew started to object. 'Even you cannot deny that it produces some very foul substances, and I dread to think what is slyly dumped in the river when Edith's ladies think no one is looking. You can ask when we visit her today.'

'We are going to see Edith? Why?'

'To warn her that I have received a lot of complaints about her reeking enterprise, and that she needs to find a way to eliminate the problem before there is serious trouble. But we had better visit Zachary first, to ascertain exactly what happened to Irby. Shall we go now?'

Bartholomew scribbled a list of passages from Galen's *De ossibus* for Langelee to read to his classes, and followed the monk across the yard to the gate, where they met Prior Joliet, Almoner Robert and Hamo, coming to put some finishing touches to the mural.

'Well?' asked Joliet pleasantly. 'Did Michaelhouse secure a wealthy benefactor last night?'

'Negotiations are under way with several interested parties,' lied Michael, and quickly changed the subject before they could press him for details. 'I heard you did rather well, too.'

Joliet's round face split into a grin of delight. 'Yes! We have been commissioned to paint King's Hall's library and Peterhouse's refectory. They said they had never seen more lifelike leaves than the ones on our oak tree.'

'And the mayor would like to see what can be done for the guildhall,' put in Robert, wincing as he tried to free his long white hair from the chain that held his pectoral cross. 'Not to mention a couple of enquiries from private individuals.'

'Good occasion,' mumbled Hamo, apparently deeming it worthy of a rare two-word sentence.

'The only unpleasant bit was when Hakeney made a scene,' said Robert, wincing. 'The man is deranged, and I wish he would find someone else to hound.'

'I shall buy him a new cross when Michaelhouse pays us at Christmas,' declared Joliet, all happy generosity. 'Wayt has offered to get one when he next visits London.'

'We had better go,' said Robert. 'The sooner we finish here, the sooner we can move to our next project.' That notion brought a sudden smile. 'The poor will not want for bread this winter!'

'It is not fair,' muttered Michael when the Austins had

gone. 'We went to all that trouble for Michaelhouse, not our hired artists.'

'Yet it is hard to begrudge their good fortune. They aim to use the profits for alms.'

'I know,' said Michael irritably. 'But that does not mean I have to like them raking in money when we still have nothing.'

They met Tulyet at the end of St Michael's Lane. Dickon was in tow, his face even brighter than it had been the previous day, suggesting the brat had contrived to acquire a private supply of dye and had reapplied it. His hair 'horns' were gone, though, no doubt a condition of being allowed to accompany his father out. Regardless, he was still attracting a lot of uneasy attention.

'His mother was keen for him to stretch his legs,' said Tulyet, when Michael enquired tentatively whether it might not have been advisable to leave him at home. 'And I am reluctant to waste good training time anyway. There is a lot to learn about being Sheriff.'

'I hope he will not be stepping into your shoes too soon,' said Michael, aware that Dickon would be a disaster for the University, and probably not very good for the town either.

'Father says I am already showing a firm hand,' said the boy with a malignant grin. 'Did you hear that I stopped that sot Hakeney from stealing your spoons yesterday? He started to shove them up his sleeve, but I told him that I would chop off his fingers if he did not put them back.'

'A crime was averted,' said Tulyet proudly. 'One that would have caused more bad feeling between the town and the University had it succeeded. I am delighted by Dickon's vigilance.'

'Have you learned anything new about Frenge?' asked Michael, unable to bring himself to praise the child. 'My own enquiries are frustratingly slow.'

'I have had scant time for anything other than keeping the peace.'

'There was a big fight last night, see,' interjected Dickon gleefully. 'I was there, so I joined in. I stabbed two scholars as hard as I could, and I bit another.'

'Who are they?' asked Bartholomew uneasily. 'Do they need medical attention?'

'He exaggerates,' said Tulyet, shooting his son a warning glance. 'He did manage to corner a trio of lads from Zachary, but they ran away before any real harm was done. Do you have a few spare moments to talk? I would like to hear what you have learned in more detail.'

'A few,' replied Michael, while Bartholomew thought it said a good deal about Dickon's fearsome reputation that he was able to rout three lads twice his age. 'But then we must visit Zachary to find out exactly why Irby died.'

He was hungry after the meagre victuals at breakfast, so suggested repairing to the Brazen George, where the landlord kept a room for his exclusive use. It was a pleasant chamber, overlooking a pretty yard where contented chickens scratched among the herb-beds. Landlord Lister came to serve them in person, chatting amiably as he regaled them with the latest gossip, although he was careful to keep well away from Dickon.

'Did you hear that everyone in Trinity Hall was ill again yesterday?' he asked. 'And do not blame the syllabub this time, Doctor – they bought it from me, and the cream was fresh.'

'Did Nigellus tend them?' asked Michael casually.

'I believe he did offer his services, although even he could not calculate horoscopes for everyone, so he told them all to don clean nether garments and stand in full moonlight for an hour.'

'That does not sound too deadly,' murmured Michael. 'But I shall visit Trinity Hall later, to ensure he did not prescribe anything else.'

'My wife was ill during the night as well,' said Tulyet. 'So was Dickon, although he has recovered, thank God. It must have been something they ate.'

'Not at Michaelhouse,' replied Michael coolly. 'None of us were unwell.'

'Suttone was,' contradicted Bartholomew. 'He called me at midnight with stomach cramps, and so did one of William's students.'

'Because they overindulged,' countered Michael sharply. 'I sampled everything on offer, and I was not ill.'

Tulyet took the opportunity to ask Lister a few questions about sucura and how it might be smuggled into the town, but while the landlord was willing to confide in an old and trusted customer like Michael, sharing confidences with the Sheriff was another matter entirely. He mumbled a vague reply and fled.

'How am I supposed to stop these illegal imports when no one will talk to me?' sighed Tulyet crossly. 'I am sure everyone knows exactly who is responsible. Everyone except me, that is.'

Michael shrugged. 'No one likes paying taxes, and why *should* the King receive money for the ingredients we put in our cakes?'

'Because it is the law,' replied Tulyet tartly.

'Then perhaps His Majesty should consider setting a more reasonable levy. Sucura is expensive without the tax, but *with* the import duty, it is beyond the reach of everyone except him and his wealthiest barons. You cannot blame folk for buying it from smugglers.'

'You buy it from smugglers?' pounced Tulyet. 'Which ones? Their names, if you please.'

'I was speaking hypothetically,' replied Michael. 'I do not shop for foodstuffs myself – I am far too busy for that sort of indulgence.'

Tulyet glared accusingly at him. 'But I imagine Agatha has laid in a store of it for Michaelhouse.'

'Chance would be a fine thing,' grumbled Michael, before remembering the trouble that had been taken to convince everyone that the College was a good proposition for potential investors. He trusted Tulyet with the truth, but Dickon was there, small eyes alight with interest, so he settled for saying, 'We do not break the law, Dick.'

Tulyet shot him a lugubrious glance, which suggested that Wauter had failed to keep him away from the marchpanes. Eager to avoid trouble, Michael changed the subject.

'Go away, Dickon. I need to discuss Frenge's murder with your father. Privately.'

'You can talk in front of my son,' said Tulyet. 'I trust him to be discreet.'

'He was not discreet when he gossiped about the physicians' experiments to refine lamp fuel last summer,' Michael shot back. 'His loose tongue caused all manner of harm.'

'He has learned his lesson.' Tulyet was stung by the reminder. 'He is older now. And anyway, what do you expect if a group of *medici* gathers in the garden next door, and sets about making explosions? Of course a bright boy will be intrigued.'

'Do you have any more tests planned, Doctor?' asked Dickon keenly. 'Because if so, I want to watch. You never meet in Meryfeld's house any more.'

And Dickon was the reason why, thought Bartholomew. 'We are too busy these days.'

'Good,' said Tulyet. 'Because it was irresponsible. But tell me about Frenge, Brother. In front of Dickon, if you please – he needs to understand how investigations are conducted.'

'Very well,' said Michael. 'We have discovered that Frenge was engaged in some very dark business, which may have led to his demise.'

Bartholomew regarded the monk askance: they had done nothing of the sort.

'What manner of dark business?' asked Tulyet curiously.

'Cattle rustling,' lied Michael. 'Which explains why he was on the King's Ditch. After all, what better way to transport stolen livestock than by water? The poison must have struck him down when he reached the Austins' convent, and he staggered towards it for help.'

'I had no idea he was a criminal,' said Tulyet wonderingly. 'Perhaps an accomplice killed him then – an argument over profits. I shall look into the matter whenever I have a spare moment.'

Michael inclined his head. 'But do you have *nothing* to report, Dick? Not even a snippet?'

'Well, I learned that Frenge visited Stephen shortly before his death,' replied Tulyet. 'I have tried to speak to Stephen, but he is never in. I am beginning to think he is avoiding me.'

'He will not avoid me,' vowed Michael. 'Leave him to us. Is there anything else?'

'Only that Morys has written to Chancellor Tynkell's mother to complain about the way his hostel is treated by the University. Word is that she is on her way to assess the situation for herself, which I sincerely hope is untrue. She is a friend of the Queen, and we do not want our troubles reported to royal ears.'

'She is a dragon,' interposed Dickon. 'Chancellor Tynkell told me so, and I am looking forward to meeting her. I hope she *can* breathe fire, because I shall be disappointed if it turns out to be one of your scholars' inventions.'

The discussion was cut short by an urgent summons for Tulyet to go to the dyeworks, where a group of burgesses had gathered to complain about the volume of water that was being extracted from the river – water that was needed for their own businesses downstream. Bartholomew stood to go with him, but Tulyet waved him away.

'The sight of the owner's brother is unlikely to help, especially one who is a scholar.'

'But she might need me,' objected Bartholomew.

Tulyet gave a wry smile. 'She will not, because she has her own little army.'

Bartholomew frowned. 'You mean her Frail Sisters? They are hardly—'

'I mean the men who used to hire her ladies when they were whores. They have gathered to protect the place, and some are very unsavoury characters. They will keep Edith safe – from disgruntled merchants *and* from scholars.'

'It is true, Matt,' said Michael, watching the Sheriff hurry away, Dickon scampering at his side. 'Your sister's women *have* garnered support from old clients. Unfortunately, there is a rumour that these men are being rewarded with the kind of favours they enjoyed when the lasses were walking the streets.'

Bartholomew groaned. 'In other words, the dyeworks is being used as a brothel. Edith cannot know – she would not condone that sort of thing.'

'Then we shall tell her. But later, once Dick has restored the peace. He is right about you being more likely to inflame than cool the situation, and we should stay away for now.'

Bartholomew turned to something else that was worrying him. 'Are you sure it was wise to tell him that Frenge was a cattle thief? When he learns the truth – which he will – he will be furious with you for wasting his time.'

'Better that than risk Dickon blabbing our suspicions to all and sundry. We do not want Nigellus to learn that he is at the top of our list of suspects just yet.'

'I am more inclined to believe that Shirwynk killed

Frenge,' said Bartholomew. 'He did it in the expectation that King's Hall would drop their lawsuit if Frenge was dead.'

'But it was Shirwynk who encouraged Frenge to invade King's Hall in the first place,' Michael pointed out. 'He is unlikely to have killed him for doing what he was told.'

'He doubtless did not anticipate that King's Hall would sue. So he miscalculated twice: once when he underestimated Wayt's capacity for revenge; and once when murdering Frenge did not result in King's Hall abandoning their case against the brewery.'

'And Shirwynk would have eager help in Peyn,' acknowledged Michael. 'However, we should not forget Stephen – the man who spoke to Frenge shortly before the murder and with Shirwynk shortly after it. And who slept with Frenge's mistress – I think he was lying when he said he had only seduced Anne once.'

'I suspect it was she who did the seducing, although I doubt she will admit it if we ask.'

'There is also Wayt,' Michael went on. 'The easy familiarity between him and Anne at Michaelhouse suggested that they were old flames. And Rumburgh said that Frenge and Wayt argued shortly before the murder . . .'

'True. Moreover, Wayt is one of the three scholars at King's Hall who have no alibi for Frenge's death.'

'Next, there is Hakeney, who hates the Austins because he thinks Robert stole his dead wife's cross. He may have sent Frenge to steal it back, and dispatched him there in the hope of embarrassing the friary.'

'That would be an extreme thing to do,' said Bartholomew doubtfully. 'Although if he were drunk . . .'

'And finally, Wauter.' Michael raised a hand when Bartholomew began to object. 'I do not believe him capable of such wickedness either, but he has said and done some very odd things of late, and until they are explained, he must remain on our list.'

'I suppose so,' said Bartholomew, albeit reluctantly.

Michael stood. 'So there are our suspects: Nigellus, Shirwynk with Peyn, Stephen, Wayt and his two alibi-less colleagues from King's Hall, Hakeney and Wauter. We had better go to Zachary before any more of the day is lost, and assess whether Nigellus has made an end of Irby.'

They knocked on Zachary's door a short while later, and were admitted to a building that was as grand as any College. It possessed a handsome hall on the ground floor, beautifully decorated with geometrical designs, and with real glass in its windows. Unlike most foundations, it did not serve as a refectory *and* lecture chamber – Zachary had designated classrooms for teaching, so that its masters did not have to compete with each other to make themselves heard.

'If you are here to fine us for improper dress, think again,' said Morys challengingly. He was wearing another yellow and black outfit, while his students had also dispensed with their uniform tabards in favour of something more colourful, and Nigellus was in red. 'We are indoors, and can do what we like in the confines of our own home.'

Michael smiled pleasantly. 'You may, of course. However, my beadles are under orders to stamp down on infractions in the streets, so you might want to change before going out.'

Morys's expression turned smug. 'You will never see the fine you levied on Saturday, though. Tynkell has quashed it for us, on the grounds that it was Hallow-tide.'

'He does not have that authority,' said Michael coolly. 'Besides, it has already been entered in our official records, so unless you want "payment refused" put next to it – which means that no Zachary man will graduate until the matter is resolved – I suggest you settle the debt.'

'You cannot—' began Morys furiously.

'I already have,' said Michael. 'So what will it be? Payment or a battle you will never win?'

Scowling angrily, Morys counted out the coins and handed them over, while Michael sat at a table to write a receipt. Nigellus made no effort to contribute to the discussion, and went instead to pick up a book and flick through it with studied disinterest. Bartholomew regarded him with dislike, thinking that here was a man who had spent so many years cowing patients with arrogant condescension that he exuded disdain as a matter of course.

'Do you not consider it demeaning to browbeat a man by telling tales to his mother, Morys?' asked Michael as he worked. 'It seems rather a shabby thing to do.'

'I am perfectly within my rights to write to my new in-laws,' declared Morys, bristling like an angry insect. 'It is hardly my fault that Tynkell is frightened of his dam.'

'If she is as terrifying as he claims, you might have done yourself a serious disservice by summoning her,' warned Michael. 'She may have words for you, too.'

Morys drew himself up to his full unimpressive height. 'Let her try! I am more than capable of standing firm against a woman, even one who counts royals among her friends.'

'Are you Principal now that Irby is dead, or will there be an election?' asked Michael, changing the subject abruptly as he scattered sand on the ink to dry it. 'I imagine you are not the only scholar who would like a stab at the post.'

'Actually, he is,' said Nigellus. 'So there will be no election, because we are all agreed: Morys is the man to lead us forward.'

Morys grinned nastily. 'Wauter will be sorry he left Zachary when he hears that Irby is dead. He wanted to be Principal himself.'

'He is happy where he is,' said Bartholomew sharply.

'You think being a Fellow is preferable to being a Principal?' sneered Morys. 'Wauter will not – he is an ambitious man. Or have you not yet seen that side of his character? Your Langelee should watch himself.'

'Irby,' said Bartholomew, declining to pursue such a distasteful discussion. 'I would like to examine him now. Where is he?'

'Examine him?' demanded Nigellus, eyes narrowing. 'Why?'

'Because I need an official cause of death to enter in the records,' replied Bartholomew. 'As is the case for any scholar who dies.'

'Nigellus conducted the only examination that is necessary,' stated Morys. 'He rested a hand on Irby's forehead after he died, to test for the presence of his soul.'

Bartholomew blinked. 'He did what?'

'It is a standard medical technique,' replied Nigellus loftily. 'As you would know if you had my extensive experience. Cadavers vibrate if the soul is still within them.'

'Regardless,' said Michael, speaking while Bartholomew was still processing the outrageous claim, 'my Corpse Examiner is duty-bound to look for himself. So where is Irby?'

'I am not telling you,' said Nigellus. 'You have no right to maul—'

'We have every right,' snapped Michael. 'Or is there a reason you want to keep him hidden? Such as the fact that his death is not all you claim?'

'Of course not!' snarled Nigellus. 'Very well – disturb his rest if you must. However, you will do it without me, because I want no part in such a vile desecration.'

'Good,' said Michael coolly. 'Because you would not have been permitted to observe anyway. It is against regulations.'

This was news to Bartholomew, although Nigellus only

gave an irritable sigh before returning to his book. This time, there was considerable agitation in his page flicking, so much so that one tore. Muttering under his breath, Morys led the way up the stairs, where Irby occupied the largest room, laid out ready to be carried to church.

'Will you be long?' Morys asked curtly. 'We have sent for a bier, and it will be here soon. We do not want to pay extra because you make the bearers wait.'

'Your grief for Irby is duly noted,' said Michael drily. 'And the answer to your question is that the examination will take as long as is necessary. Now leave us, please.'

Huffing irritably, Morys backed out and closed the door behind him. Michael took a scrap of parchment from his purse and shoved it in the keyhole. He and Bartholomew exchanged wry grins when they heard the new Principal curse softly on the other side.

'Hurry up,' Michael whispered, aiming for a large clothes chest, which he flung open. 'I suspect it will not be long before they devise some pretext to interrupt us.'

'What are you hoping to find?' asked Bartholomew, watching him begin to rifle.

'Poison – which will give us the evidence we need to arrest Nigellus.'

'It will not be in here. If Irby has been murdered, the culprit will have taken any toxins away, to ensure that no one ever knows how his victim really died.'

'We shall see.'

They were silent as they worked, Michael opening cupboards and peering under the bed, and Bartholomew intent on his examination. Unfortunately, it told him nothing. There were no marks of violence, no suggestion of illness – sudden or otherwise – and no indication that Irby had been forced to swallow poison.

'So what did kill him then?' asked Michael, exasperated. 'Not "loss of appetite" surely?'

'I do not know, Brother. However, Nigellus does not

distinguish between symptoms and diseases, so it is possible that Irby complained about not being hungry – a remark that Nigellus then took to be an ailment in itself.'

'You are too generous. Irby's lack of hunger was probably caused by some insidious poison. Do you know of any that might have such a terrible effect?'

'Plenty, although there is no way to tell whether they were fed to Irby – and dissection will not give us an answer, before you suggest it. In short, I cannot tell you why he died, and my official verdict will have to be "cause unknown".'

'Damn! Because something untoward is definitely afoot here. For a start, everything in this room belongs to Morys, and there is no sign of that grey and cream cloak Irby always wore. Morys could not even wait for Irby's corpse to be moved before claiming these quarters as his own!'

'Does that mean he is the killer, not Nigellus?'

'Not necessarily – perhaps they did it together. After all, there does seem to be a consensus in Zachary that Irby was too placid.'

'But we have no evidence. You found no sign that a toxin was used, and neither did I.'

Michael pointed to a jug on the table. 'The obvious place for it is there – it contains Shirwynk's apple wine, which we know Irby liked, because he always had a flask of it to hand. But I drank from it just now, and I am still here, so it must be innocent.'

Bartholomew gaped at him. 'You sampled wine in a room where you suspect a man was poisoned? What were you thinking?'

'That we needed answers,' replied Michael shortly. Then he looked sheepish. 'To be frank, I was thirsty, and it did not occur to me that it might be dangerous until I had taken a substantial swallow. But we are wasting our

161

time here, Matt. If Irby was murdered, his killers have covered their tracks too well. We shall have to find another way to catch them.'

Bartholomew was about to open the door when he noticed a piece of parchment adhering to the bottom of the jug – one that might have remained hidden if Michael had not indulged his greedy instincts. It was folded in half, and he was surprised to see his own name written on one side. He opened it, aware of the thudding of his heart. Was it going to be an outpouring of Irby's fears, naming Nigellus or Morys as the villain and berating Bartholomew for not coming to his aid? But there were only three words, and they made no sense whatsoever.

'*Similia similibus curantur,*' he read aloud. He looked at Michael in puzzlement as he translated. '"Like things are cured by like things". What is that supposed to mean?'

'It means that it is time we asked Nigellus a few probing questions,' said Michael with quiet determination.

'Why him?' asked Bartholomew. 'And not Morys?'

'Because of the word *cured,* which is what physicians do. Or do not do. I imagine Irby left this clue when you failed to answer his plea for help. He would have known that the Corpse Examiner would come, and it is his way of identifying his killer.'

'You are reading far too much into it, Brother! It might just be the nonsensical ramblings of a dying man.'

'Perhaps. But let us see what Nigellus has to say for himself.'

They descended the stairs to discover that Nigellus had gone to Trinity Hall, to tend those patients who had not benefited from standing under the full moon in clean underwear. Michael shot Bartholomew a look that revealed exactly what he was thinking: that Nigellus had fled to avoid being asked any awkward questions.

'I am sure he will not be long,' the monk said, sitting

on a bench and making himself comfortable. The Zachary men exchanged glances of consternation: they had expected him to leave once the Corpse Examiner had finished with Irby. 'Meanwhile, perhaps you will talk to us.'

Alarm flashed in Morys's eyes, and he ordered a student to fetch Nigellus back as quickly as possible, which had Michael flinging Bartholomew another meaningful glance, this one asking why the new Principal was unwilling to suffer an interrogation on his colleague's behalf.

'We found this.' Michael handed over the scrap of parchment. 'Is it Irby's writing?'

Morys nodded. 'He must have penned it in his delirium – a nonsense, as I am sure you can tell. Where was it?'

'Under the wine jug.'

Morys pulled a face. 'Ah, yes, the apple wine he loved so much. Personally, I would never touch anything made by Shirwynk. His hatred of our University is unnatural, and he cannot be trusted not to piss in it – or worse.'

Bartholomew regarded him thoughtfully: did the remark arise from the perfectly understandable caution of a man who hated scholars? Or was he trying to shift the blame for Irby's death on to an innocent party?

'You assumed the mantle of responsibility very quickly, Morys,' remarked Michael. 'Was Irby even cold before you took possession of his room?'

'Nigellus said Irby's soul had left his body, so where lay the harm?' shrugged Morys. 'However, I can see what you are thinking, and you are wrong. No one at Zachary would have harmed Irby. He was weak, but we liked him, and we are sorry he has gone.'

'Where are his belongings?' asked Michael, his cool expression suggesting that he did not believe a word of it. 'We need to examine those as well.'

'Why?' asked Morys suspiciously, then shrugged again

when the monk's eyebrows drew down in an irritable frown. 'They are in the shed, ready to be sent to his kin.'

A student conducted them there, but although Michael and Bartholomew went through Irby's things with the utmost care, they found nothing to help their investigation. Bartholomew paid special attention to the wineskin, but it was empty, and if it had contained something to hasten its owner's end, there was no sign of it now.

They returned to Zachary's hall, where Michael once again made himself comfortable, and Bartholomew stood behind him, tense and alert for trouble.

'What happened last night?' the monk asked. 'We know Irby tried to summon Matt.'

Morys rolled his eyes to indicate his irritation at being questioned again, but answered anyway. 'He had been unwell for two weeks or more, but woke feeling worse yesterday. Nigellus recommended that he stay in bed and told me to take his place on the *consilium*. A little later, the rest of the hostel joined us at the *disceptatio*.'

'You left a sick man alone?' Bartholomew was unimpressed.

'No – Stephen the lawyer offered to sit with him. When we came home, Irby was fading fast. He asked for you, but then Nigellus arrived back, so you were not needed. Irby died shortly after. Of loss of appetite, as I am sure you discovered. Now is there anything else? I have work to do.'

Michael smiled enigmatically. 'Then do it. Matt and I will not disturb you.'

Bristling with indignation, Morys busied himself with pens and parchment, but the presence of the Senior Proctor and his Corpse Examiner was a distraction, and although he made a good show of being inundated with important business, he did little more than shuffle documents into random piles.

Eventually, the door opened and Nigellus stalked in. The student had evidently decided that reinforcements were needed, because he had brought Kellawe and Segeforde as well, a sight that lit Morys's waspish face with relief. The Franciscan muttered something in his thick northern accent that might have been a greeting, but that might equally well have been an insult. His voice was hoarse, indicating that he had been ranting, almost certainly at the dyeworks. But it was Segeforde who caught Bartholomew's attention: the man's thick purple lips were stark against an unnaturally white face, which shone with sweat.

'Go to see if Yerland is better, Segeforde,' instructed Morys. 'Then lie down yourself. You are exhausted after the effort of preparing . . . our students for yesterday's debate . . . drilling them in the art of disputation, I mean. Not making them learn chunks of legal tract verbatim.'

'We lost because Michaelhouse cheated,' snarled Kellawe, and out went his pugnacious jaw, all bristling antagonism.

'What is wrong with Yerland?' asked Bartholomew, treating the ridiculous claim with the contempt it deserved by ignoring it.

'A headache,' replied Nigellus. 'I told him he would feel better if he recited the Lord's Prayer backwards, but he refuses to do it on the grounds that he cannot concentrate. Fool!'

'Perhaps Bartholomew has a remedy,' said Segeforde, the hope in his voice suggesting that if so, he would have a dose of it himself.

Bartholomew made for the door. 'Where is Yerland? Upstairs?'

'Yes, but there is no need for you to see him,' said Nigellus shortly. 'Just give me what you usually prescribe for severe pains in the head, and I will make sure he swallows it.'

'I cannot prescribe anything without examining him first,' said Bartholomew, surprised that Nigellus should

165

think he might. 'Headaches are symptomatic of all manner of conditions, and it would be reckless to dispense medicine without making a proper diagnosis first.'

Nigellus scowled. 'Very well, if you must, although you are wasting your time. Segeforde will take you to him, while I stay here with Morys and Kellawe. They can help me answer the Senior Proctor's questions, which I imagine will be deeply stupid.'

Segeforde took Bartholomew to the students' dormitory, where Yerland writhed in agony. A brief glance inside the lad's mouth showed no evidence that he had swallowed anything caustic, but that did not mean he had *not* been poisoned. As the student was unable to answer questions himself, Segeforde obliged. He did so in a voice that shook with fear, and Bartholomew saw he fully expected to share Yerland's fate.

'It came on suddenly. Before that, he was as hale as the rest of us.'

'Has he eaten or drunk anything different than usual?' asked Bartholomew. 'There must have been special Hallow-tide treats over the past three days.'

'Of course, but they were all from common pots, and no one else is ill. He did have a *lot* of apple pie, though.'

'What about you? Did you eat a lot of apple pie too?'

'No,' whispered Segeforde. 'I do not like fresh fruit, so I kept to the Lombard slices. I cannot imagine what is wrong with me. Do you think it is a deadly contagion that will carry us all off?'

'It is not a contagion.' Bartholomew decided to be blunt. 'Has Nigellus given you or Yerland anything to swallow? Some remedy, perhaps, which he claimed is beneficial to health?'

Segeforde would not look at him. 'He thinks such things are a waste of money, and I was surprised when he agreed to let you prescribe a cure for Yerland. Perhaps he feels the boy is beyond his skills – just as Irby was last night.'

166

Bartholomew was not sure what to think. He rummaged in the bag he always carried over his shoulder for wood betony and poppy juice, hoping Yerland's pain would subside with sleep. He mixed a milder dose for Segeforde, who gulped it down eagerly. It was not long before Yerland's breathing grew deep and regular, and the lines of agony eased from his face. The colour returned to Segeforde's cheeks, too. Bartholomew recommended that they both confine themselves to barley broth and weak ale for a few days, and to call him if there was no further improvement. Then he went downstairs, where Michael was still grilling Nigellus.

'What does *similia similibus curantur* mean to you?' he was asking. Nigellus, Morys and Kellawe sat in a row facing him, all looking like courtiers in their gorgeous robes; even Kellawe's habit was a princely garment, quite unlike those worn by most friars in his Order. 'Irby wrote it shortly before he died – addressed to Matt.'

Nigellus leaned back in his chair, all arrogant confidence. 'It means nothing – other than that his wits must have wandered as he slipped into his fatal decline.'

'What do you think killed him?' asked Michael.

'Loss of appetite,' replied Nigellus. 'How many more times do you need to be told?'

'No one starves to death in a few hours,' put in Bartholomew impatiently.

'I did not say he starved,' snapped Nigellus. 'I said he lost his appetite. Clearly, his lack of eating caused a fatal imbalance in his humours. However, he did not stop drinking, and he was fond of Shirwynk's apple wine – perhaps that played a role in his demise.'

'We will never know,' said Michael pointedly, 'because someone had emptied the wineskin he always carried.'

'Irby himself, probably,' shrugged Nigellus. 'As I said, he had a fondness for the stuff.'

167

'A lot of your patients have died recently: the Barnwell folk, Letia, Lenne, Arnold, Frenge and now Irby.'

Nigellus was unfazed by the accusation inherent in the observation. 'It happens, as Bartholomew will tell you. Indeed, he has lost two clients himself in the last month.'

'Three,' corrected Kellawe. 'I heard that the cousin of Vine the potter died an hour ago,'

'Did she?' Bartholomew was dismayed. He never had been summoned to see her, almost certainly because Vine objected to his association with the dyeworks, but he had intended to visit anyway. It had slipped his mind, and now it was too late.

'Why are you concerned about these particular fatalities anyway?' asked Morys. 'None are people who will be missed: Letia did nothing but moan, Lenne and Frenge were troublemakers, and Arnold was too old to be useful. And as for Barnwell, well, that was weeks ago, so who cares about them now?'

'You dispense some very odd cures, Nigellus,' said Michael, eyeing Morys with distaste before turning back to the Junior Physician. 'Such as telling those at Trinity Hall to stand in moonlight and wear clean undergarments.'

'And most have recovered,' asserted Nigellus haughtily. 'Thanks to me.'

'Have you heard the good news about Kellawe?' Morys spoke even as Michael drew breath for another question. 'He has been granted licence to absolve all scholars from acts of violence. It means we shall have the advantage in the looming crisis – we can dispense any lessons we like to aggravating townsmen, but nothing we do will count against our souls on Judgement Day.'

Michael's eyes narrowed. 'The University has not applied for one of those.'

'Oh, yes, we have,' said Morys. 'Chancellor Tynkell obliged, at my suggestion.'

'And we shall be needing it soon,' added Kellawe, eyes gleaming. 'Scholars will not stand mute for much longer while the town abuses us. And the biggest insults of all are the dyeworks and their scheming whores.'

Bartholomew did not often feel like punching anyone, but he experienced a very strong desire to clout the Franciscan. Michael pushed him towards the door before he could do it, informing the Zachary men curtly that he would be back with more questions another time.

'Damn Tynkell!' Michael hissed, once they were outside. 'And damn Morys, too! The town will see Kellawe's licence as a deliberate move against them. It was a stupid, wicked thing to have done when we are on the brink of serious trouble.'

'If Kellawe insults my sister again, he will be absolving *me* from an act of violence,' vowed Bartholomew. 'But what are we going to do about Irby? Just because we found no evidence against his colleagues does not mean they are innocent of harming him.'

Michael nodded. 'So we shall ask Stephen if Irby said anything significant as he lay dying.'

The lawyer lived on the High Street in one of the best houses in the town. A maid led Bartholomew and Michael to an elegant room filled with sunlight, where her master was reading. Books stood in regimented rows on shelves that lined one complete wall, so numerous that Bartholomew could not stop himself from gaping – books were expensive, given that each had to be handwritten, a task that might take a scribe several years.

'My library,' explained Stephen proudly. 'Mostly tomes on architecture.'

'You promised them to Michaelhouse,' recalled Michael. 'Then to Gonville Hall.'

'Yes,' said Stephen. 'But I have decided to keep them

for myself. They mean a great deal to me, and I do not want them to go to a place that is on the brink of collapse.'

'Michaelhouse is a very stable foundation,' lied Michael, then added spitefully, 'although I cannot say the same about Gonville. Its Master has been in Avignon for years, and shows no sign of returning.'

'Actually, I was referring to the University as a whole,' said Stephen, 'which is about to decant to the Fens, where it will not survive. Of course, I shall not mind seeing its lawyers go – it will mean more work for me.'

'There is no truth in that silly rumour,' said Michael impatiently. 'Why would we abandon Cambridge when we have everything we need here?'

'Because many of your scholars are weary of the discord between them and the town, and are delighted by the notion of a fresh start.'

'Well, we are not going anywhere,' averred Michael between gritted teeth. 'How many more times must I say it?'

'The town will be disappointed. It is looking forward to being shot of you.'

Michael scowled at him. 'Relations might be easier if *you* did not dispense inflammatory advice – such as urging King's Hall to sue Frenge, and encouraging Edith to open a dyeworks. Both have set town and University at each other's throats.'

'I suppose they have,' acknowledged Stephen carelessly. 'But it could not be helped.'

'I understand you were with Irby yesterday,' said Michael, changing the subject abruptly before his dislike of the man could start to show. 'When he was ill.'

'Yes, I sat with him for two or three hours. He was a good man and will be missed.'

'Did he say anything at all?' asked Bartholomew. 'Or write messages to anyone?'

'He was asleep most of the time. I stayed until his

170

colleagues returned from the *disceptatio,* then came home. He thanked me when I went, but those were the only words he spoke. And he certainly did not pick up a pen.'

'Why did Zachary ask you to do the honours?' asked Michael suspiciously. 'Or do you have secret nursing skills?'

'There is little nursing required for a man in slumber, as your pet physician will confirm. However, I volunteered to help because Irby was a friend, and I did not want him to be left alone while the others went out.'

'Did you know he was dying?' asked Bartholomew, manfully resisting the urge to insult Stephen back.

'No – Nigellus told me that Irby was suffering from loss of appetite, which did not sound very serious, so I was stunned when I later heard that he was dead. Unfortunately, I think I caught something from him, because I do not feel well today. Nigellus says I have the *debilitas.*'

'The what?' asked Bartholomew warily.

'The *deb-il-i-tas,*' repeated Stephen, enunciating pedantically. 'The poor have flux, fleas and boils, but the rich have the *debilitas.* Nigellus says he would not sully his hands with common sicknesses, but the *debilitas* is another matter.'

'Would you like me to examine you?' offered Bartholomew, to avoid giving an opinion on such an outlandish claim.

'No, thank you.' The lawyer eyed the physician's shabby clothes with open disdain. 'I bought a horoscope from Nigellus, and he assures me that if I avoid onions and cats, I shall feel well again in no time at all.'

'You had two visitors on the day that Frenge died,' said Michael, before Bartholomew could comment on Nigellus's peculiar advice. 'First, Frenge himself . . .'

'Yes – he came to ask whether Anne de Rumburgh might prefer marchpanes or a bale of cloth as a token of his esteem.' Stephen's face was impossible to read.

171

'He sought the opinion of a man who slept with her *once*?' asked Michael sceptically. 'Or are we to conclude that you know Anne rather better than you would have us believe?'

'You may conclude what you like, Brother.' Stephen smiled blandly. 'But Frenge respected my wisdom in the matter. What more can I say?'

'The second visitor was Shirwynk,' Michael went on. 'He—'

'We have already discussed this,' interrupted the lawyer. 'He came to hire my services against King's Hall.' He stood abruptly. 'And now, if you will excuse me, I have important business to attend. Good day.'

There was a powerful stench in the air as they emerged from Stephen's house, and Bartholomew groaned. How could Edith expect her dyeworks to be accepted when they produced such rank odours every few hours? He started to hurry there, sure the demonstrators would not let the reek pass unremarked and wanting to be to hand if she needed help. Michael followed, but they had not taken many steps before they met Wayt.

'No, I will not drop my case against the brewery,' the Acting Warden snarled in response to Michael's hopeful question. 'Cew is costing a fortune in horoscopes – Nigellus is expensive – and I do not see why King's Hall should pay for something that was Frenge's fault.'

'Really?' asked Michael. 'Michaelhouse would not baulk at the cost if one of *our* members needed specialist medical attention.'

Wayt shot him an unpleasant look. 'We did not mind at first, but it is a bottomless pit, because Cew is not getting better. Nigellus's latest advice is to apply cold compresses to the head – ones that contain some very expensive oils.'

'We have been told that you quarrelled violently with

172

Frenge shortly before he died,' said Michael, while Bartholomew thought that while Nigellus's treatment was unlikely to work, at least it would do no harm. 'Would you care to tell us why?'

Wayt eyed him coolly. 'If you must know, Frenge said that unless I dropped the case against him, he would tell my colleagues about my . . . my *indiscretion* with Anne de Rumburgh, a woman whose husband is generous to King's Hall.'

'So he tried to blackmail you, and within hours he is dead?'

Wayt gave a tight smile. 'What Frenge did not realise is that half the Fellowship have been seduced by that particular lady, so his threat was meaningless. I was angry with him for attempting extortion, but not vexed enough to do him harm. And now, if there is nothing else . . .'

He stalked away, and loath to chase after him when it was clear he was unlikely to elaborate on his answer, Bartholomew and Michael resumed their journey to the dyeworks. The smell grew stronger with every step, and people glared at the physician as he passed, knowing him to be kin to the woman responsible for it.

When they arrived, a spat was in progress. Anne was at the heart of it, skimpily dressed even by her standards, bodice straining to contain her bulging bosom. A semi-circle of Frail Sisters stood with her, hands defiantly on their hips, while behind them was a gaggle of rough men – the former clients who had rallied to protect them.

As usual, the crowd was made up of two factions. The first comprised scholars led by Kellawe, whose finger wagged furiously as he made all manner of points that no one heard over the noise of the second group, who were townsmen. Shirwynk and Peyn watched the altercation from the brewery, and their satisfied smirks suggested that they may well have aggravated the trouble. Rumburgh stood nearby. He took a sweetmeat from his scrip, and Bartholomew could tell by the way he chewed it that eating pained his sore gums.

'Thank God you are here,' said Edith, hurrying up to Michael. 'Will you tell your scholars to go away? They say they do not like the smell, but we cannot get rid of it as long as they are out there bawling and shrieking. Even Anne cannot reason with them, and she is good with men.'

'They have a point,' said Michael. 'You have stunk out the whole town, and it cannot be allowed to continue. Matt says it is only a matter of time before it kills someone.'

'I never—' began Bartholomew.

Edith silenced her brother with a look that would have blistered metal. 'It is a lot of fuss over nothing. No one will notice the aroma once they get used to it.'

'But we do not want to get used to it,' objected Michael. 'It is—'

He broke off when two Zachary scholars darted forward to engage in a fisticuffs with a pair of apprentices. With an exasperated sigh, he strode towards the mêlée. Unfortunately, his intervention meant that people stopped haranguing each other to watch, and Kellawe used the sudden silence to make an announcement.

'I have a licence to absolve any scholar who commits an act of violence against the town,' he declared in a ringing voice. Morys was next to him, nodding vigorously. 'It came from the Bishop himself. However, any townsman who harms us will land himself in serious trouble.'

'That is not fair!' cried Hakeney. 'We have the right to defend ourselves.'

'If you do, you will be doomed to the perpetual fires of Hell,' shouted Kellawe, grinning provocatively. 'Scholars, however, will be deemed blameless.'

'Not in the eyes of the Senior Proctor,' said Michael

sternly. 'I will fine any man – scholar *or* townsperson – who breaks the King's peace. And so will the Sheriff.'

'But *we* have just cause,' yelled Kellawe angrily. 'Not only does this place release dangerous vapours, but *he* said its women run a different business after dark.' He nodded towards Shirwynk. 'We do not want a brothel as a neighbour, thank you. Our students have impressionable minds.'

Bartholomew took in the Zachary lads' courtly clothes and worldly faces, and was sure there was not an impressionable mind among them. Segeforde was behind them, pale but better than he had been earlier, although there was no sign of Yerland.

'Then Shirwynk has slandered us most disgracefully,' said Edith, drawing herself up to her full height and fixing the brewer with an imperious glare. Shirwynk promptly slunk indoors, although he was a fool if he thought that was the end of the matter – Edith was not a woman to forget insults to her workforce.

'Has he?' demanded Kellawe hotly. 'Then why have you hired so many whores?'

'To dye cloth,' replied Edith tartly. 'And they are not whores: they are women reduced to desperate measures by circumstances beyond their control. You should applaud their courage, not condemn them.'

'You should,' agreed Yolande. She jabbed an accusing finger at Segeforde. 'Especially as you and many of your colleagues regularly hired our services before we started working here, so do not play the innocent with us, you damned hypocrite.'

There was a mocking cheer from the women, laughter from the townsfolk, and indignant denials from the scholars.

'These dyeworks stink,' declared Morys, once the clamour had died down. 'They made Trinity Hall sick – twice – and they claimed the life of poor Principal Irby, God rest his soul.'

'You told us that he died of loss of appetite,' pounced Michael.

Morys pointed at Bartholomew. 'Yes, but *he* said loss of appetite was a symptom, not a disease. And the disease came from here, from *this* filthy business.'

'How could you, Matthew?' whispered Edith crossly. 'I thought you admired what we are trying to do. How could you fuel these ignoramuses' vitriol by gossiping with them?'

'More importantly, there have been *town* deaths,' shouted Hakeney, before the physician could defend himself. 'Namely Will Lenne, Mistress Vine, Letia Shirwynk and poor John Frenge. Bartholomew does not care that his sister is killing us, and neither do his medical cronies. And now Stephen has the *debilitas.*'

'That sounds nasty,' gulped Isnard the bargeman. 'What does it mean?'

'It is something that afflicts only the rich,' explained Hakeney. 'Paupers are immune, so most of us need not fear it. However, it is what carried away all these hapless townsfolk.'

'If that is right, then *we* are not responsible,' said Edith. 'How can the occasional waft of bad air or bucket of sludge target only the wealthy? The answer is that they cannot. Now go away.'

'Not until you agree to leave the town,' yelled Kellawe. 'We do not want you here, and I do not see why my University should have to up sticks and move to the Fens when it is *you* causing all the trouble.'

'We cannot leave – not when we provide a valuable service to so many men,' purred Anne. She winked at Segeforde. 'And *some* scholars in particular would miss us sorely.'

Full of mortified rage, Segeforde surged towards her. The rest of Zachary followed, and there was a lot of unseemly jostling, all of which stopped when there was a piercing screech that was half indignation and half amusement. It came from Anne. Segeforde had stumbled and grabbed her dress, so that the flimsy material had come clean away in his hand. There was a shocked silence from both sides, and for a long time, no one moved.

'Well,' drawled Michael eventually, his eyes huge in his chubby face. 'That is one way to quell a spat.'

CHAPTER 7

The incident with Segeforde and Anne might have sparked a serious fight if some of Tulyet's soldiers had not arrived. They waded into the mêlée with drawn swords, which encouraged the antagonists to disperse. First to go were the men who had stood behind Edith's ladies, no doubt having fallen foul of the Sheriff's troops before, and they were followed by the other townsfolk. The scholars slunk away under Michael's withering gaze, and for the first time since the dyeworks had opened, the square was all but empty. Only the women, Rumburgh, Bartholomew and Michael remained. Edith was incandescent with outrage.

'It does not matter,' said Anne, now draped decorously in her husband's cloak. 'I wanted a new kirtle anyway, and this gives me the excuse to indulge myself.'

'It *does* matter,' fumed Edith. 'It was not the act of a gentleman.'

'No, it was not,' agreed Rumburgh, scarlet-faced with shame on his wife's behalf. 'And if my gums did not pain me so much, I would challenge Segeforde to a duel.'

'There is no need for reckless heroics, dear,' said Anne, patting his arm kindly.

'And it is not as if they have never been flaunted before,' muttered Yolande. 'Such as when she appeared naked in the mystery plays last year. It caused quite a stir.'

'It did,' agreed Michael, then felt compelled to add, albeit unconvincingly, 'though I was not there myself, of course.'

At that moment, a contingent of Austins arrived.

'What has happened?' asked Prior Joliet in a shocked voice. 'We have been regaled with such dreadful tales! Townsfolk say that Segeforde molested a helpless lady, while Kellawe informed us that she whipped off the dress herself.'

'She did not!' cried Rumburgh. 'What terrible lies!'

'We will have to decant to the Fens now,' said Almoner Robert sombrely. 'The town will never forgive Segeforde, and the University will never forgive Anne.'

'Never,' agreed Hamo.

Then Shirwynk called out from his brewery door, evidently reluctant to move closer lest Edith should decide to take issue with him for his role in the affair. 'Sue them, Rumburgh. Just as they are suing Frenge for having a little fun in King's Hall.'

'The "fun" you encouraged,' said Michael, stalking towards him. 'No, do not deny it – I have a witness. That was not the act of a friend.'

'Frenge was his own man,' said Shirwynk defiantly. 'He could have refused.'

'When he was drunk? Moreover, I find it suspicious that you consulted a lawyer just after Frenge died. Stephen says you went to hire him to sue King's Hall, but if I find out that you actually quizzed him about inheriting Frenge's half of the brewery, you will be in serious trouble.'

Shirwynk shot him an unpleasant look, then bellowed at Rumburgh. 'Are you content to let a scholar rip the clothes from your wife in a public place?'

'It was hardly—' began Michael.

Shirwynk overrode him. 'It was a clear case of assault, and dozens of witnesses will concur. If you have any respect for your wife, Rumburgh, you will restore her good name with a lawsuit.'

'Do not bother, dear,' said Anne to her husband. 'It would be so tedious.'

179

'You are a very wise lady,' said Robert, smiling approvingly. 'A lawsuit would drive yet another wedge between University and town. Besides, I doubt the compensation you would win would be worth the inconvenience of a trial.'

'Compensation?' echoed Anne sharply. 'You mean money?'

Alarm suffused Robert's face and he began to gabble. 'Very little, I imagine. Certainly not enough to warrant the trouble.'

'A paltry sum,' put in Joliet quickly. 'Especially to the wife of a rich burgess. Mere pennies.'

'Rubbish,' yelled Shirwynk. 'Zachary is a wealthy hostel. You will be awarded a fortune.'

'Do not listen to him,' ordered Michael. 'He wants you to sue a University foundation because King's Hall is prosecuting him. His advice stems from a desire for vengeance.'

'So what if it does?' asked Shirwynk, still addressing Anne. 'It does not detract from the fact that a lawsuit is an easy way to swell your coffers. Stephen will take the case, I am sure.'

'Well, now,' said Anne, exchanging a greedy glance with her husband. 'I *did* suffer when Segeforde hurled himself at me. Perhaps we had better pay Stephen a visit.'

'No, you will not,' said Edith firmly. 'A quarrel with Zachary will do no one any good, least of all us. The University is our biggest customer – we cannot afford to offend it.'

'You will not need its custom if you win funds from Zachary,' coaxed Shirwynk.

'We will make far more money by keeping its good graces,' argued Edith. 'There is—'

'The *dyeworks* will make more money: *you* will not,' called Shirwynk. 'Be a man, Rumburgh. Take what is rightfully yours.'

'I shall,' declared Rumburgh, grabbing Anne's hand

and beginning to tow her towards the High Street. 'We shall begin proceedings today, while memories are fresh.'

Michael watched Rumburgh and Anne go with a sense of helplessness, while Shirwynk filled the street with mocking laughter. Robert began to edge away, his face a mask of dismay, but Michael rounded on him before he had taken more than two or three steps.

'What were you thinking, to mention compensation?' he snarled. 'Surely you must have realised what their reaction would be?'

'I was praising her prudence,' said Robert defensively. 'Of course I did not predict that the pair of them would be seized by a sudden rush of greed.'

'Go home,' Michael ordered crossly. 'And please watch what you say in future, especially to townsfolk.'

Robert bowed his head, cheeks red against his long white hair. Joliet opened his mouth to defend his almoner, but had second thoughts when he saw the dark expression on Michael's face. He led his friars away, although Hamo felt compelled to have the final word.

'Mistake,' he murmured to Michael as he passed. 'Sorry.'

Meanwhile, Edith was still furious – about Segeforde's lunge, Shirwynk's goading, Anne's response and Bartholomew's perceived treachery. The brewer was the first to feel her tongue.

'How dare you tell Zachary that we run a brothel,' she barked, stalking towards him. 'Perhaps *I* should visit Stephen and take out a case against *you* – for slander.'

'You could try,' sneered Shirwynk. 'But no judge will convict me, because your dyeworks *do* contain prostitutes, and the men guarding them *are* repaid with sexual favours.'

'The men are paid with coins from me,' countered Edith icily. 'I assure you, nothing immoral happens here. It is a respectable establishment.'

Shirwynk attempted a sardonic laugh, although it was short-lived in the face of Edith's wrath. He became defensive. 'Well, it was not me who started that tale. Kellawe was lying when he claimed it was: I never said any such thing.'

'Insult us again and you will regret it,' hissed Edith, so venomously that the brewer blanched and retreated to his domain. When the door had closed behind him, she spun on her heel and stamped inside her dyeworks. Bartholomew followed, keen for her to know that Michael and Morys had misquoted him. He opened his mouth to explain, but the stench was far worse inside than out, and it took his breath away.

'It really is foul, Edith,' he gasped, once he had stopped coughing. 'It cannot be doing anyone any good, especially the women who work here. Can you not open some windows?'

'We could,' replied Edith coldly. 'But that would let the smell out, and we would have more complaints than ever. Besides, we barely notice it now.'

Bartholomew looked around unhappily. Several buckets of evil-smelling waste stood near the door, almost certainly destined for the river, while he did not know how anyone could bear the toxic atmosphere in the annexe, where Yolande was stirring the fermenting woad.

'This cannot continue,' he said quietly, holding his ground when Edith glowered at him. 'The protesters have a point: there *have* been mysterious deaths and illnesses over the last few weeks – roughly coinciding with the time that this place opened.'

Edith's expression went from angry to sad, which was much harder for him to bear as she doubtless knew. 'So you are against us, too?'

'I am against people becoming unwell and dying unnecessarily.'

Edith pointed at the watching women. 'If my dyeworks

are responsible for making people sick, then why are *they* not ill? They work most closely with these so-called deadly compounds.'

Bartholomew glanced at them, and thought that he had never seen a healthier horde. Every one was rosy-cheeked and sleek, and it was clear that regular meals and daytime work was doing them a power of good.

'If you want a culprit, look to your own profession,' Edith went on. 'Everyone who has died – Lenne, Irby, Frenge, Letia, Arnold, Mistress Vine – was visited by a physician first.'

'You mean Nigellus?' asked Bartholomew. 'He was not Mistress Vine's *medicus*.'

'No,' agreed Edith. '*You* were.'

Bartholomew winced. 'But I never saw her. I meant to go, but . . .'

'She was tended by Meryfeld in her final hours,' said Yolande. 'I am sure she would have preferred you, but she was too ill to argue, and Vine did not want to send for a physician who has ties to us.'

'But she had this *debilitas*, which only affects the wealthy,' added Edith stiffly. 'And as I said earlier, the waste from our dyes cannot distinguish between rich and poor, so I suggest you find something else to blame.'

And with that, she turned on her heel and stalked away.

'Come with me to talk to Shirwynk, Matt,' said Michael when Bartholomew emerged despondently from the dyeworks. 'I want to know why he is so violently opposed to our University. We have had our detractors in the past, but none as vehement as him.'

'Will you talk to Anne first?' asked Bartholomew, hopeful that trouble might yet be averted. 'She did not seem particularly upset by what happened – until Robert mentioned compensation.'

183

'I will visit her later, but the prospect of "free" money is attractive, and nothing I say will make any difference now.' Michael rubbed a hand wearily across his face. 'That stupid incident will do much harm. The town will be offended on her behalf, and scholars will rally to Segeforde, especially when he claims it was an accident.'

'Perhaps it was. I did not see what happened.'

'He *did* make a grab for her, although I doubt he intended to tear off her clothes. However, it is clear that she has a certain history with him.'

'She has a "certain history" with Stephen, Frenge and Wayt, too. Indeed, I wonder whether you and I are the only two men in Cambridge she does *not* count among her conquests.'

Michael made no reply as he hammered on the brewery door, although there was a distinct pink flush to the plump cheeks. He continued to pound, loudly enough to prevent Bartholomew from asking questions, until Peyn came to answer it.

'Have you come for a drink?' Peyn asked insolently, staggering as Michael shoved past him. 'What will you sup? Apple wine or ale?'

'Neither – not with you,' retorted Michael. '*Latet anguis in herba*, to quote Virgil.'

Peyn's eyes narrowed. 'He said that about me? Perhaps I should sue him.'

'You could try,' said Michael caustically. 'But he has been dead fourteen hundred years, so I doubt even Stephen will recommend it.' He saw Peyn's blank look and became impatient. 'He was a Roman poet. Do you have *no* education? I doubt the clerks at Westminster will be impressed.'

'Of course I know the poet Virgin,' declared Peyn. 'I read his verses when I am here at night, guarding the brewery against marauding scholars. He just slipped my mind.'

'Then maybe you should drink less apple wine,' said Michael, regarding him with dislike.

'I never drink *any* apple wine,' said Peyn sullenly. 'I dislike sweet things.'

'You prefer mud, which you enjoy lobbing at scholars. It was fortunate you missed Wayt yesterday, or you would have spent the night in my cells.'

'Fortunate for you,' sneered Peyn. 'Because if you had laid so much as a finger on me, my new employers at the Treasury would have come here and crushed you like a worm. So perhaps you *had* better take your nasty University to the Fens, Brother – it is a place where you cannot get yourself into so much trouble.'

'Was it you who started that ridiculous rumour?' asked Michael in disgust. 'I imagine it came from the town, because no scholar is foolish enough to have invented such a tale.'

'I had nothing to do with it, but it *is* true. If you will not go of your own accord, then you will have to leave once these lawsuits begin in earnest – King's Hall prosecuting us, us hitting back, and Anne suing Zachary. And if they do not force you out, the people suffering from the *debilitas* will do it – folk who are sick because *his* sister opened a dyeworks.'

Peyn jabbed an accusing finger at Bartholomew and stalked out, slamming the door behind him with a noisy crack. Thinking they had been left unattended, Michael was about to indulge in a prowl when Shirwynk emerged from the shadows.

'My son makes very good points, Brother,' the brewer said smugly.

'Your son is a fool,' retorted Michael. 'As are you, spreading lies about the dyeworks and encouraging Anne to sue Zachary. Do you *want* the town ablaze? What is wrong with you?'

'Nothing is wrong with me,' replied Shirwynk coolly.

'I just do not appreciate having my town infested with scholars. I want you gone.'

'Then you are going to be disappointed, because we are here to stay. But you have done business with us for years, so what has turned you against us all of a sudden?'

'It is not all of a sudden,' snarled Shirwynk. 'I have always disliked you, and the whole town feels the same. Now get off my property before my apprentices remove you forcibly.'

'I have questions,' said Michael, not moving. 'And if you will not answer me, the Sheriff will put them to you instead. He will arrest you and keep you in a cell until he is ready, but he is a busy man, and it might be days before he finds the time. Will Peyn delay his journey to Westminster, to make ale and apple wine while you are indisposed?'

Shirwynk scowled, trapped. 'Questions about what?'

'About your wife. I find it odd that she and Frenge died on the same day.'

'It was a nuisance. Do you have any idea how much burials cost? And I had to fund two – no joke, when I have Stephen's bills to pay as well. But all will be well when I win my case against King's Hall, because then I shall have more money than I can count.'

'Frenge was frightened of you,' said Michael, when he saw the brewer was not going to tell him anything useful about Letia. 'He—'

Shirwynk interrupted him with a braying laugh. 'Rubbish! We were the best of friends.'

'Really?' asked Michael archly. 'That is not what you said when we first discussed your relationship with him. Then you gave the impression that you were no more than working colleagues – men who endured each other's company for the sake of the business.'

'You misunderstood,' said Shirwynk sullenly. 'We were fond of each other.'

'Then why did you encourage him to invade King's Hall?'

'Not this again,' groaned Shirwynk. 'I would not have done it had I known those humourless rogues would respond by killing him. It is *them* you should be persecuting, not me. They are probably the ones stealing our apple wine, too. Some disappears almost every night, despite the precautions we take to repel burglars.'

'Ah, yes,' said Michael. 'Your precautions. They involve Peyn standing guard, which suggests one of two things: either he quaffs the stuff himself and lies when he says it is stolen; or he abandons his post to go carousing with his friends.'

Shirwynk regarded him with dislike. 'He does not drink wine, and of course he is obliged to slip away on occasion – to visit the latrine or to patrol our yard at the back. The villains wait for him to leave and then they strike.'

Michael snorted his scepticism. 'Perhaps you should consider using your apprentices instead. Or do you not trust them?'

'I trust my son,' snarled Shirwynk. 'And if he says scholars are stealing our wine, then scholars are stealing our wine.'

'It is more likely to be a villain from the town,' countered Michael. 'There are far more seculars who know about theft than academics, and if you do not believe me, look in the castle prison. It is stuffed full of them.'

It was drizzling as Michael stalked towards St Mary the Great to berate Tynkell for requesting a licence to absolve scholars from acts of violence. The Chancellor was in his office, so pale and wan that Bartholomew was concerned.

'I have the *debilitas*,' Tynkell whispered plaintively. 'And Stephen will be here in a moment, to tie me in logical knots. Please do not leave me alone with him, Brother.'

Michael's ire evaporated at such a piteous appeal, and he flopped wearily on to a bench, which groaned under his weight. Bartholomew was about to dispense the mixture for distressed stomachs that he often gave to Tynkell, when he noticed a tremor in the man's hands.

'I have had it ever since Morys and I became kin by marriage,' the Chancellor explained tearfully. 'But it is worse today, because I have just had a letter from my mother, saying she is coming to visit. If she does, it will be the end for me.'

'The end in what way?' asked Bartholomew kindly.

'In every way,' replied Tynkell miserably. 'Indeed, I might have to ask your book-bearer for a charm against evil spirits. She is a dragon, you see.'

'Please do not,' begged Bartholomew, not liking to imagine what might be made of the fact that the head of the University consulted a Michaelhouse servant on matters of superstition. 'I am sure she cannot be as dreadful as you think.'

'Easy for you to say,' muttered Tynkell disconsolately. 'You have never met her.'

'While we are on the subject of outrageous missives,' said Michael, 'perhaps you will explain why you applied to the Bishop for a certain licence.'

'Oh,' gulped Tynkell guiltily. 'You have heard about that, have you? It was not my idea. Morys said that in any battle with the town, we would be hobbled by the fact some scholars will refuse to fight lest bloodshed stains their souls. Then he recommended Kellawe as a good man to dispense absolutions. It seemed like a good idea . . .'

'It is not a good idea at all!' exploded Michael. 'It will make the town think we are planning an attack.'

'I suppose it might,' conceded Tynkell weakly, 'but Morys gave me no choice. Then he went and summoned my mother anyway – he reneged on the agreement he made, the sly rogue!'

Footsteps outside heralded the arrival of Stephen. He still looked unwell, but was clad in clothes of exceptional quality: clearly, the law was a lucrative business when clients like Edith and Shirwynk were willing to pay handsomely for sharp minds to find ways around it.

'I have just been to King's Hall to assess Cew,' he began without preamble. 'He is only pretending to be insane, purely to strengthen his College's claim against the brewery. Thus the so-called assault on him will be excluded when we go to court.'

'He is not pretending,' objected Bartholomew. 'He is genuinely disturbed – and that is my professional medical opinion.'

In truth, he was not sure what to think about Cew, but the lawyer's presumption in making a diagnosis he was not qualified to give had annoyed him.

Stephen considered for a moment. 'Then he was already a lunatic, and King's Hall aim to blame his illness on Frenge. Regardless, it will not form part of the case.'

'I wish you could find a way to persuade both parties not to proceed,' said Michael irritably. 'The situation is causing untold harm to University–town relations.'

'It will make no difference now whether they proceed or not,' replied Stephen. 'Because there is yet another suit – the assault on Anne by Segeforde. She was shamed in front of her friends and neighbours, and she is demanding substantial compensation for her anguish.'

'How much of it will you receive?' asked Michael in distaste. 'Twenty per cent? Thirty?'

Stephen regarded him coolly. 'That is my business.'

'If you do not answer, I shall tell my mother.' The gleam in Tynkell's eyes showed the pleasure he took from being on the giving end of threats for a change. 'And you have met her . . .'

'Fifty per cent,' replied Stephen quickly. He raised his

189

hands in a shrug. 'Anne could have found a lawyer who charges less, but not one who will win. Quality costs.'

Michael sent a beadle to bring Segeforde to St Mary the Great when Stephen had gone. However, it was not the purple-lipped scholar who arrived, but Morys and Kellawe. Their gloating expressions turned wary when they realised it was not the malleable Tynkell who had summoned them, but the considerably less pliable Senior Proctor.

'Anne de Rumburgh intends to sue Segeforde for assault,' said Michael. 'Where is he? We need to establish some facts if we are to defend him against Stephen.'

'Bartholomew's remedy wore off, and he is ill again,' said Morys, equally cool. 'But we are not worried about that money-grabbing whore. She has no case against Segeforde.'

Michael regarded him askance. 'Oh, yes, she does, especially with Stephen representing her. A lot of witnesses saw what happened, including myself.'

'Town louts, who will claim that Segeforde yanked at her bodice,' said Kellawe, eyes blazing with righteous indignation. His northern accent was more pronounced when he was angry, and his lower jaw thrust forward aggressively. 'But twice as many scholars, who are *decent* men, will say she did it herself. I am one of them. The harlot exposed herself deliberately.'

'That is a lie,' said Michael. 'She did nothing of the sort.'

'Does this mean you will side with the town against a scholar?' asked Morys slyly. 'I would not advise it, Brother – not if you want to be Chancellor when Tynkell resigns.'

'Tynkell will be in post for a while yet,' said Michael. 'And people have short memories.'

'He will go when I tell him or suffer his mother's wrath,' said Morys, grinning when he saw Tynkell's alarm. 'I have the power to force an election whenever I choose, so you had better do what I say, Brother, or you will lose everything you have built these last few years.'

'Then so be it,' said Michael with cool dignity. 'Because I will not lie under oath.'

'And you, Bartholomew?' Kellawe turned to the physician. 'What tale will you tell?'

'The truth, of course,' said Bartholomew haughtily, not bothering to mention that his testimony would be that he had not actually seen what had happened.

Morys's expression hardened and he turned to Tynkell. 'You had better find a way to remind them of their loyalties, or your mother is going to blame *you* for the University's troubles.'

Before anyone could argue, he had turned and strutted away, Kellawe at his heels.

Tynkell was so distressed by what might be said to his dam that Bartholomew was obliged to give him a syrup of camomile and wild lettuce to soothe his nerves, then escort him to his hostel to rest. Michael was waiting as the physician walked back past St Mary the Great.

'I can feel the tension building and I do not know how to stop it,' the monk said unhappily. 'We are at war with ourselves just when we need to present a united front.'

'You mean all the ancient rivalries between Colleges and hostels?'

'Yes, along with whether we should move to the Fens. There is a growing faction that thinks it is a good idea, while foundations like King's Hall and Gonville are just as determined to stay.'

'I am more concerned about Nigellus,' said Bartholomew. 'I am not sure he should be let loose on patients, but how can we stop him without actual evidence of wrongdoing?'

Michael was thoughtful. 'You learned nothing from Letia and Irby, but what of the others?'

'It is too late – they have been buried.'

'Lenne has not – he is in St Bene't's Church, and will not go in the ground until tomorrow.' Michael glanced up at the darkening sky. 'It will not be long now before everyone is abed . . .'

'No,' said Bartholomew. 'First, we have no authority to examine him; and second, there is no reason to think he will provide answers, given that Letia and Irby did not.'

'But Frenge did,' Michael pointed out. 'If Nigellus has been helping patients into the grave, we need to stop him – and if that means examining a corpse in the middle of the night, then so be it. Go home and try to sleep. I will wake you when the time is right.'

But Bartholomew reached Michaelhouse to find he was needed by several patients. He set off at once, and included Trinity Hall on his list, to see if he could ascertain why an entire College professed to feeling under the weather. He examined a wide range of their leftover food, paying particular attention to the syllabub, but found nothing amiss. He did, however, discover that Nigellus had been a guest of the Master on both occasions when its members had fallen ill.

It was late by the time he trudged home again. The conclave was in darkness, so he went to the kitchen, arriving at the same time as Michael, who had spent the first part of his evening in a futile attempt to persuade Anne to withdraw her complaint, and the second half with the University's lawyers, discussing the cases Stephen intended to bring against them.

The monk disappeared into the pantries in search of food, but his foray was unsuccessful, and it fell to Cynric, who made them both jump by materialising suddenly out of the gloom, to reveal where Agatha had hidden the last remnants of the feast. There were sweet cakes, some dry-cured meat, bread that was beginning to turn mouldy, and some of Shirwynk's apple wine.

Cynric was more friend than servant, and had been Bartholomew's book-bearer for years, although as the physician was unable to pay him, the title was more honorary than a description of his duties. He divided his time between helping in Michaelhouse's kitchens and working at Edith's cloth business on Milne Street – he was married to one of the seamstresses there. Bartholomew was glad he was not involved with the dyeworks, although the Welshman was by far the most able warrior in the town, and well able to take care of himself.

When he heard what Michael and Bartholomew intended to do at the witching hour, he offered to accompany them, eyes agleam at the prospect of creeping undetected through dark streets and breaking into a locked building. They were discussing details of the plan when they became aware that someone was listening in the shadows by the door. It was Wauter, wearing not his Austin habit but secular attire.

'I could not sleep,' the friar explained. 'I tried working on my *Martilogium*, but I cannot concentrate. I dressed – in clothes that will not expose me as a scholar, which would be reckless after nightfall – and was about to go for a walk when I saw lights in the kitchen.'

'Why are you restless?' asked Michael, while Bartholomew wondered why Wauter should risk going out at all when a stroll could be taken in the safety of the College's grounds.

'I keep thinking about the University's move to the Fens,' replied the Austin. 'It is a major decision, not one that should be taken lightly. However, the one thing that makes me feel we should go is the dyeworks. I am sure they are dangerous.'

'The University has been in Cambridge for a hundred and fifty years,' said Michael firmly. 'We cannot abandon all we have built over a few bad smells. We will reach some accommodation with Edith, never fear. She is a reasonable lady.'

Wauter stared at him for a moment, then continued. 'And while I hate to cast aspersions, I am worried about Nigellus. He lost six patients at Barnwell: two Augustinian canons, the reeve's wife and uncle, and two priory servants. From what I understand, they died of the *debilitas*.'

'The *debilitas*!' spat Bartholomew. 'There is no such disease. Nigellus only coined the term to make his wealthy clients feel special – to pander to their desire not to have the same ailments that afflict the poor. Moreover, the people who claim to be suffering from it display such a wide range of symptoms that they cannot possibly all have the same malady.'

'Which is why you plan to visit St Bene't's tonight,' surmised Wauter. 'To assess Lenne's remains with a view to determining whether Nigellus has done anything untoward. I will come with you, if you do not mind. Another pair of eyes to keep watch will not go amiss.'

'Good,' said Cynric, pleased. 'There are three doors, and I cannot guard them all. But before we go, you must secrete these about your persons.' He handed each scholar a packet.

'What is it?' Bartholomew opened his, and a salt-like substance poured into his hand.

'Powder,' replied Cynric, unhelpfully. 'To repel restless spirits.'

Bartholomew knew better than to argue, but Michael and Wauter were in holy orders.

'No, thank you,' said the monk, trying to pass it back. 'We shall put our trust in God.'

'A lot of prayers were said for the dead over Hallow-tide,' said Cynric, managing to make it sound sinister. 'And it has agitated their spirits, especially the ones who were murdered. Lenne's ghost will be abroad, looking for someone to haunt, but the sucura will protect you.'

'This is sucura?' asked Bartholomew, startled. 'How did you come by it? It is expensive.'

'Very,' agreed Cynric. 'Because it comes all the way from a distant place called Tyre. But its spectre-repelling properties are well worth the cost.'

'I thought it was a cooking ingredient.' Wryly, Bartholomew noted that Cynric had cleverly managed to avoid saying how he had paid for it.

'It is, but the dead cannot abide its sickliness. It will drive them away with no trouble at all, so put it in your scrips, and let us be on our way.'

'Where did you buy it?' Bartholomew persisted, staring down at the little packet in his hand. 'Dick Tulyet would like to know.'

'I am sure he would,' retorted Cynric. 'But I am not in the habit of betraying friends – who would not need to sell it in taverns if the King was not so greedy with his taxes. As things stand, he has forced the price so high that he is the only one who can afford it. Which is not right.'

He had a keen sense of social justice, and Bartholomew could tell from the jut of his chin that there was no point in reminding him that buying contraband was illegal. Moreover, Michael showed no inclination to pursue the matter, which told him yet again that the monk was unwilling to investigate a crime with which he felt some sympathy.

Bartholomew would have asked more anyway, but Cynric turned abruptly and led the way across the yard, blissfully unaware that Michael's packet went down the first drain they passed. Bartholomew wondered if he should do the same, but the truth was that he was some-times assailed with the sense that the dead did not like what he did to them in the name of justice, and so was inclined to accept any 'protection' on offer. It was rank superstition, and the rational side of his mind told him he was a fool as he slipped the sucura into his bag.

It was the darkest part of the night, and should have

been the quietest, but the town was full of shadows and whispers. Bartholomew did not see anyone, but he knew they were there, and disliked the sensation that he was being watched by eyes that were almost certainly hostile.

When they reached St Bene't's, Cynric led them up the alley that ran along the side of the graveyard, and kept them waiting for an age until he was satisfied that no one had followed. Eventually, he aimed for the priest's door, where Bartholomew – as always – was dismayed by the speed with which he picked the lock: it was hardly a talent a University servant should own. They entered a building that was pitch black and eerily silent after the rustles and murmurs in the streets.

Cynric deployed Michael and Wauter, then went with Bartholomew to the chancel, where the physician was disconcerted to see not one but three bodies. The first was Lenne, covered by a purple cloth. Irby was next to him, dressed in his Zachary uniform. The last was Yerland. Bartholomew started, shocked that the student should be dead.

'The *debilitas*,' whispered Cynric. 'I heard it in the Cardinal's Cap earlier. Will you look at him, too? You might as well, given that he is here.'

He handed Bartholomew the barest stub of a candle, and indicated that he was to make a start. The physician obliged, wanting to be finished as quickly as possible. He jumped violently when there was a crash, and waited, heart thumping until Cynric came to whisper that it was just drunks in the churchyard. Then Wauter appeared, running on silent feet.

'Douse the light,' he hissed urgently. 'Someone is coming.'

He and Bartholomew had only just ducked behind a tomb when a lamp began to bob towards them. It was a procession. Morys and Nigellus were at its head, while four students walked behind, carrying a bier. Kellawe was last, murmuring prayers. The students set the bier down and removed the blanket that had covered the body.

'Oh, no,' breathed Bartholomew. 'It is Segeforde!'

CHAPTER 8

The Zachary men did not stay long in St Bene't's. They
deposited Segeforde and left – all except one: Kellawe
had announced in a fiercely ringing voice that he would
remain there to pray by his three dead colleagues' sides.

'Now what?' whispered Bartholomew, as the Franciscan
dropped to his knees and began to intone a psalm in a
loud, important bray that seemed to suggest the Almighty
had better forget what else He was doing and listen.

'Leave it to me,' Wauter whispered back, and made a
show of 'arriving' in the church to keep a vigil of his
own.

'You are not needed,' Kellawe informed him curtly.
'My petitions will be more effective than yours, because
I am a Franciscan.'

'Very well,' said Wauter, displaying admirable restraint
in the face of such hubris. 'But come outside and share
a flask of wine with me. The night will be long and cold,
and you will need something decent inside you if you
are to give of your best.'

Kellawe allowed himself to be escorted away, and the
moment the door closed behind them, Bartholomew
darted towards the bodies, sensing he would not have
much time before the opinionated friar declared himself
suitably fortified and returned to his self-imposed duties.

It was an unpleasant business, not only rushed and
fraught with the fear that Kellawe might decide his devotions were more important than chatting to Wauter, but
because of what he was obliged to do for answers: when
an external examination of Lenne revealed nothing amiss,
Bartholomew embarked on a more invasive one using

knives and forceps. What he discovered prompted him to look inside Irby, Yerland and Segeforde as well.

'Keep your sucura to hand,' Cynric advised, glancing down as he passed by on one of his prowls, although his eyes did not linger on the body for long. 'Irby's spirit will not like you doing *that* to its mortal coil, so you will need the powder's protection for sure.'

The remark unsettled Bartholomew even more. He had no idea why, when he had long been of the belief that much could be learned from the dead and that anatomy was a valuable tool for helping the living, but it was a feeling he could not shake. He finished quickly, put all to rights, and left the church with relief. It was not long before Michael, Cynric and Wauter joined him in the graveyard, the latter pale and agitated.

'Kellawe has some very nasty opinions,' the Austin said, indicating that Cynric should lead the way home. 'He will have the entire town in flames before long. Perhaps that alone is reason enough for moving to the Fens – it will spare the town his vitriol.'

By the time they returned to the College, it was almost too late to go to bed. Bartholomew tried to sleep anyway, and passed two very restless hours before the bell rang to wake everyone for church. It was his turn to assist at the altar, and a cold chill ran down his spine when Clippesby passed him the Host and the candles guttered. The rational part of his mind reminded him that it happened all the time – St Michael's was full of unaccountable draughts – but it did make him wonder anew whether people were right to object to dissection.

'Tell me again what you discovered,' instructed Michael, when they were back in the hall, eating a plentiful but slightly peculiar breakfast of barley bread, carrots and nuts.

'Inflammation of the stomach membranes and damaged livers,' replied Bartholomew tersely. 'On all four bodies.'

'Meaning what exactly?'

'Meaning that something is wrong, but I cannot tell you what.'

'But it might indicate that they were poisoned?'

'It might. All had been ill, but with different ailments: Lenne had lung-rot, Irby complained of loss of appetite, Yerland had head pains and Segeforde had some undefined malaise – the *debilitas*, for want of a better diagnosis.'

'I can accept Lenne dying of natural causes, but not the other three. I think Nigellus killed them. And the logical extension of that conclusion is that he poisoned Letia, Arnold and the folk from Barnwell, too.'

'And Frenge – perhaps in revenge for selling sour ale to Zachary.'

'Quite,' said Michael grimly. 'So I rose before dawn and arrested him. His colleagues are furious, of course, and so is he. He thinks you put me up to it.'

Bartholomew groaned. 'If he is innocent, he will never forgive me.'

'He is not innocent, and I wish to God that I had acted the moment we found Irby's note. If I had, Yerland and Segeforde would still be alive. *Similia similibus curantur* – "like cures like". Irby knew he had been poisoned, but was too frightened to tell his colleagues lest they ran straight to Nigellus, so he wrote to you instead. It was a subtle yet clear plea for you to find an antidote.'

Bartholomew regarded him askance. 'Is that what you think it means?'

'I am sure of it, and I am only sorry that I did not understand it sooner. Twelve of Nigellus's patients are dead – thirteen, if you count Frenge – while Trinity Hall has suffered two bouts of serious sickness. This is what happens when *medici* think they are God, with the power to kill or cure.'

'He does seem to believe he is infallible,' acknowledged Bartholomew. 'But—'

'Incidentally, I have issued a statement saying that the corpses of Lenne, Irby, Yerland and Segeforde are exuding deadly miasmas. In the interests of public health, they have been sealed inside their coffins, which is the best way to ensure that no one ever sees what you did to them. It was grisly, even by your standards.'

'Thank you, Brother. The town *and* the University would have plenty to say if it became known that I invade churches at night to dissect the dead.'

'Then perhaps I should tell them,' said Michael wryly. 'It is something on which the two sides will agree, and common ground is in desperately short supply at the moment.'

When the meal was over, Langelee came to demand an update on their investigations, and the other Fellows clustered around to listen. After Michael had obliged, the conversation turned to the rumours that were circulating.

'I do not want to go to the Fens,' the Master grumbled. 'There will be no taverns, no women and no wealthy benefactors. How can we enlarge our endowment if we are not here to impress the people who matter?' He gestured to the mural. 'And this will have been wasted.'

'It might have been wasted anyway,' said William glumly. 'Folk are not exactly lining up to shower money on us.'

'I am not ready to concede defeat just yet,' said Langelee. 'Suttone, Clippesby and I will visit a few burgesses today, and tell them that they might be slaughtered in their beds if the town explodes into violence, so they should consider their immortal souls. And what better way than a benefaction to a College that will pray for them in perpetuity?'

'Do not phrase it in quite those words,' begged Michael. 'They may interpret them as a threat.'

Langelee waved away his concerns. 'Leave it to me,

Brother – I know what I am doing. You concentrate on restoring the peace. Bartholomew will help.'

'But I have not given a lecture in days,' objected Bartholomew, 'and my students are—'

'The Austins are coming to tell my lads about the nominalism–realism debate today,' interrupted Langelee. 'Yours can join them, which means you are not needed here.'

'Thank you, Master,' said Michael. 'That debate is central to all current scholarly thinking, and Prior Joliet is sure to have new insights. Your students will learn a great deal, Matt.'

'Only if they listen,' countered Bartholomew. 'Which they will not do unless someone is here to keep them in line – and most of the Fellows plan to be out.'

'Not William and Wauter,' said Langelee. 'They will prevent mischief.'

A flash of irritation crossed Wauter's face. Bartholomew did not blame him: it would not be easy to convince a lot of lively lads to listen to a multi-hour lecture on metaphysics, and Wauter would not be able to relax for an instant.

'I have other plans, Master,' said the Austin irritably.

'Cancel them,' ordered Langelee peremptorily.

'I cannot – they are important.'

Langelee's eyes narrowed. 'More than the well-being of your College? What are they then?'

Wauter's face became closed and a little sullen, an expression none of them had seen before. 'I would rather not say. They are private.'

'Then you will stay in the hall with William,' decreed Langelee with finality.

When Bartholomew had delivered his students a stern warning that any mischief would result in them cleaning the latrines for a month, he climbed the stairs to Michael's room. When he arrived, the monk began planning their day.

'First, we must visit Zachary, to ask what happened to Yerland and Segeforde. Hopefully, Nigellus's colleagues will have come to their senses now that the enormity of his crimes has been exposed, and will tell us the truth. Then we shall speak to Nigellus in the gaol.'

'I will come with you to Zachary, but not the prison. Nigellus will think I am there to gloat.'

'I do not care what he thinks and we need answers – there is no time for foolish sensitivities. Are you ready? Then let us be on our way.'

It was early, but the streets were busy, and the atmosphere was tense and dangerous. Townsmen glared at scholars, who responded in kind, and Bartholomew was shocked when some of his patients, people who had accepted his charity and professed themselves to be grateful, included him in their scowls. Perhaps more surprising was that several members of the Michaelhouse Choir hissed abuse at Michael – the man who provided them with free bread and ale. The monk did not react, but Bartholomew suspected they would be told to leave if they turned up for the next practice. Isnard was his usual friendly self, though.

'They are angry that a scholar ripped the clothes from a townswoman,' he explained. 'And they wish the University would leave Cambridge instead of just talking about it.'

'Are you among them?' asked Michael coolly, hurt by his singers' disloyalty.

'Certainly not,' replied Isnard indignantly. 'It would mean the end of the best choir in the country. And who would tend me when I am ill? I do not let any old *medicus* near me, you know – I have standards. No, Brother. You cannot let the scholars leave.'

'I shall do my best,' said Michael, mollified by the

203

warmth of the response. 'But you can help by telling folk that there will be no lawsuit between Segeforde and Anne, because Segeforde is dead. He passed away last night.'

'Yes, of the *debilitas*,' nodded Isnard. 'I heard. But it makes no difference. King's Hall is still suing Frenge's estate, even though he is dead, so Anne will still sue Segeforde's.'

'Stephen!' muttered Michael angrily. 'That will have been his idea.'

'He is skilled with the law,' agreed Isnard. He turned to Bartholomew. 'Have you seen your sister today? She had some trouble before dawn this morning.'

'Trouble?' asked Bartholomew in alarm.

'Someone broke into the dyeworks and—Wait! I have not finished!'

Bartholomew sped along Milne Street, dodging carts, horses and pedestrians. He almost fell when he took the corner into Water Lane too fast, but regained his balance and raced on. As usual, there were knots of protesters in the square at the end, some led by Kellawe and others in a cluster around Hakeney and Vine the potter. The dyeworks door was open, so Bartholomew tore through it, barely aware that the stench was so bad that day that most of the women wore scarves around their mouths and noses. Edith was on her knees with a brush and pan.

'What happened?' he demanded breathlessly.

'Matt,' said Edith, climbing to her feet. 'Do not worry. We drove him off before he could do too much harm.'

'*We?* You were here at the time?'

'Yes, with Yolande. We came to . . . to stir the woad.'

'I see.' Bartholomew drew his own conclusions when she would not look him in the eye.

'The rogue had the fright of his life when he saw us,' Edith went on, then gave a sudden impish grin. 'I have never seen anyone run so fast in all my life.'

'Who was it?'

'He wore a mask, so we could not tell. Segeforde maybe, irked because Anne intends to sue.'

'Not if it happened just before dawn – he was dead by then. I suppose it might have been one of his Zachary cronies though.'

'Dead?' asked Edith, shocked. 'How? I hope it was not the *debilitas*, because we shall be blamed if so. Zachary already thinks we caused the deaths of Letia, Lenne, Irby and Yerland, just because they lived nearby.'

Bartholomew glanced around, aware of the reek now that he was no longer worried for her safety. In the annexe, Yolande was using a ladle to remove some foul residue from the bottom of a vat, while another woman was pouring buckets of urine over the fermenting balls of woad. Then he saw that a window had been forced, showing where the invader had broken in.

'He was unlucky to find you here,' he said. 'He probably expected the place to be empty.'

'We did not hear him at first, because we were out on the pier, getting rid of the alum-lye mix that . . .' Edith trailed off in guiltily.

'You put *lye* in the river?' cried Bartholomew in horror. 'But that is caustic! It will hurt anyone who drinks it. And what about the fish? It will kill everything that—'

'No one drinks from the river at that time of the day,' interrupted Edith defensively. 'Besides, the tide is going out, so it is all washed away now.'

Bartholomew smothered his exasperation. 'The tide is on the turn, which means some will come back again. And what about the people downstream, not to mention their animals? Besides, you are meant to be transporting of that sort of thing to the Fens.'

'We do, usually, but it is a long way on isolated tracks, and two or three buckets of sludge hardly warrant the trouble.'

'Two or three buckets *a day*,' Bartholomew pointed out. 'It adds up. You should store them until you have enough to make the journey worthwhile.'

'We have tried that, but your colleagues will insist on moaning about the smell.' Edith fixed him with a hard glare. 'You criticise us, but what about all the Colleges, hostels and convents that throw sewage, kitchen waste and God knows what else into the water? And besides, a few pails in an entire river will do no harm. They will dilute.'

'Will they?' demanded Bartholomew. Lye could have caused the burns he had seen on Frenge – the King's Ditch was not the river, but they were still connected. Could Frenge have been poisoned as he rowed to the Austin Priory, and the bruises on his face were not from someone forcing him to drink, but him clawing at himself in agony? 'Are you sure? Because I am not.'

'Our waste looks bad because it is brightly coloured,' Edith went on, 'whereas the stuff produced by everyone else just looks like dirty water. But theirs is just as dangerous.'

'You cannot know that,' Bartholomew said tiredly. 'And what if the protestors are right – what if the spate of recent deaths *is* because of you?'

Edith scowled at him. 'Use your wits, Matthew. Who drinks from the river and eats its fish? Paupers! And are paupers falling ill? No, the dead are all wealthy folk who go nowhere near the Cam for victuals. Besides, if you want a culprit, you should look to your own profession, as I have told you before. All the victims consulted a physician before they died.'

'Yes – Nigellus mostly,' sighed Bartholomew. 'So Michael arrested him last night.'

'Good,' said Edith harshly. 'He is certainly the kind of man to let an innocent dyeworks take the blame for something he has done.'

'He still might, so perhaps you should close until the situation is resolved.'

'And what happens to my ladies in the interim? Do they go back on the streets until you give us permission to reopen? I am sorry, Matt, but I am proud of what we have achieved here, and I cannot abandon them. They need me.'

Bartholomew smiled despite his concern, touched by her dedication to a sector of the community that did not often win champions. 'Then Cynric will stay with you until this is over.'

Edith smiled back, and Bartholomew was glad the quarrel was over, even if it was only a temporary truce. 'Thank you. His presence will be greatly appreciated.'

The door opened then, and Anne sauntered in wearing a kirtle that was cut even more revealingly than the one that had caused all the trouble the previous day. It looked new, and he wondered if she was already spending the money she expected to win from her lawsuit.

'I thought we had agreed that you would stay away until the matter with Segeforde is sorted out,' said Edith coolly, eyeing the gown with open disapproval. 'You being here is incendiary, especially with Kellawe outside.'

'Why should *he* dictate what I do?' pouted Anne. 'I am a free woman.'

'Very free – that is the problem,' muttered Edith.

'I have money invested in these dyeworks,' Anne went on. 'So I have a right to reassure myself that they are running smoothly. Besides, no one has my experience with the sales side of the business, so you need me here.'

'True,' acknowledged Edith. 'We do. Very well, then, but stay in the back and keep a low profile. We do not want your presence to aggravate the University – our biggest customer.'

'I know you are vexed with me for suing Segeforde,' said Anne, coming to take her hand. 'But he deserves it for what he did to me. Besides, I shall invest some of my compensation here, so the dyeworks will certainly benefit.'

'Segeforde is dead,' said Bartholomew. 'He will not be paying you anything.'

'I heard,' shrugged Anne. 'But Stephen says we can just transfer our grievance to his estate. And better I get the money than Segeforde's vile colleagues at Zachary Hostel. It would not surprise me if *they* dispatched him, in a desperate attempt to make me drop my complaint.'

Having had her say, she flounced off, all swinging hips and heaving bosom.

'Do not let her beguile you, Matt,' warned Edith, clearly of the opinion that no man would be able to resist such a tempting display. 'Her husband might be impotent, but they are still married, and I doubt she would make you happy anyway.'

'She hardly compares to Matilde and Julitta,' said Bartholomew, offended that Edith should think he might allow himself to be enticed. He had standards and Anne was well below them.

'No,' agreed Edith softly. 'She does not.'

Bartholomew left the dyeworks to find Michael and Kellawe outside, glaring furiously at each other, while Hakeney and his cronies watched intently from the other side of the road.

'Here,' said Kellawe, thrusting a flask at the physician. 'Swallow this.'

'What is it?' asked Bartholomew suspiciously, declining to take it.

'Water from the river. If your sister's business is doing no harm, you will not mind downing it, to prove to everyone that it is safe.'

'The river has *never* been safe,' said Bartholomew shortly. 'And I have been advising people not to drink from it ever since I became a physician.'

'You are refusing?' pounced Kellawe triumphantly.

'Yes. Not because of the dyeworks, but because of the

sewage that is discharged into it from Trinity Hall, Clare College, the Carmelite Friary and every house and hostel in between.'

'We know the truth,' called a verbose but stupid priest named Gilby. 'The Cam *is* poisoned, thanks to your sister and her whores. Her husband must be spinning in his grave.'

Oswald probably *would* have deplored Edith helping prostitutes, thought Bartholomew, but it was not for Gilby to say so. He reined in his temper with difficulty, ignoring the jeers that followed when Kellawe theatrically poured away the flask's contents.

'I am glad you refused, Matt,' murmured Michael. 'They probably added something to make you ill regardless. They are so determined to see Edith fail that no sly tactic is beneath them.'

'Now perhaps *you* will answer some questions.' Bartholomew addressed Kellawe, pointing at the Franciscan's boots as he did so: they were speckled with spots of red, yellow and blue. Clearly, the friar had not gone straight home after finishing his vigil for Segeforde, Irby and Yerland in St Bene't's Church, but had made a detour. 'Such as how did that happen?'

Kellawe flushed scarlet. 'Painting,' he replied, chin jutting out defiantly. 'Touching up the murals in our hall. And you cannot prove otherwise.'

Bartholomew felt his blood boil. What if the Franciscan's felonious antics had put Edith and her women in danger? He was about to launch into an accusatory tirade when Michael grabbed his arm and pulled him away, much to Kellawe's obvious relief.

'Exposing him as a burglar here will do nothing for the cause of peace,' he muttered. 'I shall fine him later, in the privacy of his hostel, where there will be no witnesses to turn it into an excuse for a fight.'

Bartholomew was not sure he agreed, but allowed

himself to be steered away. 'I will go to Barnwell this afternoon,' he said, wondering if the Franciscan and his followers would leave the dyeworks alone if Nigellus was proven guilty. 'To ask about the six people who died there.'

'Go now,' instructed Michael. 'We should have as many facts at our fingertips as possible when we interrogate Nigellus.'

He was about to add more when he noticed Shirwynk and Peyn outside their brewery. Peyn was slouched in an attitude of sullen indolence, and Bartholomew felt like remarking that the lad would have to make himself more amenable if he aimed to succeed at the Treasury.

'If you want the villain who invaded the dyeworks,' Peyn said as the two scholars approached, 'you need look no further than there.' He nodded to Kellawe and his supporters.

'My son is right,' said Shirwynk, and there was pride and love in the way he looked at the youth. 'The culprit will not be a townsman.'

'Moreover,' Peyn went on, 'the sudden outbreak of the *debilitas* is a sly plot by academics to kill all the burgesses, so there will be no one left to challenge the University's authority.'

'If that were true, the *debilitas* would only affect towns-folk,' said Michael coolly. 'But scholars are suffering, too.'

'But not at Michaelhouse,' Peyn flashed back. 'Which is more affluent than all the other Colleges put together. You should be dying, too, yet you remain suspiciously healthy. You are sacrificing colleagues from other foundations to strike a blow at the town.'

Langelee would be pleased to hear that his scheme to conceal Michaelhouse's poverty had been so successful, thought Bartholomew, amused by the irony. 'No one is—'

'You are ruthless and dangerous,' interrupted Shirwynk.

'And if we can do anything to oust your University from our town, we will not hesitate.'

Michael regarded them both thoughtfully. 'I ask again: why have you taken so violently against us after years of peaceful coexistence?'

'Because we have had enough of your arrogance, condescension and dishonesty,' snapped Shirwynk. 'More of my apple wine was stolen last night, and I *know* a scholar took it.'

'How can that have happened?' demanded Bartholomew archly. 'I thought Peyn stayed here all night to guard it.'

He did not voice the thoughts that sprang instantly to mind – that Kellawe had gone to avail himself of a courage-generating tipple before turning his attention to the dyeworks next door. Or that Michael had hit the nail on the head when the matter had been raised before – that Peyn had either supped the stuff himself or he was not as assiduous with his duties as he would have his father believe.

Shirwynk glared at him. 'The poor boy fell asleep for a few moments – protecting our property from thieving scholars is exhausting. The cunning bastards waited until he closed his eyes, and then they crept in.'

Unwilling to waste time arguing, Bartholomew and Michael went on their way, the physician wondering how Peyn had managed to persuade his father to be sympathetic to his napping on duty.

'He adores the lad,' said Michael. 'God knows why. I should be ashamed if he were mine, and I cannot imagine the Treasury being very impressed when he appears on its doorstep, expecting access to the King's money.'

The atmosphere was poisonous as Bartholomew and Michael walked up Water Lane – figuratively and literally. The dyeworks had started a process that involved a lot of foul-smelling ochre smoke, while it felt dangerous to be abroad in an academic tabard.

Bartholomew went directly to Michaelhouse, where Cynric was proud to learn that he was now responsible for Edith's safety. Then, while Michael set about strengthening his case against Nigellus, Bartholomew aimed for the Barnwell road. He was relieved when it began to rain, giving him an excuse to raise his hood. It concealed his face, enabling him to walk without being subjected to a barrage of insults.

The Barnwell Causeway was a desolate place to be, even in good weather. It was elevated above the marshes through which it snaked, leaving its users cruelly exposed to the elements. That day, rain scudded across it in sheets and everything dripped. Bartholomew walked briskly, while wind hissed among the reeds and made his cloak billow around him. Eventually, he reached the huddle of buildings that comprised the Augustinian convent, and hammered on the door.

A lay-brother conducted him to the warm, cosy solar occupied by Prior Norton, a man who might have been nondescript were it not for a pair of unusually protuberant eyes. Bartholomew stated the purpose of his visit quickly, wanting to waste neither his time nor the Prior's with aimless chatter. Norton listened carefully, then sent a canon to fetch Birton the reeve.

'We lost Cellarer Wrattlesworth and his friend Canterbury in quick succession,' Norton said while they waited. 'And our cook and gardener the week before. All four were tended by Nigellus – I would have summoned you, but you were away. He assured me that he could cure them by calculating their horoscopes and prescribing specific remedies.'

'Medicines?'

Norton nodded. 'Electuaries, infusions, tonics, decoctions. His last recommendation was Gilbert Water, which was very expensive, although it did scant good.'

'Were you happy with his suggestions at the time?'

'At first. However, I began to doubt his wisdom when he blamed our elderflower wine for the deaths. We have been drinking it for years with no ill effects, so his claims were a nonsense.'

Bartholomew had been provided with a cup of it when he had arrived, and although it was generally believed that the Augustinians' devotion to their beverage was undeserved, he had to admit that the one he sipped now was sweeter than usual, and so almost palatable.

'Of course, we did not part on the best of terms,' confessed Norton sheepishly. 'I was fond of Wrattlesworth, and was angry that Nigellus had failed to save him. I am afraid I said some rather cruel things about his competence – things of which I am now ashamed.'

'Physicians understand grief,' said Bartholomew kindly. 'And we have learned not to take such remarks to heart. Nigellus will not have been offended.'

'Actually, I think he was,' said Norton ruefully. 'Indeed, I believe he still is. I have tried to apologise several times, but he will not give me the time of day.'

The reeve arrived at that moment, a gruff, competent man in middle years with thick-fingered hands and skin that was reddened from time spent out of doors.

'My wife died the same day as Wrattlesworth,' he said, when he heard what Bartholomew wanted to know. 'The day after my Uncle Egbert. Nigellus said it was my fault, because I refused to rub snail juice on Olma's face, but she was a fastidious woman and would not have liked it. Of course, now I wish I had done as he ordered . . .'

'It would have made no difference,' said Bartholomew. He did not usually gainsay his colleagues' opinions, but he did not see why Birton should torture himself with needless guilt. 'It might even have caused distress in her final hours. You were right to refuse.'

Birton's eyes filled with tears, and he grasped

Bartholomew's hand gratefully before he took an abrupt leave. Norton watched him go unhappily.

'Olma was never in good health, while Egbert, Wrattlesworth and Canterbury were elderly. However, the cook and the gardener were in their prime, and should not have been taken from us so soon. They did spend too much time in the kitchen eating – both were very fat – but they had never suffered a day's illness in their lives until the *debilitas* struck them down.'

'How do you know it was the *debilitas*?' asked Bartholomew.

'Because Nigellus told us,' replied Norton. 'Not at the time – he was always rather vague about what was wrong – but he said so a few weeks later.'

'Did any of them drink from the river? Or eat fish caught in it?'

'None of us would touch river water,' said Norton with a moue of distaste. 'We may live in the marshes, but we are not insane! However, we all eat fish, and Wrattlesworth and Canterbury liked it especially well, particularly when served with a cup of our elderflower wine.'

'Did Olma and Egbert eat fish, too?'

'Of course. Nigellus recommends it for anyone who is frail or elderly, because it is easy to digest. Do you think we should avoid it then? I know your sister puts unpleasant things in the Cam, but they will surely be diluted by the time it reaches us?'

'It might be wise to avoid river-caught foods until we have identified the problem,' replied Bartholomew, although he felt disloyal to Edith for saying so.

'Then please do not take too long, Bartholomew. We rely on it in the winter when game is scarce. And our victuals are miserable enough as it is.'

'Are they?' Bartholomew was surprised to hear it, given that the priory was comfortably wealthy, and he had always been extremely well fed when he had been invited to dine there.

214

'Mealtimes are no longer as enjoyable as they were,' confided Norton with a sorrowful sigh. 'You see, the elderflower wine we made this year was the best we have ever produced – pure nectar. You have the honour of drinking the very last cup. Is it not exquisite?'

'Indeed,' replied Bartholomew dutifully, although he would not have accepted a refill. Clearly, Norton's definition of 'exquisite' was rather different from his own.

'But now it is gone, and our older brews are rough by comparison. It was the sun, you see – it ripened the grapes at exactly the right time.'

There was something about the remark that made Bartholomew wonder if he was being told the whole truth, but the Prior asked him to tend two lay-brothers at that point – a sprain and a festering finger – obliging him to turn his mind to medicine. When he had finished, he walked home, thinking about what he had learned.

He had identified two common factors in the six deaths: Nigellus and fish from the river. He was inclined to dismiss the fish, because far more people would have died or become ill if those had been the culprit. Which left Nigellus.

When Bartholomew arrived home, Michael listened carefully to everything the physician had reasoned, then gave a brief account of his own discoveries.

'Everyone who is ill or who has died of the *debilitas* was treated by a physician – most by Nigellus, but a few by you, Rougham and Meryfeld. Yet you say there is no such thing as the *debilitas* – it is a fiction invented by Nigellus.'

'Not a fiction, but a grand term for a whole host of ailments, designed to make the wealthy think they have something more distinguished than stomach cramps, headaches, muscle weakness, constipation and so forth.' Bartholomew's expression was wry. 'I imagine anyone with two pennies to rub together will be claiming to have it soon. It is fast becoming a status symbol.'

'Then do not tell Langelee, or he will order everyone in Michaelhouse to acquire one.'

They walked to Water Lane, where Zachary's door was answered by Morys, who was so angry that he seemed to have swollen in size – more hornet than wasp. Meanwhile, Kellawe had slunk home to change his shoes and glared challengingly as the visitors were shown into the hall. The students came to their feet as one, hands resting on the daggers they carried in their belts.

'There is a statute forbidding the toting of arms,' said Michael sharply.

'It is no longer safe to be without them,' retorted Kellawe. 'And I have a licence to absolve scholars from violent acts, so protecting ourselves is not a problem.'

'Your licence might save you time in Purgatory, but it will not protect you from a fine,' said Michael. 'And your warlike attitude has just won you one, as has your invasion of the dyeworks.'

'I never—' began Kellawe furiously.

'The drips on your spoiled boots do not match the colours of the murals here,' snapped Michael. 'Do not take me for a fool.'

'I did it for everyone,' snarled Kellawe, not bothering to deny it further. 'University *and* town. The dyeworks are a filthy abomination, and if you will not take steps to close them down, what choice do I have other than to take matters into my own hands?'

'Five shillings,' said Michael. 'That is the fine for burglary. And three more for bearing arms. You will pay by the end of today or you can all enjoy a spell in the proctors' cells.'

'Is that why you came, Brother?' asked Morys icily. 'To demand yet more money and issue threats? Was not arresting Nigellus enough?'

'It is an outrage,' put in Kellawe hotly. 'You had no right to—'

'I have every right,' snarled Michael. 'His patients are dying like flies, and I would be remiss to ignore it. Yerland, Segeforde and Irby—'

'Nigellus did not harm them.' Kellawe was almost screaming. 'You are a fool to suggest it. And why have you sealed them in their coffins? When I went to pay my last respects, one of your beadles refused to remove the lids.'

'Because they are expelling poisonous miasmas,' snapped Michael, although Bartholomew hoped *he* would not be asked to elaborate, given that he was not very good at telling convincing lies. 'It happens on occasion, when a person has been fed toxic substances shortly before death. Lenne is similarly affected – another of Nigellus's clients.'

'What toxic substances?' asked Kellawe, his voice dripping disbelief.

'Ones that are sold to physicians and no one else,' lied Michael, watching intently for a reaction. The only one he saw was an abrupt shying away from Bartholomew. 'No, not him! He no longer uses them, on account of them being so dangerous.'

'Then search Nigellus's room,' sneered Kellawe. 'You will find nothing untoward there.'

'Thank you,' said Michael, although Morys shot the Franciscan an irritable scowl. 'I will.'

Nigellus's chamber was luxurious, and every piece of furniture was of the very highest quality. It did not, however, contain much in the way of medical paraphernalia, other than a urine flask that was dusty with disuse, a pile of astrological tables and a jar of liquorice root. If Nigellus had been dosing his customers with something deadly, he did not keep it at Zachary.

'Or his colleagues have been here before us,' muttered

217

Michael, finally conceding defeat. 'They would certainly conceal evidence of a crime to protect their hostel's reputation.'

'Would they?' asked Bartholomew. 'If Nigellus *has* killed three of their colleagues, they might be wondering who will be next.'

They returned to the hall, where Michael began to put questions to the entire hostel. The atmosphere was glacial – Kellawe had been preaching insurrection while Bartholomew and Michael had been upstairs.

'Tell us what happened yesterday,' ordered the monk. 'Start with Yerland.'

There was a moment when it seemed they would refuse to cooperate, but then Morys spoke.

'He slept peacefully after Bartholomew gave him that draught. A few hours later, he woke and asked for more. Nigellus thought it too soon and told him to wait. Segeforde reported that Yerland slipped into an uneasy sort of doze thereafter, and died without uttering another word.'

'So obviously, it was *your* medicine that sent him to his grave,' hissed Kellawe. 'Not Nigellus, who gave him nothing.'

'How do you know Nigellus gave him nothing?' asked Bartholomew. 'Did someone stay with Yerland the whole time, and so can swear to it?'

'Yes,' said the Franciscan coldly. 'Segeforde did.'

'I see,' said Michael flatly. 'So tell us what happened to *him.*'

'He shut himself in his room after Yerland breathed his last,' replied Morys. 'Nigellus became worried after a while, and found him dead when he went to check on his well-being.'

'Nigellus did?' pounced Michael. 'Fascinating. And Segeforde sleeps alone?'

'Yes.' Morys glared at him. 'But that does not mean Nigellus sneaked in and killed him.'

218

No,' conceded Michael. 'Yet it is suspicious that the sole witness to Yerland's death is dead himself, *and* that the man we suspect of murder is the one to discover Segeforde's body.'

'It is not *suspicious* at all,' snarled Kellawe. 'Nigellus has done nothing wrong, and you know it. He will sue you for wrongful arrest when you release him.'

'What happened next?' asked Michael, ignoring the threat.

'Kellawe suggested taking Segeforde to the church,' replied Morys. 'Which was fortunate, given that you say his corpse is leaking nasty vapours. Normally, we would have kept him here.'

'God told me to remove him to St Bene't's,' said Kellawe smugly. 'I am one of His chosen, so clearly He wanted to protect me from harm.'

Bartholomew itched to retort that God obviously did not care that much, given that Kellawe had then spent much of the night on his knees next to the bodies, but was afraid that observation might make Kellawe question Michael's claim. And the last thing he wanted was for the lids to be removed and the victims examined.

'Are you sure it is not because Segeforde had a better room?' Michael was asking acidly. 'And you wanted it empty so you could move into it yourself?'

Kellawe's face was as black as thunder, especially when several students exchanged amused glances. 'Perhaps I did lay claim to it this morning, but—'

'At least you had the decency to remove the body first,' said Michael.

Morys had the grace to blush.

'That was helpful,' said Michael brightly, once they were out in the street. 'Nigellus almost certainly *did* give Yerland medicine, and Segeforde was murdered because he witnessed it.'

'Perhaps, but you cannot prove it,' Bartholomew pointed out.

'I can prove that both victims – and Lenne and Irby, too – consumed something that damaged their livers and stomachs. Or rather, you can.'

'Yes, but not that Nigellus was responsible. It might have been someone else. Kellawe or Morys, for example.'

'Kellawe and Morys would not have murdered Lenne,' argued Michael. 'Whereas Nigellus was his physician. Moreover, you are forgetting that crucial piece of evidence – the note Irby wrote to you, in which he virtually *names* Nigellus as his killer.'

'He does not,' said Bartholomew, feeling that the monk was putting far too much store in a message that was ambiguous at best.

Michael sighed irritably. 'Then we shall visit Lenne's wife and see what she can tell us. She will not enjoy an invasion from scholars, but it cannot be helped.'

Bartholomew fell into step beside him. They met the Austin friars on Milne Street – they had finished teaching the nominalism–realism debate to Michaelhouse's students, and were on their way home. Prior Joliet was clutching his elbow, his round face creased with pain, while Robert had a solicitous arm around his shoulders and the burly Hamo toted a thick staff. Wauter was with them, looking angrier than Bartholomew had ever seen him.

'Someone threw a rock,' he said tightly. 'The whole town has gone insane, and not even priests are safe now.'

'Who?' demanded Michael. 'Tell me, and I will arrest him.'

'I was not there,' replied Wauter bitterly. 'I wish I had been, because I would have—'

'No,' interrupted Joliet, gently but firmly. 'We will not sink to violent thoughts.' He turned to Michael. 'We did not see the culprit, Brother. I just felt the stone land.'

'We do not know if the attack was because we are

scholars,' added Robert, 'or because we were emerging from Michaelhouse, which is home to a physician.'

'There is a rumour that *medici* are dispatching their patients, you see,' explained Joliet, when Bartholomew frowned his puzzlement. 'One has been arrested for it.'

'Segeforde,' grunted Hamo.

'Yes, let us not forget that damned fool,' spat Wauter. 'He assaulted a popular lady in front of dozens of witnesses. And do not say it was an accident, because it was not.'

'It certainly looked deliberate to me,' said Joliet. He shook his head tearfully when Bartholomew offered to examine his arm. 'It is just a bruise, and I would rather not stay out longer than necessary – I want to be safely inside my convent with the gate locked. I dislike the town when it takes against the University.'

'Fens,' growled Hamo, gripping the stave. 'Good.'

'You are right, Hamo,' said Robert, wincing when a group of passing apprentices took the opportunity to howl abuse. 'Because as soon as one problem is solved in this place, another raises its head. Like my cross – Hakeney stole it today.'

'How do you know it was him?' asked Michael tiredly.

'Because he raced up to me, tore it from my person and danced away laughing,' replied Robert sourly. He rubbed his neck. 'And it hurt.'

'When they heard, the head of every convent in Cambridge demanded an audience with me,' added Joliet. 'They all said the same: that attacks on priests cannot be tolerated and action must be taken. They ordered me to report Hakeney to the Sheriff immediately.'

'Which he did, but Tulyet was reluctant to make an arrest, lest it ignited a riot,' Robert went on bitterly. 'He said that Hakeney is clearly not in his right wits, and it would be wiser to resolve the matter without recourse to a process that might see him hanged.'

'So we decided to let the matter go,' said Joliet, 'but then my fellow priors descended on me *again*, this time with Stephen, who recommended a civil suit instead.'

'No!' cried Michael, horrified. 'The University cannot sue another townsman. Dick Tulyet was right: it will cause no end of trouble. The priors should have minded their own business.'

'I disagree,' said Wauter stiffly. 'If we ignore this vicious assault, what message will it send to those who wish us harm? A lawsuit is the only way to keep us all safe.'

'Let me speak to Hakeney,' said Michael wearily. 'I will tell him to give back the cross and apologise. Then you can tell Stephen that his services will not be required, and the matter can be quietly forgotten.'

'Very well,' said Joliet, sadness etched into a face that was meant for laughter. 'I should like to avoid bad feeling if possible, so please try your best.'

'But if Hakeney refuses, we will have no choice but to proceed,' warned Robert. 'We cannot risk people thinking it is acceptable to assault clerics – which some may already believe, given that Prior Joliet has just been injured. It is—'

He was interrupted by another barrage of waved fists and combative yells, this time from a gaggle of bakers. Joliet whimpered his distress, Robert and Wauter flinched, and Hamo took a firmer grip on his staff. Michael saw the culprits on their way with a few sharp words, but Bartholomew was unnerved. The Austins were by far the most popular Order in the town, and if they were not safe, what hope did the rest of the University have?

Not many moments passed before Bartholomew and Michael were stopped again, this time by Wayt and Dodenho from King's Hall. They were at the head of a phalange of students who wore leather jerkins under their tabards, and carried swords or bows. One even had a mace, a weapon rarely seen off the battlefield. Several were wan, and clearly not in the best of health. Bartholomew stared at a lad whose hand was to his stomach; the student saw him looking and sneered, which revealed a thin grey line around the tops of his incisors.

'Are you aware that strutting around armed to the teeth is a finable offence?' asked Michael.

'We are,' replied Wayt arrogantly. 'But we do not care. We would rather lose a few shillings than our lives – and the town is not safe for scholars at the moment.'

'It is safe if you stay indoors,' retorted Michael. 'You do not have to venture out.'

'We do if we want to pray in St Mary the Great for Cew,' Wayt flashed back. 'Or do you suggest that we forget our religious obligations while the town is being difficult?'

'That does not excuse—' began Michael.

'Cew is worse,' blurted Dodenho. His expression was so full of unhappy concern that Michael elected to over-look the interruption. 'He has a weakness in his muscles now.'

'And he still thinks he is the King of France,' said the Acting Warden unpleasantly. 'Your medicine did nothing to cure him of that delusion, Bartholomew.'

'Meanwhile, three more of our lads have come down with the *debilitas*,' added Dodenho. 'Would you mind visiting them later, to see what might be done to ease their discomfort?'

'No,' said Wayt sharply. 'What if the reason for their malaise is his sister's dyeworks? He is not the man we should trust with our students' welfare.'

Bartholomew opened his mouth to object, but Dodenho was wise enough to know that offending *medici* was not a good idea when the University was on the verge of a major brawl. After all, who else would sew up wounds and set broken bones?

223

'Please come when you can, Bartholomew,' he said quietly, shooting the Acting Warden a glance that warned him to hold his tongue. 'We would be most grateful. Perhaps you will be able to persuade Cew to eat something other than oysters and soul-cakes as well.'

'Now that would be useful,' acknowledged Wayt. 'Oysters are expensive, while soul-cakes should not be baked outside Hallow-tide.'

'They also contain sucura, which is risky to buy with the Sheriff on the warpath about it,' added Dodenho, then flushed sheepishly when he realised that he had just admitted to breaking the law. He changed the subject hastily. 'I hear Nigellus has been arrested for killing Frenge. Pity. It would have been better for the University if the culprit had been a townsman.'

'Fortunately, he has not been a scholar for very long,' said Michael. 'He was a resident of Barnwell until a couple of months ago – a fact we shall be sure to emphasise.' He turned to Wayt. 'Are you *sure* it was your relationship with Anne de Rumburgh that Frenge threatened to expose unless you dropped the lawsuit against him? Not something else?'

'Of course,' replied Wayt, curtly enough to be suspicious. 'And now, if you will excuse us, we have business to attend.'

'You are going the wrong way,' said Michael, stepping in front of him. 'St Mary the Great is in the opposite direction.'

'We have another matter to attend first,' explained Dodenho. 'Namely asking if Stephen will change his mind about representing us. We have our own lawyers, of course, but none of them have his experience or cunning.'

Michael watched them go, then he and Bartholomew resumed their walk to the Lenne house.

'King's Hall has all manner of nasty secrets,' he said, 'illicit supplies of sucura among them. But we have no time to explore that now, so I shall leave it for later.'

'Will you?' asked Bartholomew. 'I was under the impression that you were willing to turn a blind eye to that particular crime.'

'I turn a blind eye if the culprits are discreet, but Wayt is brazen and arrogant. Indeed, if I did not think it would cause more trouble than it was worth, I would tell Dick Tulyet about him.'

Bartholomew had expected a frosty reception from Isabel Lenne, so he was startled and wary when she smiled warmly at him. Her cordiality was quickly explained, though.

'It was good of you to give Will a free coffin, Doctor,' she said. 'I always thought you did not like him, because of his sour temper and sharp tongue.'

'Oh,' said Bartholomew uncomfortably, feeling the colour rise into his cheeks. Michael poked him hard, warning him against declaring that the 'gift' had had nothing to do with him.

'It is not the fanciest of caskets,' she went on, 'but it would have suited Will's simple tastes.'

'It is our pleasure, Mistress Lenne,' the monk said smoothly.

'He went in the ground this afternoon,' sighed Isabel. 'Which you will know, of course. That is why you are here – to offer your condolences.'

'Yes,' lied Michael. 'Nigellus tells us that your husband died of metal in the mouth.'

She nodded. 'Which is a common symptom of the *debilitas*, apparently. Nigellus says it occurs most frequently in men who swear a lot, and Will did love to curse.'

'Nigellus said that?' Bartholomew could not keep the astonishment from his voice.

She nodded again. 'But Will's suffering did not last long. After the metal came a recurrence of his old apoplexy, which is what carried him off.'

'So he died of an apoplexy?' pounced Bartholomew. 'Not the *debilitas*?'

She flushed. 'It *was* the *debilitas*, but it manifested itself in apoplexy-like symptoms. I will not have it said that Will died of anything vulgar.'

'What happened exactly?' asked Bartholomew, declining to comment.

Isabel's voice grew unsteady as she described how Lenne had returned from the tavern feeling ill. He had mentioned an unpleasant taste that Nigellus had diagnosed as metal in the mouth, the remedy for which was to suck raw garlic. Not long after, Lenne had exhibited all the classic symptoms of a major apoplectic attack and had died an hour later. As far as Isabel knew, nothing other than garlic had been recommended, and Nigellus had been the only visitor.

'Your anatomising should have told us that he died of natural causes,' said Michael crossly, once they were outside. 'We could have saved the cost of a coffin.'

'It is not as simple as that. Perhaps Lenne did die of an apoplexy – Isabel's testimony certainly suggests it – but what about the damage to his liver and stomach? Moreover, this metal in the mouth is peculiar. I have never heard of it before, and I am puzzled as to what caused it.'

'So did Nigellus murder Lenne or not?' asked Michael impatiently.

'I do not know,' replied Bartholomew, equally irritable. 'There is no way to tell.'

'You are no help,' said Michael in disgust. 'But you can make up for your inadequacy in the Corpse Examining department by accompanying me to interrogate Nigellus.'

'No, Brother. I told you: he will think I am there to gloat.'

'You must – he will try to confuse me with complex medical explanations, and I shall need you to tell me

whether they are reasonable. Come on. The sooner we
see him, the sooner we can go home. Even I feel vulner-
able wandering about today.'

CHAPTER 9

The proctors' gaol was a nasty, damp building behind St Mary the Great. Bartholomew only visited it when prisoners needed medical attention, and each time he went, he remembered how much he disliked it. The cells were in the basement, on the grounds that this would reduce the risk of the inmates being broken out by indignant cronies.

Although he complained about the unhealthy atmosphere, it was not bad as such places went. There were vents to supply fresh air, and the beadles kept it fairly clean. The food was often better than what was served in Michaelhouse, and there were reasonable arrangements for sanitation. Nigellus had been provided with a lamp, books, parchment, pens and blankets. He was writing when the beadle unlocked the door, taking the opportunity to prepare lectures for the following week – underlining the fact that he expected to be free to give them.

'Have you come to release me?' he asked archly, when Michael and Bartholomew entered. 'If so, do not bother with apologies. You have offended me so deeply that only financial restitution will salve my distress. You will be hearing from Stephen first thing in the morning.'

'We are here for answers,' said Michael, sitting on the bed; Bartholomew leaned against the doorframe. 'The matter is far from over, I am afraid. At least a dozen of your patients are dead, and if your feathers are ruffled in our search for the truth, then so be it.'

'I am surprised at you, Bartholomew,' said Nigellus coldly. 'You are a colleague, and I had expected your support. How can you betray me in this manner?'

'Shall we begin with Barnwell?' asked Michael, ignoring the remark. 'And the six people who died within days of each other while under your care?'

'Three very elderly men, two servants who did nothing but sit around and eat, and a woman with a wasting sickness,' replied Nigellus dismissively. He glanced archly at Bartholomew. 'Or do you think these are folk you might have saved?'

'Then what about Frenge?' demanded Michael. 'He was your patient, and he was neither ancient, fat, nor cursed with poor health.'

'Yes, but his last visit to me was more than a week ago. You cannot lay his fate at my door.'

'You have seen him since,' countered Michael. 'We have witnesses who say you argued with him over the sour ale he sold Zachary. Please do not lie: it will only make matters worse.'

'Oh, yes,' said Nigellus shortly. 'I had forgotten – it was an unmemorable event. I did inform him that selling us inferior wares was unacceptable, but that is not a crime. However, I had nothing to do with his demise. Or do you imagine that I lurk in convents waiting to strike my victims?'

'I am not in a position to say – yet,' replied Michael. 'Now tell me about Letia.'

'Shirwynk summoned me too late to save her,' said Nigellus, treating the monk to an unpleasant look. 'Personally, I think he did it deliberately, because he wanted her dead. When I arrived, she was so dizzy that she barely knew her name.'

'You mean she was delirious?' asked Bartholomew.

Nigellus shot him a disdainful glance, and when he spoke, it was as if he was addressing an annoying and particularly stupid child. 'No, because she was not suffering from hallucinations. You cannot have one without the other. Surely you know that?'

229

'Actually, it is perfectly possible to be in an acute confused state without delusions,' said Bartholomew, surprised that Nigellus might think otherwise. 'What were her other symptoms?'

'She was hot and she had vomited, but those were irrelevant to my diagnosis. Dizziness is a serious and often fatal condition, and it was obvious to me that she was going to die.'

Bartholomew did not bother to argue. 'And Lenne?' he asked.

'Metal in the mouth, a disease described by Hippocrates. I prescribed garlic, not only to remove the taste, but to rebalance the humours. Garlic is hot and wet in the second degree, as I am sure you know.'

Bartholomew knew no such thing, and was also sure that Hippocrates would never have considered 'metal in the mouth' a disease. He regarded his colleague intently, trying to decide whether Nigellus was simply a terrible physician, or a very clever one attempting to conceal his crimes with a show of bumbling ineptitude.

'Brother Arnold,' he said eventually. 'You claimed he died of insomnia.'

'Yes, which can be deadly in elderly patients, as the Greek physician Xenocrates says. If they do not have access to the rejuvenating powers of sleep, they sicken and die. And before you ask, Irby was suffering from a loss of appetite, another dangerous disease.'

'It takes longer than a few hours for a loss of appetite to prove fatal,' said Bartholomew, whose only knowledge of Xenocrates was that the infinitely more famous and trustworthy Galen had criticised him for making 'remedies' out of particularly unpleasant ingredients.

'Irby had a pre-existing condition that required a regular intake of nutrients,' Nigellus flashed back. 'When he failed to eat, he fell into a torpid state, and that was the end of him.'

Bartholomew struggled to understand what might actually have happened. 'Did he suffer a sudden loss of weight, accompanied by excessive urination and—'

'Hah! You do know of the ailment. Your training is not as flawed as I was beginning to fear. His urine was sweet on my tongue, and was obviously abnormal.'

'You *tasted* it?' Bartholomew was repelled.

Nigellus's composure slipped a little. 'Of course, as the great Aretaeus of Cappadocia recommended we do. Why? How do you do it?'

'By seeing whether it attracts ants,' replied Bartholomew, regarding him askance.

Nigellus waved a dismissive hand, although a flush in his cheeks indicated his chagrin at having been found lacking. 'But Yerland is the one who will prove my innocence. *I* did not give him medicine for his headache, *you* did. Ergo, you are the one who should be sitting here, not me.'

'You gave him nothing at all?' asked Michael.

'No – I have one cure for headaches: sleeping in a darkened room. I have learned through the years that they either get better on their own or they become worse and the patient dies. Nothing the *medicus* does affects the outcome one way or the other, so I never bother to try.'

'Did Segeforde have a headache, too?' asked Bartholomew.

'He had a pallor,' replied Nigellus. 'So all I did for him was recommend an early night.'

'Now what about this *debilitas* you have been diagnosing?' asked Michael. 'Matt tells me that there is no such sickness.'

Nigellus scowled. 'Of course there is, and his remark does nothing but underline the fact that I am a better, more experienced *medicus* than he. He claims to have University degrees, but all I can say is that he cannot have paid much attention in class. I, on the other hand, listened to every word my tutors told me.'

'When did you study at Oxford?' asked Michael, aiming to make enquiries to see if Nigellus was telling the truth about his education.

'Before you were born,' came the sharp response. He shot Bartholomew an unpleasant sneer. 'When medical students were of a much higher calibre.'

'*Similia similibus curantur*,' persisted Michael, while Bartholomew felt himself begin to lose patience with Nigellus, and struggled against the urge to turn on his heel and march out. 'Irby wrote it just before he died. What did he mean?'

'Clearly, he was reflecting on the best way to counteract the stench caused by Edith Stanmore's dyeworks.' The speed of Nigellus's response indicated that he had already given the question serious consideration. 'He was pondering whether creating odours of his own would neutralise hers.'

'Can you prove that?' asked Michael.

'Can you *dis*prove it?' Nigellus flashed back. 'You think I harmed all these people, but you have no evidence to support your theories, or you would not be here now, fishing for answers.'

Michael stood, refusing to rise to the bait. 'Thank you for your time. You will no doubt be seeing more of us in the coming days.'

'I cannot wait,' said Nigellus acidly. 'However, do not forget to ask Tynkell how much money is in the University Chest. You will need every penny once Stephen is through with you.'

'Well?' asked Michael once they were outside. 'He had an answer for everything, but only a fellow *medicus* will know whether his replies were reasonable.'

'There is something to be said for treating headaches

by sending the patient to rest in a dark room, although I suspect he misremembered the sources he quoted.'

'That does not answer my question.'

'Letia's high temperature and sickness should have formed part of Nigellus's diagnosis, but he chose to ignore them. And it is common knowledge that patients with Irby's condition can slip into a fatal decline if they fail to eat. Nigellus should have taken steps to prevent it.'

'So ineptitude rather than malice killed Irby and Letia? What about the others?'

Bartholomew shrugged. 'He assumed the symptoms exhibited by Lenne and Arnold were diseases, and elected to treat those rather than identify the underlying causes. They might have lived if he had approached them differently, but they might not. We will never know.'

'Then what about the damage to stomachs and livers that you found in the three Zachary men and Lenne?' Michael was sounding exasperated. 'You said that might be evidence of poison.'

'Yes – *might* be evidence of poison. But I cannot prove it.'

'I am not very impressed with your help in this matter, Matt. If you do not give me something useful soon, I may be forced to let him go.'

'Well, if you do, it should be on condition that he does not practise medicine again. Do you have the authority to enforce that?'

'Yes, but only temporarily. He will contest my decision and Stephen will argue that he be permitted to trade until the case is resolved in court. Thank God we have Irby's note – the only truly compelling piece of evidence against him.'

Bartholomew was thoughtful. 'His explanation of the note made no sense: if Irby *had* been reflecting on how best to combat the reek from the dyeworks, why did he address his letter to me, the brother of the owner? Why not Nigellus, the *medicus* in his hostel? Or one of his colleagues?'

'Those are good questions,' said Michael. 'And one we shall ponder while he sits in my gaol.'

While Michael went to do battle with Stephen, Bartholomew trudged home to Michaelhouse, wanting no more than a quiet evening in the conclave. Unfortunately, the porter handed him a long list of patients who needed to see him. Given the uneasy atmosphere, Bartholomew was reluctant to venture out alone, and as Cynric was with Edith, he took two students instead – Melton and Bell.

'Prior Joliet is a gifted speaker,' said Melton, as they walked to the home of a wealthy merchant. Bartholomew did not have many rich patients, but Rob Upton did a lot of business with Edith and thought hiring her brother was an easy way to stay in her good books. 'But Father William refused to let us take any breaks, so it was one long, continuous session.'

'What about the noonday meal?'

'Cancelled,' scowled Melton. 'To save money after the lavish display we put on over Hallow-tide. So now we are *starving.*'

Upton claimed he was suffering from the *debilitas*, although Bartholomew suspected that the half-empty plate of marchpanes might have more than a little to do with the patient's 'griping in the guts'. He asked enough questions to prove himself right, and set about writing out the remedy for over-indulgence that he was often obliged to dispense to those with more money than sense.

'Three other burgesses fell ill with the *debilitas* today,' whispered Upton miserably, 'while it killed Lenne, Arnold, Letia and the scholars from Zachary.'

'You will feel better tomorrow,' Bartholomew assured

234

him, 'although you should abstain from rich foods for a few days. And that includes marchpanes.'

'Let me try one,' begged Bell plaintively. 'To assess whether they are safe.'

Bartholomew shot him an admonishing glance, but that did not stop the lad from snagging one on the way out anyway.

'Too sweet,' was the verdict once they were outside. 'Like eating pure honey. No wonder Upton was queasy. But now I am hungrier than ever, and I doubt I shall sleep tonight.'

'Nor will I,' moaned Melton. 'The pangs are growing worse by the moment.'

Bartholomew took them to the Brazen George, where Landlord Lister provided a large plate of tasty scraps for a very reasonable price. When they had finished, they went to Gonville Hall, where a Fellow named Osborne was suffering from a weakness in the legs. As Osborne reeked of claret, Bartholomew could not imagine why Rougham should want a second opinion as to what was wrong.

'It came on him gradually,' Rougham explained. 'He cannot stand without falling over.'

When he heard how much Osborne had imbibed, Bartholomew was not surprised.

'He drank to help with the discomfort of his *debilitas*,' added another Fellow. 'His knees were wobbly before his three jugs of wine.'

Declining to comment, Bartholomew prescribed a large bowl of his favourite cure-all – boiled barley water – and an early night. Afterwards, he accepted the offer of refreshments in Rougham's quarters, where he was provided with wine so dry as to be almost unpalatable. While he warmed himself by the fire, he told Rougham what Nigellus had claimed about the patients he had lost.

'I cannot imagine why Zachary recruited him,' said Rougham in distaste. 'He is the worst combination of unshakable conceit and incompetence. And Oxford-trained into the bargain.'

'They probably hope he will leave them all his money,' said Bartholomew, disinclined to remind him that Nigellus was not the only one who had studied at the Other Place. 'He is a wealthy man, after all.'

'He is a charlatan,' spat Rougham. 'If you do not want more folk to die – which we dare not risk when the town is in such turmoil – Michael should keep him under lock and key.'

'The *debilitas* was his invention,' mused Bartholomew. 'He probably blurted it out when he was stumped for a diagnosis, and it has become a popular term for a whole range of unrelated symptoms – headaches, stomach pains, nausea, constipation, weakness in the limbs . . .'

'Perhaps you and I should rename it the Devil's Pox,' suggested Rougham wryly. 'Then we would never see another case again. But you are wrong to say these symptoms are unrelated, Bartholomew. I have seen more of the *debilitas* than you – all my patients are rich, while yours tend to be paupers – and nearly everyone complains of two or three problems, not just one.'

'Osborne did not. He just had weak legs.'

'Along with a mild headache and nausea,' corrected Rougham. 'He did not mention them to you because he was more concerned about not being able to walk. I hate to admit it, but Nigellus might have stumbled across a new disease. It would be galling if he did – him being such an ass.'

'Do you think my sister's dyeworks are responsible?' asked Bartholomew, voicing the worry that had been with him all day. He supposed Gonville's strong wine must have loosened his tongue, because he was not sure he wanted to hear Rougham's answer.

'No, I do not,' replied Rougham promptly. 'Or rich and poor alike would be afflicted. However, the venture *will* claim lives eventually, because nothing can smell that bad and not be harmful. If you can persuade her to move to the marshes – or better yet, close down – you will be doing the town a great service.'

They talked a while longer, then Bartholomew stood to leave, wondering if he should claim to have the *debilitas* when he found himself decidedly light-headed.

'You were pale and unhappy when you arrived,' explained Rougham. 'So I added poppy juice to your wine. It will give you a good night's sleep, and restore the balance of your humours.'

'You dosed me with soporific?' Bartholomew was horrified.

'Yes, and do not glower at me – it was for your own good. As the great Galen said, the body knows what it needs, so one should pay heed to it. Yours must require restorative sleep, or it would have vomited my mixture out. So go home now and rest well.'

Bartholomew did rest well, sleeping so deeply that he did not hear the bell when it rang the following morning, and nor did he stir when his students indulged in a pillow fight over his head. They left him to his slumbers, and went to assemble in the yard for church. However, he was not the only one who had failed to appear: Wauter was also absent.

'Perhaps we need a bigger bell,' muttered Langelee, striding towards the Austin's room. 'Because I cannot have my Fellows oversleeping. It sets a bad example to the students.'

Wauter was not there, although his undergraduates were, still in bed and claiming they could not rise because they had the *debilitas*.

'He did not come home last night, sir,' said one, which

237

explained why there were several empty wineskins on the floor and all four looked decidedly seedy.

'Where did he sleep then?' demanded Langelee.

'We do not know,' replied the lad wretchedly. 'At his old hostel, perhaps.'

Langelee's expression was dangerous as he stalked across the yard to deal with his other missing Fellow, and it darkened further still when Michael regaled him with an account of how he had spent *his* evening: a throng of students from Zachary had invaded the King's Head, a rough tavern where scholars were not welcome. Not surprisingly, there had been a fight.

'Was anyone hurt?' asked Langelee, shaking Bartholomew's shoulder with considerable vigour. When the physician only turned over and went back to sleep, he drew a blade – a wicked little thing that had been intended for use as a letter-opener, but that he had honed to extraordinary sharpness. It had been nowhere near a missive in years.

'No, but someone will be if you brandish that thing around,' said Michael in alarm. 'What are you going to do?'

Langelee used it to prick the back of Bartholomew's hand, and his eyebrows shot up in astonishment when the only response was a twitch. 'I have never known that not to work before! I used to do it all the time when I was in the Archbishop of York's employ. Of course, I usually applied my blade to the throat . . .'

'No!' snapped Michael, as the Master leaned down purposefully. He grabbed a bowl of water and splattered some on the physician's face. Bartholomew sat up blinking.

'Rougham gave me a soporific,' he said defensively, surmising that it may have required some effort to wake him. He struggled to clear his muddy wits, then frowned when he saw the bead of blood on his hand and the blade that Langelee was putting away. 'Did you *stab* me?'

'No, I *nicked* you. You barely moved, so I should have jabbed harder.'

Bartholomew eyed him coolly. 'You will never win wealthy benefactors if word gets out that you spear your Fellows while they sleep.'

'On the contrary, I will probably win their approbation. They will all wish they had the courage to do the same to lazy minions. Besides, it was only a poke with a letter-opener.'

'So that explains why I did not feel it,' muttered Bartholomew, well aware of what the Master had done to what had once been an innocent little implement. 'Blunt blades always hurt more than sharp ones.'

He rose and dressed quickly when the bell sounded again, and had to run to catch up with the procession, much to the delight of his students. He barely heard William's Mass, overcome as he was with the frequent and annoying urge to yawn. As they walked home, Michael confessed that Nigellus's arrest had done nothing to calm troubled waters.

'Meanwhile, Anne is refusing to drop her case against Segeforde's estate, and King's Hall is just as stubborn about Frenge and the brewery.'

'What about the Austins?' asked Bartholomew, trying hard to concentrate. 'Do they still aim to sue Hakeney for snatching Robert's cross?'

Michael nodded. 'I did suggest to Dick Tulyet that we put an end to the nonsense by arresting Hakeney for robbery, but Dick insists that the fellow is not in his right wits, and thinks putting him in custody would ignite a major riot. Unfortunately – as it galls me to see Hakeney strutting free after so brazen a crime – I suspect he is right.'

'The Austins suing a townsman might ignite a major riot, too.'

'Yes, but not immediately, and who knows what Dick

and I might be able to achieve for the cause of peace in the interim?'

'Stephen,' said Bartholomew bitterly. 'I wager anything you like that it was *he* who encouraged the other priors to bully Joliet into suing Hakeney – and all so he could win himself another client.'

'Of course it was Stephen,' growled Michael. 'And I shall visit him first thing this morning, and demand to know why he is so eager to see his town in flames.'

They ate a hasty breakfast in the hall, listening to William grumble about the fact that Wauter had selfishly abandoned him the previous day, leaving him to supervise the entire College alone.

'He just disappeared! He was there one moment and gone the next, without so much as a word of explanation. And he has not been seen since.'

'Where has he gone?' asked Bartholomew. It was curious behaviour for a Fellow, especially one who was new and so still needed to win the respect of his colleagues.

'I have no idea, but we should have known better than to recruit an Austin,' spat William. 'They are all the same: lazy and unreliable.'

'That is untrue, Father,' objected Clippesby, who had a toad on the table and was trying to feed it pieces of meat. 'Prior Joliet and Almoner Robert have worked extremely hard on our behalf, and my students say their lecture yesterday was a masterpiece.'

'I would not know,' said William acidly. 'I did not hear any of it because I was trying to control a lot of unruly medics. Moreover, it is not the first time that Wauter has played truant. He vanished on All Souls' Day, too, when the rest of us clerics were frantically trying to prepare the church for our founder's Requiem Mass.'

'Oh, yes,' recalled Michael. 'He returned breathless and dishevelled, and made that odd remark about us being "perceived as having an unstained soul despite our many blemishes". I did not know what he meant then, and I do not know now.'

'This toad heard Kellawe say—' began Clippesby.

'Kellawe!' said William in distaste. 'My Order should never have accepted him. And now he has a licence to absolve scholars from acts of violence. It is not fair! He will only use it on men from Zachary, leaving the rest of us stained with sin.'

'You will not be stained with sin if you commit no crimes,' Bartholomew pointed out.

'*This toad*,' repeated Clippesby loudly, cutting across William's tart response, 'heard Kellawe say that Wauter left the town on horseback yesterday. Wauter had a fat saddlebag, and it appeared as though he intended to be gone for some time.'

'Without asking his Master's permission?' demanded Langelee angrily. 'Well, when he returns he will learn that Michaelhouse is not Zachary – *we* do not permit Fellows to trot off in the middle of term. What about his teaching? Ah! Here is Prior Joliet and his helpers. We shall ask them about their fellow Austin's antics.'

'But where would he go?' asked Prior Joliet worriedly, when Langelee explained what had happened. His arm was in a sling – a scrap of orange material that was very bright against the sober habit of his Order. 'He has no family, and all his friends are here.'

'I will ask our brethren,' offered Robert. 'Perhaps one of them will know.'

'Will you teach his classes?' asked William belligerently. 'Because I am not doing it.'

'Of course,' replied Joliet. 'Robert and I shall lecture on St Augustine's *Sermones* while Hamo tries to finish the mural. And finish we must, as we start work in King's Hall next week.'

'Your Hallow-tide celebrations did much to secure us new commissions,' said Robert with a smile that held

241

the hint of a gloat. 'I hope fortune shone on you as brightly.'

'Of course it did,' lied Langelee, unwilling to admit that it had not.

Assuming he was no longer needed now that Nigellus was in custody – Michael was more than capable of finding the evidence needed to prove the *medicus*'s crimes himself – Bartholomew informed his students that he planned to test them on Galen's *De ossibus* that morning. He was irked by the relief on their faces when Michael announced that the investigation was still a long way from over, and that the physician could not return to his regular duties just yet.

'A terrible thought struck me earlier,' the monk confided, once it had been agreed that Robert would read the relevant passages to the medics on the understanding that they would have them verbatim by the end of the week.

'That my students will never become physicians as long as you keep tearing me away from my teaching?' asked Bartholomew sourly.

Michael's expression was bleak. 'I am serious, Matt. A lot of things are going wrong at the moment – the various lawsuits, the murders, the assault on Anne, the trouble at the dyeworks. And now Wauter has vanished.'

Bartholomew regarded him blankly. 'I do not understand—'

'I have assumed they are all unrelated, a random collection of nasty events. But there are so many of them, and they all do one thing: damage the relationship between town and University. In short, I think someone is orchestrating the whole lot – someone who *wants* the situation to explode into violence.'

'Why would anyone want that?' asked Bartholomew doubtfully. 'Who would benefit?'

'Those who would like us to move to the Fens. What began as a silly rumour has become a movement with growing support. A *lot* of our scholars think it is a very good idea. And if there is open war between us and the town, even more will agree.'

'But there is nothing in the Fens. It is a stupid notion.'

'Is it? The priests among us have long deplored the University's growing secularism, and a move to the marshes would make us more like a monastery – a self-sufficient foundation set apart from the vices of the laity.'

Bartholomew rubbed a hand through his hair. 'Let us assume you are right. Is Nigellus the sly mastermind behind this scheme?'

'It is possible: he does think we should go. But so does another suspect, one who is much closer to home.'

Bartholomew regarded Michael in alarm. 'You mean Wauter?'

'Yes. He was a scholar in Zachary until the beginning of term – Nigellus's hostel. Their terms of tenure did not overlap, but they still had dealings with each other.'

'You think Wauter encouraged Nigellus to . . . No, Brother! This is too outlandish.'

'Perhaps. Yet Zachary lies at the heart of all our problems: one of its masters assaulted Anne; he and two other members lie dead in odd circumstances; another has a licence to absolve scholars from violent acts; its new Principal has an unsavoury hold over the Chancellor; it lies on the same street as the brewery and the dyeworks; and its resident *medicus* stands accused of murder.'

'And an *ex*-member is a strong supporter for a move to the Fens,' added Bartholomew reluctantly. 'Although I do not see Wauter as an arch villain who would sacrifice lives to get what he wants.'

'I do not know what to think. However, there is only one way forward: Frenge's murder started it all, and I have the sense that finding *his* killer will allow us to make sense of everything. You have never been happy with the evidence against Nigellus, so let us explore our other suspects for a while instead – the men of King's Hall, Shirwynk and Peyn, Hakeney and Stephen.'

'The last four would be glad to see the University leave Cambridge,' said Bartholomew. 'But the King's Hall men would rather it stayed.'

'So they claim – they may be lying in an effort to confuse us. We shall ask them as soon as we have had words with Stephen about his sly manipulation of our gullible priors.'

They walked directly to Stephen's house on the High Street, only to be informed by his maid that her master was out with a client, although she was unable to say which one.

'Tell him we called,' ordered Michael, not bothering to hide his irritation. 'And that he had better be in when we visit later, or there will be trouble.'

The girl gulped, clearly loath to repeat that sort of message to the man who paid her wages. 'Then come in and wait for him,' she suggested. 'He will not be long – he is still not very well, so he will be keen to come home and lie down. He has pains in his wrists and he keeps being sick.'

'I hope he will not use ill health as an excuse to avoid answering our questions – if he is fit enough to dash out after customers, then he is fit enough to speak to us,' said Michael unsympathetically. 'You can tell him *that* when he returns as well.'

Without waiting for a response, he turned on his heel and began to stalk towards King's Hall. However, he and Bartholomew had not taken many steps before they met Tulyet and Dickon. The boy's face was as vividly scarlet as ever, so he remained an unsettling sight. He favoured the two scholars with a wide grin, and they blinked their astonishment: his teeth were blue.

244

'You cannot blame that on the dyeworks,' said Bartholomew to the Sheriff.

'He drank some woad,' said Tulyet, giving his son a disapproving glare. 'It was a stupid thing to have done. He might have poisoned himself.'

'I did not *drink* it,' Dickon informed him chirpily. 'I just took a mouthful, kept it there during Mass, then spat it out.'

'I wondered why you were so quiet.' Tulyet turned anxiously to Bartholomew. 'It will not stain him permanently, will it?'

'No, although he might want to remember in future that one of the ingredients of blue dye is urine.'

Horror stole over the lad's face, and there followed a good deal of agitated spitting.

'Relations continue to deteriorate between us and the University,' Tulyet said to Michael, dragging his eyes away from the spectacle. 'The situation is not helped by that tale you told me about Frenge.'

'That he was a cattle thief,' put in Dickon. 'Which he was not, so you lied.'

'Dickon!' snapped Tulyet. He turned back to Michael. 'I am sure it was an honest mistake on your part, Brother, but the fact is that you were wrong. Frenge's only real failing was a fondness for his own wares, which led him to do reckless things.'

'Like invading King's Hall and the Austins,' said Dickon. 'It was stupid when he could have gone somewhere like Zachary, which has lots of lovely things to steal, but not much in the way of defences.'

Michael and Bartholomew regarded him askance, both unsettled that he should know which University foundation would be best to burgle. Tulyet hastened to change the subject.

'I do not know how best to keep the peace,' he confided unhappily. 'Flooding the streets with troops amounts to martial law, which is more likely to inflame than soothe.'

'Then do it,' suggested Dickon keenly. 'A massacre will show everyone who is in charge.'

A soldier arrived at that point to announce trouble in the Market Square. Tulyet hurried away to deal with it, Dickon dancing at his heels, flashing his blue fangs at anyone who glanced in his direction.

'Why are men so blind when it comes to their offspring?' said Michael wonderingly as he watched them go. 'Shirwynk is another example: Peyn is a sullen lout who is barely literate—'

'And who has never heard of Virgil,' put in Bartholomew.

'—but Shirwynk thinks he will sail into the Treasury and make his fortune. Perhaps it is as well I will never have brats. I should not like folk to see *me* as a doting fool, fawning blindly over some useless young wastrel.'

King's Hall was ready to repel an invasion. Its gates were barred, its walls were patrolled by archers, and a stone smacked into the ground when Michael and Bartholomew approached, as a warning that they should come no closer. The monk stopped dead in his tracks and scowled upwards, outraged that anyone should dare try to prevent the Senior Proctor from going about his lawful business. Alarmed, the culprit dipped out of sight.

'No, I will *not* withdraw my complaint against Frenge's estate,' snarled Wayt, when they had been admitted to his solar by a porter who wore full battle armour and carried a bow. 'We suffered shamefully at his hands, so why should we not sue for compensation?'

'Because it is damaging the fragile relations between the University and the town,' Michael snapped back, watching intently as he tried to assess whether he was speaking to a killer.

'I care nothing for the town's paltry efforts to make

war,' spat Wayt. 'And Frenge's prank destroyed Cew's mind, so we owe it to him to persist.'

'Frenge is dead,' said Michael sharply. 'Is that not punishment enough?'

'Not as far as we are concerned. And speaking of Frenge, I do not believe that Nigellus dispatched him. The culprit is far more likely to be Shirwynk, in the expectation that we would drop our case against him. Which is another reason why we will not do it.'

'Let us consider Frenge's last movements again,' said Michael, struggling for patience. 'He claimed he was bringing ale here, to King's Hall. Your porters say such a delivery was never made, but you were seen arguing with him shortly before he died – about Anne Rumburgh allegedly, with whom you both had relations.'

'How many more times must I repeat myself? First, if Frenge claimed he was supplying us with ale, he was lying: we have never done business with his brewery and we never will. And second, yes, he threatened to tell my colleagues about Anne, but his attempt to blackmail me failed: they already know, because most of them have had her themselves.'

'Was it your colleagues he threatened to tell?' probed Michael. 'Or the wronged husband?'

Wayt smiled without humour. 'He could hardly take that sort of tale to Rumburgh when he was enjoying Anne's favours himself!'

'But *he* did not stand to lose princely benefactions from an indignant donor,' Michael pointed out. 'I would say the power lay with him in this disagreement, and that you had very good reason to want him silenced.'

Wayt's face turned pale with anger. 'How dare you! *We* are the victims here. It was our pigs and geese who were set running amok in his foolish japes, and our colleague who was frightened out of his wits.'

Michael folded his arms thoughtfully. 'Are you sure

there is not another dark secret in King's Hall? One Frenge discovered when he came raiding?'

Alarm flared in Wayt's eyes: Michael had hit a nerve. He began to lash out defensively. 'You have no idea what you are talking about. Now come with me, both of you. At once!'

'Go with you where?' asked Michael, not moving.

'To see Frenge's victim. Then you will see who is in the right and who is in the wrong.'

He stalked out, so Bartholomew and Michael followed him along a corridor to where curious hooting sounds could be heard. It seemed the King of France had been replaced by an ape.

Bartholomew was shocked by the decline in Cew. The logician was no longer able to walk, as he had lost control of his left foot, which dragged whenever he tried to raise it. He loped about on all fours instead, making animal-like grunts while Dodenho tried in vain to persuade him back to bed.

When the Michaelhouse men approached, Cew bared his teeth, and Bartholomew saw a thin grey line around the top of them. It was identical to the one he had seen in the student the previous day, and similar to the problem suffered by Rumburgh. But there was no time to ponder its significance, because Cew began to gibber in a manner that made Dodenho back away in alarm.

'Garlic and onions. Put them in my soul-cakes. List the syllogisms – Barbara, Celarent, Darii, Ferio. Dodenho does not know them. Garlic in the oysters, onion in the pastries.'

'You see?' snapped Wayt, although there was more sorrow than anger in his voice. 'Now tell us why we should care about the man who did this to him.'

'He will not eat oysters now.' Dodenho sounded sad and frustrated in equal measure. 'Just soul-cakes. God knows why – they are far too sickly for me.'

'You sweeten them with sucura,' said Bartholomew, recalling what Dodenho had let slip the last time they had met.

'Not any more,' averred Wayt. 'We use honey instead.'

'Honey is not a syllogism,' babbled Cew. 'Baroco, Bocardo. Nasty, sticky stuff to dissolve my orb and sceptre. I hate honey, so give me onions. Onions and garlic.'

'He keeps asking for those,' said Dodenho worriedly. 'But he cannot mean it.'

Bartholomew was about to agree when he remembered Rougham quoting Galen the night before, about the body knowing what it needed. Nigellus had mentioned it, too, at a meeting of the *consilium*, when he and Bartholomew had argued about the importance of a balanced diet. But before he could suggest that they give Cew what he wanted, Wayt tried to propel him and Michael towards the door. Outraged that anyone should dare lay hands on the august person of the Senior Proctor, Michael resisted with a snarl, so Wayt ordered Dodenho to see the Michaelhouse men off the premises, loath to risk his dignity in a shoving contest he would not win.

'He means no harm,' said Dodenho apologetically, once they were in the yard. 'Although I shall be glad when Master Shropham comes home. Can you help Cew, Bartholomew? Or did Wayt not allow you sufficient time to judge?'

Suspecting Dodenho might baulk if anything as vulgar as onions and garlic was recommended for the patient, Bartholomew mumbled something about a remedy he kept at home.

'I will prepare it now and bring it as soon as it is ready,' he promised.

Leaving Michael to visit Stephen alone, Bartholomew hurried back to College, where he solicited Agatha's help. Together, they produced a stew that contained plenty of onions and garlic, along with barley and sundry other vegetables. When they were soft, he mashed them to a paste, which he coloured with saffron left over from Hallow-tide, aiming to disguise the mundane ingredients with an exotic splash of colour. Then he added boiled water to turn the concoction into a smooth soup. Agatha grinned when he asked her to keep the recipe secret, delighted to indulge in a conspiracy with a Fellow.

He returned to King's Hall, where Dodenho was waiting anxiously. He was whisked quickly to Cew before Wayt could see him, and was pleased when the patient gulped down a whole bowl.

'What is it?' asked Dodenho curiously, as Cew indicated that he wanted more.

'Royal Broth,' lied Bartholomew, smiling encouragingly at Cew. 'It is full of expensive ingredients that only monarchs can afford.'

The logician wolfed down a second helping, after which he curled up and went to sleep.

'We shall have some of this Royal Broth for our ailing students as well,' declared Dodenho, watching in relief. 'Nigellus calculated their horoscopes, but we are not sure we can trust those now that he stands charged with murder.'

'What else did Nigellus do?' probed Bartholomew. 'What medicines did he prescribe?'

'No medicines,' replied Dodenho. 'Only advice – mostly about foods that should be avoided when the moon and stars are in certain positions. It was all very complicated, and I am not surprised our lads made mistakes – it is not always easy to see where these celestial bodies are at specific times, and we cannot spend all night gazing at the sky.'

'He gave them nothing at all to swallow?'

'No – just a long list of instructions about the ascendancy of Venus and that kind of thing. When he first arrived in Cambridge, he confided in his cups that he planned not to accept any sick clients, and that he aimed to acquire a practice comprised solely of healthy ones.'

'Well, a lot of them are sick now,' remarked Bartholomew. 'And some have died.'

'He should have realised that no one stays hale and hearty for ever, and his was an impractical aspiration. He must be livid that the *debilitas* has come to haunt us, given that he is not very good at curing it. Unlike you with your magical Royal Broth. What did you say was in it?'

To ensure that Dodenho continued to feed it to Cew, Bartholomew took a leaf from Nigellus's book and became haughty. 'I am afraid I cannot share my professional secrets with laymen. Suffice to say that it contains a wide variety of costly and efficacious compounds.'

'Fair enough,' said Dodenho pleasantly, and handed him a shilling, a fee far in excess of what the physician had intended to charge. 'Is that enough, or do you require more?'

Bartholomew wanted to refuse it, feeling that to accept would be tantamount to theft. However, if he did, Dodenho would probably be suspicious, and he was loath to risk Cew's well-being over a few pennies. He took the coin with a sheepish nod of thanks.

Dodenho spirited him to the students' dormitory afterwards, both keeping a wary eye out for the bellicose Wayt. When he had examined his new patients, Bartholomew trailed back to Michaelhouse and handed the shilling to a delighted Agatha. She immediately set to work on a much larger pot of 'Royal Broth', promising to deliver it to King's Hall herself when it was ready.

Bartholomew met Michael in the yard. The monk was disconsolate that interviews with Shirwynk, Peyn and Hakeney had yielded nothing of value, while Stephen could not have been as ill as his maid had claimed, because he was still out.

'I discovered that Cew and Wauter were friends, though. Very *good* friends.'

'We already knew that,' said Bartholomew. 'He told us so himself.'

'No – he told us that he visited Cew to debate points of logic. It is not the same, and by all accounts he is deeply distressed by Cew's descent into madness. And now he has disappeared.'

Bartholomew frowned. 'I hope you are not suggesting that Frenge's attack on Cew sent Wauter on a spree of revenge that involves murder and the removal of the University to the Fens.'

'It does sound outlandish,' admitted Michael. 'But we have both encountered stranger motives in the past, and we should not discount this one until we are sure it is wrong. I suggest we visit Zachary now, to see what Wauter's old colleagues can tell us about him.'

They arrived to find the Zachary students sitting in their hall on benches, while Morys held his lecture notes upside down and Kellawe looked shifty. Bartholomew interpreted this as meaning that the pair had been giving incendiary speeches, but did not want the Senior Proctor to know.

'We will not talk to you until Nigellus is released,' stated Morys, to a chorus of defiant cheers. He was wearing hose with yellow and black stripes, a black gipon with an amber belt, and a hat stippled in the same colours. Bartholomew wondered why one of his friends did not do him the kindness of advising him to choose attire that did not scream 'unpopular stinging insect'.

'That would be foolish,' said Michael coldly. 'It will only prolong his incarceration.'

'If you are here to suggest we apologise for what Segeforde is *alleged* to have done to Anne, you have had a wasted journey,' said Morys. 'It was an accident, and we are not giving that money-grubbing harlot a penny.'

'She exposed herself deliberately,' declared Kellawe, all wild eyes and outthrust jaw. 'And poor Segeforde was so appalled by the sight that he fell into a fatal *debilitas*.'

One lad in the front row began to splutter, struggling to turn laughter into a cough when the Franciscan glared at him, while his cronies looked away or pretended to wipe their noses in an effort to conceal their own amusement. Clearly, the late Segeforde had been rather more worldly than Kellawe would have the Senior Proctor and his Corpse Examiner believe.

'Segeforde's demise puzzles me,' said Bartholomew, wishing he could reveal what his illicit dissection had told him – one of the Zachary men might have an explanation. 'He was well enough to protest outside the dyeworks and launch himself at Anne. But all of a sudden he is dead.'

'It was not "all of a sudden",' snapped Morys. 'He had been unwell with the *debilitas* all day, which you know perfectly well, because you physicked him.'

'Along with Yerland,' added Kellawe pointedly. 'Yet it is poor Nigellus who is locked away accused of malpractice. You are fortunate the Senior Proctor is your friend, because otherwise it would be *you* in that cell.'

'While I am here, you can tell me why you went to the King's Head last night,' said Michael, ignoring the accusation and glaring at the students, although Bartholomew took a step towards the door, fearing the situation might turn ugly. 'You should not have visited a notorious town stronghold.'

'We have the right to go wherever we please,' declared Morys. 'However, in the light of what happened, we have advised all University men to arm themselves. We have also recommended that they do not wear their academic tabards, on the grounds that it makes them too visible a target. I have already seen a number of lads following our advice.'

'Then the proctors' coffers will soon be overflowing,' said Michael. 'And speaking of fines, you owe three shillings for the fracas last night. If you do not pay by noon tomorrow, I shall send beadles to seize the equivalent amount in goods. I am sure you have plenty of books we can take.'

Morys was furious. 'You cannot! The Chancellor will not permit it.'

'You have already summoned his mother, so he has nothing to gain by opposing me now.' Michael smiled archly. 'You should have confined yourself to threats, because then he would have been yours to manipulate as long as you wanted. You made a tactical error, Morys.'

'How dare you—' began Morys, but Michael overrode him.

'Have any of you seen Wauter? He has disappeared, and while you may look the other way while your scholars wander where they please, we have rules at Michaelhouse. Unless Wauter returns immediately, he will lose his Fellowship.'

'We no longer consider him a friend,' said Kellawe sullenly. 'He made a serious mistake when he abandoned us for another foundation. As far as I am concerned, he is dead.'

'Figuratively speaking,' added Morys quickly, shooting his colleague a warning glance. 'We do not mean him physical harm, obviously.'

'Obviously,' agreed Michael flatly. 'But when he was still alive in your eyes, did you ever talk about the University moving to the Fens?'

The Zachary men exchanged glances that were impossible to interpret.

'No,' replied Kellawe shiftily. 'But we are not discussing him or anything else with you. Now go away or we will—'

He was interrupted by the sound of a door being thrust open, after which Cynric burst in.

'A number of scholars have marched against the dyeworks,' the book-bearer gasped. 'And Mistress Stanmore needs you to disperse them.'

CHAPTER 10

Bartholomew was out of Zachary before Cynric had finished speaking, deftly jigging away when the book-bearer tried to grab his arm to explain further. However, Cynric had dealt with far more awkward customers than agitated physicians, and Bartholomew had not gone far down Water Lane before he found himself jerked roughly to a standstill. He tried in vain to struggle free.

'Mistress Stanmore is safely inside with the door locked,' Cynric said briskly, 'as are her ladies and their guards. They are in no danger, but *you* will be if you race up to the protesters alone. Everyone knows she is your sister, and they will consider you a target. Now wait for Brother Michael and his men.'

Bartholomew wanted to argue, but the monk was puffing towards them anyway, a dozen beadles at his heels. Gripping the physician's sleeve to ensure he did not outrun them, Cynric fell in behind. They arrived to find thirty or so scholars in a howling throng in front of the dyeworks. All had demonstrated there before, but never at the same time.

Bartholomew felt the cold hand of fear grip him. Was it coincidence that they should all decide to come at once, or had someone whispered in suggestive ears?

'Here comes Zachary to swell their number,' muttered Michael. 'Damn it, Cynric! I wish you had taken us outside before announcing what was happening.'

It was not just scholars who were massing in the square. So were a number of townsmen, led by Hakeney, who brazenly sported Robert's cross around his neck. As it would be like a red flag to a bull if the demonstrating scholars saw it, Bartholomew went to suggest that he tuck it inside his tunic. Only when the townsmen surrounded him menacingly did it occur to him that it had been stupid to move away from the beadles.

'No, I will not hide it,' snarled Hakeney indignantly. 'I *want* everyone to know that I retrieved it from that thieving Robert.'

The townsmen closed in even tighter, and Bartholomew braced himself for a trouncing, but suddenly Cynric was among them, hand on the sword at his side.

'We were just talking,' said Hakeney quickly, evidently aware of the Welshman's military prowess. 'No harm has been done, eh, Bartholomew? But you had better go and defend Brother Michael – those scholars look ready to attack him.'

He was right: tempers were running high in the University faction. The situation was aggravated by Kellawe, who directed a stream of invective not only against the dyeworks, but also against some of his fellow protesters. Bartholomew wondered if the Franciscan would be quite so vociferous if someone took a swipe at his pugnacious jaw and broke it.

'We want those whores out!' he screeched. 'They are not welcome near Zachary. Put them by White Hostel instead – their members are not fussy about the company they keep.'

'Now just a moment,' objected the dim-witted but vocal priest named Gilby, who happened to be a member of that particular foundation. 'We are not—'

'Do not call us names,' bellowed Yolande from inside the besieged building. 'Especially as most of you have been our customers for years – from Zachary *and* from White.'

'We can prove it, too,' called another woman. 'We know all your little foibles. Go on, Brother. Ask us a question about any of this rabble, and we will tell you exactly what he likes to do behind closed doors. You will be entertained royally, I promise.'

'Lies,' cried Morys, although his flaming cheeks and uneasy eyes suggested otherwise.

'The *debilitas* is in Physwick Hostel now,' raged Kellawe, not about to be sidetracked. 'And these whores put it there. They are as base and corrupt as the filth they hurl in the river.'

Bartholomew's heart lurched as the dyeworks door opened and Edith strode out. She was not particularly tall, but she was like a giant when she was angry, and the power of her personality had been known to cow even Dickon. Everyone fell silent as her eyes raked across them.

'My workers are good women,' she said frostily, once the protesters had gone so quiet that a pin could have been heard dropping, 'who are doing their best for their families. Now, I suggest we dispense with this unseemly hollering and resolve our differences with proper decorum. I shall listen to your complaints, and you will listen to my replies.'

'Listen to you?' spluttered Kellawe. 'I do not think so! Decent men are dying all over the University, thanks to you and your trollops.'

Morys and a few Zachary men cheered, but support from the other foundations was suddenly half-hearted – Edith's quiet dignity had unnerved them. She waited for the clamour to die away before speaking again.

'First, they are not trollops, they are women who have fallen on hard times. We have rectified the matter, and they are now gainfully employed. And second, we accept your objection about the river. In future, we shall ensure that *all* our waste is transported to the Fens.'

'To the Fens?' cried Morys. 'But that is where we plan to move our University.'

'Then you cannot complain about us poisoning the

town,' called Yolande provocatively. 'Not if you do not intend to live here.'

Edith shot her a warning scowl, then turned back to the scholars. 'It is a large area, Principal Morys. You cannot occupy it all.'

'But even if you do cart your rubbish away, there will still be a smell.' Kellawe appealed to his students. 'Will we listen to her? She is a strumpet, just like her women!'

Bartholomew took a furious step forward, but Cynric was there to stop him from taking another. Unfortunately, the movement had attracted attention.

'There is her brother,' shrieked Kellawe, stabbing a vengeful finger. 'A member of the University, but not really one of us because of his ties to her. We should eject him, because we do not want scholars who are tainted with links to the town. All townsfolk are scum, after all.'

There was an indignant roar from Hakeney and his followers, whose numbers had increased as the argument had unfolded. They now outnumbered the scholars by a considerable margin.

'There is no point discussing this further now,' said Morys, alarmed by the fury his colleague's words had elicited, and so beginning to ease towards the safety of his hostel. 'We are wasting our time. However, we shall return later to—'

'No, you will not,' stated Michael firmly. 'I have had enough of this nonsense. Anyone who is still here by the time I count to five will be fined sixpence. One. Two—'

'Ours is a legitimate protest, and we shall do it where we please,' screeched Kellawe. 'Is that not so, Morys? Morys? *Morys!*'

An expression of alarm filled his face when he saw his supporters had disappeared. There was a cheer from the townsfolk when he turned and fled, although it petered out when Michael whipped around to glare at them.

'You cannot fine *me* sixpence,' said Hakeney challeng-ingly. 'I do not have any money.'

'Then you can join Nigellus in my gaol,' retorted Michael. 'And that goes for you, too, Isnard. I see you hiding behind Vine. You should know better than to take sides against the University – you, a member of the Michaelhouse Choir.'

The bargeman was not the only singer in the horde, and afraid their free bread and ale might be at risk, many slunk away, heads down against recognition. The remainder hesitated uncertainly, but it took only one more imperious glare from Michael to send them on their way, too. Soon, only he, Bartholomew and the beadles were left.

'Thank you, Brother,' said Edith. 'And now, if you will excuse us, we have work to do.'

'We had better visit the Austins next,' said Michael, glancing up at the sky as he and Bartholomew left Water Lane. The light was beginning to fade, and it would be dark soon. 'Robert offered to ask the other friars if they know where Wauter might have gone, and we are in desperate need of answers – I sense time fast running out for us.'

They began to hurry towards the friary, using lanes rather than the main streets, to reduce the possibility of running into trouble. Michael's beadles and Tulyet's soldiers were everywhere, faces strained as they struggled to prevent skirmishes from breaking out. It was time for vespers, which meant scholar-priests were obliged to go to church. They assembled in large groups to walk there, and Bartholomew despaired when he saw how many were armed. He had no doubt that word was out that Kellawe would absolve anyone obliged to use weapons, and was glad that Cynric had agreed not to leave Edith's side until the crisis was over.

'There will be trouble before the night is out,' predicted Michael. 'I can sense it building. It is an unpleasant feeling, being pulled this way and that like a puppet – one no Senior Proctor should experience. Yet I do not know how to stop it.'

'Yes, we *are* puppets,' agreed Bartholomew soberly. 'Because I think you are right to see a connection between the murders, the lawsuits and the aggravation at the dyeworks – everything *is* designed to exacerbate the tension between University and town. Whoever is behind it is very clever – more than us, I fear.'

'Not more than me,' declared Michael indignantly. He took a deep breath, and Bartholomew saw his resolve strengthen. 'I am the Senior Proctor, and no one – whether it is Wauter or anyone else – is going to harm my University.'

Filled with new determination, he strode the rest of the way to the convent, this time not bothering to slink along alleys. He walked openly and confidently, and those whose hearts quickened at the prospect of catching him while he was virtually alone and unprotected quickly melted away when they read what was in his face.

The priory was locked when he and Bartholomew arrived, and it was some time before his knock was answered. Then the door swung open to reveal the friars standing in an uncertain semicircle beyond, wielding an eclectic array of 'weapons'. Most were wildly impractical, and included a ladle, a trumpet and part of a spinning wheel. Hamo, whose bulk might have been a deterrent in itself, was not among them.

'We do not feel safe here any longer,' said Joliet, who gripped a chair leg in his good hand; the other was still cradled in the orange sling. 'Folk are angry that a townsman was murdered in our grounds, and we have been discussing an escape to the Fens – while we still can.'

'There is no need,' said Michael briskly. 'The tension will ease. It always does.'

'Until the next time,' said Robert bitterly. He alone of the friars was not brandishing something with which to hit someone. 'When it will start all over again. We are tired of it, Brother. We have done our best with alms and charity, even when it has meant personal hardship, yet still the town turns against us.'

'Because you are suing Hakeney,' said Michael curtly. 'A poor man who will never be able to pay whatever the courts decide.'

'I would withdraw the suit,' said Joliet. 'But the other Orders say that if I do, everyone will think that priests are fair game for robbers. They threatened to denounce us if we weakened.'

'So?' shrugged Michael. 'You are an independent house. You do not need their blessing.'

'But we *do*, Brother,' whispered Joliet. 'We would be sacked for certain if word leaked out that the other convents will not come to our aid in the event of trouble.'

'And besides,' added Robert, 'Hakeney ripped the cross from my neck with considerable force. It would be cowardly to pretend it did not happen. Yet there might be a way . . .'

'Yes?' asked Michael sharply.

'We could put the matter in the Bishop's hands and let *him* decide the outcome. He is neither scholar nor townsman, and thus the perfect arbiter.'

'What an excellent notion!' cried Joliet. 'I shall write first thing in the morning, with your permission, Brother.'

'Granted,' said Michael in relief, a sentiment that was echoed in the faces of all the Austins. 'I shall tell Stephen to forget your case until we have the Bishop's reply. It was criminally reckless of him to recommend this course of action.'

'It was not just Stephen,' said Robert. 'There was also a letter . . .'

'A letter?'

'From someone who just signed himself as a well-wisher,' explained the almoner. 'Hamo found it shoved under our front gate.'

'Prior Etone of the Carmelites had one as well,' added Joliet. 'It urged him to convince us to sue.' He glanced at Robert. 'Personally, I suspect both were from Stephen, touting for business, although he denies it, of course.'

'Do you still have this missive?' asked Michael urgently.

Joliet shook his head. 'Parchment is expensive, so we scraped it clean and used it for something else. Why? Is it important?'

'Possibly,' sighed Michael. 'But the reason we came was to ask after Wauter. Robert offered to find out if any of you know where he might have gone.'

'Robert did question us,' said a portly, balding Austin named Overe. 'But all we could tell him is that Wauter likes the Fens. Perhaps he went there in search of serenity – something that is sadly lacking in Cambridge at the moment.'

'Without telling anyone?' asked Michael dubiously. 'That does not sound very likely.'

'Then maybe he went to find a good place for the University to settle,' suggested Robert. 'He would not be the first. The Dominicans have sent out a party, and the Carmelites plan to do likewise.'

'They are wise,' said Joliet softly. 'I sense that the town will soon make our position untenable, and we should have some idea of where to go when they drive us out.'

'No one will drive us out,' said Michael firmly, but his words carried little weight when they were followed by a sudden clash of arms from the High Street. The friars exchanged grim looks.

'You look harried, Brother,' said Joliet kindly, 'and in

263

need of the peace that only communion with God can bring. Will you join us for vespers? Hamo is already preparing the chapel, so we can start straight away.'

'Thank you,' said Michael, and began to walk there, although Bartholomew knew it was more for the opportunity to quiz Hamo about the anonymous letter than to pray.

Night was approaching fast, and the precinct was full of shadows. All the brothers were uneasy, and each time there was a yell or a clatter from outside, they jumped in alarm. Several stopped in the little cemetery that held Arnold, though, declining to let their nervousness interfere with their obligations to a colleague's soul.

'Do you really think Nigellus killed him?' asked Joliet softly. 'He was old and in poor health, and I cannot imagine why anyone would want to dispatch a man with so little time left.'

'The ways of felonious minds are not for us to fathom,' replied Michael, as a roundabout way of saying that he had no answer.

They entered the chapel, the Austins carefully stacking their 'weapons' in the porch first. It was very dark inside, the only light coming from a candle burning on the altar. Suddenly, a huge shadow loomed, causing Robert to squawk in shock and the others to scatter in alarm.

'Hamo!' exclaimed Joliet, hand to his chest. 'You frightened the life out of us! Why have you not set the altar? What have you been doing all this time?'

Hamo made no reply, and simply stood with his huge hands dangling at his sides.

'Hamo,' said Robert sharply. 'The Prior asked you a question.'

'There is something wrong!' Bartholomew darted forward, and just managed to catch the hulking friar before he fell. He staggered under the weight. 'Bring a lamp, quickly!'

The feeble glow from the lantern that was produced showed Hamo's face to be unnaturally pale. It also revealed a spreading stain on the floor. Hamo had been stabbed.

'Save him!' cried Joliet, while the other Austins clamoured their horror and disbelief. 'You must save him!'

But the wound, although small, had sliced deeply into Hamo's lung, and Bartholomew could hear that it had already filled with blood. There was nothing he or anyone else could do, and he read in Hamo's eyes that he knew it.

'He needs last rites,' he said to Joliet, hating to see the Austins' instant dismay.

Hamo took a handful of Bartholomew's tunic and tugged, indicating that he wanted to speak. Bartholomew put his ear close to the dying man's mouth, but what emerged was so low as to be virtually inaudible. When he sat back, the others clamoured to know what had been said.

'I am not sure,' replied Bartholomew. 'It sounded like "all".'

'All what?' demanded Michael.

'Perhaps he was beginning a prayer,' suggested Robert, white-faced with shock. 'Almighty God, have mercy upon me . . .'

'Or he wanted to say *aliteum*,' added Overe. 'Meaning a crime – because one has certainly been committed here.'

'Fetch some water,' ordered Joliet urgently. 'It may unlock his throat. Hurry!'

'Who did this to you, Hamo?' asked Michael, ignoring the panicky confusion that ensued as the friars blundered around in a frantic attempt to locate a cup. 'Did you see?'

He crouched next to Bartholomew, but this time the whispered word was even softer.

'Where is the water?' cried Joliet, his voice cracking with desperation. 'Overe!'

Hamo fixed Bartholomew with a bright-eyed stare, and the physician was sure he was trying to convey a message. The dying man held his gaze a moment longer, before giving a brief, conspiratorial nod. Then he closed his eyes and breathed his last.

Joliet began to intone a final absolution in a voice that was unsteady with shock, and one by one, his priests joined in. Some looked around fearfully as they did so, afraid the killer might still lurk, ready to claim another victim.

'There is no one else here,' said Michael, the only one who had thought to check. 'The culprit must have committed his vile deed and fled.'

Resolve filled Joliet's round face. 'Our prayers for Hamo's soul can wait – God will understand. Search the grounds. We cannot let this villain escape. He may kill again!'

Bartholomew went to help, leaving Michael to question those friars who were too old or infirm to join in the hunt. The obvious place to start as far as the physician was concerned was the back gate – Overe assured him that the front one had been locked and guarded all day – so he grabbed a pitch torch and hurried there at once, Robert at his heels. It was ajar when they arrived. Robert tugged it open and pointed at the priory's boat.

'We got a better mooring rope after Frenge died,' he said, and Bartholomew noted that the little craft was now secured to the pier with a serious tangle of knots. 'The killer cannot have used our boat to cross the ditch this time, so he must have swum across.'

'Not unless he is a lunatic,' said Bartholomew eyeing the still, black, stinking waters in revulsion. 'However, I noticed that the gate was open – I thought you were going to keep it locked after what happened to Frenge.'

'We meant to mend it,' said Robert sheepishly, 'but then other concerns assailed us, and I am afraid and we made the foolish assumption that lightning would not strike twice . . .'

'So this is definitely how the culprit came in, then,' said Bartholomew, sure such an unforgiveable oversight would not have happened at Michaelhouse. 'He must have taken a boat from somewhere else. It would not be difficult – there are dozens of them further downstream.'

'I suppose so,' said Robert miserably. 'Poor Hamo. How could such a terrible thing happen?'

Easily, thought Bartholomew, when his brethren were so cavalier about security.

News of Hamo's stabbing spread like wildfire, and the town was soon abuzz with rumours. Bartholomew volunteered to help keep the peace, but first a gaggle of lawyers from Gonville Hall howled insults at him for being kin to the woman who hired whores, then a band of townsmen accused him of encouraging Edith to poison people in order to drum up trade for himself.

'You are more liability than help, Matt,' said Michael. 'But your offer is appreciated, as are the ones from Michaelhouse and the Austins. No one else has bothered, presumably because they would rather be fighting.'

'Or because they are too frightened to venture out,' suggested Bartholomew.

Michael snorted his disbelief at that notion. 'But I am worried about Wauter. *Has* he gone to find a nice spot for the University in the Fens? Or is there another, darker reason for his absence?'

Bartholomew stared at him. 'You think that *he* might have killed Hamo?'

'Well, he is an Austin, who knows his way around their priory.'

'No,' said Bartholomew, shaking his head. 'I cannot

believe that of him. The killer is more likely to be Hakeney, who has a grudge against the Order.'

'Against Robert,' corrected Michael.

'He is a drunk and the chapel is poorly lit. Perhaps it is a case of mistaken identity.'

'I doubt that even the most pickled of minds could confuse Hamo with Robert, even in the dark.' Michael turned when his favourite beadle approached. 'Well, Meadowman? Will there be a battle between us and the townsfolk tonight?'

'No, thank God,' replied the beadle tiredly. 'But there may be one tomorrow, when the troublemakers use Hamo's murder to whip up more bad feeling. We are going to be busy if we want to avert a crisis, Brother.'

Bartholomew walked back to College, grateful when Meadowman offered to escort him. The beadle's burly presence saved him both from a spat with Zachary and from trouble with Shirwynk's apprentices. It was the role Cynric usually fulfilled, but Bartholomew was glad he had detailed the book-bearer to stand guard over Edith instead.

As it was late, his students were already in bed, but Bartholomew was too unsettled to sleep. He sat in the hall, reading works by Aretaeus of Cappadocia, aiming to learn whether Nigellus had misquoted him. A little after midnight, Michael came to report that the town was quiet – partly because it had started to rain, but mostly because Tulyet had given Dickon charge of a patrol.

'Which did more to send would-be rioters home than all my beadles and the drizzle put together,' said the monk. 'The boy is a hellion. What are you reading?'

Bartholomew told him. 'I have found nowhere yet that recommends quaffing urine to assess it for sweetness.'

'And nor will you, I warrant,' said Michael. 'But do not stay up too late. We shall have another busy day tomorrow if we are to catch a killer and avert a war.'

Bartholomew was soon absorbed in the book again and time ticked by. He closed his eyes when oily fumes and the flickering light from the lamp gave him a headache, aiming to rest them briefly, so was surprised when someone shook him awake several hours later.

'You are not supposed to sleep in here,' said Deynman accusingly. 'It is a library. What will benefactors think? We shall be banished to the Fens for certain.'

Bartholomew sat up, hand to his stiff neck. 'Is it time for church?'

'Not yet, but I was restless, so I thought I would come here to think. It is a good place during the hours of darkness, when there is no one clamouring at me to borrow my treasures. Sometimes, I wish you would all go away and let me do my work in peace.'

'But we *are* your work,' Bartholomew pointed out. 'You are supposed to lend us books.'

'Not the way I see it,' retorted Deynman archly. 'And there is a nasty tendency in this University to take me for granted – to use me for menial tasks. Well, I am not a messenger-boy – I am a *librarian*.' He spoke the word grandly, still delighted by the way it sounded.

Bartholomew regarded him in alarm. 'Please do not say a patient asked you to tell me something and you refused. Or forgot.'

'Not a patient. I would make an exception for those. It was Irby from Zachary – before he died, obviously. He shoved a note in my hand and ordered me to give it to you. I told him I was Michaelhouse's *inlitteratus*, and thus above running errands, but he only laughed.'

Bartholomew regarded him wonderingly. '*Inlitteratus?*'

'It is Latin for librarian,' explained Deynman. 'Thelnetham told me so.'

'It means illiterate,' said Bartholomew, wondering how Deynman's grasp of the language could remain so dismal when he spent his whole life among books written in it.

'Thelnetham was being unkind, and Irby must have thought you were making a joke.'

Deynman's face crumpled in dismay. 'You mean I have been going around telling all and sundry that I am unlettered? No wonder people have looked at me so oddly! How could he?'

'How indeed?' murmured Bartholomew. 'Do you still have Irby's letter?'

Deynman went to rummage in a pile of parchments, his expression sullen. 'Thelnetham will not get away with this,' he vowed. 'I shall send him an anonymous gift of that apple wine he likes so much – in the hope that it will make him sick again.'

'Apple wine? You mean the stuff Shirwynk makes?'

'Thelnetham is a glutton for it, and is sure to drink it all without sharing with his brethren. He told me that the last barrel he purchased brought on a bout of the *debilitas* – it turned him silly and he had to spend a whole week in bed.'

'Then why would he drink a second one?' asked Bartholomew, thinking the Librarian's plans for sly revenge needed some serious revision.

'Because he is a pig and will be unable to resist it,' replied Deynman. 'And I hope my gift makes him ill for a lot longer than a week. Hah! Here is Irby's note.'

Bartholomew groaned when he read what was written. '*Similia similibus curantur.*'

'Currants are similar to each other,' translated Deynman liberally. 'But why—'

'No! It means like things are cured by like things.' Bartholomew waved the letter at him. 'And here he explains that it is his suggestion for the *disceptatio*. He and I were on the committee appointed to choose the topic, but he was ill for the final meeting. Morys took his place.'

'And promptly picked a boring discussion about giving

270

away property that one doesn't own,' recalled Deynman. He nodded to the letter. 'Irby's idea would have been much more entertaining.'

'When did he give you this message?'

Deynman thought carefully. 'Saturday – the day before his death. Why?'

'Because when he received no reply, he started to write another – the one I found under a jug in his room. It is not a clue revealing the identity of the man who took his life: it is a piece of routine correspondence.'

Deynman regarded him uneasily. 'Are you saying it was important?'

Bartholomew nodded unhappily. 'We wasted valuable time trying to work out its significance. And worse yet, Michael arrested Nigellus on the strength of it.'

Deynman's expression was scornful. 'I am surprised he has lasted so long as Senior Proctor, because everyone knows that Nigellus never *cures* anything. He calculates horoscopes that prevent people from becoming ill, but once they have a disease, he does nothing at all.'

'How do you know?' asked Bartholomew absently, his mind on Nigellus's probable reaction when told his arrest had been a mistake. It would not be pleasant.

'Because my brother got the *debilitas,* and Nigellus told him to abstain from food and drink for a day, but refused to prescribe a remedy. He also declined to give anything to Trinity Hall when they got the *debilitas* – twice – and the Gilbertine Priory.'

Bartholomew scrubbed hard at his face, wishing Deynman had acted like a responsible, rational being, and passed the letter on. He left the hall, and when he saw a lamp burning in Michael's room, he climbed the stairs to tell him what had happened. The monk was horrified.

'But that was our best piece of evidence against Nigellus!'

271

'I did tell you it was unsafe,' said Bartholomew tiredly. 'You will have to let him go.'

'Let him go?' cried Michael, loudly enough to wake the novices who shared his room. They sat up, rubbing sleep from their eyes. 'Even if he did not dispatch Irby, his incompetence still made an end of Letia, Lenne, Arnold and God knows how many others.'

'Did it? I am no longer sure about that. The Prior of Barnwell told me that Nigellus recommended all manner of tonics, infusions, electuaries and decoctions to help the canons who were ill, but nothing worked. Then Nigellus came here, where his "cures" entail eating garlic, wearing certain clothes or standing in the moonlight.'

'Meaning what?' asked Michael impatiently. 'Do not speak in riddles, Matt.'

'Meaning that I think the Barnwell losses shook his confidence, so when he came here, he elected not to prescribe anything. His diagnoses are outlandish, and he almost certainly has never read Aretaeus of Cappadocia, but I have not encountered a single person who has said that Nigellus has given him medicine.'

'You are right, sir,' put in one of the students. 'I have friends in Ovyng Hostel, and all he did when they had the *debilitas* was tell them to avoid being looked at by rabbits.'

'Prior Norton probably contributed to Nigellus's self-doubt,' continued Bartholomew. 'He confessed that he said some cruel things when his people failed to recover.'

Michael stared at him. 'But Nigellus will sue me if I release him, and we cannot afford yet another source of discord. I will have to keep him until the current trouble is over.'

'That might be some time,' said the student. 'Because the disturbances will not stop until the University has moved to the Fens – and that will not be organised overnight.'

'We are not going,' said Michael firmly.

'That is not what the town thinks,' said the student, 'while half our scholars would go tomorrow if they could. Regardless, the trouble will not subside very quickly, if at all.'

Dawn was touching the eastern sky when Bartholomew and Michael left the College, but the streets were mercifully empty, and when they met Meadowman, the beadle reported that it had been a quiet night. The gaol was full, though, of those who had made a nuisance of themselves before the rain and Dickon had driven people home. All would be released later that morning on payment of a fine – or languish until their friends managed to raise the requisite amount.

As the prison was filled to capacity, Nigellus no longer had the luxury of a room to himself, but he had made the most of the situation, and when Bartholomew and Michael arrived he was delivering an acid-tongued sermon to his cellmates. It comprised a poisonous diatribe against everyone who annoyed him: the dyeworks; the folk at Barnwell, whom he claimed had spread lies about him; and *medici* jealous of his superior abilities.

'Here comes the Devil Incarnate,' he sneered when he saw Michael. His hateful gaze shifted to Bartholomew. 'And his helpmeet. You will both go to Hell for what you have done to me, and I shall sue the University for every penny it has.'

'Good,' said a lad from Bene't College. 'Because I do not want to move to the Fens, and if you deprive the University of funds, its officers will not have the money to bring it about.'

'I would not mind going,' countered a Carmelite novice. 'There are no Frail Sisters in the Fens, and I shall not find myself tempted by their invitations. I never think about them when they are not around, but when they appear in front of me . . .'

'Stand up, Nigellus,' instructed Michael. 'I am letting you go.'

There was a resounding cheer and Nigellus smirked. It was an unpleasant expression, designed to annoy, and Bartholomew found himself wishing his colleague *had* been guilty.

'I shall see Stephen the lawyer this morning,' Nigellus declared. 'My reputation has been severely damaged, and for that you must pay.'

'On the contrary,' said the Carmelite. 'Your reputation is enhanced – you are a martyr for the cause and we all admire you. You will certainly find your practice swollen with new patients now.'

Nigellus shot him a foul look. 'I do not want new patients. I want compensation.'

He stalked through the door, and made a show of brushing himself off once he was in the street, declaring in a ringing voice that the University had never had any real evidence against him. He had been arrested, he informed passers-by, purely to conceal the fact that Edith was poisoning the town with her dyeworks, aided and abetted by her brother.

'Edith has harmed no one,' said Bartholomew, trying to sound as though he believed it.

'You would say that,' jeered Nigellus. 'Michaelhouse has become fabulously rich of late – mostly because she is giving you half her profits.'

Bartholomew doubted even that would be enough to save the College from fiscal ruin. 'No,' he began. 'She would never—'

But Nigellus was already stalking away.

It was Suttone's turn to officiate at Mass, and as he was inclined to be wordy, it went on longer than usual. The scholars arrived home to see smoke billowing from the kitchen, and the breakfast pottage was full of crunchy black bits. Agatha had attempted to disguise the damage with an additional dose of salt and a generous sprinkling of parsley.

'Perhaps we *should* go to the Fens,' said Michael, poking at the mess without enthusiasm. 'Living off the land cannot be worse than this. I am glad no benefactor is here to see what we really eat, or he might be forgiven for thinking we will not last the term.'

'We won't,' said Langelee in a low, strained voice. 'Our creditors are demanding payment, and our coffers are empty. Word will soon spread that we cannot pay our debts, and that will be the end of us. If we had secured even one donation, we might have weathered the storm, but we have won nothing.'

'It is your fault,' said William sullenly to Michael. 'The University has never been so unpopular, and as Senior Proctor, you should have taken steps to maintain good relations.'

'The town does hate us,' agreed Suttone unhappily. 'Our College is usually exempt from animosity, because Matt tends the poor and Michael feeds the choir. But those vile dyeworks are owned by Matt's sister, while Michael keeps arresting people for breaching the peace.'

'At least we have a nice mural to look at in our final days as Fellows,' said Clippesby, who was holding a pot on his lap, in which swam several fish. 'Aristotle, Plato, Galen and Aquinas, all teaching eager students.'

'It *is* a nice mural,' said Suttone sadly. 'And I *like* that oak tree – it reminds me of the one I used to scale when I was a boy.'

'I wish we had commissioned a tapestry instead,' said Langelee, after a brief silence during which they all tried to imagine the portly Suttone ever being lithe enough to climb anything. 'We could have sold a tapestry, but we cannot sell a wall.'

'The mural was Wauter's idea,' said William bitterly. 'Perhaps he realises it was sheer folly, and that is why he has disappeared.'

'I searched his room,' said Langelee. 'His *Martilogium* has gone, which makes me suspect that he plans to be away for some time – perhaps even permanently.'

When the meal was over, even the abstemious Bartholomew felt the need for something else to eat, so he went to see what Michael had in his private pantry. He tended not to buy spare food – called *commons* – himself because he either forgot it was there or his students got to it first. He was impressed when Michael produced smoked ham, an excellent cheese, several boiled eggs and half a loaf of bread. Obligingly, his students went to the hall to study, leaving the two Fellows alone to discuss their investigation. Michael began.

'Our culprit – I shall call him the *strategist*, on account of the cunning way he manipulates us all – knows exactly how to stir up trouble between University and town, both with real events and with rumours.'

Bartholomew agreed. 'Our so-called removal to the Fens; what or who is causing the *debilitas*; the murder of Frenge. All have aggravated the situation, especially when combined with the ill-feeling about the various lawsuits and the dyeworks.'

'I visited every convent in Cambridge last night, and all had received an anonymous letter urging them to persuade the Austins to sue Hakeney.'

'Then our culprit is Stephen,' said Bartholomew promptly. 'He is the one who will profit from all this legal activity.'

'I managed to catch him in a tavern last night, and he says *he* had a missive as well. I am inclined to believe him. However, even the Senior Proctor is fallible, so he had better remain on our list of suspects for now.'

Bartholomew was thoughtful. 'These messages *prove*

276

the strategist exists – that someone *is* prepared to do whatever it takes to achieve his ends.'

'Even kill,' said Michael sombrely.

'I do not suppose Stephen or the priors showed you these letters, did they? In other words, could you match the writing to any of our suspects?'

'None of the priors kept them, while Stephen was in the Cardinal's Cap, and so not in a position to oblige. However, Hamo saw the one that was sent to Joliet, so perhaps he was killed because he recognised the hand.' Michael regarded Bartholomew soberly. 'He would have recognised Wauter's – a fellow Austin.'

'I suppose he would,' acknowledged Bartholomew reluctantly.

'So let us consider what happened in the chapel last night. Hamo went to prepare it for vespers. He was alone, and while he was there, someone slipped in and stabbed him. He was no weakling, so his attacker either approached very stealthily or it was someone Hamo did not perceive as a threat. Such as a colleague.'

'But no one else saw Wauter in the convent last night.'

'Because the culprit entered via the broken back gate, as you yourself discovered. Of course, it could just be a townsman, aiming to win justice for Frenge. Did Hamo's body provide any clues?'

'All I can say is that he lived for some time after he was attacked. He lay a while by the altar, but managed to rise and lurch to the door. I could tell by the way the blood had splattered.'

Michael regarded him in distaste. 'What a ghoul you are!'

'Most people in his position would have called for help or staggered out to find some, but he stayed in the chapel.'

'He probably wanted to die in a holy place. He was a friar – these things are important.'

Bartholomew shook his head slowly. 'Perhaps, but

something is not right about the affair. He spoke one word – "all" – but what did it mean? He did not look as though he was praying to the Almighty.'

'Then perhaps Overe was right, and he started to say *aliteum* – a crime.'

'He would not have wasted his final breath stating the obvious,' said Bartholomew impatiently. 'And why did he not just tell us who stabbed him?'

'The chapel was dark and he was stabbed from behind. He may not have seen his attacker.'

But Bartholomew remained troubled. 'I cannot shake the conviction that he was trying to convey a message in that final word – one he mistakenly thought I understood. I have the sense that I have failed him.'

'Then let us return to the friary now. Perhaps he left a clue, and all will become clear in the full light of day.'

Bartholomew and Michael were about to leave Michaelhouse when the gate opened, and Joliet and Robert walked in. Both were pale, and Joliet's red eyes suggested he had been crying.

'You need not teach today,' said Langelee kindly. 'Not after the nasty shock you had last night. I know from experience what it is like to lose a colleague. Go home and pray for his soul.'

Joliet looked away. 'You are good, Master Langelee. However, we did not come to work, but to ask what Brother Michael plans to do about finding Hamo's killer.'

'All I can,' replied Michael simply. 'So perhaps we can walk to the friary now, to view the chapel in daylight.'

Joliet smiled wanly. 'I hoped you would, so we shut it up after we took Hamo to the charnel house. No one has been in it since.'

They walked to the High Street, where they were hailed by Gilby, the dim-witted priest from White Hostel. He was riding on a cart that was piled high with his belongings. He was grey-faced, and one hand was clasped to his stomach.

'I have the *debilitas*,' he whimpered. 'I do not want to die, so I have decided to leave Cambridge while I can. Three other scholars from White will follow me this afternoon, along with four from Trinity Hall and two from Peterhouse.'

'We shall be sorry to lose you,' lied Michael. 'Where will you go?'

'The Fens,' replied Gilby with a vague flap of his hand. 'We shall establish a new University where members can be free of poison – of the body *and* the mind. In time, this one will fade into oblivion, and we shall be regarded as the true *studium generale.*'

'Are you sure it is wise to travel while you are ill?' asked Bartholomew.

'Of course it is,' said Michael quickly, scowling at him. He turned back to the priest with a bright smile. 'Go and found your university, Gilby. I wish you every success.'

'I do not want to leave,' said Gilby, eyes narrowing when he saw the monk was glad to be rid of him. 'But your ineptitude as Senior Proctor leaves me no choice. And do not come crying to me when the town destroys you, because you will not be welcome.' He turned to the Austins. 'But you will.'

'Thank you,' said Joliet. He glanced nervously around him. 'If the town continues to descend into chaos, you might be seeing us sooner than you know.'

'How can *you* think of going?' asked Michael reproachfully. 'What about the paupers who rely on you – the ones you starved yourselves to feed last winter, and who you will help with the money you have earned by teaching and painting at Michaelhouse?'

Joliet looked away. 'I pity them, but I must consider the safety of my people. This week has proved beyond all doubt that the town loathes us, despite all our sacrifices.'

'And one of them killed Hamo,' added Robert. 'We cannot fight such deeply held hatred.'

'You are quite right,' agreed Gilby. 'So do not wait too long before joining us.'

He cracked the reins and the vehicle rumbled forward. Another followed, bearing two men from Gonville Hall, one of whom was the drunken Osborne. Both looked wan.

'Where they will sleep?' asked Bartholomew, watching the wagons clatter away. Joliet and Robert dropped behind to talk in low voices, obviously giving serious consideration to Gilby's invitation. 'All are used to comfort, and I doubt they will enjoy bedding down under a cart, especially if they are ill.'

'They will not sleep under a cart,' predicted Michael. 'I suspect they will aim for a specific location – one the strategist has already chosen. A settlement left empty after the plague, perhaps.'

'Then they will be disappointed. It has been a decade since those were abandoned, and few will be habitable now. However, I suspect the strategist wants our scholars to think as you have – that his new university has decent buildings free for the taking.'

'Then his foundation will not survive long – his cronies will not stay if they are forced to live like peasants. And they cannot come back to us, because I will not allow it. They will have tasted independence, so will be a divisive force. Yet we will not survive either if we are stripped of too many members, but how can we stop them from trickling away?'

'There is only one way: find the strategist.'

It was not an easy journey to the Austin friary. Townsmen hurled abuse at them, although none was quite brave enough to launch a physical attack on the princely bulk of the Senior Proctor, while students roamed in belligerent packs.

'We *should* follow Gilby,' gulped Robert. 'We will be safe in the marshes.'

'Safe, but not comfortable,' said Michael. 'Do not abandon your lovely convent just yet.'

'I am not comfortable here,' averred Joliet, waving a hand in front of his face as a particularly noxious waft blew from the dyeworks.

They reached the priory, where Bartholomew and Michael surveyed every inch of the chapel for clues, but found nothing useful. The blood that had been dripped and smeared on the floor confirmed what the physician had already surmised – that Hamo had been attacked near the altar, but had managed to stagger to the door where he had died.

'There is no suggestion that the culprit broke into the church,' said Bartholomew, inspecting the lock. 'He walked inside freely.'

'Of course he did,' said Robert bitterly. He and his brethren were standing in the porch, watching the search with troubled expressions. 'The door was open, because we were about to say vespers – and Hamo was in here, preparing the altar.'

'I have been wickedly remiss,' said Joliet, tears rolling down his round cheeks. 'I saw how easy it was to invade our holy grounds when Frenge died, but I never imagined the killer would strike again. I should have posted guards, or barricaded the gates. And Hamo paid the price for my complacency.'

'We will find the culprit,' promised Michael, as the friars hastened to comfort their leader. 'And we shall start by questioning Hakeney.'

CHAPTER 11

Hakeney was not at home or protesting at the dyeworks, and Bartholomew and Michael were not sure where else to look for him. As they pondered, Isnard the bargeman swung up on his crutches, and began to regale them with his opinion of the latest rumour that was surging around the town.

'Hakeney did *not* kill Hamo,' he declared. 'It is a vicious lie – one put about by the Austins, probably, so we will all support their legal case against him. Well, it will not work.'

'Who told you this tale?' demanded Michael irritably.

'Dozens of folk,' replied Isnard, and began to list them. 'Landlord Lister, Noll Verius, Thelnetham of the Gilbertines, Dickon Tulyet, Peyn and Shirwynk the brewers—'

'What makes you so sure that Hakeney is innocent?' interrupted Michael, seeing the recitation would continue for some time if he let it.

'Because he was with me in the King's Head when Hamo was stabbed,' replied Isnard. 'We were there all night, and he is still there now. I am his alibi, and you know you can trust me.'

'Right,' said Michael, aware that Isnard was not always conscious after visiting that particular tavern, and Hakeney could have wandered out, committed a dozen murders and returned to his tankard with the bargeman none the wiser.

A hurt expression suffused Isnard's face when he saw what Michael was thinking. 'I barely touched a drop all night, Brother. We kept clear heads for making plans, see.'

'What plans?' asked Michael in alarm.

'Me and some of the choir aim to stop the University from slinking off to the Fens,' replied the bargeman. 'Our musical evenings would not be the same without you, Brother, and we want you to stay.'

'I am glad someone does.'

'It might be dangerous to intervene,' warned Bartholomew, not liking to imagine what wild and reckless scheme the patrons of the King's Head might have hatched, regardless of whether they had stayed sober. 'Please do not—'

'We care nothing for danger,' declared Isnard grandly. 'Not when we are doing what we believe is right. Do not worry – we will not let the fanatics in the town drive you away.'

'I am more concerned about the fanatics in the University,' muttered Michael. 'But leave the matter to me, Isnard. I have no intention of leaving Cambridge.'

'But some of you have already gone,' Isnard pointed out worriedly. 'Wauter yesterday, Gilby and others this morning, with more set to follow tonight. It is the beginning of the end.'

'It is not,' said Michael firmly. 'I repeat: leave the matter to me. Now, you say Hakeney is in the King's Head still?'

'Yes, lying on the floor. Do you want a word with him? Then I had better accompany you, to make sure you come to no harm.'

The King's Head was a sprawling tavern on the edge of the town, famous for strong ale, vicious fights and rabid opinions. Scholars were not welcome, although Bartholomew and Michael were tolerated, one for physicking the poor and the other for running the choir. Even so, both were uneasy as they entered the dark, smelly room with its reek of spilled ale and rushes that needed changing. The clatter of conversation immediately died away.

'They are with me,' announced Isnard. 'Come to disprove these lies about Hakeney.'

'Good,' said the landlord, a burly brute with scars. 'Because he came here shortly after the squabble at the dyeworks and he has not left since. A dozen witnesses will tell you the same. Besides, can you really imagine a skinny wretch like him dispatching a great lump like Hamo?'

'You would be surprised,' said Michael. 'Not all murderers are . . .' He waved a vague hand, suddenly aware that if he attempted a description of the classic notion of a killer, any number of men in the room, including the landlord, might take it personally.

Bartholomew left the monk to verify Hakeney's alibi, while he followed Isnard to the back of the tavern, where the vintner was fast asleep on a straw pallet, one of several thoughtfully provided for those patrons who found themselves unable to walk home. Isnard woke him with a jab from a crutch, and Hakeney sat up blinking stupidly. He wore a knife on his belt, but it was too large to be the murder weapon.

'Why would I stab Hamo?' he asked, when Isnard explained what was being said about him. 'It is Robert who stole my cross.'

'Perhaps you aimed to deter the Austins from suing you,' suggested Bartholomew.

'Is that a possibility?' asked Hakeney eagerly, and the physician could see it was a notion that had not occurred to him before. The vintner was not the culprit.

'Why choose now to snatch the cross?' asked Bartholomew. Then a thought occurred to him. 'Or did someone encourage you to do it?'

'I did meet a man who told me I was a fool to let myself be so wronged,' confided Hakeney. 'He suggested the best way to get my property back was just to take it.'

'Who was he?' asked Bartholomew urgently.

Hakeney shrugged, and the red-rimmed eyes and sallow features suggested he would not be a reliable witness anyway. 'I never saw his face, and the tavern where he got me was one of the dark ones. He was a townsman, though. No scholar would have dispensed such sensible advice.'

'Give it back, Hakeney,' said Isnard disapprovingly. 'You told me last night that Robert's cross is different from your wife's. Do the decent thing and admit you made a mistake.'

'No, I shall keep it,' said Hakeney, taking it in his hand and staring down at it. 'It reminds me of Lilith, even if it *was* never hers in the first place.'

Bartholomew considered grabbing it himself, knowing that the vintner was not strong enough to stop him, but then came to his senses. They were in the King's Head, and even Isnard would not be able to protect him if he assaulted one of its regulars.

'The Austins are going to ask the Bishop to decide the case,' he said instead. 'It is a good idea – he will be an impartial judge.'

'Oh, no, he won't,' declared Hakeney fervently. 'I have crossed swords with him before – over a pig that was mine, but which he claimed was his. I will not get a fair hearing from the Bishop of Ely, and I refuse to accept him as an arbiter.'

'Then stay low until Hamo's killer is caught,' advised Bartholomew, sure the sight of the vintner strolling free would infuriate some of the University's feistier members, and the last thing they needed was another murder. 'Do you have somewhere to hide?'

'Yes,' agreed Hakeney, reaching for the jug of wine that he had not finished the previous night and taking a deep draught. 'Right here. The landlord will not mind.'

*　　*　　*

Bartholomew and Michael left the tavern, and as they crossed the bridge over the King's Ditch, the physician stopped to stare down at the sluggish, murky waters. When he looked up again, he saw the top of the Austins' chapel over the chaos of rooftops in between, while several boats were tied up on the bank below. None were secure, and anyone might have jumped into one, rowed the short distance to the convent and gone in to commit murder.

'I have been looking for you,' came a voice at his side. It was Dodenho from King's Hall. 'Two more of our students have gone down with the *debilitas*, and we need another pot of your miraculous Royal Broth. It has eased all Cew's symptoms, and he is better than he has been in days, although he is still mad, unfortunately. Still, one thing at a time.'

Loath to dispense a remedy, even vegetable soup, without examining the patients first, Bartholomew offered to accompany him to King's Hall while Michael went to question the Austins again. As they walked, Dodenho regaled the physician with opinions, one hand on the sword he wore at his side. Bartholomew was grateful for his martial presence, given the amount of hostility he himself was attracting.

'If the University does go to the Fens, we shall not join it,' Dodenho declared. 'It would be a bleak and impoverished existence, and our scholars are all from noble households, so they expect a degree of comfort. I imagine you feel the same, given the luxury in which you live.'

Bartholomew gave a noncommittal grunt, thinking that Langelee's ruse had been successful indeed if even the elegant King's Hall was convinced of Michaelhouse's affluence.

When they arrived, Wayt gave reluctant permission for Bartholomew to examine the men who were ill. There were seven in total, exhibiting symptoms as varied as nausea, stomach pains, headaches, insomnia and dizziness. One lad, who had been ill longer than the rest, showed Bartholomew how his foot dropped when he tried to walk, a peculiar problem that had afflicted Cew, too.

Cew, on the other hand, was considerably improved. His gait was back to normal, there was colour in his cheeks, and he seemed much stronger. Unfortunately, he was again convinced that he was the King of France.

'The metal has gone,' he confided. 'We cannot taste it any longer. It must have been in the oysters. They were brought here on the river, you see, and we all know the Seine is poisoned.'

'He means the Cam,' put in Dodenho helpfully. 'The Seine is in France.'

'Our sucura is imported via the Seine,' Cew went on. 'Our courtiers adore sweet things, and it is our pleasure to indulge them, especially as they put extra in our own soul-cakes as a reward. King's Hall is awash with it, although Wayt will tell you otherwise. But Frenge knew.'

Bartholomew glanced at the Acting Warden, and when he saw the expression of weary exasperation on the hirsute face, something suddenly became abundantly clear.

'You lied!' he exclaimed. 'You did not argue with Frenge about Anne the day he died – you quarrelled about sucura.'

Wayt opened his mouth to deny the accusation, but Cew clapped his hands in delight. 'You have it! You have it! What a clever fool you are!'

Wayt cast a venomous glare at his colleague, who rocked back and forth, grinning wildly. There was a moment when Bartholomew thought the Acting Warden would attempt to dismiss the claims as the unfounded ravings of a lunatic, but then he threw up his hands in resignation.

'Very well,' he sighed irritably. 'Yes – Frenge threatened to tell the Sheriff that we bought illegal sucura, and King's Hall cannot afford to be seen breaking the law. However, I did not kill him. I merely informed him that if he ever breathed a word of our doings to another living soul, I would sue him for slander.'

'You should have told Michael the truth,' said Bartholomew accusingly. 'It was—'

'And risk him betraying us to Tulyet? Do not be stupid! However, *you* cannot go running to him with this tale, because physicians are morally bound to keep their patients' ramblings quiet. Ergo, anything that Cew brays is confidential.'

'No one from Michaelhouse would blab about sucura anyway,' interposed Dodenho. 'Being so affluent, they purchase it by the bucket load themselves.'

Bartholomew regarded him thoughtfully. Every College and wealthy hostel in the University had reported cases of the *debilitas* except one: Michaelhouse. Was it because no one there could afford sucura – that it was the illegally imported sweetener that was making everyone ill? Had it become contaminated somehow, perhaps from the dyeworks? Was that why no pauper had been afflicted by the *debilitas*, and why it remained exclusively a 'disease' of the rich?

He pulled the little packet that Cynric had given him from his bag, ignoring Dodenho's triumphant hoot that he had been right, and poured some into his hand. He licked it cautiously. It did not taste as though it would do him harm, but only a fool thought that everything with a pleasant flavour was safe to eat.

'Your theory is flawed,' said Wayt, when Bartholomew explained tentatively what he was thinking, careful not to reveal that while Agatha had used sucura in the Hallow-tide marchpanes, all the other cakes had been made using the considerably cheaper honey. 'Osborne of

Gonville Hall has the *debilitas,* but he never touches sweet foods.'

'The same is true of Lenne and the Barnwell folk,' said Dodenho. 'They had the *debilitas* so badly that it killed them, but they never ate sweetmeats either.'

But the more Bartholomew pondered the matter, the more he was sure that sucura had played a central role in the sudden rise of the *debilitas.* He decided to experiment, and sent to Michaelhouse for more Royal Broth. When it arrived, he gave instructions that the sick men were to consume nothing but it and boiled barley water for a week. Assuming they followed his advice, he might soon have the beginnings of a solution.

Michael was waiting for him outside King's Hall, gloomily reporting that none of the Austins had remembered anything new. The killer had probably entered the convent at dusk, when there had been deep shadows to hide in, and there were no witnesses to the crime – at least, none that he had been able to find.

'And now Kellawe has disappeared,' the monk added. 'Morys came to me in a panic about it an hour ago, although I suspect the fellow has just joined the exodus to the Fens.'

'Have you checked the dyeworks? He may be making a nuisance of himself there.'

'Come with me, then,' said the monk tiredly. 'Even I do not feel safe walking alone today, but the company of the Hero of Poitiers should serve to protect me.'

Bartholomew winced. Cynric had been with him when the tiny English army had met the much larger French one, and gloried in the fact that he and the physician had played a part in the ensuing battle. Bartholomew's contribution to the fighting had been adequate at best, although he had been invaluable in tending the wounded afterwards. However, Cynric, with the blood of bards in his veins, had exaggerated their performance to the point where the rest of the Black Prince's troops might as well have stayed at home.

They arrived to find the dyeworks closed. Unusually, there were no protesters outside, so Water Lane was strangely quiet. Then Edith appeared, Cynric hovering watchfully at her side, with a complex explanation about how long woad needed to soak, and as the previous day's trouble had caused delays, the next stage of the process could not start until noon. It was midday now, so her women were beginning to trickle in. Anne de Rumburgh was among them, sensuously seductive in a new scarlet kirtle, which was not Bartholomew's idea of obeying Edith's instruction to 'stay in the back and keep a low profile'.

'We will be busy this afternoon with the first batch of Michaelhouse tabards,' chattered Edith as she unlocked the door. 'We dyed them with weld – yellow pigment – yesterday, so now we will overdye them with woad to make them green. Of course, we had to treat them with . . . certain substances first, because the garments are black.'

'Toxic substances?' asked Bartholomew archly. 'Which produce nasty residues?'

Edith glared. 'Of course not. But do not ask me for details, because they are a trade secret.'

At that moment, Anne flung open the rear door, and then gave a cry of horror when light flooded in to reveal what had hitherto been in darkness. The entire back half of the dyeworks' floor was submerged in a multicoloured lake – one that had seeped under the door and oozed towards the river in trails of yellow, red and orange. Her howl brought the other women running, and they stood at the edge of the spillage, gazing at it in stunned disbelief.

'Our crimson!' wailed Yolande. 'Some spiteful beast has emptied out every bucket we made! And the weld, too! Who could have done such a terrible thing? It represents *weeks* of hard work!'

'The window has been forced again,' said Cynric, going to inspect it.

'By the same villain as last time, I imagine,' said Anne angrily. 'For spite, because we almost caught him.'

'He did it to "prove" that we pollute the river,' said Edith in a strangled voice, while Bartholomew wondered if Kellawe had returned to finish the mischief he had started two days ago, before disappearing to the Fens to avoid another fine. 'That we let our colorants escape into the water. And how can we deny it when the "evidence" is here for all to see?'

'Then rinse it away before anyone sees,' advised Michael urgently. 'I have no idea if it is dangerous, but it *looks* terrible.'

'It will be too late,' said Yolande hoarsely. 'The demonstrators are already gathering. They must have seen us coming to work . . .'

In the vanguard of the deputation was Morys, who looked small, mean and angry in his trademark yellow and black. When he saw the vivid stains, his eyes shone with delighted malice.

'Look! Look!' he yelled triumphantly. 'The whores have poisoned the river again, and this time the Senior Proctor and his Corpse Examiner *cannot* pretend they do not know what we are talking about, because they are staring right at it!'

At his nod, several Zachary students slipped away, clearly aiming to spread word of the outrage. In response, Edith clapped her hands, bringing her workers out of their shocked immobility. Immediately, they set about hauling buckets of water from the river to sluice the offending mess away, although Cynric's strategy of digging it in with a spade was ultimately more successful. Unfortunately, their labours were all for naught, as the

Zachary lads did their work all too well, and people were soon flocking to inspect the damage. Morys was on hand to explain what had happened.

'The strategist has excelled himself this time,' muttered Michael. 'This will certainly cause trouble. And do not say we cannot prove he was behind this – of course he was.'

Bartholomew followed Edith back inside, where the light from the door revealed multihued footprints, made when the invader had hurried about wreaking his destruction. He bent to inspect them, and was surprised to identify not one but two different sets. One was larger and a mark on the sole was indicative of a hole. The other might have belonged to anyone.

He stood, and his eyes were drawn to the largest of the three great dyeing vats. The outside was liberally splashed with yellow, as it was where Michaelhouse's tabards were soaking. The ladder, which allowed the women to climb up and inspect the contents, was lying on the floor, and his stomach began to churn when it occurred to him that the staff would never have left it like that. He set it in its clips and began to ascend, aware that Michael, Cynric and the ladies had caught his unease and were watching him intently. He reached the top, but all he could see was sodden material. Then he spotted a hand.

Appalled, he grabbed it and began to pull, although the rational part of his brain told him that its owner was beyond any help he could provide. The bright yellow face that emerged, eyes open in death, meant nothing to him at first, but then he recognised the pugnacious jaw.

'Christ God,' he swore. 'It is Kellawe.'

As they were worldly women, Edith's staff were not unduly perturbed by the news that a Franciscan friar was dead in one of their vats, and were eager to scale the ladder and look for themselves. Bartholomew was hard-pressed to stop them, and it took a sharp word from his sister before they fell back. She was white-faced with shock.

'Kellawe must have climbed up there for mischief, lost his balance and pitched in,' surmised Yolande. 'His accomplice, being a cowardly brute, ran away and left him to drown.'

Bartholomew thought she might be right, given that Kellawe had invaded the dyeworks once already, and the ladder was unstable, so it would have been easy to slip. While Yolande elaborated on her theory to the others, Bartholomew glared at Michael.

'You should have arrested him the last time,' he whispered accusingly. 'Not just levied a fine. Then he might have been less inclined to reoffend.'

'I thought five shillings would make him think twice about re-indulging his penchant for burglary – it is a veritable fortune,' Michael hissed back. 'And keep your voice down. I did not tell Edith that Kellawe was the guilty party, lest she or her ladies decided to take matters into their own hands. She will skin me alive if she learns the truth.'

She might, thought Bartholomew, and it would serve him right. But quarrelling with Michael was doing no good, so he forced down his irritation. 'So what does this tell us – that Kellawe was the strategist and our troubles are over? Or that Kellawe was in the strategist's pay, and came here under orders to cause all this damage?'

'Who knows?' Wearily, Michael turned to the women. 'Are you *sure* you know nothing about this? You did not find him here and decided to deal with the matter yourselves? I understand why you might – he had no business breaking in and you are understandably indignant.'

'Yes, we are,' replied Yolande frostily. 'However, if we had killed him, do you really think we would have left him in one of our vats? Of course not! We would have buried him in the Fens, where his corpse would never be found.'

'That is a good point, Brother,' said Bartholomew. 'Kellawe's demise will do the dyeworks immeasurable harm, and may even see them closed down.'

'So the bastard will achieve in death what he could not do in life,' spat Yolande in disgust. 'God damn him to Hell!'

Michael began to look around, noting that the footprints were dry, which suggested that Kellawe and his accomplice had broken in some hours before.

'Morys told me earlier that Kellawe left home at midnight, to keep vigil in St Bene't's Church for his dead colleagues,' he mused. 'He—'

'We finished work at roughly that time,' interrupted Yolande. 'However, I can tell you two things: first, I can see St Bene't's from my house, and there were no lights there all night – I would have noticed – which means Kellawe said no prayers for his friends. And second, we all have alibis in each other from midnight until now.'

'It is true,' nodded Edith. 'Half came home with me and half went with Yolande, because it was late, and we did not want them walking home alone lest they were accused of . . .'

'Plying their former trade,' finished Yolande. 'So none of us shoved your acid-tongued Franciscan in the dye, Brother.'

Bartholomew was relieved, as he had not liked the notion of investigating his sister's workforce. He and Cynric began the complex operation of removing Kellawe from the vat without pulling the whole thing over. It was a messy business, even with the smocks and gloves that Edith lent them, and when they had finished, there were several shilling-sized stains on their clothes and skin that would be difficult to remove. Bartholomew began his examination, although he found the saffron-coloured face disconcerting, and so covered it with a cloth.

'Do not tell the students what happened, boy,' murmured Cynric. 'They will refuse to wear tabards that have been soaking with a corpse. And who can blame them?'

'That is a good point,' whispered Michael. 'We cannot afford to buy the material for new ones. So how did he die? Drowned? Overcome by fumes? That vat does reek.'

'Unfortunately not,' said Bartholomew sombrely. 'He was strangled. Look, you can see the twine still embedded in his neck. Someone came up behind him, looped it over his head, and pulled until he was dead.'

'Murdered?' groaned Michael. 'Not an accident? Are you sure?'

Bartholomew nodded. 'Then he was toted up the ladder and dropped into the vat – not to hide the body, given that even I know that these tanks are inspected and stirred multiple times a day, but for its shock value.'

Michael's expression hardened. 'And all to exacerbate the trouble between us and the town. Is there anything to say who did this terrible thing?'

'No, but our first task should be to check all our suspects' footwear.' Bartholomew pointed at the tracks that crisscrossed the floor. 'The large ones are Kellawe's – they match the hole in his heel. The others came from a pair of sturdy outside boots, almost certainly his killer's.'

'We shall do it at once,' determined Michael. 'Particularly Zachary's. Kellawe is the fourth member of that place to die in odd circumstances, so something untoward is unfolding there. However, I can tell you someone who is innocent: Nigellus, who was in my gaol all night. Of course, there is an *ex*-Zachary man who is mysteriously missing . . .'

* * *

While Michael asked more questions of Edith's staff, Bartholomew fetched a bier from St Mary the Great. He commandeered four beadles to carry it at the same time, and had just ushered them inside the dyeworks when he heard a commotion coming from the brewery next door. Beadle Meadowman followed him there to see what was happening.

They were greeted by a curious sight. Principal Morys was racing from barrel to barrel, attempting to peer behind them, while Shirwynk was trying to stop him. The brewer was large and powerful, but Morys buzzed about like an agile fly and easily evaded the bigger man. Peyn leaned against a wall and laughed at the commotion, although his tone was more mocking than amused, and did nothing to soothe ragged tempers.

'Morys is looking for someone,' Peyn replied in answer to Bartholomew's questioning glance. 'But he is wasting his time: we do not allow our nice clean brewery to be infested by grubby scholars.'

'I know he is in here,' shouted Morys. Bartholomew glanced at his boots, but if the Principal had been in the dyeworks, he had had the sense to change, because they were spotless. The same was true of the shoes worn by Shirwynk and Peyn. 'What have you done with him?'

'We do not know what you are talking about,' declared Shirwynk, although his tone was taunting, and aggravated Morys even further.

'Kellawe!' Morys screeched furiously. 'Where is he?'

Bartholomew watched him. Did his agitation mean he had no idea that his colleague was dead? Or was it a ploy to make the Senior Proctor believe him innocent of murder?

'How should we know, hornet-face?' asked Peyn, so insolently that Morys lunged at him.

Peyn jerked back in alarm, but his devoted father was there to protect him, and managed to grab Morys by the neck. When the Principal began to make unpleasant choking sounds, Bartholomew went to intervene, but one of Shirwynk's meaty paws lashed out and caught him on the nose. Shock rather than pain caused him to stagger back, and when Meadowman surged to the physician's rescue, Morys took the opportunity to slither free and resume his hunt.

'I think it is time you left, Principal Morys,' said Meadowman, releasing Shirwynk when Bartholomew indicated that he was unharmed. 'You are not wanted here.'

Morys ignored him, and went instead to one of the big lead cisterns and peered inside.

'Your friend will not be in there,' jeered Shirwynk.

'We have found Kellawe,' said Meadowman. 'He is in the dyeworks.'

'He would never set foot in that place,' declared Morys, darting around Shirwynk and aiming for another vat. 'It is full of whores.'

'He is dead,' said Meadowman bluntly. Bartholomew winced: he had intended to break the news somewhere more private. 'He forced his way in for mischief and was murdered there.'

Morys stopped dead in his tracks and stared at him, while Shirwynk and Peyn exchanged a glance that was impossible to interpret.

'Murdered?' echoed Morys, fists clenched at his side. 'How?'

'He was strangled and his corpse tossed in a vat,' replied Meadowman, before Bartholomew could phrase it more delicately.

'So,' snarled Morys, more angry than distressed, 'yet another scholar killed by the town.'

'Do not blame us,' Shirwynk flashed back challengingly. 'It is far more likely to have been another academic. God knows, you all hate each other enough.'

'Lies!' hissed Morys. 'The town dispatched him for certain. I will hunt out the culprit and—'

He stopped when realisation came that threatening vengeance in front of a beadle was hardly wise. His lips clamped together and he stalked out to stand in the street, breathing heavily as he fought to control his temper. Bartholomew and Meadowman followed.

'Is it true that Kellawe went out at midnight?' Bartholomew supposed it was as good a time as any to ask questions. 'To pray for Irby, Yerland and Segeforde?'

Morys nodded tightly. 'He took his religious duties seriously, God bless his sainted soul. I saw him out, then retired to bed. When there was no sign of him this morning, I reported my concerns to the Senior Proctor – who ignored them.'

'Why were you both still up at midnight? It seems an odd time to—'

'Losing three members of our hostel in such quick succession has been upsetting, and neither of us felt like sleep. We sat talking until he decided to go to church. And before you ask, I went to bed alone. However, you accused Nigellus of murder without foundation, so do not make the same mistake with me.'

'Did Kellawe take anyone with him to St Bene't's?' pressed Bartholomew. 'Or were other Zachary men already there?'

'I do not recall,' replied Morys shortly.

'Footprints tell us that Kellawe was with someone,' put in Meadowman. Bartholomew winced again, and wished the beadle would be quiet. 'We shall be wanting to inspect all of Zachary's boots today.'

Morys glared at him. 'Then I shall go and assemble my scholars.'

He raced away before they could stop him. Meadowman followed, but the Principal scuttled up the road with impressive speed, shot inside his hostel and slammed the door. Bartholomew stifled a groan. Michael would find no stained footwear now, and any culprit would be told exactly what to say to exonerate himself.

From the door of the brewery Peyn laughed, a forced, jeering cackle that Bartholomew found intensely irritating. Ignoring the fact that he did not have the authority to interrogate townsmen, the physician strode towards him. Peyn promptly disappeared inside, but as he neglected to close the door, Bartholomew was able to barge in after him.

'Where were *you* between midnight and dawn?' he demanded.

'In here,' replied Peyn, bold again now that his father was there to protect him. 'Guarding our wares against the scholars who come to steal.'

'And I was asleep in the room at the back,' added Shirwynk. 'But before you ask, no one was with us. I am recently widowed, while Peyn was too busy being vigilant for company.'

'So you will have to take our word for it,' smirked Peyn. 'You have no choice – the town will not take kindly to you trying to blame one of us for Kellawe's murder.'

'Of course, the *University* will not be pleased when it learns that I am going to sue Morys for trespass,' said Shirwynk slyly. 'But I do not care. Look at the mess he made. And you and your beadle will be our witnesses.'

'There will be a riot!' chortled Peyn in delight. 'After which the University will be ousted from our town once and for all. We do not want you here, and I cannot imagine why I ever thought I might become a scholar.'

'Did you?' asked Bartholomew in surprise, thinking of the lad's awful writing and the fact that he had never heard of Virgil. He seriously doubted Peyn would have been accepted, even at those foundations where academic merit came second to the size of parents' donations.

Sensitive to any perceived slight against his son,

Shirwynk shoved the physician rather vigorously, so that he stumbled against one of the wine tanks. 'It was a passing phase, and one he grew out of, thank God. Now get out, before I sue you for trespass, too.'

Bartholomew was glad to leave the brewery, although he wished he had more to take with him than a host of unanswered questions and suspicions. He returned to the dyeworks to find that Michael had already gone to Zachary, and hoped the monk had arrived before Morys had warned everyone to hide any stained footwear.

'What is this?' asked Edith, turning him around to inspect the back of his tabard. 'You are covered in white dust. Take it off. I will wash it and then dye it with the others.'

'No, thank you,' said Bartholomew, not wanting a garment he was obliged to wear every day to go in a vat that had recently held a corpse. It was silly, he knew, especially given his occupation, but he could not help it. 'Shirwynk pushed me against one of his tanks. That dust must have—'

'If he pushes you again, tell me,' instructed Cynric grimly. 'And I will push him back.'

While Bartholomew had been gone, the women had done their best to return the Franciscan to some semblance of normality. They had scrubbed his hands and face, and although he was still more amber than he should have been, at least he was recognisably human. They had been unable to do much with his habit, though, so Edith had sent Cynric to Michaelhouse to beg one from William. What had arrived was a vile article, thick with filth and fleas, but Bartholomew put it on the body anyway. Then he loaded Kellawe on the bier and sent the beadles away with it.

He walked to Zachary Hostel, and arrived to find Morys refusing to let Michael inside. He was at an upstairs window, Nigellus at his side.

'You cannot keep me out,' Michael was stating indignantly. 'I am the Senior Proctor.'

'You arrested me on patently false charges,' shouted Nigellus. 'So I took legal advice from Stephen. He says that any contact with you should be through him from now on.'

'It is not you I want,' snapped Michael. 'It is everyone else.'

'Then you should have thought about that before hounding an innocent man,' Morys shot back. 'Because you are not coming in.'

Michael spread his hands. 'How am I supposed to solve Kellawe's murder if you will not help me? Do you want his killer to go free?'

'*You* will not solve it,' sneered Nigellus. 'You are an incompetent. Now go away. If you have questions for us, you can ask them through our lawyer. But not today. Stephen's *debilitas* is worse and keeps him in his bed. However, he was not too ill to assure me that your University will be obliged to pay me a fortune.'

'It is your University, too,' Michael pointed out. 'And suing it is hardly the best use of its resources. We should be channelling them into averting the trouble with—'

'We do not want to be a part of it any more,' interrupted Nigellus. 'It is corrupt and rotten, and Kellawe was right to want a new one in the Fens. We shall leave in the next few days, to join those who have gone before us. Our new *studium generale* will be free of vice and cronyism.'

'There speaks the hostel that controls Tynkell with threats over his mother,' muttered Michael, as the window slammed closed. 'I shall be glad to be rid of them. Unfortunately, the fact that they are not leaving immediately suggests they aim to use the intervening time to recruit more scholars to their cause.'

'Almost certainly,' agreed Bartholomew. 'And Morys

301

has no alibi for Kellawe's murder – perhaps he killed him to make scholars think they are in danger here, and will be safer in the Fens.'

'Surely Morys would have preferred Kellawe alive? Kellawe was fervent in his support of the move, not to mention the fact that he held the licence to absolve Zachary's scholars from acts of violence.'

'Would you want a man like Kellawe in *your* new University? He might be popular with malcontents and fanatics, but rational, decent scholars would recoil.'

'Rational, decent scholars will not be considering removing to the Fens.'

'But they are, Brother. The Austins think it is a sensible idea, and other good men will follow. Unless you do something to stop it, your University will be torn in half.'

CHAPTER 12

Although Bartholomew and Michael spent the rest of the day in a determined effort to identify Kellawe's killer, they met with no success. Bartholomew lost count of the boots he examined for red and yellow splashes, but whoever had been with the Franciscan in the dyeworks had been clever enough to dispose of any incriminating evidence. In the end they gave up and went home, exhausted by their efforts.

'We have a number of suspects, both for killing Kellawe and for being the strategist,' said Michael, as he and Bartholomew stood outside the hall after breakfast the following day. 'First, Morys, because Kellawe's fierce tongue was a liability—'

'And he killed Frenge to cause a rift between University and town,' nodded Bartholomew, 'thus encouraging a lot of scholars to think they might be safer in the Fens. Nigellus is innocent of the first, but might have had a hand in the latter.'

'Second, Shirwynk and Peyn, who live next door to the dyeworks and hate all scholars. Third, Hakeney, because he is under the delusion that Robert stole his cross, and his assault to get it back has certainly encouraged the Austins to want to leave us for the marshes.'

'I am less convinced about those three. The strategist is clever, and I am not sure they are sufficiently well organised, especially Hakeney.'

'Fourth, Wauter,' continued Michael, 'because we do not know where he is or what he is doing. He is certainly intelligent enough to organise all this trouble. Fifth, Stephen, because he will have more work from townsmen if the University's lawyers move to the Fens. He denied sending the messages urging the priors to convince Joliet to sue Hakeney, and I *thought* he was telling the truth, but perhaps I was wrong to be so trusting . . .'

'But Nigellus – and Stephen's maid – said that he has the *debilitas*. Sick men do not strangle their victims and toss them in vats.'

'The *debilitas* comprises a lot of symptoms that cannot be proved – headaches, nausea, stomach pains, constipation, so how do you *know* he is ill? Have you examined him?'

Bartholomew shook his head. 'I offered, but he refused.'

'Interesting,' said Michael. 'So I suggest we pay him a visit today and repeat the invitation. His response will be revealing in itself. And sixth, we have the men of King's Hall. They are violently opposed to a move to the Fens, and killing one of its most vocal proponents might serve to damage its cause. Of course, if so, it means that none of them is the strategist.'

'I doubt Cew is the culprit, while Dodenho is no more capable of ingenious subterfuge than Shirwynk, Peyn and Hakeney. That leaves Wayt . . .'

'Cew also has the *debilitas*,' mused Michael, 'but *his* sickness has turned him insane. Yet how do we know his madness is real? He might be acting.'

'I really do not think so, Brother. It seems genuine to me.'

Michael turned to another subject. 'Edith and Yolande did not tell us the truth, you know.'

Bartholomew regarded him uneasily. 'About what?'

'They said their women were with them all night, but Cynric confided that there was actually a good deal of coming and going – some still engage in their old business, despite your sister's efforts to reform them. I am afraid we cannot discount them as suspects for Kellawe's murder, so they are seventh on our list.'

'None of them will be the strategist though – they will not want the University to go, because scholars buy a lot of dyed cloth and . . . other services.'

'True, but the strategist might have encouraged one of them to kill Kellawe. Most are impetuous ladies who would not need much convincing that dispatching a thorn in their side would be to their advantage. They are unlikely to have sat down and considered the repercussions. Like so many others, they would have been clay in his manipulative hands.'

Bartholomew was silent for a while, thinking. 'There are other deaths that should not be forgotten either – Letia, Lenne, Arnold, Irby, Yerland, Segeforde and the Barnwell folk. We do not know why they died, but four of them suffered damage to their stomachs and livers, which I am sure was not natural . . .'

'Damage that cannot be attributed to Nigellus, because he does not dispense medicines,' sighed Michael, then shook his head. 'And those are the deaths we know about. It occurs to me that this strategist might have claimed dozens of other lives to get what he wants.'

Bartholomew rubbed a hand though his hair. 'We had better visit Stephen then. Unfortunately, being a lawyer, he is unlikely to be tripped up by our questions.'

'Do not be so sure.' Determination gleamed in Michael's green eyes. 'I am the Senior Proctor, and no sly killer has bested me yet.'

Before they started their enquiries, Bartholomew stopped at King's Hall, where he was pleased to learn that all seven patients were showing signs of improvement. He started to tell Michael why he thought his Royal Broth was working, but the monk waved his explanation away with an irritable flap of a plump hand, more interested in holding forth about their suspects.

As they walked along the High Street, Bartholomew recalled the stone that had been lobbed at Prior Joliet, just for associating with Michaelhouse, and sensed that it would not be long before someone from the College suffered serious physical harm. It was not a comforting thought, and when they met Thelnetham the Gilbertine, who favoured them with a friendly smile, it was a welcome relief.

'You cannot still want to be reinstated as a Fellow at Michaelhouse,' said Michael ruefully. 'It is a dangerous place to be at the moment.'

'No worse than any other University foundation,' replied Thelnetham. 'And I will take my chances. I hear that Wauter has abandoned you, probably to facilitate the new *studium generale* in the Fens, so you have a vacancy . . .'

'You will not be joining him there?' asked Michael. 'To make a cleaner life away from the polluting effects of the town?'

Thelnetham shuddered. 'Certainly not! It will be damp, uncivilised and full of fanatics. And speaking of fanatics, have you heard that Shirwynk is suing Morys for trespass? Morys invaded his brewery yesterday, apparently, looking for Kellawe.'

Michael groaned. 'Yet another incident to cause dissent. Will it never end?'

'Not as long as we enrol undesirables like Kellawe, Morys, Segeforde and Wayt,' said Thelnetham ruefully. 'But I am glad we met, Bartholomew, because I have a touch of the *debilitas* and I am in need of relief.'

'Deynman said you had been unwell,' recalled Bartholomew, and regarded the Gilbertine coolly. 'After he mentioned that you called him an *inlitteratus*.'

Thelnetham shrugged, unrepentant. 'I needed a diver-

sion from my discomforts, just as I need one now – I
should not have drunk that second cask of apple wine,
given that the first made me so ill, but it was a gift from
an admirer and I could not resist it.'

'It was from Deynman,' said Bartholomew, a little gleefully – he was fond of the dim-witted Librarian, and
disliked Thelnetham's supercilious attitude towards him.
'To avenge himself for your unkindness. If you are ill, it
seems his plan worked.'

Thelnetham was stunned to learn that he was the victim
of a scheme devised by Deynman. 'What a vile thing to
do! I shall sue him for damages unless you give me some
of your Royal Broth. I feel dreadful – my head is swimming in a most unpleasant manner.'

Bartholomew frowned. 'Deynman said the first lot of
wine made you silly and drove you to bed for a week.
Does that mean your head swam then as well?'

The Gilbertine nodded. 'In an identical manner. What
does—'

'What about difficulty in sleeping, nausea, headaches
and a metallic taste in your mouth?'

'Yes, but to a lesser degree. I went to Nigellus for a
cure, but all he did was calculate my horoscope and advise
me to avoid going anywhere near sheep – which is easier
said than done when one's priory lies on a main road,
and the creatures are taken to and from market all day.'

'When you did not recover, did he tell you it was because
you had failed to follow his precise instructions?'

'Yes, he did. Why?'

Bartholomew's mind was racing as he turned to
Michael. 'Perhaps Nigellus's diagnoses are not so
outlandish after all. Lenne tasted metal in his mouth,
Letia was dizzy, Arnold had insomnia, Yerland had headaches, Irby lost his appetite, while others have suffered
from nausea, heavy limbs – including foot drop – and
stomach pains.'

'Other than the foot-drop, I have had all those,' interposed Thelnetham. 'But the swimming head is the worst – quite distressing, in fact.'

'The other victims also had one symptom that affected them more severely than the others,' Bartholomew went on, excitement in his voice as answers blossomed. 'The rest were there, but to a lesser degree. Rougham was right: they *are* all indications of the same disease.'

'Yes – the *debilitas*,' said Thelnetham drily.

Bartholomew ignored him. 'Cew, who has been ill for several weeks, has exhibited all these signs, along with constipation. However, I suspect he was witless long before Frenge jumped out at him, but King's Hall does not want to admit it – it is better to blame a townsman for his condition than to confess that one of their scholars went mad for no reason.'

'Perhaps,' said Michael. 'But I—'

'Cew will only eat oysters and soul-cakes – soul-cakes containing sucura.'

'Containing *honey*,' corrected Thelnetham. 'King's Hall does not use sucura, because it is illegal. Wayt told me so himself.'

'He was lying,' said Bartholomew impatiently. 'Besides, Cew expressed a dislike for honey, so why would one of his two chosen foods contain it? The answer is that it would not.'

'Are you saying that sucura is responsible for all these ailments?' asked Michael doubtfully. 'If so, you are wrong. We used some in the marchpanes we served after the *disceptatio*, and no one suffered any ill effects from those. Moreover, I ate some of King's Hall's soul-cakes but I am hale and hearty, as you can see.'

'I doubt a few will be harmful, but Cew has been devouring platefuls of them for weeks. And there was the syllabub at Trinity Hall. I blamed bad cream, but the entire episode was repeated, even though fresh ingredi-

308

ents were used the second time. The culprit was the masses of sucura used to sweeten it – not sufficient to kill, but enough to lay everyone low for a day or two.'

'Arnold liked sweet cakes,' mused Michael. 'So did Letia and Segeforde.'

'Well, I do not,' put in Thelnetham. 'I have the *debilitas*, but I have never touched sucura. My Prior issued a ban on it when the Sheriff declared it illegal. Your theory is flawed, Matthew.'

'But you like apple wine,' said Bartholomew. '*Sweet* apple wine, so syrupy that I cannot bear more than a sip. And we have been told that Irby and Lenne loved it, too.'

'No,' said Michael firmly. 'Shirwynk does not add sucura to his wine. If he did, it would be a lot more expensive. You are mistaken, Matt.'

'I am not,' insisted Bartholomew. 'The apple wine and the sucura are *both* responsible for the *debilitas*, which is why my seven patients in King's Hall are recovering – they have been told to eat Royal Broth and nothing else. The source of the trouble has been removed, you see.'

'But the wine comes from Shirwynk, while sucura is whisked through the Fens,' Thelnetham pointed out. 'You cannot link them, just because both are sweet.'

'But they *are* linked,' insisted Bartholomew. 'I should have seen it days ago. The sucura is not "whisked through the Fens", which is why Dick Tulyet has had so little success in tracing it. It comes from the brewery. Look at my tabard – Shirwynk shoved me against one of his tanks earlier, and I came away covered in the stuff.'

He hauled the garment over his head, and pointed at the white dust that still adhered to it, despite Edith's efforts to brush it off. When Thelnetham and Michael continued to look blank, he produced the packet of sucura that Cynric had given him. It and the dust were identical, and a lick proved they tasted the same as well.

Michael was stunned. 'So sucura is brewery dust? But it cannot be, Matt! It has been sold in London for years, and I know for a fact that it is imported at great cost from Tyre.'

'Not this "sucura",' said Bartholomew. 'It is different.'

Michael rubbed his jaw. 'So are you saying that Shirwynk is the strategist?'

'I do not know about that – only that the source of the *debilitas* is his brewery. The apple wine and sucura do not kill instantly, but work over a period of time – although a heavy dose, as was in Trinity Hall's syllabub or Thelnetham's whole cask of apple wine, will have a more immediate effect. And they are fatal to those weakened by age or sickness, like Lenne, Letia, Irby and Arnold.'

'Lord!' gulped Thelnetham. 'I shall never drink wine again.'

He grimaced as he spoke, which allowed Bartholomew to see a faint line of grey on his gums. It was identical to the ones on the scholars from King's Hall and Rumburgh.

'Go to Michaelhouse and ask Agatha for some Royal Broth,' Bartholomew instructed. 'If you eat it with nothing but plain bread and watered ale for a week, you will be cured.'

He suspected that just avoiding the white powder would be enough to do the trick, but patients liked to be given 'medicine' and tended to get better more quickly if they thought they were taking a remedy that worked. Besides, a diet of vegetables, bread and weak ale would do no one any harm. Thelnetham nodded his thanks and hurried away, eager to start the treatment as soon as possible.

'We cannot march into the brewery and accuse Shirwynk,' warned Michael. 'We tried it with Nigellus and look how that turned out. We dare not make another mistake.'

310

'There is evidence at Barnwell. The canons' elderflower wine has a reputation for being sour, but they gave me a cup on Tuesday and it was unbelievably sweet. Two clerics died, along with a cook and a gardener – who would certainly have been in a position to filch it from the kitchens. At first, I thought the culprit might have been river fish . . .'

'You mean fish that had been poisoned by the dyeworks?'

Bartholomew nodded. 'Nigellus identified the wine as the cause, which offended Prior Norton, but he was right. The two dead canons were elderly and in frail health, while the servants were fat, and probably sat around downing a lot of it.'

Michael was still unconvinced. 'Did Norton admit that sucura had been added?'

'Of course not. He claimed the wine's sweetness was due to the sun ripening the grapes at the right time, but I could tell he was lying. Send a beadle to Barnwell to get the truth. Norton will confess if he knows it is important.'

Michael did so at once, urging the man to hurry. Then Bartholomew spotted Rumburgh scurrying along with his head down, aiming to conceal himself from scholars who thought that Anne had torn off her own dress in the fracas outside the dyeworks. The burgess blanched when Bartholomew ordered him to tip his head back and open his mouth. The grey line on his gums was thicker than it had been a few days before.

'Do you like apple wine?' Bartholomew demanded.

Rumburgh shook his head. 'I am an ale man myself. There is nothing more delicious than ale and a cake of a morning. It—'

'*Sweet* cakes?' interrupted Bartholomew. 'Ones flavoured with sucura?'

'Oh, no,' gulped Rumburgh unconvincingly. 'That would be illegal.'

'This is not evidence, Matt,' warned Michael, after Rumburgh had scuttled away. 'Shirwynk will claim that you are trying to protect Edith by sacrificing him. And others will agree.'

'Stephen wanted to be an architect, did he not?' asked Bartholomew. 'And he has a lot of books on the subject?'

Michael blinked at the abrupt change of topic. 'Yes – a library that should have come to Michaelhouse. Why?'

But Bartholomew was already running towards the High Street. Michael hurried after him, and caught up just as he was hammering on Stephen's door.

'Why are you interested in architecture all of a sudden? How will Stephen's books prove that Shirwynk is the poisoner?'

'Years ago, I read something in *De architectura* by the Roman engineer Marcus Vitruvius Pollio,' replied Bartholomew. 'Michaelhouse does not have a copy, but Stephen will.'

'I still do not understand,' snapped Michael. 'Explain.'

'I will,' promised Bartholomew. 'When I am sure myself.'

A servant conducted them to the pleasant room at the back of the house, where the lawyer was lying full length on a cushioned bench. The number of pots and packets on the table besides him suggested that he had been frantically dosing himself with all manner of medicines from the apothecary. He was pale, frightened, and the room had the unmistakeable odour of sickness.

'You came fast, Bartholomew,' he whispered with pathetic gratitude. 'I thought you might refuse, given that I have aggravated the situation between town and University with my lawsuits, and our last meeting was less than amiable . . .'

'Scholars are not vindictive men,' averred Michael, before Bartholomew could remark that he had not received a summons. 'But before Matt helps you, tell me whether you advised Shirwynk to sue Morys for trespass.'

Stephen paled even further. 'Yes, but it is not for me to judge the ethics or wisdom of such cases, Brother. All I do is apply the law.'

'Speaking of asinine counsel, did you urge the drunken Hakeney to steal Robert's cross?' asked Michael. 'An honest answer, please, or you will get no cure from Matt.'

Stephen licked dry lips. 'We have been through this, Brother – I had a letter from a well-wisher, saying that if Hakeney stole the almoner's crucifix, I might win myself another client . . .'

'That is not what I asked,' said Michael sharply. 'I want to know if you sneaked into a tavern wearing a disguise and incited Hakeney to commit a crime.'

'You would have worn a disguise, too, if you had been obliged to enter that particular inn,' retorted the lawyer, which Michael supposed was as close to an admission of guilt that they were likely to get. 'And then I offered the Austins my legal services, as I told you yesterday.'

'Who sent you this letter?'

'I do not know, but it was good advice, because I *did* win myself another client.' Stephen turned terrified eyes to Bartholomew. 'I have answered your friend's questions, so now you must help me. I have no strength in my wrists, and I feel dreadful. I hear you have cured several King's Hall men, so do the same for me.'

'How much sucura have you had recently?' asked Bartholomew.

'Sucura? Me? Do I look like the kind of man to buy illegal substances?'

Bartholomew eyed him in distaste. 'I cannot make an accurate diagnosis if you lie to me.'

Stephen gulped. 'Well, then, perhaps a few grains do slip into the pastries I enjoy before I go to bed at night. They taste so much better than when made with honey, and it is difficult to deny oneself when the stuff is so freely available. If the Sheriff does not want us to have it, then he should restrict its import.'

'He tries,' said Michael. 'But he is hampered by the fact that arrogant folk with money undermine his efforts to stamp the business out.'

While the monk went to fetch some Royal Broth from Agatha – although not before he had extracted a substantial fee to cover the cost of the 'expensive ingredients' – Bartholomew examined Stephen. It did not take him long to ascertain that the lawyer was suffering from all the same symptoms as Thelnetham, although he was most concerned about the weakness in his wrists.

'May I consult your books while we wait for Michael to return?' Bartholomew asked.

Stephen winced at what he mistakenly thought was a bald reminder of past shabby dealings. 'Cure me, and I will willingly donate them to Michaelhouse. But you cannot blame me for withdrawing the original offer.'

Bartholomew went to the shelves and ran his finger along the displayed spines. The problem was that *De architectura* comprised ten volumes, and he could not recall in which one he had seen the section he wanted to check. While he began to look, Stephen continued to talk.

'Blame the letters I was sent, warning me that Michaelhouse aims to move to the Fens. I asked Rougham about it, and he said the tale was true, but that Gonville would never leave, so I decided to favour them instead – until I had a message saying that they were going, too.'

'The sender was lying – neither foundation has any intention of uprooting.' Bartholomew was thoughtful. 'Did you tell anyone else that our Colleges might be relocating?'

'I might have mentioned it to one or two people.' The lawyer's cagey response told Bartholomew that he had probably gossiped to anyone who would listen. 'However, the story *is* true, because some scholars have already left. Not from Michaelhouse or Gonville, perhaps, but from other foundations. And more are set to follow.'

'Your rumour-mongering is probably responsible for that – the notion that two powerful Colleges might be on the verge of departure is rather different than the defection of a handful of malcontents from the hostels. Where are these messages? Do you still have them, or did you throw them away?' Like the priors had done, Bartholomew thought.

'I keep everything that is sent to me,' came the unexpected but welcome reply. 'Lawyers like records of correspondence. They are on the table, along with the one about Hakeney.'

Eagerly, Bartholomew snatched up the notes, and inspected them carefully. The writing was identical on each, and the message brisk and to the point. Unfortunately, there was nothing to reveal the sender's identity: the parchment was undistinguished, and the ink a standard black. However, the culprit needed to invest in a new pen, because a split nib meant that every upstroke was bifurcated.

'I am surprised you acted on these,' remarked Bartholomew, disappointment rendering him testy. 'Surely you must be suspicious of unsolicited anonymous advice?'

'Why, when the sender clearly means me well? He must be a scholar, though, because who else knows Latin and has access to writing materials?'

'Lawyers,' replied Bartholomew promptly. 'Town priests and vicars. Wealthy merchants with their own clerks.' There was no reply, so he went on. 'Are you sure you have no idea who sent them? *Please* tell me if you do – it is important.'

'Well, no one from Michaelhouse or Gonville Hall,'

said Stephen drily. 'It deprived them of a generous gift. Perhaps it was someone from the hostels, jealous of your good fortune.'

The obvious suspects would be from Zachary, thought Bartholomew, wondering if it was enough to exonerate Wauter. But would they really be so petty? Then the faces of the hostel men paraded through his mind – Kellawe, Nigellus, Segeforde, Morys – and he knew they would.

'Tell me one more thing,' he said. 'What did you and Frenge discuss shortly before his death? You claimed earlier that he wanted your advice about gifts for Anne.'

Stephen looked away miserably. 'He came to bring me some sucura.'

Bartholomew turned back to *De architectura*, and found the answer he was hunting in the eighth volume, just as Michael returned with the broth and young Bell, who had volunteered to feed it to the patient and sit with him afterwards. Briefly, Bartholomew told Michael what he had reasoned, speaking in a low voice so as not to be overheard by the loose-tongued lawyer.

'But are you *sure* the brewery is to blame for the *debilitas*?' the monk asked worriedly. 'Because if you are wrong, there will be a rift between us and the town that will never heal – Shirwynk will not let it.'

'I cannot be absolutely certain until I have inspected his vats, but it makes sense.'

'Does it mean he is the strategist, too? His hatred of the University gives him a powerful motive, and Peyn would not be beneath penning sly letters to greedy lawyers – although he must have had help, given that his Latin is poor and his handwriting worse.'

'They could have hired a scribe. However, all this means that the dyeworks are innocent.'

'That is what worries me, Matt. You have a vested interest in proving that the *debilitas* is not Edith's fault, and I am afraid it might have clouded your judgement.'

Bartholomew was too fraught to be indignant that his professional opinion should be questioned, or to remark that Michael should know him better than to think he would fabricate or misread evidence where matters of health were concerned.

'There is only one way to find out,' was all he said.

Bartholomew was astonished to find the beadle who had been sent to Barnwell waiting for them when he and Michael emerged from Stephen's house – not enough time had passed for the man to have run all the way there, spoken to the canons and trotted back.

'Prior Norton is in town,' the beadle explained. 'So I was saved a journey. He was reluctant to admit to buying sucura at first, but confessed when I told him why I needed to know. He said Canon Wrattlesworth, who was the first to become ill, stirred some into a cup of elderflower wine one night, because he thought the priory's brew was overly sour—'

Bartholomew groaned. 'That would not do it – the exposure needs to be continuous over a period of weeks or even months.'

'You did not let me finish,' said the beadle. 'He declared his sweetened drink so much nicer than the usual vintage that he added a massive dose of sucura to every vat made this year. Everyone agreed it was better, and it was quickly consumed. Wrattlesworth was the cellarer, and Norton thinks that he and his friend Canterbury – the other dead canon – had far more than anyone else.'

'What about the cook and the gardener?' asked Bartholomew.

'The same, because both spent a lot of time in the kitchen. Moreover, Norton gave several casks to Birton the reeve, who thought it too sweet, but his frail wife and elderly uncle loved it. And they are the other two who died.'

317

'So you were right, Matt,' said Michael. 'The sucura *is* to blame, and we were wrong to accuse Nigellus. Damn! He will not let us forget this in a hurry. Still, Stephen will not represent him – unless he wants to be deprived of your healing Royal Broth.'

'Prior Norton also told me that *Shirwynk* uses a lot of sucura in his apple wine,' the beadle went on. 'Shirwynk offered him some once, and being a man who knows his beverages, he was able to tell exactly what was in it. He says it is loaded with the stuff.'

'Go to the castle and repeat all this to the Sheriff,' ordered Michael. 'Then ask him to come to the brewery as soon as he can. Matt and I will meet him there.'

Unfortunately, he and Bartholomew reached Shirwynk's domain to find a cart piled high with boxes and a horse already in harness – Peyn was about to leave for Westminster. The apprentices were waiting, ready to make their farewells when he emerged.

'No!' whispered Bartholomew urgently, as the monk prepared to stride through them. 'We should wait for Dick. There are too many of them, and if the situation turns ugly—'

'We have no choice,' Michael hissed. 'Peyn is just as much to blame as his father, and we cannot risk losing him. And we certainly cannot have him appearing for work at the Treasury!'

Unhappily, Bartholomew followed him inside, the apprentices a menacing presence at their heels. They were just in time to see Shirwynk hugging his son. The brewer was furious, mortified that strangers should witness the unmanly tears that glittered in his eyes.

'What do you want?' he snarled. 'Get out!'

'We have reason to believe that your apple wine is giving people the *debilitas*,' began Michael briskly. 'It is—'

'Do you see what they are doing, Peyn?' asked Shirwynk angrily. 'They want me to drop my case of trespass against

318

Morys, so they aim to bully me into submission by attacking my wares. It is sly and mean, but that is to be expected of the University.'

'The architects of ancient Rome knew not to use lead containers for making wine,' said Bartholomew, walking to the nearest vat and inspecting it closely. 'But you ferment yours in these metal tanks, which you recently bought from—'

'Ancient Rome?' echoed Shirwynk in disbelief. He addressed Peyn a second time. 'They must be desperate indeed if they are forced to quote examples from ancient Rome!'

'Listen to me,' said Bartholomew quietly. 'Vitruvius was a very wise man, and he recommended clay for storing foodstuffs, because lead has compounds that leach—'

'There is nothing wrong with my wine,' snapped Shirwynk, and to prove it, he went to the nearest vat, dipped a beaker into it and drank deeply. 'Delicious! But am I dead? No, I am not. Now leave, before my lads toss you out.'

'Wine is acidic,' persisted Bartholomew, jigging away from the burly youth who tried to grab his arm. 'It *dissolves* lead. You must have noticed the white granules that grow where—'

'No,' interrupted Peyn shortly. 'We have not.'

Bartholomew ran his finger down the tank, then held it up so they could see the whitish powder that adhered to it. 'Lead salts – formed when the acid from the fermenting apples eats into the metal. They are sweet to the taste, which is why your wine has a sickly flavour. It is not the kind of sucura you can buy in London, imported from Tyre and taxed at ninety per cent, but something else altogether.'

'Most of Cambridge does not call my apple nectar sickly,' said Shirwynk dangerously. 'It is extremely popular.'

'I am sure it is – far more than the sour stuff you could

319

brew in wooden barrels. But you bought these metal ones from the Austin Priory this year—'

'Then it is their fault, not ours,' Peyn interrupted again. 'Not that it matters, because you are wrong anyway. You say our wine is causing the *debilitas,* but my mother died of that disease, and she never touched wine of any description.'

'But she ate food made with your "sucura",' argued Bartholomew. He raised his finger again. 'And this is it – a by-product of brewing apple wine in lead tanks. It is not smuggled into the town, but manufactured here. *You* are the ones who have flooded Cambridge with it.'

'We most certainly are not,' declared Shirwynk indignantly. 'Yes, there is usually a white crust in the vats, but not enough to "flood" an entire town. As everyone knows – except you, it would seem – sucura comes through the Fens.'

'No, it does not, which is why the Sheriff has never been able to catch anyone bringing it in. You have complained several times that someone steals your wine at night, yet Peyn stays here to keep guard, so how can thieves break in? But I know the answer.'

'Do not listen,' Peyn instructed his father nervously. 'He is just jealous that I am about to become a successful Treasury clerk. He wishes it was him that was going to Westminster.'

'I will hear no slander against my son, Bartholomew,' warned Shirwynk. He nodded to his apprentices. 'Throw him out.'

'He has been boiling the wine down while you are tucked up in bed and he is here alone,' said Bartholomew, ducking behind the vat to escape the hands that came to lay hold of him. 'A process that sees it crystallise as white powder – which he passes off as sucura. I wager anything you please that it will no longer be available once he leaves home.'

Peyn was shaking his head, but he wore a heavy bag looped over his shoulder, and his hand kept dropping to it in a very furtive manner. Michael made a lunge for it. Peyn tried to jerk away, and the ensuing tussle saw several packets drop out on to the floor.

'Those are mine,' shouted Peyn. 'I bought them to . . . to bake my father a farewell cake.'

'And when do you propose to do that?' demanded Michael archly. The apprentices stopped trying to seize Bartholomew and stared at Peyn instead, equally unconvinced by the claim. 'On the open road? And that is enough for twenty cakes, anyway.'

Shirwynk's open mouth and pale face suggested that he had no idea what his son had been doing, but he rallied quickly. He ordered his apprentices out and told them to close the door behind them, unwilling for them to hear more of the discussion.

'Peyn is a good lad,' he said, when they had gone. 'If he says he bought the sucura, then he did. It is illegal, but we all do stupid things from time to time, and one foolish mistake should not cost him his Treasury career. I am sure we can come to an arrangement.'

Michael reached under a table and retrieved something from the floor – several pieces of parchment that had been folded to make tiny envelopes, all of which were identical to the ones Cynric had given the Michaelhouse Fellows to protect them against restless spirits.

'Then why is there a lot of unused sucura wrapping here? And I imagine the Sheriff will find even more evidence once he starts looking.'

'We will make good on the tax,' blurted Shirwynk, capitulating abruptly as the case against Peyn went from strength to strength. 'We will offer Tulyet a settlement he cannot refuse. However, it is none of the University's concern so—'

'Oh, yes it is,' said Michael sternly. 'Scholars are dead

because *you* have been selling contaminated wine, while your greedy son has been manufacturing lead salts and calling them sucura.'

'Lead salts are not poisonous,' said Peyn, licking dry lips. 'Physicians and apothecaries use them in medicine. Even if you can prove these charges, we have harmed no one.'

'They may have benefits in small doses,' acknowledged Bartholomew. 'But people have been swallowing lots of them.' He turned to Shirwynk. 'Including you, probably. Can you honestly say that you have not recently suffered from headaches, a metallic taste in your mouth, dizziness, stomach cramps, insomnia, loss of appetite, weakness in the limbs or nausea?'

'I might have felt a little shabby of late,' conceded Shirwynk. 'But you cannot prove it is because of my wine or sucura.'

'Yes, I can,' countered Bartholomew. 'All it needs are a few simple tests.'

'You have been listening to that imbecile Nigellus,' sneered Shirwynk, although a tremor in his voice revealed his growing fear that the physician might actually be right. 'He does not know what he is talking about either.'

'Other symptoms of lead poisoning include irritability and increased aggression,' said Bartholomew. 'Which may explain why so many people have been unusually short-tempered these last few weeks. Yourself among them.'

Shirwynk stared at him. 'If I am angry, it is because your University tries my patience. It has nothing to do with any so-called lead salts.'

'Peyn has told us twice now that he does not touch apple wine or sweet foods,' said Bartholomew. 'And he has exhibited none of these symptoms. He—'

He stopped speaking when Shirwynk whipped around and grabbed a long metal hook from the wall. He jabbed at the scholars with it, forcing them to retreat or risk being disembowelled.

'Put that down,' ordered Michael imperiously. 'Or I shall—'

'You are in no position to make threats,' snarled Shirwynk. 'And I have heard enough. I cannot allow you to harm Peyn as he stands on the brink of his new life. I am afraid you must die.'

CHAPTER 13

The cold determination in Shirwynk's eyes told Bartholomew and Michael that he meant to kill them where they stood. Peyn knew it, too, and his face was hard with savage glee as he drew the long knife he carried at his side, aiming to lend a hand.

Bartholomew pulled a pair of heavy childbirth forceps from his medical bag. They were not much of a weapon, but they did serve to deflect Shirwynk's first blow, although he knew it was only a matter of time before the hook found its mark.

'I know why you hate the University,' the monk said, wholly unfazed by the danger. 'Peyn made such a point about not wanting to be a scholar that I looked in our records. And what did I find? That he *did* apply, but was soundly rejected. You are both bitter—'

Bartholomew only just managed to counter the furious swipe that Peyn aimed at the monk's vitals, although Michael did not flinch, perhaps because there had been no time. The resulting clash made Peyn yelp in pain and he fell back, nursing a wrenched elbow.

'King's Hall,' he hissed between gritted teeth, flexing his damaged joint. 'How dare they refuse me! And they were followed by Gonville, Peterhouse and all the hostels.'

'Even Zachary!' said Michael tauntingly. 'A place with no academic standards whatsoever. You must have cut a miserable figure indeed for them to turn you down.'

Bartholomew was hard-pressed to fend off Shirwynk's indignant assault, and was aware that if father and son attacked together, he and Michael would be dead. Shirwynk fell back eventually, circling as he considered his next move. Peyn had recovered sufficiently to try a jab or two, but he was tentative, unwilling to risk further injury.

'If you must antagonise them, Brother, then at least grab a weapon,' hissed Bartholomew urgently. 'I cannot defend you indefinitely.'

Michael picked up a ladle from the floor and feinted at Peyn, who staggered backwards with an alarmed squeak.

'You should have accepted my son,' said Shirwynk coldly. 'He would have been an asset to you, and I had set my heart on him becoming a lawyer. But his talent is such that he does not need your paltry degrees anyway. Not now he has won his post in Westminster.'

Confident in his father's devotion, Peyn began to gloat. 'It was so easy to fool you! I read how to make lead salts when I was preparing my application for King's Hall – Stephen let me use his library. *No one* guessed it was me making and selling the sucura.'

'Peyn!' barked Shirwynk, horrified. 'Say no more.'

'Why?' shrugged Peyn. 'They will never repeat this conversation to anyone else, and they *should* know that their stupid University made a mistake by declining to take me.'

'So I am beginning to understand,' murmured Michael, 'given that you promptly turned around and started to poison everyone.'

'I have been making sucura for months,' said Peyn tauntingly. 'At first, I only sold it in Barnwell, thinking to keep the venture modest, but it was so successful that I could not resist expanding into Cambridge. People want it so badly that they pay stupidly high prices, and it has made me rich. How do you think I got my post at Westminster?'

Shirwynk blinked. 'Because the Treasury heard about your remarkable abilities and invited you to join them, just as I have been telling everyone.'

Peyn laughed, although it was a bitter sound. 'Nothing

is free in this world, Father. I *bought* the position – with money from my sucura.'

'But if the stuff *has* been causing the *debilitas*, as these scholars say, then it means you killed Letia,' breathed Shirwynk, shocked. 'Your mother.'

'She was dying anyway,' shrugged Peyn. 'Or so she claimed. Personally, I thought it was just an excuse to lie around in bed eating cakes.'

'You did not know your sucura might be dangerous,' said Shirwynk. It was a statement, not a question, and there was a pathetic desperation in his eyes. 'You sold it in all innocence.'

Peyn grinned malevolently, a response that made his sire's face crumple in dismay. 'I had my suspicions, which is why I never touch it myself. Not the sucura *or* the apple wine.'

'But you let me drink it.' Shirwynk's voice was low and strained.

Knowing where his best interests lay, Peyn abandoned his air of gloating insouciance and became ingratiating. 'I would not have let you come to harm. And I am not responsible for the deaths anyway. All the victims were old, ill or overly greedy.'

'Was *Frenge* overly greedy?' asked Michael. 'I assume you poisoned him as well?'

Peyn shook his head. 'His death was a nuisance, actually, because he was the one who took the sucura out to sell.'

'No!' snapped Michael. 'I questioned any number of people who bought the stuff – Agatha, Cynric, Mistress Tulyet, Dodenho, Chancellor Tynkell – and none of them got it from Frenge.'

'Stephen did,' said Bartholomew. 'He told me so a few months ago.'

Peyn shot them both a pitying glance. 'Frenge did not deal with the bulk of our customers himself, stupid! He hired petty criminals to do it – men who are used to hawking goods of dubious origin around the town's taverns.'

'Then it was all Frenge's idea,' said Shirwynk, still unwilling to see his beloved son in the role of arch villain. 'He was a thief . . . there was a rumour that he stole cattle—'

'He did not have the wits to devise a scheme of this audacity and cunning,' interrupted Peyn. 'Only I did.' He smirked challengingly at Michael. 'And incidentally, he never delivered ale to King's Hall on the day he died. I made that up to confuse you.'

'But you told me that tale as well,' said Shirwynk hoarsely. 'And I repeated it to others . . .'

'Just as I intended,' said Peyn, all smug triumph. 'It put suspicion on King's Hall, which serves them right for suing us.'

There was a moment when Bartholomew thought Shirwynk would be so stunned by his son's nasty revelations that he would lay down his hook and surrender, but only a fleeting one. Peyn also sensed his sire's weakening resolve, so took steps to remedy the situation. He put a loving arm around his father's shoulders, and murmured in his ear. Whatever he said caused Shirwynk to take a deep breath and become businesslike.

'Go and wait outside. I do not want your last memories of Cambridge tainted by murder.'

'No, we shall dispatch them together,' said Peyn, obviously not trusting him to go through with it. He gripped his blade purposefully. 'Ready?'

Shirwynk nodded, his expression grim, and they advanced side by side. Bartholomew held his forceps in one hand and let his medical bag slide into the other, aiming to swing it in the hope of entangling one of their weapons.

'Stop!' ordered Michael, raising the ladle. 'Desist immediately, or I will—'

327

'Will what?' sneered Peyn. 'Arrest us? How? We are the ones with the pointed implements.'

'By summoning HELP!' Michael bawled the last word at the top of his voice, and the brewery door flew open to reveal Tulyet and several soldiers. Dickon was there, too, his face still scarlet, although his teeth were back to their normal yellowish white.

Shirwynk and Peyn whipped around in horror. In a frantic but ill-advised effort to save the day, Shirwynk went on a wild offensive, but a hook, however sharp, was no match for broadswords, and Tulyet disarmed him with ease. When he saw his father defeated, Peyn dropped his knife and held his hands in front of him, to show he was unarmed. They shook with fear.

'I assume you heard everything, Dick?' asked Michael, while Bartholomew leaned against the wall and wished *he* had known that the Sheriff had been poised for rescue. No wonder Michael had been all cool composure in the face of death!

'I did,' replied Tulyet. 'Every word.'

'It was all Frenge's idea,' bleated Peyn. 'I swear! He forced me to help him and—'

'How?' asked Tulyet mildly. 'You just said he did not have the wits.'

'No, but he does,' said Peyn, pointing at his father. 'I did learn about lead salts in Stephen's books, but when I told *him* about them, he devised a way to make himself rich *and* to rid himself of an unwanted wife into the bargain. I did nothing wrong. It was all him.'

The blood drained from Shirwynk's face, but even this final evidence of his son's perfidy did not dent his devotion. 'Yes,' he said softly. 'The scheme was all mine. Peyn knew nothing about any of it. He is innocent of any wrongdoing.'

There was a flicker of something in Peyn's eyes, but it was gone too quickly to say whether it was remorse.

'So release me,' the boy said. 'I shall go to Westminster and our paths will never cross again. Unless you ever need a favour, of course, in which case I shall be delighted to oblige.'

'Take them away,' said Tulyet, eyeing him with disgust. 'Thank God I have an upright, noble son, because I think I should die of shame if I had one like you.'

Once Shirwynk and Peyn had been marched to the castle, Bartholomew examined the metal vats, to assure himself that his conclusions were right. He was, and Michael and Tulyet listened aghast as he explained in more detail how Peyn had made 'sucura', both appalled by the lad's brazen disregard for the people who had sickened or died.

'So it and the apple wine are insidious poisons,' said Tulyet when Bartholomew had finished. 'Ones that work gradually. Once they are unavailable, will the *debilitas* disappear?'

'There should be no further cases, and I hope the symptoms of those already affected will be eased by certain treatments.' Bartholomew glanced at Michael. 'Lead poisoning explains the damage I saw in the stomachs and livers of Lenne, Yerland, Segeforde and Irby.'

'We shall have to apologise to Nigellus,' said Michael unhappily. 'Damn! It is certain to cost an absolute fortune – one he will doubtless use to fund his new *studium generale* in the Fens.'

'You will have to apologise to Edith as well,' added Bartholomew. 'She said from the start that her dyeworks were innocent, and she was right.'

'What about Frenge?' asked Tulyet. 'Can we attribute his death to sucura or apple wine?'

Bartholomew shook his head. 'He was fed an acidic substance that killed him quickly, one quite different from lead salts.'

'Yes – we still have a killer at large,' agreed Michael. 'A person who stabbed Hamo and strangled Kellawe as well. Unfortunately, we are running out of suspects. Or do you think Shirwynk and Peyn are responsible?'

'Not Shirwynk,' said Tulyet. 'He was too shocked by his son's admissions to be a seasoned murderer himself. And to be frank, I do not think Peyn is brave enough to claim his victims face to face. What about Cew? His madness has always seemed rather convenient to me. After all, who will suspect a lunatic?'

'I am fairly sure his affliction is genuine,' said Bartholomew.

'Perhaps so, but that does not preclude him from being the strategist,' said Michael, and explained his theory about the criminal mastermind to the Sheriff. 'After all, it requires a certain type of insanity to bring all this about – one that entails a good deal of ruthless cunning.'

'Then perhaps the strategist is Stephen,' suggested Tulyet. 'He is ruthlessly cunning.'

'He is currently suffering from a weakness in his wrists,' said Bartholomew. 'One that would make strangling anyone impossible.'

'Who, then?' demanded Tulyet, beginning to be exasperated. 'Wauter, who rode away into the Fens, where he is welcoming scholars with open arms?'

'We cannot know that,' said Bartholomew sharply. 'There may be a perfectly innocent explanation for his disappearance.'

'Unlikely,' said Tulyet. 'But I appreciate that you do not want this strategist to be from Michaelhouse. I have a fondness for your College myself, and would far rather the culprit came from somewhere else – such as King's Hall or Zachary.'

'Not King's Hall,' said Michael. 'They are determined to keep the University in Cambridge, no matter what they have to do to achieve it. The best suspects are Nigellus and Morys, who are leading proponents for the *studium generale* in the Fens.'

'If it is Nigellus, you will not have to apologise for arresting him on suspicion of killing his patients,' remarked Tulyet. 'And I admit that it would give me pleasure to see such an arrogant devil behind bars.'

Michael smiled wanly. 'I am with you there, Dick, so Matt and I will speak to him and Morys as soon as I have had something to eat. It is not something to be attempted on an empty stomach, and the confrontation with Shirwynk and Peyn has quite sapped my energy.'

'There is no time for gorging,' said Tulyet. 'I should have told you at once: trouble is brewing between King's Hall and some of the scholars who want to leave. I tried to quell it, but they took exception to my inter-ference. You are the only one who can prevent a pitched battle.'

'I am sure there are townsmen to hand, though,' said Michael acidly. 'Ready to join in. We must stand together if we are to keep the peace, so come with me.'

They secured the brewery and hurried to the High Street, where raised voices could be heard. Afternoon was fading to evening, and it would not be long before it was dark, at which point it was obvious from the tense atmosphere that fights would break out.

'How long have you known that the University rejected Peyn?' asked Bartholomew.

'Ever since he admitted it just now.' Michael shrugged at the physician's astonishment. 'It was a guess, Matt. We do not keep records of failed applications.'

The quarrel was centred on the Trumpington Gate, where scholars from King's Hall, along with students from several other Colleges, had taken up station, all armed to the teeth. Facing them was a horde from the hostels, many wearing religious habits and carrying bundles of belongings. Crowds of townsfolk had gathered to watch, clearly intending to weigh in should there be a brawl.

'The hostels are appalled that Shirwynk is prosecuting Morys for trespass,' explained Beadle Meadowman worriedly. 'And fear they will suffer similar charges if *they* inadvertently set foot in the wrong place. Thus the sanctuary of the Fens is attractive, but the wealthier foundations want to stop them from going.'

'We have arrested Shirwynk,' said Michael. 'He cannot sue anyone.'

'That news was broken a few moments ago, but it has made the situation worse,' said Meadowman. 'The hostels think it is a lie – a ruse to keep them here.'

'We must put an end to this nonsense fast, Brother,' said Tulyet. 'Your University is tearing itself apart over this Fen business, and my town will certainly home in on any weakness.'

'You have soldiers and Michael has beadles,' said Bartholomew. 'Send both groups in to disperse this gathering.'

Michael and Tulyet shot him withering looks. 'That would ignite a riot for certain,' said Tulyet. 'This is not a situation that will be resolved by brute force.'

While he and Michael discussed strategies, Bartholomew turned his attention to the mob. Not surprisingly, some voices were louder than others. Nigellus and Morys were in the vanguard of those who wanted to leave, although neither had a pack, suggesting that they did not intend to stay long in the marshes – they would return for more converts.

Meanwhile, Wayt led the faction that aimed to stop them. He was yelling that the hostels had a duty to stay, but was unable to explain why, and side-stepped the issue when his opponents claimed, not without cause, that King's Hall was prepared to put comfortable buildings before a better atmosphere for teaching. Then Nigellus bawled that scholars would be able to devote themselves to the lofty goal of learning far more readily when away from the filthy habits of seculars, and Tulyet's men were hard-pressed to prevent offended townsmen from responding to the insult with their fists.

The soldiers were heavily armed, but were under strict orders not to use their weapons. Dickon ignored the edict, and scampered around with a drawn sword. Townsmen and scholars alike fell back whenever he was near, all eyeing the red-faced figure uneasily. Bartholomew took the opportunity afforded by the distraction to approach Wayt and Dodenho.

'Take your men home,' he begged. 'Without them, the other Colleges will give up and—'

'And the hostel rabble will escape,' snapped Wayt, eyeing the opposition with icy disdain. 'Which I refuse to allow.'

'You cannot keep them here against their will,' argued Bartholomew.

'Oh, yes, I can,' averred Wayt. 'Personally, I would just as soon be rid of the scum, but we cannot let them establish a rival *studium generale* elsewhere. It might grow bigger than our own, and we have carved a nice niche for ourselves in Cambridge.'

'It is not just selfishness,' added Dodenho hastily. 'We may not survive if half of us defect, especially if Oxford takes advantage of our weakness and comes to poach our remaining best thinkers.'

'These hostel men are fools,' declared Wayt, 'driven to recklessness by the mealy-mouthed nonsense spouted by Nigellus, Morys and the Austins. It is for their own good, as much as ours, that we intend to stop them from going.'

'The Austins?' asked Bartholomew in surprise. 'They are no fanatics.'

'They are less bombastic than the rest,' conceded Wayt. 'But they still think the University would be better off in the bogs. The damned imbeciles!'

It occurred to Bartholomew that King's Hall's arrogance might have done more to drive the hostel men away than anything the Austins had said. And when he glanced at the fleshy, dissipated faces around him, he wondered if the rebels were right to think the University would fare better away from the town and its worldly distractions.

'Hamo getting himself killed did not help either,' said Dodenho. 'Prior Joliet should have done more to prevent another murder in his domain, especially given what happened to Frenge.'

'Hamo probably poisoned Frenge,' spat Wayt venomously. 'Which is why a townsman invaded the convent and dispatched Hamo in his turn. It is a pity the man did not use his dying breath to identify his assailant. I heard all he did was blather about the Almighty.'

'I suppose he was in pain,' surmised Dodenho. 'And did not know what he was saying.'

'Nonsense – the killer would have used a sharp knife,' argued Wayt, 'which means that Hamo would have felt nothing at all. And it was remiss of him to go to his grave without sharing the name of his murderer.'

Bartholomew started to tell Wayt that being fatally stabbed certainly would hurt, sharp blade or no, but the Acting Warden ignored him and began haranguing the hostel men again. Unwilling to stand next to him while he did it, Bartholomew slunk away.

Yet Wayt's words sparked a sudden memory of Poitiers, when men with terrible injuries had still found the strength to fight on and even celebrate when the battle was over. In some cases, it had been hours before they had complained of pain, so perhaps Wayt *was* right to claim that Hamo had not felt much. A solution began to unfold in his mind, so he grabbed Michael's sleeve and pulled the monk away from the howling mob, where he could make himself heard.

'Hamo lived for some time after he was stabbed,' he

began. 'Long enough to lurch from the chancel to the porch, and then to whisper his dying words. Or rather, *word*, in the singular.'

'A word that made no sense,' said Michael distractedly. He tried to pull away. 'I cannot talk about this now, Matt. We are on the verge of a riot, in case you had not noticed.'

Bartholomew gripped his arm harder. 'The other morning, Langelee jabbed my hand with his letter-opener, but I did not feel it bite because the blade was so sharp. The same thing happened to Hamo – I think there was no or little pain when he was first stabbed. He was weakened certainly, but still able to move about. It was only when we found him that the agony struck and he died.'

'What are you talking about?' cried Michael. 'Please, Matt! We have more serious matters to consider right now – such as the survival of our University.'

'I think Hamo *did* see his killer,' Bartholomew went on. 'But the culprit did not care – he left him to die, confident that he would not live long enough to talk. *He* was the strategist, Michael – a man so sure of himself that he thinks he is infallible. He—'

Tulyet bustled up at that moment, to make a terse report. 'The hostel men are retreating, thank God. Order King's Hall to stand down, Brother, and I will deal with the townsfolk. However, it is only a temporary reprieve: the hostels will try to leave again, and the Colleges will attempt to stop them. Tonight, probably.'

Michael shoved Bartholomew aside and went to do as he was told. 'You have won the confrontation,' he said to Wayt, speaking softly so that no one from the hostels would hear and beg to differ. 'Now go home before any of your lads are hurt. It is getting late anyway. You must be tired.'

'Not at all,' declared Wayt, although Dodenho began chivvying their students away. Few went willingly. Meanwhile, Peterhouse, Bene't and the Hall of Valence Marie – the Colleges with buildings closest to the

Trumpington Gate – offered hospitality to their supporters, which meant that most were not going very far at all.

'Listen to me, Brother,' Bartholomew said urgently, pulling the monk away from his duties a second time. 'Hamo *did* tell us his killer's identity. Or rather, he told us where he had left something that will give us the answer.'

Michael shook his head in incomprehension. 'He said "all". How can that—'

'I think I only heard part of the word he was trying to say. He was preparing the chapel for vespers when he was attacked – his killer chose a time and a place when he knew his victim would be alone. Hamo was stabbed in the chancel – we know that because of the blood that spilled there. I think he was trying to say "altar".'

'Meaning what?'

'Meaning that he left something on or near the altar and he expected us to find it. He believed he had communicated something important with his dying breath, because I saw satisfaction and relief in his face.'

'What manner of something?' demanded Michael.

'We must go to the Austins' chapel and look. And hope that the strategist has not guessed what Hamo tried to do and has been there before us.'

Tulyet was irked when Michael told him that he was going the Austin Priory, feeling he was being left to handle a potentially explosive situation on his own. The monk promised to return as soon as possible, and left Meadowman in charge in his stead.

'Then do not be long,' ordered Tulyet curtly. 'It will be dark soon, at which point the hostel men will try to slip away under cover of night – and the Colleges will be waiting.'

'Hopefully, we will return with the news that the strategist is arrested,' said Michael. 'That might calm troubled waters.'

'It is far too late for that,' said Tulyet bleakly. 'And while Meadowman is an admirable fellow, he is not the Senior Proctor. Come back as soon as you can.'

Michael and Bartholomew hurried to the convent. At a glance, the streets appeared to be deserted, folk obediently obeying the curfew that had been imposed by Senior Proctor and Sheriff, but there were flickers of movement in the smaller alleys, and doors were ajar in every house as people peered out. Bene't College's gates were closed, but a rumble of feisty voices from within indicated that its residents were busily inciting each other to mischief.

'There is no point speaking to them,' said Bartholomew, seeing Michael falter, torn between exploring the Austins' chapel and issuing a warning to a College known for its fondness for brawls. 'They will not listen, and you will have wasted valuable time.'

The monk knew he was right, and they resumed their journey without a word. It was not long before they arrived. The front gate was locked, and the Austins were evidently not expecting visitors, because no one was on duty to answer their knocks. Fraught with frustration, Bartholomew gave it a heavy thump with his shoulder, and was disconcerted to discover it so rotten that it almost gave way.

'They spend all their money on alms,' said Michael. 'Unlike King's Hall, or even Michaelhouse, where security is considered more important. Hit it again.'

'But if I break it, they will have no way to keep marauders out,' argued Bartholomew, disliking the notion of vandalising a religious house.

'A rotten door will provide scant protection anyway,' Michael pointed out, and when the physician still hesitated, he charged at it himself, causing it to fly to pieces under the onslaught.

'God's teeth, Brother!' hissed Bartholomew, surveying the shattered remnants in dismay. 'Now we cannot even begin to disguise the damage.'

'It was more fragile than I anticipated,' said Michael defensively. 'And do not blaspheme.'

The priory grounds were empty, but a voice could be heard emanating from the refectory: the friars were eating, listening to their Bible Scholar read aloud as they did so. Rather than waste time in explanations, Michael trotted straight towards the chapel.

The building was shadowy and as silent as the grave, which Bartholomew found unnerving, especially when he remembered that it had been about the same time of day that Hamo had been killed. He glanced around anxiously, half expecting the strategist to leap out at them with his sharp little blade, but the place was deserted. He followed Michael to the altar.

'There is nothing here,' said Michael accusingly, whispering because it seemed wrong for loud voices to shatter the building's peace. 'You were wrong!'

Bartholomew dropped to his hands and knees, and pushed aside the cloth that covered the table to peer underneath. At first, he thought Michael was right, but then he saw dark smudges in the ancient dust of the floor. He stood, grabbed a candle, and crouched back down.

'Writing,' he said excitedly. 'Or rather letters drawn in blood. Hamo must have put his hand beneath and—'

'I understand what he did,' interrupted Michael sharply. 'What does it say?'

'Robert,' replied Bartholomew, staring up at him.

'He cannot mean the almoner. He must mean Robert de Hakeney.'

'Hakeney has an alibi for Hamo's murder – he was in the King's Head.'

'Then perhaps he hired a crony to do it. God knows, there are dozens of men in that rough place who would oblige him.'

'It costs money to rent a killer, and Hakeney does not

have any. Moreover, his behaviour on the night of the murder was not commensurate with a man who had commissioned a crime. I think Hamo *did* mean his fellow Austin.'

Michael glanced around uncomfortably, although they were still alone. 'Why?'

'First, because he wrote this message in a place where it would not be seen by any of his brethren. And second, because he told *us*, rather than one of them, what he had done.'

Michael made an impatient movement with his hand. 'You are reading too much into the unfathomable actions of a dying man.'

'*Think*, Brother! Hamo was badly wounded, but did not try to summon help. Why? Because he knew his killer would be among those who came. And why did he not reveal the name of his assailant as he breathed his last? Because Robert was there, and would have found a way to dismiss or explain away whatever Hamo had managed to gasp.'

Michael started to argue, but then stopped and became thoughtful. 'You said at the time that he was trying to communicate something. Failing that, the message would eventually have been found by whoever changes the altar cloth – the sacristan or his assistants, but definitely not the almoner. But *why* would Robert kill Hamo? He is a friar, and a good one. Such men do not usually dispatch their colleagues.'

'Because Robert is the strategist.' Bartholomew continued quickly when he saw Michael's immediate disbelief. 'He is one of those who thinks the University should decant to the Fens.'

'So does half the University,' Michael pointed out.

'But it makes sense! Frenge also died here – in a place that Robert knows. But this is no time to speculate. Our best option now is to go to the refectory and see what

Robert has to say about his name written in blood beneath the altar.'

He began to hurry there before Michael could object, arriving to find the friars concluding a modest repast of bread and ale. They were standing and Prior Joliet had just finished saying grace. They all looked up in astonishment when Bartholomew burst in. Robert was not there.

'Where is your almoner?' Bartholomew demanded.

Joliet blinked at the abrupt question. 'He has gone to Michaelhouse. Why? And how did you get in? Our front gate is locked.'

'Gone to Michaelhouse to do what?' asked Bartholomew in alarm.

'To deliver wine,' said Joliet, regarding Bartholomew in bemusement. 'It is a gift from your sister, but the mood of the town is such that she was too afraid to take it herself, so she asked Robert to oblige. I advised him to leave it until tomorrow, but he—'

'Edith is not in the habit of sending us wine,' interrupted Bartholomew. 'And even if she were, she has a whole household to do her bidding and would not have asked Robert. Moreover, she would not think it necessary for the stuff to arrive tonight, when the town is alive with unrest.'

'So what does it—' began Michael.

Bartholomew cut across him. 'Robert aims to do Michaelhouse harm, no doubt to cause further strife between University and town. Which is more evidence that he is the strategist!'

'Now just a moment,' objected Joliet indignantly. 'Edith probably chose Robert to be her agent because he is an almoner, used to giving things away. He—'

'*How* did she ask him?' demanded Bartholomew. 'Did she come here?'

'No, she sent a message.' It was Overe who replied. 'I have it here.' He reached into the scrip that hung from his belt and produced a folded piece of parchment.

'I have seen this writing before,' said Bartholomew, snatching it from him. 'Or rather, I have seen letters penned with this nib – it has a nick, which makes all its upstrokes distinctive.'

'Where have you seen it?' asked Joliet warily.

'On letters to Stephen. Two informed him that Michaelhouse and Gonville are on the brink of moving to the Fens, and a third told him to persuade Hakeney to steal Robert's cross.'

'*Robert's* cross,' pounced Michael. 'He is unlikely to encourage a crime against himself. And why would he bother to forge a note from Edith? He could have just told everyone that she asked him to deliver the wine and no one would know any different. You are wrong, Matt.'

'He would not have been allowed out without one,' said Overe. 'The rest of us would have refused to let him go – on account of the danger – but this letter is very persuasive . . .'

'It is,' agreed Bartholomew, scanning it again. 'It is also nothing Edith would have written. Ergo, Robert penned it himself, aiming to escape the convent and further his nasty plans.'

'My almoner is a good man,' said Joliet quietly. 'Like all my brethren. Indeed, there is only one Austin whose character I would question – the one in your College.'

'Wauter?' asked Bartholomew, his stomach churning.

'Well, he did charge off to the Fens without asking permission,' Joliet went on. 'And I am told he took his *Martilogium* with him, which means he is unlikely to return.'

'Go to your chapel and lock the door,' instructed Michael. 'I am afraid your front gate will no longer protect you. Do not come out until I tell you it is safe to do so.'

'And if you see Robert, toll the bell,' added Bartholomew. 'Michael will send help.'

'But why?' cried Joliet, distressed. 'I thought we had

just proved that you are wrong, and that Robert is innocent of . . . whatever it is you think he has done.'

'There is no time to explain,' said Bartholomew. 'You will just have to trust us.'

Dusk had settled across Cambridge as Bartholomew and Michael ran along the High Street, and mischief was in the air. Lights blazed from Gonville Hall, and its gates were open to reveal scholars massing in its yard. Michael stopped to demand whether they had heard about the curfew.

'Yes, but we shall have no University left if we do not stop the defectors from disappearing into the marshes,' said an undergraduate, a burly youth whose missing front teeth suggested he was no stranger to brawls. 'You should thank us for what we aim to do tonight.'

'You will stay in and behave,' said Michael sharply. 'Where is Rougham?'

'Out with a patient,' replied the lad, 'and the other Fellows have locked themselves in the conclave. Perhaps you should join them there, Brother. It will be safer for you.'

Michael struggled not to lose his temper. 'Where are your academic tabards? You do know I can fine you for not wearing them?'

'They make too obvious a target for our enemies, so we elected to don secular garb tonight,' replied the lad. He flicked imaginary dust from his fur-trimmed gipon, a gesture that suggested vanity had played no small role in the decision to defy the University's rules on what constituted suitable attire.

Michael was used to dealing with insolent youths, and his steely glance had caused many a knee to wobble, but Gonville's boys had been drinking. It was also too dark for the full force of his proctorly glower to be felt, and Bartholomew knew that, although they meekly closed

342

their gates as the Senior Proctor ordered, it would not be long before they marched out.

In St Michael's Lane, a few scholars from Ovyng and Physwick hostels were slinking along in the shadows, cloaked and hooded against recognition, many with bundles over their shoulders. Others were calling them back, some issuing threats and ultimatums that were unlikely to encourage the renegades to stay.

'It is like trying to stem the tide,' said Michael in dismay, as he hammered on Michaelhouse's sturdy gate. 'The strategist has been clever indeed.'

The porter opened the door to reveal a scene of efficient activity. Some students had been set to patrol the walls, while others were filling butts with water should there be a fire. Langelee was in charge, standing serenely in the middle of the yard as he issued instructions to Fellows, students and staff alike. Even Agatha was scurrying to obey, and was in the process of putting all the College's valuables in a box so it could be buried.

'Buried?' asked Michael in alarm.

'It is the best way to keep it safe from looters,' explained the Master. 'I have been in enough dangerous situations to know that our very existence is in question tonight. Vengeful hostel men or townsfolk may batter their way in, but they will not get our precious treasures. Such as they are.'

'Good.' Michael cast a quick glance around. 'Is everyone here?'

Langelee nodded. 'Do not worry, Brother. The other Heads of Houses might have lost control of their lads, but I still command Michaelhouse.'

'Robert,' said Bartholomew urgently. 'Did he come to deliver wine?'

'Yes – some of that nasty apple brew from Shirwynk, which he said was a gift from your sister, although I should be surprised if that were true. She knows I do not like it.'

'Has anyone had any?' demanded Bartholomew.

'Not yet. Robert said we should share it out tonight, to fortify ourselves for the coming battle, but Clippesby started clamouring some tale about pigeons and poison and he unsettled me, to be frank, so I put it in your storeroom. Why—'

Bartholomew shoved past him and ran to his quarters, where the cask was standing in the middle of the floor. He decanted some of its contents into a cup, and sniffed it before swirling it around to inspect its consistency. It looked and smelled innocuous enough. He stared at it. It was reckless to sip something he was sure was dangerous, but time was short and he needed answers. He put a drop on his tongue, and immediately tasted the sickly sweetness of the wine. It was followed by a slight burning sensation. He spat it out of the window.

'He added a caustic substance to it,' he told Langelee and Michael. 'Not enough to kill instantly – like the stuff he forced Frenge to swallow – but enough to make us very ill. And all so that Edith would be blamed.'

'Why would Robert want that?' asked Langelee, startled.

'To create another reason for the University to be angry with the town,' explained Bartholomew. 'And another reason for people to rail against the dyeworks. Robert is a clever man – the strategist is a good name for him.' He turned to Michael. 'Well? Is this evidence enough for you to accept that he is the mastermind behind all this mayhem?'

Michael nodded slowly.

'Then go and stop him,' ordered Langelee. 'I will dispose of this "gift" and keep the College safe. Now hurry, before he destroys us all.'

'Perhaps there are advantages to having a battle-honed Master,' said Bartholomew, as he and Michael raced back towards to the Austin Priory in the hope that Robert had returned. 'At least we know that Michaelhouse is safe in his hands.'

344

'Nowhere is safe tonight,' said Michael grimly. 'And Langelee knows it. Why do you think he is burying our valuables? He has never done that before.'

Bartholomew shot him a sidelong glance. 'Do you think it is that bad?'

'I would not be surprised if the whole town was in flames by tomorrow,' came the sombre response. 'Especially if we do not find Robert and prevent him from implementing more of his felonious plans.'

CHAPTER 14

Trouble found Bartholomew and Michael long before they reached the Austin Priory. Gonville's students were out, and they had been joined by lads from King's Hall. They were facing a small pack of scholars from the hostels, led by Gilby, the vociferous priest from White. Some carried pitch torches, and the light they shed cast eerie shadows on the surrounding houses.

'I thought you had gone to the Fens,' said Michael, displeased to see Gilby in the thick of more disorder. 'And that you were sick with the *debilitas.*'

'I made a miraculous recovery,' replied the priest. 'God be praised.'

'Is there any apple wine in the marshes?' asked Bartholomew. 'Or sweet foods?'

'No,' replied the priest shortly. 'There is nothing debauched about our new *studium generale.* It is a fine place, based on sober virtues. And it is growing fast, which is why I am here – to encourage other decent men to join us. But these louts will not let us pass.'

'Stand aside,' Michael told the College men tiredly. 'We are not tyrants, to keep them here by force. If they want to live in rush hovels and listen to lectures given under dripping trees, then that is their decision.'

'There should be a statute forbidding anyone from slinking off in the middle of term,' said the gap-toothed Gonville boy. Michael took a step towards him, at which point he decided it was imprudent to challenge the Senior Proctor and so shuffled to one side. His cronies did likewise.

'Go,' said Michael to Gilby, indicating the path to freedom. 'But bear in mind that once you do, you can never return. We will not reinstate rebels.'

'Why would we return?' asked Gilby haughtily. 'Your University is steeped in corruption – especially Michaelhouse, which was as poor as a church mouse last year, but now is drowning in money. And I know why: donations from the dyeworks. The latest bribe was a cask of wine. Poor Almoner Robert said that Edith Stanmore insisted he deliver it immediately, despite the perils of being abroad tonight.'

Before Bartholomew could inform him that Edith had done no such thing, there was a shout, and they turned to see the scholars of Zachary Hostel marching towards them. They were led by Nigellus, although Morys was nowhere to be seen. Every man was sumptuously attired and carried an impressive array of weapons – swords, daggers, cudgels and even crossbows. There was a collective hiss as King's Hall drew their own blades and took up fighting formation. Gilby barked an order, and his followers did likewise.

'No,' snapped Michael. 'The town would love to see us tear each other to pieces. Do you *want* to provide their entertainment tonight?'

'We will defeat the hostel scum, then teach the town a lesson,' shouted someone from King's Hall to cheers from his cronies. 'The priest who promised to absolve them of the sin of attacking us is dead, so we will all burn in Hell together.'

'Almoner Robert has been granted a licence to take his place,' announced Nigellus, although Bartholomew was sure it could not be true – there had not been enough time to make such arrangements with the Bishop. 'So you will burn alone.'

'Take your students home, Nigellus,' begged

Bartholomew, seeing the hostels take courage from his words and square up for a brawl. 'You are a physician. You cannot want a battle that—'

The rest of his sentence was lost as the Colleges surged forward with a baying roar, and for a moment, all was a blur of flailing weapons, screams and curses. Those who had been holding torches dropped them in order to fight, with the result that the street was suddenly plunged into darkness, making it all but impossible to tell friend from foe. A few torches continued to flicker on the ground, but rather than illuminating what was happening, they posed a fire hazard, and more than one combatant backed away to slap at burning clothing.

Fortunately, the skirmish did not last long, and Bartholomew had done no more than haul out his child-birth forceps to defend himself before he sensed some of the belligerents running away. The trickle quickly became a rout, and then the street was full of the rattle of fleeing footsteps and the cheers of the victors. The dropped torches were snatched up to show that the hostels had won the encounter, thanks to a timely influx of reinforcements from the foundations along Water Lane.

'That showed the rogues!' howled Gilby, his voice only just audible over the triumphant yells. 'Now we shall hunt down more of those College vermin and show them what—'

'No, you will not,' bellowed Michael furiously. Bartholomew was relieved to see him unharmed. 'Take your recruits and go – and do not show your face here again.'

'Not until I have trounced King's Hall,' countered Gilby, and before Michael could stop him, he had dashed away, his torch acting as a bobbing beacon to his followers.

Soon all that remained were the injured, a dozen or so scattered across the street, moaning or crying for help.

Bartholomew grabbed a light and went to see what might be done for them.

'Does anyone need last rites, Matt?' asked Michael urgently. 'Or may I go?'

'No one from Zachary needs a priest,' came a familiar voice. It was Nigellus, one hand clasped to his hip. His voice was gloating even in his pain. 'Almoner Robert has already absolved us for anything we might do tonight. But come here, Brother. I have something to tell you.'

Michael knelt next to him, but Bartholomew's attention was snagged by the student who lay groaning at his feet, and he did not hear what Nigellus whispered to the monk. He glanced up several minutes later to see Michael disappearing into the darkness, leaving him alone with the casualties of the encounter, all of whom pleaded with him to tend them first. For the second time that evening, he found himself thinking of Poitiers – of the battle's aftermath, when he had been similarly inundated with piteous calls for help.

He moved from one to the next, determining quickly who could be saved and who was a lost cause. He stemmed bleeding from five serious wounds, reset a broken arm and reduced a dislocated shoulder before reaching Nigellus, who had a crossbow bolt lodged in his hip. It was not easy to remove, and Nigellus howled so loudly that Bartholomew feared the screams would bring back the hostel men, who would almost certainly assume he was being deliberately heavy-handed.

He was acutely aware of movements in the shadows nearby, as people slunk this way and that, but it was too dark to see whether they were friendly or hostile. All he could do was keep working and hope they would realise that he was not a 'damned butcher' as Nigellus was shrieking, and that his aim was to mend, not torture, the injured.

By the time he had finished with Nigellus, the other

casualties had either staggered away by themselves or been carried home by friends – only two corpses remained. He was as taut as a bowstring, wondering how he was going to tote Nigellus to safety on his own. He was relieved when Tulyet, Dickon and a band of soldiers arrived.

'The whole town is running mad,' the Sheriff reported tersely. 'We are a hair's breadth from a riot such as we have never seen.'

Dickon covered the faces of the dead with their cloaks, and Tulyet nodded silent approval – although a cold shiver ran down Bartholomew's spine when he read not compassion in the eerie red face, but ghoulish fascination. More sounds of violence were carried on the wind, and Tulyet issued a stream of orders to his men that had them scurrying off in all directions.

'I should have stayed in Barnwell,' Nigellus was muttering. His face was ashen, and Bartholomew wondered if he would survive the shock of the wound and what had been necessary to treat it. 'I had a good life there, but Robert said I was wasted, and should become a scholar . . .'

'*Almoner* Robert?' demanded Bartholomew, crouching next to him. 'Why? He is not a member of Zachary. Or was he actually inviting you to become an Austin?'

'He has friends in Zachary – friends who support his contention that the University is corrupt and bloated. He aims to lead it to a better future, where scholars do not live in constant fear of attacks by the town, and where whores do not entice students to sin.'

'Right,' said Bartholomew, too tired to argue. He stared at the wounded *medicus*, then decided it was as good a time as any to ask the questions that were plaguing him. 'You prescribed medicines in Barnwell, but not here. Why?'

'Because none of them really work,' replied Nigellus

bitterly. 'And Prior Norton made some nasty remarks about the expense. I did not want Cambridge folk making the same accusations, so I decided only to accept healthy clients. But then the *debilitas* struck here as well . . .'

Bartholomew was surprised that Nigellus had allowed the wild words of a grieving man to wound him. He could only suppose that years of working in a small community, where his skills and training – whether adequate or not – had given him a godlike status, meant Nigellus was unused to criticism. He stood, not sure what to say to a physician who thought more of his reputation than his ability to serve the people who needed his help.

'Robert means well,' Nigellus went on softly. 'But I fear he may have done terrible things to effect a solution. Irby died of natural causes, but Yerland, Segeforde and Kellawe . . . I think Robert might have dispatched them because they questioned his methods. *I* never hurt anyone, though, despite what you think.'

'I know,' said Bartholomew gently. 'You are a healer, not a killer.'

Nigellus winced at the kindness in his voice, and his expression turned stricken and very guilty. 'Yet I may have sent a man to his doom even so,' he whispered. 'Robert's request was so odd . . . I should not have done what he ordered . . .'

'Done what?' asked Bartholomew anxiously.

'He told me that if I were to see the Senior Proctor, I should send him to the Austin Priory. I did as he asked, but now I wonder whether I should have held my tongue. I have a bad feeling that Robert means Brother Michael harm.'

Briskly, Bartholomew ordered two passing beadles to carry Nigellus to Zachary, but he had taken no more than two or three steps towards the Austins' domain when a huge crowd of hostel men suddenly materialised in front of him. He faltered, wondering if they would chase him if he darted down an alley. Then Tulyet strode forward, several soldiers and Dickon at his back.

'Go home,' the Sheriff roared. 'Or you will answer to the King for disturbing his peace.'

The hostels jeered, careless that they were challenging a royally appointed official, and there was a moment when it seemed there would be another bloody skirmish. But then came the sound of clashing arms from the Market Square, and as one, the horde whipped around and raced off to join it.

'Your strategist has done his work well, Matt,' growled Tulyet. 'So far, no scholar has listened to me, and the beadles say that no townsman will listen to them. The only way to restore order is for Michael and me to stand together.'

'I will bring him as soon as I have rescued him from Robert,' said Bartholomew, hoping he could reach the convent unscathed. 'Until then, use Chancellor Tynkell.'

'Take Dickon with you,' said Tulyet. 'He carries my authority and is proficient with a blade.'

'No, thank you!' gulped Bartholomew. Tulyet's eyes narrowed, so he flailed around for an excuse that would be believed. 'He is too young for—'

'No, I am not,' interrupted Dickon crossly. 'I am bigger than some of our soldiers.'

It was no time to argue, and Bartholomew supposed that the sight of Dickon's fierce scarlet face might be enough to save him from attacks en route – and may even frighten Robert into an easy surrender. 'Very well, but only if he does what I tell him.'

'Do you agree, Dickon?' asked Tulyet. 'Yes? Good. And remember what I have taught you: the appearance of a confident, well-armed soldier is often enough to bring about a peaceful solution, without recourse to violence.'

Dickon nodded dutifully, although Bartholomew

doubted the homily would do much to keep the brat in check – it should have been obvious even to the most besotted of parents that Dickon was itching for battle. He grabbed a torch from the ground and set off with the boy in tow, immediately disconcerted to note how comfortable Dickon was with his armour and weapons.

They reached the Austin Priory without incident, at which point Bartholomew faltered. Now what? He might endanger Michael if he just charged in. And what if Robert had persuaded his brethren to his way of thinking? Bartholomew could not tackle an entire convent alone – or even with Dickon. He jumped when there was a chorus of ear-piercing cheers from the Market Square: one side had scored a victory, although there was no way to know who, or how many casualties might have resulted from the clash.

'Hurry up,' hissed Dickon irritably. 'Or you will make me miss the next fight, too.'

Bartholomew crept forward, where the torch revealed that the gate's shattered remains had been replaced by a refectory table, which had been upended and jammed into the gap. He pushed it, tentatively at first but then with growing urgency. It did not budge.

He stared at it. Did it mean that Michael had not been able to get in either, and had given up and gone else-where? Or had the opening been secured once the monk was inside – that he had already been 'dealt with' and Robert was in control?

Then Bartholomew felt himself shoved out of the way. Dickon took his sword, inserted it between table and gatepost, and levered furiously until a gap appeared.

'That is no way to treat your weapon,' remarked Bartholomew, stepping forward to lend his greater strength to the task – an easy one now that the table was loose.

'It is still sharp enough for what we need it to do,'

replied Dickon with cool pragmatism. Then he grinned, small eyes glittering. 'Besides, my father will get me another if this one breaks, and I want a bigger blade anyway.'

Bartholomew was sure he did. He hauled him back by the scruff of his neck when the lad started to enter the priory first, earning himself a venomous look in the process.

'Robert might be armed,' he explained.

Dickon grinned again. 'Good. Then I will kill him.'

'Stay behind me, and do as I say,' ordered Bartholomew, heartily wishing it was the father, not the son, who was with him.

He doused the torch in a trough of water – there was no point in advertising their arrival – and stepped through the gate, heart thudding so loudly that he was sure Dickon would be able to hear it. The convent was pitch black inside, and the only lamps were in the chapel.

'We had better put the table back as we found it,' he whispered. 'Leaving the entrance unsecured might encourage looters inside.'

'They will not find much in here,' muttered Dickon disparagingly. 'The Austins live like paupers, and some only have one pair of boots. I have six.'

Bartholomew ignored the lad's self-important bragging, and shoved the table back into place. As an added precaution, he placed a thick plank across it, sliding the ends into two conveniently placed recesses in the doorway to either side. It would now be impossible to break in without some serious pounding.

'It is a good thing Robert did not do that,' remarked Dickon. 'Or I could have levered all night and not got in.'

'Perhaps he is not here,' said Bartholomew. 'And I doubt his brethren have much experience with this sort of thing.'

'No,' agreed Dickon. 'Priests are nearly all useless at warfare.'

He spat, to indicate his disdain for such an unpardonable failing, making Bartholomew wonder afresh whether he wanted the boy at his side that night. Then came the sound of voices: the friars were chanting a psalm. Bartholomew heaved a sigh of relief – they would not be performing their religious devotions if they were helping Robert with his grand designs. Or if they had just helped him to murder Michael, for that matter. He crept towards the chapel, and spent several moments peering through a crack in the door, trying to assess whether the almoner was in there with them.

'They are in the chancel,' reported Dickon, and Bartholomew saw that he had climbed on to a tombstone and prised open a window shutter, again using his trusty sword. 'But Robert and your fat friend are not among them.'

Bartholomew tried to open the door, aiming to ask if they knew where the almoner might be, but it was locked. Then he remembered Michael telling Joliet and his flock to retreat to the building and shut everyone inside. He hammered hard.

'Who is it?' came Joliet's voice. 'Robert?'

'No, it is Dickon Tulyet and Doctor Bartholomew,' piped the boy. 'Open up in the name of the law.' He smirked at the physician and added *sotto voce*, 'I have always wanted to say that.'

'We cannot,' replied Joliet. 'Robert has the key, but he is not here. What is happening out there? We keep hearing terrible battle cries.'

'Your almoner is the villain who has been killing everyone and setting the University against our town,' explained Dickon bluntly.

Bartholomew shot him a withering glance. Joliet would have plenty to say about such a claim, and arguing would waste time – time Michael might not have. There was a brief silence from behind the door, followed by a clamour of objections and queries. Joliet's voice rose above it.

'You are wrong, as I told you earlier. However, something odd is happening, or Robert would not have trapped us in here. Let us out and we shall work together to find the truth. Hurry!'

'Is there another key?' called Bartholomew urgently, after a quick inspection told him that the chapel door was rather more robust than the gate and was unlikely to fall to pieces if he charged at it. 'Think quickly! We need your help to search the grounds.'

'For Robert?' asked Joliet doubtfully. 'You think he is here?'

'I think he may have taken Michael prisoner.' Bartholomew's voice cracked with tension. 'And the Senior Proctor is desperately needed if we are to avert a riot. Please – the key!'

'Robert has the only one.' There was a brief pause before Joliet asked in an uncertain voice, 'Have you seen Wauter today?'

'No, why?'

'Because he sent me his *Martilogium* to mind an hour ago, which means he is back in town. But why give us his work to look after? Do you think he has an inkling that Michaelhouse might be destroyed in these riots? But how would he know such a thing, unless . . .'

Bartholomew closed his eyes in despair. So Wauter was involved after all. He turned frantic attention to the lock, but he had no idea how to pick one, so it was no surprise when he failed. Dickon jabbed at it frenziedly with his sword, but met with no more success than the physician.

'Climb through the windows, Father,' called Bartholomew. 'Or is there another door?'

'Just this one,' replied Joliet. 'And the windows are too narrow.'

356

'We will have to smash the door down,' said Dickon, eyes gleaming. 'With a battering ram.'

'Then fetch one,' snapped Joliet. 'Quickly! I am sure your father has one at the castle.'

'We should find Michael first,' replied Dickon, loath to be sent on an errand that would take time and might mean missing more fun. 'Where would Robert take him?'

Joliet ignored him. 'Please, Matthew! Time trickles away with this jabbering. Go to the castle and fetch the battering ram. But do not ask anyone for help. It is impossible to tell friend from foe at the moment, and we do not want someone deciding that an entire convent of trapped friars would make for an interesting pyre.'

'Which it would,' declared Dickon gleefully. 'And what a sight it would be!'

As Joliet and his brethren were in no immediate danger, Bartholomew thought that freeing them was far less urgent than rescuing Michael. He began to search the priory himself, Dickon at his side, but it did not take him long to ascertain that the dormitory, refectory and outbuildings were empty. He stood in the grounds, trying to quell the panicky roiling of his stomach – the fear that Michael was already dead, and that if so, nothing would stop the town from erupting into violence from which it might never recover.

'Go back to the main entrance and waylay some soldiers,' he told Dickon, racking his brain for other places where Robert might be. 'I am sure they can break down the chapel door without resorting to war machines.'

'The back gate,' whispered Dickon, ignoring the order. 'The one that opens on to the King's Ditch. Robert got away with murder there once, so he will think he can do it again. *That* is where he will have taken the fat monk.'

He had a point, although Bartholomew was disconcerted that a child should have such a clear notion of the way killers thought. They set off towards it, although moving quietly in the pitch dark took longer than when they had been there in daylight. They reached the rear wall, and groped their way along it until they found the gate. Outside it, voices came from the direction of the pier.

'I told you so.' Dickon could not resist a gloat.

'Your plan will not work, Robert,' Michael was saying. 'Someone will come.'

Bartholomew and Dickon inched forward. A lantern illuminated the scene. The Austins' boat had been pushed three or four feet out into the King's Ditch, and Michael had been made to sit on the central thwart – the seat that spanned the middle of the craft – to which he was bound securely. Morys stood in front of him, holding an axe, while Robert and two Zachary students watched from the bank. The students were large, sturdy lads armed with swords, and Bartholomew supposed he should not be surprised that the hostel was involved in Robert's machinations.

'They are going to hack a hole in the boat, so it will sink and drag Michael to the bottom,' whispered Dickon, as if he imagined Bartholomew might not understand what he was seeing. 'Clever! It will keep the corpse hidden for ages, and no one will ever know what happened to him.'

Bartholomew stared at the little tableau with a sense of helplessness. He might have managed to overwhelm Robert and Morys, but he could not defeat the students as well, and Dickon was still a child for all his vicious bluster.

'Fetch help,' he whispered. 'There will be scholars in the streets. Go!'

'How will I know if they are on our side?' asked Dickon, not unreasonably. 'You heard what Prior Joliet said about not trusting anyone. Moreover, they might kill me for being the Sheriff's son. So you do it, while I stay here and watch.'

Bartholomew was halfway to the gate when he had second thoughts. It might be some time before he managed to waylay scholars who would help him, and it was clear that Morys and Robert intended to kill Michael quickly before moving on to the next part of their plan. He stopped and hurried back again. He would just have to devise a way to best four armed and cunning men using a set of childbirth forceps and an unpredictable boy.

'I would not have stopped you from leaving, Robert,' Michael was saying. There was a tremor in his voice: he could not swim, and had a mortal terror of drowning. 'There was no need to destroy the town and tear the University apart.'

'Of course there was,' retorted Robert shortly. 'The Colleges enjoy a comfortable existence here, and will never abandon it willingly. But after tonight, the town will be so enraged by the University's antics that no scholar will be able to stay.'

Morys smirked. 'It will not be long now before all our dreams are realised.'

Robert nodded to Morys, and the axe began to rise. Bartholomew braced himself to race forward, regardless of the unfavourable odds, but Michael spoke quickly to delay the inevitable. Desperately, Bartholomew tried to think of a rescue plan, but his mind was frighteningly blank, and all he could do was listen with mounting horror.

'So you poisoned Frenge,' Michael said. 'A townsman killed on University property was sure to cause discord, especially one who had already invaded King's Hall.'

'And it *did* cause discord,' said Robert smugly. 'Although that was not why we did it. The truth is that he came to bring Father Arnold some sucura – unlike you, we guessed it came from the brewery, and I secured a good price for the stuff in return for keeping Peyn's little secret.'

'Which explains why Frenge sneaked across the King's Ditch in the boat,' surmised Michael. He glanced down. 'This boat. You did not buy his brewery's ale, so he could not come here openly, claiming you as customers. He was obliged to visit slyly, using the back gate . . .'

'Where he overheard Morys and me discussing our plans. The fool tried to blackmail us – to raise the money he would need to buy lawyers to defend him from King's Hall, ironically.'

'So we agreed to pay and offered wine to seal the pact.' Morys took up the tale. 'Wine dosed with a toxic substance taken from the dyeworks. Unfortunately, one sip was not enough, so we had to force him to finish the rest. Then we left him here, where his corpse proved very useful in furthering our designs.'

'You helped, Brother.' Robert's smile was gloating. 'With the tale about him being a cattle thief – an accusation that infuriated the town. And another truth will circulate tomorrow – one that will reveal it was poison from the dyeworks that claimed his life.'

'It will be our parting gift to the town,' said Morys. 'A story that will see that place closed down once and for all.'

Bartholomew's stomach lurched at the notion that Edith should be so used, and he looked around frantically for something that might help him defeat them. There was nothing.

Robert's expression turned earnest. 'But you must see we are right, Michael. The town has never wanted us. Its residents fight us constantly, despite all we have done to win their affection – such as starving ourselves last winter so that the poor could eat – but still they hate us. And their antipathy turns our scholars aggressive, arrogant and overbearing.'

'So you set out to make it worse,' said Michael in distaste. 'You identified folk with grudges and manipulated them – to add fuel to the fire.'

Robert nodded. 'It was easy. I persuaded Shirwynk that his son had suffered an injustice when he was rejected from the University; I wrote letters to the greedy and selfish Stephen; I sent Kellawe, Gilby and Hakeney to stir up trouble at the dyeworks . . .'

'Using Stephen was a clever touch,' bragged Morys. 'He gossiped, as we knew he would, and made scholars think that a move to the Fens was being discussed at the very highest levels.'

Michael ignored him and addressed Robert pleadingly. 'How can you think of abandoning the paupers who rely on you? And what about the commissions for the murals that you have won? I thought you were pleased by them?'

'We shall still execute those,' said Robert. 'But on buildings in the marshes. And I am afraid the poor will have to manage without us. It might have been different if they had sprung to our defence when the trouble started, but they stood back and watched in delight.'

'The cross that created such a rumpus,' said Michael quickly, as Morys fingered the axe. '*Did* you buy it in London?'

'Of course not,' replied Robert scathingly. 'My documents are forgeries. I took the thing from Hakeney solely to demonstrate how the town will always side with one of their own, regardless of the "evidence". I also knew he would refuse to have the case judged by the Bishop – again showing the town's disinclination to be reasonable and fair in its dealings with us.'

'And there was Anne,' said Michael, unable to keep the resignation from his voice. 'She would have overlooked Segeforde's assault, but you were there to mention compensation . . .'

'Which I suspected would snag her avaricious interest,' smirked Robert.

Michael turned to Morys. 'Are you sure you want to go to the Fens with a man who has murdered four Zachary scholars? Who is to say that you will not be next?'

Robert laughed. 'I did not kill them. *He* did.'

'Not Irby.' Morys's wasplike face was bright with spiteful triumph. 'He died of disease. And not Kellawe either. Why would I? He was one of our most fervent supporters. But Yerland and Segeforde began to have second thoughts about our scheme, so I fed them fatally large doses of sucura – one in some apple pie and the other in Lombard slices. And before you ask, yes, we know all about lead salts.'

'But you gave them to Arnold!' cried Michael, addressing Robert. 'A fellow Austin!'

'To end his suffering,' explained Robert. 'He was old and in pain, so why not hasten his end? It was an act of mercy, as he would have been the first to agree.'

There was a roar of angry voices on the High Street, and Robert nodded at Morys a second time to smash the boat, but Michael had another question.

'Which of you will be Chancellor of your University in the Bogs?' he asked contemptuously.

Robert smiled enigmatically. 'Neither. We are followers, not leaders.'

Bartholomew frowned. Did that mean Robert was not the strategist? Then who was? Wauter? He glanced behind him uneasily, half expecting the geometrician to be standing there listening, but the priory was deserted and eerily still. The scent of rain was in the air, and a distant part of his mind wondered how long it would be before there was a downpour.

'Our Chancellor will be a better man than Tynkell,' said Morys with a moue of distaste. 'What a weakling! Frightened of his mother!'

'I know you killed Hamo, Robert,' gabbled Michael as the axe went up again. 'When we came here on the night of his murder, you were the only friar who was unarmed – you had no knife because you had used it to stab him. But you should have made sure he was dead – he lived to write your name under the altar. It is still there, and your brethren are looking at it as I speak.'

Robert's reply was lost in a sudden frenzy of yells from the street, and footsteps hammered along outside – towns-folk, judging by their voices. Bobbing torches lit the night, so many that it seemed the whole of Cambridge had turned out to make mischief. Then there was a boom that sounded as though it came from the priory's front gate.

'Looters,' said Morys in satisfaction. 'Just as we expected. The last stage of our plan is about to unfold.'

The axe cracked down and water began to fountain into the little craft. With a yell of victory, Morys dropped the axe into the boat and leapt for the safety of the pier.

CHAPTER 15

No ingenious scheme to save Michael had occurred to Bartholomew, so he did the only thing he could – he leapt up and powered forward, bowling into the plotters and managing to carry Robert and one of the students into the King's Ditch with him.

His world went dark as he hit the water, the lamp's frail gleam unequal to penetrating its filthy blackness. It was shockingly cold, and he tried not to swallow, suspecting it would kill him if his opponents did not. His hands touched the soft sludge on the bottom, so he kicked upwards – and was startled to find himself standing in water that barely reached his waist.

'No!' cried Robert in dismay, also on his feet. 'The ditch has silted up! The boat will not sink far enough to hide the monk's corpse!'

Michael, struggling frantically against the ropes that held him as the boat began to sink, did not seem very comforted, and was looking more frightened than Bartholomew had ever seen him. Then a clash of metal drew the physician's eyes to the bank. Dickon was fighting the remaining student. Bartholomew watched in horror. Dickon was large for his age, but he was still a child, and could not possibly win a battle with a full-grown man.

While he hesitated, not sure whether to rescue Dickon or Michael first, he heard a splash and whipped around to see Morys wading towards him. He tried to back away, but mud and weeds snagged his feet, and he could not move quickly enough. Morys grabbed his tabard, but Bartholomew jerked it back, pulling Morys

364

off balance. While the Zachary man floundered, Bartholomew seized his hair and forced Morys's face so deeply under the water that he felt it squelch into the slime on the bottom.

Meanwhile, the boat was sinking fast, and even with the silt, Bartholomew knew that Michael's head would not clear the surface once the vessel settled on the bottom. He surged towards it, but a hand caught his shoulder. It was the student he had knocked into the ditch. Bartholomew lashed out with a punch that hit home more by luck than design, then resumed his agonisingly slow journey towards Michael.

'Matt!' shrieked the monk in terror. 'Cut me free!'

Bartholomew reached for his medical bag where he kept several surgical blades, only to find he no longer had it – in the panic following Nigellus's confession he had left it on the High Street. Then he remembered the axe – Morys had dropped it into the boat before leaping to safety. He plunged beneath the surface, cold-numbed fingers groping wildly in the blackness. It was not there! Had it fallen out? Then his questing fingers touched the handle. He took hold of it and stood.

'Hurry!' howled Michael. The water had reached his chin.

Both took breaths at the same time, Michael as the ditch surged towards his nose, and Bartholomew as he dived, desperately hoping that the axe would be sharp enough to hack through the ropes. He found Michael's legs, then groped for the cords, sawing frantically at one that was stretched taut from the monk's frenzied struggles to break free. He could not tell whether it was working, and was about to surface for air when he was thrust down so hard that his head cracked against the gunwale.

He tried to push upwards, but someone was holding him down. He struggled, violently at first, but with decreasing vigour as he felt himself begin to black out. Then, just when he thought his lungs would explode, he was released. He surfaced, gasping, to see that he must have cut enough of the rope to let Michael snap the rest, because the monk was standing up.

He looked around wildly, and saw it had been the student who had tried to drown him; Michael had knocked him away with his shoulder, and the lad was floating face-down nearby. Morys was clawing at the mud that filled his eyes and nose, while Dickon and the other student were still engaged in their deadly dance. Bartholomew looked for Robert.

'Behind you, Matt!' howled Michael.

Bartholomew spun around to see that the almoner had managed to grab the axe. With a vengeful grin, Robert raised it above his head in readiness for the fatal blow. Bartholomew threw up an arm to defend himself, but then came an imperious voice.

'What is going on?'

Bartholomew sagged in relief. It was Prior Joliet. Robert lowered the axe, while on the bank, Dickon and the student stopped fighting.

'You are making too much noise,' said Joliet angrily. 'Do you *want* the beadles to rush in and see what is happening?'

Numbly, Bartholomew noticed that the Prior's arm was no longer in its orange sling, and there seemed to be nothing wrong with it.

'So *you* are the strategist!' spat Michael in disgust. 'I might have guessed.'

'Might you?' mumbled Bartholomew, hating the sour taste of defeat. It had not occurred to *him* that the jolly, round little Prior should be involved in such a wicked scheme. 'Why?'

'The mural in our hall,' said Michael. 'What does it depict?'

'Aristotle, Plato, Galen and Aquinas,' replied Bartholomew, struggling to understand why the monk should consider the painting relevant. 'Teaching under a tree.'

'Quite,' said Michael. 'Under a *tree* – not in an academic hall or a church. I wondered from the start why that should be, but now I understand. It was *Joliet's* idea to move the University to the Fens. He painted his vision of the future.'

Many things became clear to Bartholomew as the last clue fell into place, but there was no time to analyse them, because a fury of sound from the High Street suggested that a pitched battle was in progress. There would be injuries and deaths, particularly among the townsmen, whose sticks and tools were no match for the scholars' swords and bows.

He glanced at Joliet and saw satisfaction in the plump face. It was exactly what the Prior wanted: no scholar could stay in a place that burned with resentment over the uneven number of casualties, so the University would have to flee to the Fens, where his dream of a *studium generale* away from the trappings of a town would be realised. Bartholomew felt a small spark of satisfaction, though: the sacking of the Austin Priory would not contribute to the trouble, because the bar he had placed across the door would keep looters out – at least until Joliet and Robert realised what he had done and went to remove it.

'Pull that student out of the water,' instructed Joliet, when the clamour had eased and he could make himself heard again. 'Or he will drown.'

Robert tossed the axe to Morys and went to oblige, although Bartholomew could see it was too late. So could Joliet, who scowled angrily.

'If you had dispatched Michael quickly, as I ordered,

Bartholomew would have gone away in ignorance and that lad would still be alive. Now we shall have to kill Bartholomew, too, which is a pity – another physician would have been be useful in the Fens.'

'Do not use the axe to do it, Morys,' advised Robert. 'A knife will be cleaner.'

He was proven right when Bartholomew evaded Morys's wild swing with ease. Swearing under his breath, the Principal tossed the axe on to the pier and drew a dagger instead.

'How did you escape from the chapel, Father Prior?' asked Bartholomew, edging away.

'By unlocking the door,' replied Joliet shortly. 'Do you really think I would allow myself to be shut inside when a riot was in progress?'

'You tried to make us think that Wauter was the strategist,' said Bartholomew accusingly, jerking away from Morys' next lunge, which came far too close for comfort. 'You claimed he left you his *Martilogium* to—'

'To ensure you did not suspect me,' interrupted Joliet briskly. 'Yes. Not that it matters now. And I do have the *Martilogium*. It is a valuable work, and I could not risk it being destroyed in the riots. I took it when I last visited your College.'

'Wauter was never one of us,' said Morys, grimacing when yet another swipe missed. 'He would have disapproved.'

'So who is involved?' asked Michael. 'All Zachary, I suppose, which is why they refuse to wear their tabards – a ploy to aggravate the town with a flaunting of riches. And the Austins.'

'Not the Austins,' said Joliet. 'It is best my brethren remain ignorant of what needs to be done, so they are still locked in the chapel, praying for peace.'

'And not Nigellus either,' surmised Bartholomew. 'Or he would have treated you with more respect at the *discep-*

tatio. Instead he blackmailed you over the sucura you acquired from Frenge.'

'I will make him regret that,' vowed Joliet unpleasantly, then turned to his helpmeets. 'Enough talk. Make an end of them.'

Obediently, the surviving student renewed his assault on Dickon, while Morys advanced on Bartholomew again. Robert jumped into the ditch and waded purposefully towards Michael.

'You sold Shirwynk those lead tanks, knowing exactly what would happen if he fermented wine in them,' said Michael, twisting suddenly so that Robert was knocked backwards. 'And you have pretended to be calm and reasonable, but your "innocent" remarks have made matters worse.'

'Hurry up,' Joliet snapped to his helpmeets. 'This distasteful confrontation has gone on quite long enough.'

'You were never hurt by a rock either,' said Michael. 'You claimed a townsman had lobbed one, hoping the University would rebel at an assault on a priest, and you wore a bright orange sling to draw attention to the "injury". But it was yet another ruse, aimed to encourage more—'

'It worked,' interrupted Joliet curtly. 'Which is even more reason to leave this turbulent town. If we can stir up such hatred with a few rumours, lawsuits, lies and deaths, imagine what would happen if someone wicked tried to do it.'

'Someone wicked?' echoed Michael in disbelief. 'I think you will find that *you* qualify for that particular description – as you will learn when your sins are weighed on Judgement Day.'

'We are in the right,' snarled Joliet, and as he spoke, he stepped into the flickering lamplight to reveal what he was wearing on his feet. 'It is fat and corrupt Colleges that—'

'*You* killed Kellawe!' breathed Bartholomew when he saw the colourful smears. He recalled what Dickon had said: that the Austins did not have the luxury of spare boots. Joliet had worn sandals in his refectory earlier, but something sturdier was needed for hurrying around outside in the dark, so the Prior had had no choice but to don the footwear he had worn to the dyeworks.

'He was a liability,' snapped Joliet crossly. 'And put more moderate men off joining us. I told him to stay away from your sister's business after he was almost caught there the first time, but he ignored me and went again anyway. I followed and—'

He was interrupted by an agonised scream. The surviving student had been distracted by the discussion, which allowed Dickon to dart forward and plunge his sword into the lad's foot. Then Dickon whipped around and rushed at Joliet. The Prior tried to turn, but lost his footing on the slippery wood. He landed on his back, where he made a peculiar sound, half whimper, half groan.

Bartholomew also capitalised on the distraction, lashing out with a punch that sent Morys flying. When the Principal regained his feet, he was within reach of Dickon's sword. There was an unpleasant crunch as metal met bone, and Morys went limp.

'Untie me, Matt,' shouted Michael, ramming a meaty elbow into Robert's face. The almoner reeled, dazed. 'The University needs its Senior Proctor out on the streets, or these misguided fools are going to get their wish of a University in the Fens.'

'Not Morys – he is dead,' said Dickon with enormous satisfaction. 'I can see his brains.'

'So is Joliet,' added Bartholomew, as he slashed away the ropes from Michael's wrists with his trusty dagger. 'He landed on the axe that Morys dropped just now, and it must have punctured his . . .'

He trailed off when he saw Dickon listening with far too much interest.

'Get the chapel key from his purse,' instructed Michael, climbing out of the ditch and pulling the dazed Robert with him. 'Hurry!'

Bartholomew obliged, then used Dickon's sword to urge Robert and the limping student towards the chapel. He glanced up at the sky as they went. Dawn would come soon, and he wondered what horrors daylight would reveal.

They reached the chapel to find that the Austins had been suspicious when Joliet had accused Robert of shutting them in when they knew he had the key himself. One had also seen Morys forcing Michael towards the King's Ditch at knifepoint. They were sorry when the monk gave a brief summary of what had happened, but not surprised, and informed him that their concerns had been mounting for some time.

'The Zachary men often visit at night,' said Overe, watching Dickon shove the two prisoners into the chapel and lock the door. 'And Prior Joliet hated the fact that the University is surrounded by what he called the corrupting influence of the town.'

'But we want to stay,' said another. 'How can we succour the poor from the marshes?'

'A move would have gone against everything we believe in,' said Overe. 'Yet Joliet and Robert were not bad men – just ones who did what they thought was right.'

'Setting an entire town alight with hatred and bigotry is right?' asked Michael archly.

Bartholomew, Michael and Dickon hurried to the High Street to see that Bene't College was under siege from a gang of hostel men, while a mob from the town was looting a house that had been left empty when its residents had decanted to the Fens. More trouble was brewing at the Trumpington Gate, where a host of scholars had again gathered to leave, and a rival contingent led by King's Hall aimed to stop them. Townsfolk had gravitated towards the confrontation.

'Where have you been, Brother?' demanded Tulyet between gritted teeth. 'Your hostel men have not brought travelling packs with them this time – they carry staves and knives, and they intend to do battle with the Colleges.'

'Where is Tynkell?' asked Michael. 'Did he not tell them to go home?'

'They are well past taking orders,' said Tulyet. 'We need a miracle if we are to avert a massacre.'

'Their leader is dead,' said Michael grimly. 'But it seems his plan might work anyway.'

'It was Prior Joliet and Master Morys,' piped Dickon. 'Prior Joliet fell on an axe that punctured something, while I killed Master Morys with a blow that sliced clean through his head.'

Tulyet grimaced irritably, clearly thinking it was another of his son's exaggerations. Michael did not enlighten him, but hurried to interpose himself between the two factions, calling for his beadles as he went. Unfortunately, the lines were blurred, so it was impossible to know where one ended and the other began. Townsfolk were everywhere, adding to the confusion and the din.

He started to shout, but although those closest to him turned to listen, the general racket was so great that his words were inaudible to most. Then another voice joined in, one that *did* still the cacophony.

'Brother Michael is talking,' roared Isnard the bargeman, his powerful voice explaining why the Michaelhouse Choir had a reputation for being able to sing at such a tremendous volume. 'So shut your mouths and listen.'

'Why should we?' demanded Gilby. He carried a stave, and had a pack of hostel men at his heels, all of whom looked as though they would rather skirmish than embark on a life of scholarly contemplation in the marshes. 'He is friends with the woman who is poisoning our river – which is another reason why we should abandon this filthy place.'

'No one is poisoning the river,' shouted Bartholomew, eager to clear his sister's name. He baulked at adding more, though, suspecting that naming the brewery as the culprit was unlikely to help the cause of peace.

'He is right,' boomed Michael. 'It was a misunderstanding, which will be explained in full later this morning. So go home and wait there for news.'

'You heard him,' bellowed Tulyet, going to stand next to the monk in a gesture of unity. His voice was hoarse from previous appeals. 'Stand down, all of you.'

'We will stand down when these hostel vermin slink back to their hovels,' declared Wayt, who was clad in full armour and carried a halberd. 'Until then, we stay here.'

'We want you *all* to leave our town,' shrieked Hakeney. He had abandoned the sanctuary of the King's Head, and was with a contingent of heavily armed cronies who looked delighted at the prospect of going to war with scholars. 'None of you are welcome here.'

Howls of fury vied with cheers and a lot of menacingly brandished weapons. Then Michael's eye lit on the Chancellor, who had donned his ceremonial finery in the hope of rendering himself more imposing. It had not worked, and he looked like a frightened man wearing robes that were too big for him. Michael was desperate enough to make an appeal anyway.

'Do something, Tynkell,' he begged. 'For God's sake, *help* me!'

Tynkell cleared his throat nervously as the clamour began to die down. 'This is all very silly,' he began feebly. 'So go home. It looks like rain anyway, and you will not want to get wet.'

There was a startled silence, followed by jeering laughter from townsmen and scholars alike. But the atmosphere soon turned menacing again.

'Will we listen to a man who is afraid of his mother?' asked Wayt sneeringly of his cronies. 'Or shall we leave that sort of nonsense to the hostels?'

'*We* are not afraid of women,' declared Gilby. He turned to the men who were ranged at his back. 'Are you ready? Then let us attack and be away from this evil place once and for all!'

Gilby's charge never materialised, because there was a sudden rumble of hoofs on the road outside the gate. A cavalcade was thundering towards it, comprising an elegant carriage, two heavily loaded wagons and a pack of liveried knights on horseback. There was immediate curiosity – and consternation – as only nobility or high-ranking churchmen travelled in that sort of style.

The vehicles clattered through the gate and rolled to a standstill. The warriors took up station on either side of them, their faces dark and unsmiling. A nervous murmur ran through the crowd, but it petered out quickly, and the silence was absolute as one horseman flung back his hood and dismounted.

'Wauter!' breathed Bartholomew. 'Now what?'

The geometrician strode towards the carriage and offered his hand to its occupant. A woman alighted. She was well past her prime and not very tall, but there was a gleam in her eye and a set to her chin that indicated she was not someone to trifle with.

'Oh, Lord!' gulped Tynkell, as she gazed around with an imperious stare that caused more than one person in the crowd to shuffle his feet and look away. 'It is my mother!'

'Lady Joan de Hereford,' announced Wauter in a ringing voice. 'Wife of Robert Morys of Brington Manor and friend of Her Majesty the Queen. And with her are members of the royal guard – men who know how to deal with those who break the King's peace.'

'What is going on here?' demanded Joan. 'Why are you not at your devotions? It is time for morning service, is it not? To be attended by scholars *and* townsfolk.'

'We are about to teach the University a lesson,' shouted Hakeney, hopping from foot to foot in excitement, so that the cross he wore around his neck bounced wildly and was in danger of knocking his teeth out. However, if he was expecting support from his ruffianly friends, he was disappointed, because they shot away from him as though he had the plague.

Joan fixed him with a hard stare. 'You intend to attack my son?'

Hakeney swallowed hard when he found himself standing in splendid isolation. 'Not him, specifically, but scholars in general. They are an unruly horde, given to stealing crucifixes and suing people. Not to mention wearing clothes that make them look like courtiers. Not that there is anything wrong with courtiers, of course,' he added prudently.

'I am glad to hear you think so,' said Joan coolly, then brought her basilisk gaze to bear on the assembled scholars. 'The King will not be pleased to learn that you would rather brawl than attend your religious duties. So shall I tell him, or will you go to your churches and chapels?'

Wayt opened his mouth to argue, but she fixed him with a steely glare, and the words died in his throat. However, it was the knights who convinced him to stand down – one spurred his enormous destrier forward and the Acting Warden was obliged to scramble away or risk being knocked over. The other warriors followed suit, drawing broadswords as they did so, and the crowd scattered like leaves in the wind. A skirmish had been

375

averted, aided by the fact that dawn had brought a drenching drizzle that encouraged people not to linger anyway.

'Hello, Mother,' said Tynkell, advancing with a curious crab-like scuttle that made those watching wonder if he aimed to embrace her or fall at her feet.

Lady Joan regarded him stonily. 'I thought Master Wauter was exaggerating when he came to tell me to hurry because there was trouble. I am not impressed, William. You are Chancellor – you should nip this sort of thing in the bud. As should the Sheriff.'

'He tried,' shouted Dickon indignantly. 'He is my father, and a very good leader. He has been teaching me things.'

Joan's eyebrows went up when she saw the scarlet face, but then her expression softened. 'And you are a worthy pupil, I am sure. Come here, and tell me your name.'

'Why am I not surprised that she has taken a liking to him?' muttered Wauter, coming to stand next to Bartholomew and Michael. 'The Devil sees his own like, I suppose.'

'Where have you been?' demanded Michael frostily.

'Fetching her,' replied Wauter. 'I wrote a letter explaining why, and left it with Prior Joliet. Did he not give it to you? Lady Joan and I are old friends, and I thought she would give her son the strength he needs to lead the University in its time of crisis.'

'You consider Dick and me unequal to the task?' asked Michael coolly.

'I thought you might need help,' said Wauter quietly. 'That is all.'

'Well, I am glad you brought the King's knights,' said Tulyet, watching Lady Joan and Dickon talk animatedly. 'I am not sure we could have quelled that battle without them, and people would have died.'

'How long will she and her entourage stay?' asked

Bartholomew, suspecting the turmoil would start again the moment they left.

'Until Christmas at least,' replied Wauter. 'Quite long enough to put us all in order.'

EPILOGUE

About a month after the incident at the Trumpington Gate, Michael was able to report with satisfaction that the fledgling *studium generale* in the Fens was no more. When the first serious frost settled across the marshes, most of its scholars decided that it was no place to spend the winter, and began to trickle away. Eventually only a stubborn handful remained, but not enough to warrant being called a university or even a college.

The same evening, he and Bartholomew met in the conclave. It was bitterly cold, but there was no fire, because Michaelhouse's finances did not stretch to wood, and the only refreshments on offer were sour ale and stale bread. They joined William and Wauter at the table where, as usual, the discussion turned to the strategist and his schemes.

'Joliet manipulated everything and everyone to achieve what he wanted,' said Wauter, shaking his head sadly. 'He persuaded Stephen to find a way around the town's by-laws for Edith to start her dyeworks, knowing that people would object and there would be trouble—'

'Stephen, who was so miserly that he insisted on finishing the expensive sucura he had bought, which brought about his death last week,' said William with unfriarly satisfaction.

'He added it secretly to his Royal Broth,' said Bartholomew, wishing he had guessed sooner why the lawyer had failed to rally. 'He told me just before he died that he found the mixture unpalatable on its own.'

'It is difficult to mourn him, though,' said Michael. 'Even on his deathbed, he was encouraging people to sue each other over the slightest offence. I shall not miss his agitating.'

'The apple wine and sucura claimed twenty-five lives in the end,' said Bartholomew. 'Six from Barnwell, Letia, Lenne, Arnold, Irby, Yerland, Segeforde and Stephen, plus three of my patients, four of Rougham's and five more of Nigellus's. Other than Yerland and Segeforde, all would probably have survived had they been younger or fitter.'

'I wonder how Nigellus likes practising in the Fens,' said William smugly. 'It is a far cry from his comfortable existence here, and I am sure he cannot be happy with only half a dozen impoverished fanatics to tend.'

'Well, he did want the University to move there,' said Michael, 'so he cannot object to the choices he was offered: prison or permanent exile in the marshes. And at least out in the bogs he can call himself Senior Physician, although it is not a title he deserves. Did I tell you that he was lying when he claimed to have trained at Oxford? He was there less than a month before they tired of his arrogance and threw him out. He certainly never graduated.'

'So he was a fraud,' mused Wauter. 'I always sensed something unsavoury about him, which was one reason why I was glad to accept a post here when Irby told me that Nigellus had been invited to join Zachary.'

'Along with the promise of decent company, of course,' put in Michael.

'Joliet had his just deserts, though,' said William. 'The Austins refused to have him in their cemetery, so he went behind the compost heap in St Botolph's. Personally, I think his helpmeets should join him there, but some still live.'

'Not Robert,' said Michael. 'He hanged himself in his cell after a visit from Lady Joan. Meanwhile, everyone else from Zachary has been banished to France.'

'They did a lot of harm,' said Wauter sadly. 'Robert

killed Arnold and Hamo, Morys poisoned Segeforde and Yerland, and they both worked together to dispatch Frenge. And Joliet strangled Kellawe.'

'But not before Kellawe had run amok in the dyeworks,' said William disapprovingly. 'Twice. He should never have been allowed to wear a Franciscan habit – he should have been an Austin instead.'

'I am going to resign my Michaelhouse Fellowship,' said Wauter. He raised a hand when a startled William began to blurt an apology. 'Not because you just insulted my Order, Father, but because my colleagues have asked me to be their Prior. I think I must accept.'

'Why?' demanded William, speaking belligerently to mask his dismay. The weeks since the crisis at the Trumpington Gate had allowed Wauter to become a popular and trusted colleague, and the Franciscan did not want to lose him. 'If you go anywhere, it should be to the Fens – you did say that you thought the University should decant there.'

'I was mistaken,' said Wauter quietly. 'Our future is here. The townsfolk do not want us, so it is our duty to change their minds – which I can do better in a convent that dispenses alms than in a college that can barely afford to feed itself.'

'You will be an excellent Head of House,' said Michael warmly. 'And as Joliet and Robert are no longer available to teach our students, you can do it instead. We will not let you escape from us that easily!'

Wauter laughed. 'You have no money to pay me, and I should concentrate on my *Martilogium* anyway. Prior Joliet was right about that, at least – it is an important work.'

He stood to leave, and his place at the table was taken by Clippesby, who had the College cat in his arms. The Dominican was sorry when he heard the news about Wauter.

'Please do not invite Thelnetham to take his place,'

he begged. 'He was such a divisive force, and the College is much nicer without him. But what a pity about Wauter! He is a good man.'

'He is,' agreed Michael. 'Although there was a time when I thought he might be the strategist. For example, when he left us to do all the work in the church on All Souls' Day, then returned to make that enigmatic remark about Michaelhouse's stained soul, I thought he had been up to no good. But do you know where he went?'

'Yes – to move the remains of the shed that was set alight behind the church,' replied Clippesby. 'He thought it was unsightly and might count against us as we tried to attract benefactors. The pigeons that live in the grave-yard told me.'

Michael sighed irritably. 'You knew? You might have told me!'

'You did not ask,' replied the Dominican serenely.

'Still, at least some good came out of this miserable affair,' Michael went on. 'Matt is hailed as the man who discovered a cure for the *debilitas*.'

'Royal Broth is not a cure,' said Bartholomew. 'It is an easily digestible—'

'It is a cure,' said Michael firmly. 'Our reputation is shaky at the moment, and we need all the goodwill we can muster. Having the physician responsible for elimin-ating the *debilitas* helps.'

'But I did not eliminate it,' objected Bartholomew. 'The removal of lead salts from the town's diet means there have been no further cases, but the victims still—'

'Royal Broth is selling as fast as Agatha can make it,' grinned William. 'The money is just pouring in.'

'She charges for it?' asked Bartholomew in dismay.

'Yes,' said William. 'But do not look so horrified. Only rich folk were able to buy sucura and apple wine, so they are the ones who need the remedy. They can afford to pay her inflated prices. Of course, I am not sure we shall ever rid the College of the stench of onion and garlic . . .'

'Not everyone has recovered, though,' said Clippesby sadly. 'Cew remains mad.'

'I do not think his affliction was caused by lead salts,' said Bartholomew. 'Although I am at a loss as to what else it could have been. Ailments of the mind are a mystery to me.'

'No they are not – they are just so complex that you cannot explain them to laymen.' William shrugged when Bartholomew shot him an uncomprehending glance. 'People will think less of you if you confess that you are as perplexed by his condition as everyone else.'

'But I *am* perplexed.'

'Then ask King's Hall for Cew's head when he dies,' suggested William. 'You can anatomise it and find the answers you need. But until then – bluster. For the good of the College.'

'Now that Warden Shropham is back, and Wayt no longer runs King's Hall, Dodenho has admitted that Cew lost his reason several weeks before Frenge frightened him,' said Bartholomew. 'Wayt lied purely to win easy money from the brewery.'

'Wayt was not the only one to spout untruths,' said Michael. 'So did Hakeney.'

'You mean his claim that Frenge knew Wauter?' asked William. 'Yes – it was pure malice on his part. I challenged him about it and he made a full confession.'

'And speaking of Frenge, we were suspicious that he and Letia died within hours of each other,' said Michael. 'But it *was* coincidence. Of course, Frenge was no innocent victim. On the day he was killed, he made two separate attempts at blackmail – King's Hall over the sucura he himself had sold them, and then Robert and Morys over a conversation he overheard.'

The door opened at that point, and Langelee entered,

his face grey with worry and fatigue. He looked so unwell that William, not usually a man to concern himself with the needs of others, scrambled to his feet so the Master could sit.

'We failed,' said Langelee hoarsely. 'We gambled everything we had – and more – to win a benefactor, but the bad feeling Joliet generated in the town means that donors are withdrawing offers, not making them. Michaelhouse will be dissolved before the end of term.'

'Perhaps not,' said Bartholomew, speaking over the immediate chorus of dismay. 'Lady Joan was impressed by Edith's efforts to reform the Frail Sisters, but thinks that dyeing is too arduous a trade for ladies. She told Tynkell to award my sister the contract for sewing the University's robes instead.'

'And Tynkell did it?' cried William. 'Our colleagues will wear garments made by whores? What will Oxford think?'

'*Ex*-whores,' corrected Bartholomew. 'Well, mostly. Edith is relieved – she has accepted that the dyeworks are problematic, and is delighted to be able to provide her staff with safer work.'

'I am glad the dyeworks will close,' sighed Langelee. 'They stink to high heaven. But what does this have to do with Michaelhouse? Or will your sister employ us as seamstresses? I might accept – I shall need to earn a crust somehow once the College folds.'

'She has given the dyeworks to us,' explained Bartholomew. He held out a piece of parchment. 'I have the deed here. It includes not just the building, but a sizeable tract of land and that nice new pier.'

Langelee snatched it from him and the colour slowly seeped back into his cheeks. When he looked up, his eyes were bright with tears. 'We are saved! God bless her.'

'The revenue from the dock alone will keep us in

victuals and fuel,' said Clippesby, beaming happily. 'And we can sell the building to—'

'Sell?' interrupted Langelee. 'We most certainly shall not! Dyeing is a lucrative business. We shall take over the running of it, and it will earn us a fortune.'

'But you have just explained why we cannot do that,' said Bartholomew irritably. 'The stench—'

'What stench?' interrupted William. 'I cannot say I find it particularly noxious.'

'On reflection, neither do I,' said Langelee breezily. 'In fact, it is extremely pleasant.'

For the rest of that term, Lady Joan became a familiar sight on the streets of Cambridge as Chancellor Tynkell showed her around his domain. She insisted on visiting every College, convent and hostel in the University, often multiple times, and it quickly became a point of honour for each to impress her more than their rivals. The frantic primping that took place, along with the numerous disputations arranged by Michael, served to keep the scholars far too busy to contemplate squabbling with each other.

'It is a pity she is the wrong sex,' sighed Michael. 'She would make an excellent Chancellor – far better than her son.'

The town proved less easy to distract, and there was bitter disappointment that the promised exodus of scholars was not going to take place after all. Spats between them and the academics grew more frequent and increasingly violent. Michael, Bartholomew and Tulyet met to discuss them in the Brazen George one day just before Christmas.

'Perhaps Prior Joliet was right,' said Bartholomew, weary after dealing with the injuries arising from yet another brawl. 'The town will never be easy with us in it, and it might be better for everyone if we go to live in the Fens.'

'It will not,' said Tulyet firmly. 'Without the University, we would be nothing.'

Michael gazed wonderingly at him. 'And this from a townsman?'

'We sell you our ale, bread, meat, cloth, pots and fuel; and we rent you our houses and inns. In return, you provide us with scribes, physicians and priests, while the friaries do good work with the poor, despite the recent hiccup with the Austins.'

'Then why do I feel as though we are not welcome?' asked Michael.

'Because you are arrogant, miserly and condescending; you make nuisances of yourselves with our womenfolk; and you do not pay fair prices for our goods. You belittle and cheat us at every turn, and you are rarely good neighbours.'

'Well, yes,' acknowledged Michael. 'But we cannot help that.'

HISTORICAL NOTE

In 2009, the University of Cambridge celebrated eight hundred years in the city, although the exact date that scholars arrived in the town is not known. It probably came about because a riot in Oxford had caused scholars to flee, and some of them chose to settle in Cambridge, almost certainly because they had family connections there. As the foundation grew and the academics began to assert themselves, trouble boiled between them and the townsfolk, and the next eight centuries are peppered with brawls, disagreements, rows and riots. One of the most serious was in 1381, during the Peasants' Revolt, when many University records were destroyed and its buildings attacked, so ill-feeling would certainly have existed between University and town in the 1350s.

The problem was compounded by the fact that there were rivalries and quarrels within the University, too. The Colleges were stable foundations with endowments, which meant their scholars tended to live more comfortable existences than those in the hostels, a fact that caused resentment and led to spats. Hostels came and went with their principals, although some, like Ovyng and Physick, were fairly long lived. There is a reference to a hostel named St Zachary Inn, but little is known about it, except that it probably took its name from the Church of St John Zachary, which stood on the junction of Milne Street and Water Lane. The church was eventually demolished to make way for King's College Chapel.

As always with the Bartholomew books, *A Poisonous Plot* is based around real people and events. In 1340, a clerk named Stephen of Cambridge, acting for the town, successfully argued that a case of assault should be brought by Anne de Rumburgh against Peter Segeforde. I could find no Peter Segeforde in the University's records, but Walter Segeforde was vicar of St Edward's Church – he was appointed in 1344 and stayed until 1359.

In the same year, Robert de Hakeney was accused of stealing property from Robert de Comberton. Again, there was no Robert de Comberton in the University, but there was a John Comberton. He was an Austin friar, based at the convent that once stood near St Bene't's Church, between what is now Wheeler Street and the New Museums Site.

In 1358, there was another lawsuit in which John Frenge was sued for trespassing on the property of John Wayt (there was a John Wayt de Warefeld at King's Hall in the 1370s, although it is unclear if these were one and the same). And five years later, a similar case had William Shirwynk as the plaintiff and John Morys as the defendant. Morys was the name of an influential family in the town, and a William Morys was enrolled in the University in the 1370s.

Other real people include Nigellus Thornton, who was a physician in Cambridge in the thirteenth century. He owned several properties in the town and in nearby Barnwell, and left some of them to the University, probably in exchange for Masses for his soul. Richard de Kellawe, a Franciscan, was appointed in 1341 as Commissary of the Chancellor (at this time William Tynkell) by the Bishop of Ely to absolve scholars who were guilty of acts of violence. He came from Carlisle, and was Warden of the Cambridge Franciscans in the 1330s.

John Wauter (or Water) was a Fellow of Michaelhouse in the early 1400s. As a priest, he was licensed to hear confessions in the Ely diocese, and he gave a *Martilogium* to Peterhouse. Ralph de Langelee was probably Master of Michaelhouse in the 1350s, and his Fellows included Michael (de Causton), John Clippesby, William (de Gotham), Thomas Suttone and William de Thelnetham. William Melton and William Bell were later members, and their names appear in records at the beginning of the fifteenth century.

William Irby was a scholar in the 1370s, nominated three times for the Mastership of Peterhouse, and was later rector of Norton in Suffolk, where he was buried. John Yerland studied at the University in the 1370s, after which he took holy orders. He became rector of Limpsfield in Surrey. Poor John Cew (or Coo), a King's Hall Fellow appointed in 1432, is reported to have 'lost his reason' fifteen years later. John Gilby studied in Cambridge in 1381, and was ordained as a subdeacon. He became vicar of Chesterfield and rector of Kneesall in Nottinghamshire.

To avoid confusion, 'Austin' has been used to denote the friars, and 'Augustinian' to refer to the canons whose priory was at nearby Barnwell, although the two terms are interchangeable. Ralph Norton was Prior at Barnwell in the 1350s, and his contemporaries included John Wrattlesworth and John of Canterbury. Hamo de Hythe was an Austin friar, and the Prior of his convent was John Joliet (or Julyet). Tulyet and Lenne were important mercantile families in fourteenth-century Cambridge, while John de Birton was reeve of Barnwell in the 1380s.

The Roman architect Marcus Vitruvius Pollio did indeed warn of the perils of using lead vats to store foodstuffs, and fermenting apples in them might well have led to a variety of unpleasant side effects among those who enjoyed the resulting brews.